# VICTORIES OF THE SPACE MARINES

ACROSS COUNTLESS BATTLEFIELDS on myriad worlds, the Adeptus Astartes fight valiantly to defend the Imperium of Mankind and its Emperor entombed within his Golden Throne. Against insidious xenos and foul warp-bred denizens, these superhuman warriors are bred for battle and victory is encoded in their very genes.

But the Emperor's light no longer shines upon all of his sons and some have strayed from the path, turned renegade and now wage war against those they would once have called brother. For these Traitor Marines their existence is fraught but the rewards, should they gain the favour of their patron god, can be manifold and immortality – literally – awaits.

This anthology collects the best new Space Marine stories from some of the Black Library's leading authors including James Swallow, Gav Thorpe, Ben Counter, Chris Wraight and Steve Parker.

WARHAMMER 40,000 STORIES

# VICTORIES OF THE SPACE MARINES

### Edited by
### Christian Dunn

BLACK LIBRARY

**A BLACK LIBRARY PUBLICATION**

First published in Great Britain in 2011 by
The Black Library,
Games Workshop Ltd.,
Willow Road, Nottingham,
NG7 2WS, UK.

10 9 8 7 6 5 4 3 2 1

Cover illustration by Hardy Fowler.

A CIP record for this book is available from the British Library.

ISBN 13: 978 1 84970 043 6

Distributed in the US by Simon & Schuster
1230 Avenue of the Americas, New York, NY 10020, US.

See the Black Library on the internet at
**www.blacklibrary.com**

Find out more about Games Workshop
and the world of Warhammer 40,000 at
**www.games-workshop.com**

Printed and bound in the US.

IT IS THE 41st millennium. For more than a hundred centuries the Emperor has sat immobile on the Golden Throne of Earth. He is the master of mankind by the will of the gods, and master of a million worlds by the might of his inexhaustible armies. He is a rotting carcass writhing invisibly with power from the Dark Age of Technology. He is the Carrion Lord of the Imperium for whom a thousand souls are sacrificed every day, so that he may never truly die.

YET EVEN IN his deathless state, the Emperor continues his eternal vigilance. Mighty battlefleets cross the daemon-infested miasma of the warp, the only route between distant stars, their way lit by the Astronomican, the psychic manifestation of the Emperor's will. Vast armies give battle in His name on uncounted worlds. Greatest amongst his soldiers are the Adeptus Astartes, the Space Marines, bio-engineered super-warriors. Their comrades in arms are legion: the Imperial Guard and countless Planetary Defence Forces, the ever-vigilant Inquisition and the tech-priests of the Adeptus Mechanicus to name only a few. But for all their multitudes, they are barely enough to hold off the ever-present threat from aliens, heretics, mutants - and worse.

TO BE A man in such times is to be one amongst untold billions. It is to live in the cruellest and most bloody regime imaginable. These are the tales of those times. Forget the power of technology and science, for so much has been forgotten, never to be re-learned. Forget the promise of progress and understanding, for in the grim dark future there is only war. There is no peace amongst the stars, only an eternity of carnage and slaughter, and the laughter of thirsting gods.

# CONTENTS

# RUNES

## by Chris Wraight

BALDR SVELOK SLAMMED hard into the acid-laced rock.
His plate crunched against the stone, sending warning runes flashing across his helm-feed. Instinct told
him another blow was coming in fast, and the Wolf
Guard ducked. A massive tight-balled fist tore into
the rock where his head had been, showering him
with shards where the impact had obliterated the
cliff.

Svelok dodged the next crashing fist, his augmented limbs moving with preternatural speed. He
almost made it, but the monster's talons raked down
across his right shoulder-guard, sending him sprawl-
ing to the ground and skidding across pools of acid.
He landed with a heavy crack, and something
snapped across his barrel chest boneplate. He felt
blood in his mouth, and his head jerked back from
the impact.

Throne, he was being taken apart. That did *not* happen.

He spun onto his back, ignoring the heavy crunch as the creature's clawed foot stamped down just millimetres from his arm. It towered into the storm-wracked sky, a living wall of obsidian, five metres high and crowned with dark, curving spikes. Lightning reflected from the facets of its organic armour, glinting off the slick ebony. Somewhere in the whirl of jagged, serrated limbs was a monotasking mind, a basic alien intelligence filled with an urge to protect its territory and drive the infiltrating humans back into space.

Svelok had never seen a xenos like it. The closest he could get was a creature of demi-myth on Fenris, the Grendel, but these bastards were encased in plates of rock and had talons like lightning claws.

'You all die the same way,' he growled. His voice was a jagged-edged rasp, scraped into savagery by old throat wounds. He sounded as terrifying as he looked.

The storm bolter screamed out a juddering stream of mass-reactive bolts, sending ice-white impact flares across the creature's armoured hide. It staggered, rocking back on its heels, clutching at the hail of rounds as if trying to pluck them from the air. The torrent was relentless, perfectly aimed and deadly.

The magazine clicked empty. Boosted by his armour-servos, Svelok leapt to his feet, mag-locked the bolter and grabbed a krak grenade.

Amazingly, the leviathan still stood. It was reeling now, its hide cracked and driven in by the barrage of bolter fire, but some spark of defiance within it hadn't died. A jagged maw, black as Morkai's pelt, cracked open, revealing teeth like a row of stalactites. It lurched back into the attack, talons outstretched.

Whip-fast, Svelok hurled the grenade through the open mouth. The massive jaws snapped shut in reflex and the Space Wolf crouched down against the oncoming blast. There was a muffled boom and the xenos was blown apart, its iron-hard shell smashed open and spread out like a splayed ribcage. The behemoth crumbled in a storm of shards, toppled, and was gone.

'Feel the wrath of Russ, filth!' roared Svelok, leaping back to his feet, fangs bared inside his helmet. He seized a fresh magazine, spun round and slammed the rounds into the storm bolter's chamber. There'd been three of them, massive stalking beasts carved from the stone around them, horrors of black, tortured rock bigger than a Dreadnought.

Now there were none. Rune Priest Ravenblade loomed over the smoking remains of the largest, his runestaff thrumming with angry, spitting witchfire. Lokjr and Varek had taken out the third, though the Grey Hunters' armour was scarred and dented from the assault. The xenos monsters were tough as leviathan-hide.

'What in *Hel* are these things?' Lokjr spat over the comm, releasing the angry churn of his frostblade power axe.

'Scions of this world, brother,' replied Ravenblade coolly.

'Just find me more to kill,' growled Varek, reloading

his bolter and sweeping the muzzle over the barren landscape.

Svelok snarled. His blood was up, pumping round his massive frame and filling his bunched muscles with the need for movement. The wolf-spirit was roused, and he could feel its feral power coiled round his hearts. He suppressed the kill-urge with difficulty. His irritation with Ravenblade was finding other outlets, and that was dangerous.

'How far, and how long?' he spat, flexing his gauntlet impatiently.

'Three kilometres south,' said Ravenblade, consulting the auspex. 'One hour left.'

'Then we go now,' ordered Svelok, combat-readiness flooding his body again. 'There'll be more xenos, and I still haven't seen one bleed.'

KOLJA RAVENBLADE LOPED alongside the others, feeling his armoured boots thud against the unyielding rock. Gath Rimmon, the planetoid they'd been on for less than an hour, was a hellish maelstrom of acid-flecked storms. The sky was near-black, lit only by boiling electrical torment that scored the heavens with a tracery of silver fire. In every direction the landscape was dark and glossy, cut from unyielding rock and glinting dully in the flickering light. Acid pooled across the jagged edges, hissing and spitting as it splashed against the Astartes' armour. The four Space Wolves ran south through narrow defiles of jet, each worn down by millennia of erosion, each as pitiless and terrible as the ice-fields of Fenris in the heart of the Long Winter.

This world was angry. Angry with them, angry with itself. Somewhere, close by, Ravenblade could feel it. It was like the beat of a heart, sullen and deep. That was the sound that had drawn him here, echoing across the void, lodged in the psychic flesh of the universe. Something was hidden on Gath Rimmon, something that screamed of perversion.

And it was being guarded.

'Incoming!' bellowed Varek, halting suddenly and sending a volley of bolter fire into the air.

Ravenblade pulled out of his run and swept his staff from its mag-lock. His helm-display ran red with signals – they were coming from the sky. He spoke a single word and the shaft blazed with fluorescent power, flooding the land around.

Above them, dozens of creatures were flinging themselves from the high rock, talons of stone outstretched. They were carved from the same material as the planet, each of them crudely animated creatures of inorganic, immutable armour. Eight spindly legs curved down from angular abdomens, crowned with extended rigid plates for controlled gliding. At the end of the metre-long body, wide jaws gaped, lined with teeth of rending daggers. They plummeted towards the Space Marines soundlessly, like ghosts carved out of solid adamantium.

'Fell them!' ordered Svelok, his storm bolter spitting controlled bursts at the swooping xenos. The rounds all hit, sparking and exploding in showers of shattered rock. The Wolf Guard made killing look simple. A shame, thought Ravenblade, that he had no time for anything else.

Varek's bolter joined in the chorus of destruction, but some xenos still got through, wheeling down and twisting through the corridors of fire.

For those that made it, Lokjr waited. The massive warrior, his armour draped in the pelt of a white bear and hung with the skulls of a dozen kills, spun arcs of death with the whirring blade of his frost axe.

'For the honour of Fenris!' he roared, slamming the monomolecular edge in wide loops, slicing through the glistening rock-hide and tearing the flyers apart as they reached him.

Watching the carnage unfold, Ravenblade grasped his staff in both hands, feeling the power of his calling well up within him. The wind spun faster around his body, coursing over the rune-wound armour. Acid flecks spat against his ancient vambraces, fizzing into vapour as raw aether rippled across steel-grey ceramite.

'In the name of the Allfather,' he whispered, feeling the dark wolf within him snarl into life. The runes on his plate blazed with witchlight, blood-red like the heart of a dying star. He raised the staff above his head, and the wind accelerated into a frenzied whine. A vortex opened, swirling and cascading above the four Space Marines, billowing into the tortured air above them.

'Unleash!'

A column of lightning blazed down from the skies. As it reached Ravenblade's outstretched staff it exploded into a corona of writhing, white-hot fire, lashing out from the Rune Priest in whip-fronds of dazzling brilliance.

The surviving flyers were blasted open, ripped into slivers by the leaping blades of lightning, crushed and flayed by the atomising power of the storm. The Rune Priest had spoken, and the creatures of Gath Rimmon had no answer to his elemental wrath.

As the last of them crunched to the ground, Raven-blade released the power from the staff. The skirling corona rippled out of existence and a shudder seemed to bloom through the air.

By contrast with the fury of the storm, the Rune Priest stood as still and calm as ever. Unlike his brothers, his pack-manner was stealthy. If he hadn't been picked out by Stormcaller, perhaps the path of the Lone Wolf would have called for him.

Kilometres above them, the natural storm growled unabated. The planet had been cowed, but remained angry.

'Russ damn you, priest,' rasped Svelok, crushing a fallen flyer beneath his boot and crunching the stone to rubble. His helm was carved in the shape of a black wolf's head, locked in a perpetual curling grimace. In the flickering light its fangs glistened like tears. 'You'll bring more to us.'

'Let them come!' shouted Varek, laughing harshly over the comm.

Svelok turned on him. The Wolf Guard was a hand's breadth taller and broader than the Grey Hunter, though the aura of his ever-present battle-lust made him twice as terrifying. His armour was pitted and studded with old scars, and they laced the surface like badges of honour. Rage was forever present with him, frothing under the surface. Ravenblade could sense it through the layers of battle-plate, pulsing like an exposed vein.

'Don't be a fool!' Svelok growled. 'There's no time for this.'

Ravenblade regarded the Wolf Guard coldly. Svelok was as angry as the planet, his hackles raised by a mission he saw no use or glory in, but he was right. Time was running out. They all knew the acid tide was racing towards them. In less than an hour the ravines would be filling up, and ceramite was no protection against those torrents.

'I'll be the judge of that, brother,' warned the Rune Priest. 'We're close.'

Svelok turned to face him, his bolter still poised for assault. For a moment, the two Space Wolves faced one another, saying nothing. Svelok had no patience with the scrying arts, and no faith in anything but his bolter. He had almost a century more experience on the battle-front than Ravenblade, and took orders from no one but his Wolf Lord and Grimnar. Handling him would be a test.

'We'd better be,' he snarled at last, his voice thick with disdain. 'Move out.'

SIX KILOMETRES TO the north, Gath Rimmon's dark plains were deserted. The tearing wind scoured the stone, whipping up the acid that remained on it and sending curls of vapour twisting into the air.

In the centre of a vast, tumbled plateau of rock was a circular platform. Exposed to the atmosphere, it looked raw and out of place. Lightning flashed across the heavens, picking out the smooth edge of the aberration.

Suddenly, without any signal or warning, a crystalline pinprick began to spiral over the platform. It span rapidly, picking up speed and flashing with increasing intensity. It moulded itself, forming into a tall oval twice the height of a man. At its edge, psychic energy coursed and crackled. The rain whipped through it, vaporising and bouncing from the perimeter.

Then there was a rip. The surface of the ellipse sheered away. One by one, figures emerged from the portal. Eight of them. As the last stepped lightly from the oval, the perimeter collapsed into nothingness, howling back into a single point of nullity.

The arrivals were man-shaped, though far slighter than humans, let alone Space Marines. Six were clad in dark green segmented armour. They carried a chainsword in one hand and a shuriken pistol in the other. Their closed-faced helmets were sleek and tapered, and all had twin blasters set into the jowls. They fell into position around the platform, their movements silent and efficient.

Their leader remained in the centre. He was arrayed in the same armour, though his right hand was enclosed in a powerclaw and the mark of his shrine had been emblazoned across his chest. He moved with a smooth, palpable menace.

Beside him stood a figure in a white mask carrying a two-handed force sword. The blade swam with pale fire, sending tendrils of glistening energy snaking towards the ground. He wore black armour lined with bone-coloured sigils and warding runes. Ruby spirit-stones studded the surface, glowing angrily from the passage through the webway. He wore no robes of rank over his interlocking armour plates, but his calling was unmistakable. He was a psyker and a warrior. Humans, in their ignorance, called such figures warlocks, knowing little of what they spoke.

'You sense it, Valiel?' asked the claw-fisted warrior.

'South,' nodded the warlock. 'Be quick, exarch; the tides already approach.'

The exarch made a quick gesture with his chainsword, and the bodyguard clustered around him.

'Go fast,' he hissed. 'Go silent.'

As one, the eldar broke into a run, negotiating the treacherous terrain with cool agility. Like a train of ghosts, they slipped across the broken rocks, heading south.

SVELOK FELT BATTLE-FURY burning in his blood, filling his muscles and flooding his senses. He was a Space Wolf, a warrior of Fenris, and his one purpose was to kill. This chase, this *running*, was horrifying to him. Only the sanctity of his mission orders restrained him from turning and taking the wrath of Russ to every Grendel-clone on the planet. He knew the acid ocean was coming. He knew that the entire globe would soon be engulfed in boiling death. Even so, turning aside from the path of the hunt for the sake of a Rune Priest's dreams sickened him.

They were coming to the end of a long, narrow defile. The stone walls, serrated and near-vertical, blocked any route but south. A few metres ahead, hidden by a jutting buttress of rock, the route turned sharply right.

Svelok's helm-display flickered, and he blink-clicked to augment the feed. There were proximity signals on the far side of the buttress. Plenty of them.

Varek whooped with pleasure. 'Prey!' he bellowed, picking up the pace. By his side, the bear-like Lokjr kicked his frost axe into shimmering life and returned a throaty cry of aggression. 'Fodder for my blade, brother!'

Only Ravenblade remained silent, and his wolf-spirit remained dark. Svelok ignored him. Energy coursed through his own superhuman limbs, energy that needed to be dissipated. He was a Wolf Guard, a demigod of combat, the mightiest and purest of the Allfather's instruments of death, and this is what he'd been bred for.

'Kill them all!' he roared, his hearts pounding as he tore round the final corner and into the ravine beyond. His muscles tensed for impact, suffused with the expectation of righteous murder. A kind of elation bled into the fanged smile under his helm.

Past the buttress, tall cliffs of stone soared away on either side, cradling a narrow stretch of open ground. The massive Grendel-creatures were there, stalking like Titans across the stone, silent and dark. Flyers swooped among them. There were smaller creatures too, all encased in the acid-washed rock-hide of their kind, multi-faceted and covered in diamond-hard spikes and growths. Their vast mouths opened, each ringed with armour-shredding incisors.

Something was in their midst, hunted and cowering. The xenos had come to slay.

'Humans!' called out Lokjr, barrelling into the nearest walker. His frost axe slammed against its trailing leg, throwing up shards and sparks.

'Preserve them,' ordered Ravenblade, dropping to one knee and spraying bolter fire up at the circling flyers.

Svelok charged into the nearest spiked xenos, ducking under a clumsy swipe and punching up with his power fist. The stone chest shattered as the crackling disruption field tore through it. He threw an uppercut at the monster's head, ripping away spikes, before cracking it apart with a savage back-handed lunge. What was left of the xenos fell away and he ploughed on, heading to the heart of the melee.

A dozen weapon-servitors, grey-skinned and fizzing from the acid in the air, were being torn apart by two of the Grendels. Even as Svelok raced to intercept, a big one was ripped limb from limb by a talon-thrust, its pallid flesh impaled on the tips of massive claws, implanted machinery snapping and crunching. Las-blasts spat out in all directions, bouncing harmlessly from the rock-hide of the xenos.

'What are they doing here?' growled Varek, taking down his target with a volley of superbly positioned bolter rounds and whirling to confront the first of the slower-moving walkers.

Svelok sent a column of bolter shells into another spiked creature and charged into assault range. Above him, a Grendel was turning, its massive fists clenching with intent.

'Russ only knows,' he snapped. 'Just finish them!'

There was a crack of thunder above them and forks of lightning plunged from the sky. As coolly as ever, Ravenblade had got to work. Bolts of searing witch-fire slammed down, punching through rock-hide and breaking limbs apart. The rain of whining destruction was withering, and the smaller flyers were cut down from the air.

Svelok engaged the nearest Grendel, glorying in the crackling aura of his power fist. The wolf-spirit howled within him, and he crunched his fist into the creature's leading knee-joint. The stone shell shattered, bringing the massive xenos down. It plunged its own fist at Svelok's head, but the Space Wolf was already moving, darting to the left and releasing a barrage of rounds at the Grendel's open mouth. The bolts exploded, dousing the monster in a cataclysm of sparks.

'Death to the alien!' roared Svelok, his ragged voice ringing out of his helm's vox-unit and echoing across the ravine. His fist clenched around the trigger, and the twin barrels spat more streams of rock-tearing bolts.

Thrown back by the fury of the assault, the Grendel toppled, broken limbs grasping for purchase. Svelok leapt after it. His armour powered him into the air and on top of the creature's chest. He plunged down, pinning the monster, his power fist thrumming. Twice, three, four times he punched, his arm moving like a piston, his disruptor-shrouded gauntlet tearing up stone and delving into the heart of the xenos. It cracked, stove, crunched, shattered.

Then he leapt free, whirling to face his next target, clenching the power fist for another assault.

The Space Marines had sliced through the xenos as they'd been made to do. Only one of the big walkers remained. Ravenblade had it enclosed in an aura of blazing light, raised from the ground, coils of lightning crackling between it and the Rune Priest's staff. Helpless, it writhed within the nimbus of psychic power, trapped inside like an insect in amber. Ravenblade uttered a single word. The cracks in the creature's armour blazed white-hot, frozen for a second in a lattice of blazing tracery, then it blew itself apart in an orgy of bursting aether-fuelled immolation. Massive chunks of broken hide tore through the air, smoking and fizzing from the Rune Priest's warpborn energies.

Varek and Lokjr let their heads fall back and howled their victory, swinging their weapons around them like the barbarous warriors of Fenris they'd once been.

'For the Allfather!' Svelok bellowed, giving vent to his battle-fury. As Lokjr raised his massive arms in a gesture of defiance and triumph, the skulls at his belt clattered and swirled around him.

Only the Rune Priest remained unmoved. He let the vast power at his command bleed away and strode silently forwards. The bodies of servitors lay before him, ripped to shreds by the acid, or the xenos, or both. In the middle of them all hunched a human shape, clad in some kind of suit and unsteadily regaining its feet.

Svelok cursed under his breath. What was *wrong*

with the priest? Were his fangs so blunted by med-dling in runes that he couldn't revel in the joy of victory like a Son of Russ should? He reined in his own exuberance grudgingly, and made his way to the cowering form on the ground. Varek and Lokjr took up guard around them, no doubt eager for more combat.

The survivor was clad in bulky armour of an ancient template, blood-red in colour and fully covering his body. It looked obsolete, scored with the patina of years and covered in esoteric devices Svelok didn't recognise. Brass-coloured implants studded the surface, humming sclerotically and issuing hisses of steam. As the human rose, servos whined in protest and a thicket of mechadendrites scuttled out from hidden panels at his shoulders to begin repairing surface damage. Across his chest was the skull of the Adeptus Mechanicus, pitted and worn from age.

The man's face was hidden beneath a translucent dome of plexiglass filled with a thin blue mist. His head was little more than a dark shadow within that clouded interior, though the spidery shapes of augmetic rebreathers and sensor couplings could be made out.

'Speak, mortal,' ordered Svelok in Low Gothic, determined to interrogate him before Ravenblade could.

A series of clicks emerged from the dome. Eventually, hidden behind a wall of distortion, speech emerged from a vox-unit mounted on his sternum. There was no emotion in it, barely any humanity. It had been filtered through some proxy mechanism, cleansed of its imperfections and rendered blank and sterile. Svelok felt nothing but disgust.

'Adeptus Astartes,' came the voice. Then a train of jumbled clicks. 'Low Gothic, dialect Fenris Vulgaris. Recalling.'

Ravenblade stayed silent. Even through the barrier of the runic armour, Svelok could feel his keen interest in the pheromones his pack-brother emitted. Something had got the prophet worked up. Another vision? Or something else? He suppressed a low throat-rattle of irritation. There was no time for this.

'Identify as Logis Alsmo 3/66 Charis. Departmento Archeotech IV Gamma.'

Another pause.

'I should add,' he said. 'Thank you.'

THEY CAME TO a standstill. As they'd headed south, the plains had given way to twisting, steep-sided gorges. Pools of fluid could be seen glistening at the base of the defiles, harbingers of the deluge to come. They were closing on their quarry, but time was running out. The acid was coming.

'What do you sense?' asked the exarch.

The warlock remained silent, his head inclined to one side. Above him, the sides of the gorge soared upwards.

'Mon-keigh,' he said at last. 'And something else.'

Even as Valiel finished speaking, there was a crack in the rock face closest to him. The warriors snapped into a defensive cordon around the warlock.

A pillar of rock seemed to detach from the cliff nearest them. As it did so, jagged arms broke free from the torso, showering corrosive fluid. Silent as death, an eyeless creature, obsidian-clad and uncurling talons of stone, began to move towards them. Further down the gully, spiked variants detached, unfurling glossy limbs and exposing gem-like teeth.

'This world dislikes intruders,' said Valiel.

The exarch hissed an order, and the troops fanned out into a line in front of the warlock. The creatures lumbered nearer.

'Was *this* in your visions?' asked the exarch over his shoulder.

Valiel let the psychic surface of his witchblade fill with energy. These creatures hadn't been, but then glimpses of the future were always imperfect. That was what made the universe so interesting.

'You don't need to know. Just kill them.'

RAVENBLADE GLANCED AT his auspex. Thirty-nine minutes.

'Your purpose here, tech-priest,' he said, towering over the logis. 'Speak quickly – I can kill you as well as those xenos.'

He could still feel the dark wolf within him panting, circling impatiently, thirsting for more release. It would have to wait. There was also a shard of fear from the logis, generated by the vestigial part of whatever humanity he'd once had. The Space Wolves towered over him, their massive war-plate draped in gruesome trophies and adorned with runes of destruction.

'Rune Priest,' said the logis. 'Artificer armour, Fenris-pattern.'

Svelok growled his displeasure. 'Stop babbling, mortal, or I'll rip your arms off. Answer him.'

The logis shrank back, cogitators whirring. Communication in anything other than binaric seemed difficult.

'Gath Rimmon,' Charis said. 'Third world Iopheas Secundus system. Acid surface, total coverage, impenetrable, sensor-resistant, hyper-corrosive. No settlement possible, no surveys archived.'

Svelok took a half-step forwards, his gauntlet curling into a fist. 'We know this!' he rasped over the mission channel to Ravenblade. 'He's wasting our time.'

'Let him speak,' replied Ravenblade. His voice was calm, but firm.

'Single satellite, class Tertius, designation Riapax. Orbit highly irregular. Period 5,467 solar years. Proximity induces tidal withdrawal across polar massif for three local days, total exposure thirty-four standard hours. Opportunity for exploration. Sensors detect artefact. Mission dispatched. Xenos infiltration unanticipated.'

'What kind of artefact?'

'Unknown. Benefit analysis determined by age. Assessed Majoris Beta in priority rank system Philexus. Resources deployed accordingly.'

'You have a location?'

'Signal intermittent, 2.34 kilometres, bearing 5/66/774.'

'Then we need him,' said Ravenblade to Svelok on the closed channel.

'Forget it,' said Svelok. 'Too weak.'

'He has a lock. We don't have time to waste looking.'

'Morkai take you, prophet!' cried Svelok, spitting with vehemence. 'What *is* this thing? We diverted a *strike cruiser* for your visions.'

Ravenblade remained impassive. Svelok was the deadliest killer he'd ever seen, a single-minded inferno of perfectly controlled rage and zeal. Despite all of that, the Wolf Guard had no idea of the power of the Wyrd and the knowledge it gave Ravenblade. How could he? How could anyone but a Rune Priest understand?

'He comes with us. We have less than an hour to find it and return to the pick-up coordinates. The acid is returning, brother. When it comes, the chance will have gone for another five millennia.'

'Then let it lie. This worm can scurry after it.'

Ravenblade felt the dark wolf issue a low psychic growl, hidden to all but his aether-attuned instinct. Svelok was a stubborn bastard, as stubborn as the Great Wolf himself, but there were other ways of deciding this.

'Enough.'

He twisted open a casket hanging from his neck to reveal a dozen pieces of bone, each inscribed with a single rune on both sides. He spilled the pieces into his gauntlet's palm, marking how each fell. As he worked, he saw Svelok turn away in exasperation. The Wolf Guard had no time for the runes. That was his problem.

Ravenblade studied the sigils. Rune patterns were complex and subtle things. He opened his mind to the patterns in the abstract shapes. Across time and space, the angular outlines locked into their sacred formation. The sequence fell into place. He had his sign.

'The runes never lie, brother,' he said. 'We are meant to be here, and we are on the right course. The strands of fate demand it. And there's something else.'

He looked at Svelok, and this time spoke over the standard vox. Another element had emerged, one he'd not foreseen.

'I sense xenos,' he announced. 'They are here.'

THE EXARCH CALLED his warriors back. None of the creatures remained alive. Two had died in the assault, their fragile armour rent by the talons of the world's guardians. Once the shell was broken, the acid rain did the rest.

'Safeguard the spirit stones,' ordered Valiel, sheathing his witchblade and bringing his breathing under control. The survivors did his bidding silently.

'Are we near?' The exarch's voice, muffled by a damaged speech matrix, was tainted with accusation. Valiel regarded him carefully. The exarch was the deadliest killer he'd ever seen, a relentless master of close-ranged combat. Despite all of that, the warrior had little idea of the full power of the warp and the knowledge it gave Valiel. How could he? How could anyone but a warlock understand?

'See for yourself.'

Before them, the series of winding gullies opened out into a wide valley which ran towards the southern horizon. At the far end of the valley was a cliff of cloud, flecked with pale lightning at its base. A distant roar came from it, just like the sea coming in.

'The tides approach,' said the exarch, resentment still in his voice. He feared nothing but that which he couldn't fight. So it was with all those lost on the warrior path.

'What we seek lies on the precipice of danger,' said Valiel. 'Remember your vows, killer.'

The warriors returned and waited. Valiel could sense their doubt, just like their master's.

'Follow me,' said the warlock. He didn't wait for the exarch's assent. Now, above all else, he trusted in the vindication of his vision. The artefact was at hand. Ignoring the acid rain as it streaked across his armour, the warlock strode down the floor of the gorge and into the valley beyond.

SVELOK'S PACK BROKE from the cover of the gorges and into a wide, bowl-shaped valley. At its far end, a few kilometres distant, the storm raged unabated. A low roar echoed from the mountain walls on either side. The tide-line was almost visible. Even now the rocks underfoot were sodden with puddles of gently hissing fluid. The planet's inhabitants had been driven off for now, but the pack was still being shadowed by flyers, circling out of bolter range like vultures.

They kept running, kept the pace tight. Twenty-five minutes. Ravenblade could taste the acrid stench of the distant acid ocean. Readings scrolled down his helm-display detailing atmospheric toxicity. Nothing his armour couldn't handle. For now.

'Bearing,' he ordered over the mission channel.

'Imminent, Space Marine,' responded the logis, struggling to match the pace in his archaic armour. 'Recommend halt.'

The Space Wolves came to a standstill and waited for Charis to catch up. The rain streaked and steamed from their battle-plate. Lokjr's bear pelt was being eaten away, and the runes of Ravenblade's pauldrons were still glowing an angry red, like wounds washed in iodine.

'Located,' said Charis. A laser-sight extended from his right shoulder and pointed out a piece of flat rock a few metres distant.

'Russ, that's nothing!' mocked Varek.

'Silence!' ordered Svelok, his mood clearly still dark. 'We'll examine it.'

As Ravenblade approached the site he had a sudden lurch of remembrance. He'd seen it before. Like a déjà vu, the blank gap in the stone loomed up towards him. He had no doubts. This was where he'd been drawn to.

No more than five metres square, a shaft had been bored directly down into the valley floor. It plunged vertically, sides smooth and open to the elements. It was perfectly black, as if it went all the way down to Hel. There were no steps, and few hand-holds. Far above them, the thunder growled, echoing from the valley sides.

'That's it?' demanded Svelok.

Ravenblade nodded, mag-locking his staff. 'Where we're meant to be, brother.'

'You *sense* it?'

The psychic signal filled Ravenblade's mind, drowning out the pheromone-signatures of his battle-brothers. All that he could sense was the thing that had drawn him, and the stench of the xenos. Both were close.

'Trust me.'

Svelok turned away. 'Lokjr, you'll hold. Drop anything that gets close. Varek, take point. We're going down.'

Panels on Charis's gauntlets and vambraces opened up, revealing clawed extensions capable of gripping the rock face. The Space Marines, with their occulobe-enhanced vision and superhuman poise, needed no such aids.

Varek swung himself over the edge, his boots finding instant purchases against the rock, and started to descend.

Ravenblade turned away, reaching for the runes again. Surreptitiously, keeping them shielded from Svelok, he spilled the bone fragments into his palm once more.

'What do you see?' The rumbling voice was Lokjr's. Unlike his superior, the Grey Hunter had a pious respect for the readings.

Ravenblade stared at the figures resting on his gauntlet. The fragments glistened pale in the darkness. Shapes swam before his eyes, resisting interpretation. Elk, Fire, Axe, Death, Ice. None of them stood in their proper relations. There was no pattern. Ravenblade felt a rare pang of unease. For the first time in his life, over a hundred years of service, the runes were blank. There was nothing.

'All is at it should be,' he said, snatching up the bones and putting them away. 'Time to go.'

SVELOK WENT CAREFULLY but quickly, testing each hold before placing his weight on it. He knew as well as the others that when the tide came up the valley floor it would cascade down the shaft on top of them. Whatever happened, they had to be back up on the surface before then. Damn that priest. This mission was pointlessly dangerous. They didn't even know what they were hunting down. His pack-brothers respected the Wyrd, but he'd never trusted it. There was a thin line between augmentation and corruption, and Rune Priests walked it perilously.

He blink-clicked a feed from Ravenblade's auspex to his helm display. Twenty minutes.

'Report,' he snapped.

There was a low thud from below him as Varek leapt to the bottom of the shaft.

'At the base,' he responded. 'No targets.'

Svelok checked his proximity readings.

'Teeth of Russ,' he spat. 'Where are those xenos?'

He crunched to the ground beside Varek. On three sides, the stone walls continued to the level of the floor. The fourth opened out into a small underground chamber carved roughly from the rock. As Ravenblade and Charis completed the descent, the lumen-beams of the Space Marines' helms ran across the enclosed space.

A circular access hatch had been carved into the floor of the chamber. Svelok's helm detected the force field across it – one strong enough to withstand five thousand years of acid erosion.

'The mechanism may prove–' started Charis.

A blast rang out across the chamber, and the embedded control panel exploded with a gout of oily smoke. The field shimmered and gave out.

'Varek, with me,' barked Svelok, his bolter barrel glowing from the discharge. 'Priest, keep an eye on the mortal.'

Then he leapt through the hatch, landing heavily several metres down and throwing up a cloud of fragile debris. He sprang away, whirling his bolter round.

Still no targets. His lumen-beam ran over banks of equipment. Cogitators, they looked like, ancient and dark. He heard a crash behind him as Varek joined him. Together they swept the space with their weapon muzzles.

Nothing. The room was empty. It had been empty for millennia. A chamber no more than ten metres square, packed with defunct machinery, heavy with decay. Coils of translucent piping lay breached and desiccated in the dust. Bundles of machine-spirit conduits led from cogitator banks to an elaborate brass altar, black with age, studded with skulls and obscure control runes. There was a faint hum from somewhere, as if the force field had a counterpart hidden in the chamber. Cracked crystal viewports were as dark and lifeless as the shaft above them, and the floor was thick with ancient dust.

Ravenblade and Charis clambered down from the hatch via footholds in the wall. Svelok lowered his bolter and widened his lumen-beam.

The altar was the centrepiece. Though tarnished

and old, the pipes and embellishments were massively complex. The hum came from its base, and a faint power reading registered on his helm display. Sitting on the altar was a box. A small, black box. Fascinated, Charis edged towards it.

Svelok turned to Ravenblade.

'You sensed xenos,' he said. 'Where are they?'

The Rune Priest didn't reply. He was looking at the space where Svelok had landed. There was a shattered ribcage on the floor, brittle with age. Other bones littered the floor. Ravenblade snapped his gaze towards the altar.

'They're here, Space Wolf.'

Charis's voice had taken on a fresh clarity, and he suddenly seemed to have no trouble with rendering Gothic. Svelok and Varek spun round to face him. The logis withdrew his gauntlet and exposed a grey-fleshed claw of a hand, riddled with mechanical components. He took the box.

'They've always been here.'

VALIEL DROPPED THROUGH the hatch, landing lightly on the pristine metal floor. He sprang clear, making room for the warriors to follow. The dark green figures leapt into the room, rolling away and uncoiling into attack poses, the exarch close behind.

The chamber was harshly lit and lined with gleaming machinery. Coils of translucent pipes pumped coolant from cogitator banks to an elaborate brass altar, studded with skull-and-cog devices and surmounted by a humming containment field. Runes flickered across crystal viewports as the arcane clusters of machinery clicked through their protocols. A low humming gave away the power stored in the room, enough to supply a protective field of prodigious strength.

The chamber's lone occupant whirled round to face them. A human, wearing bright red armour. The close-fitting plates were covered in gleaming mechadendrites, all clicking animatedly, sparkling under the bright strip lighting. His domed helmet had been retracted, revealing a thin, young face. Only a few augmetics marred the taut skin, though there already fresh incisions on his cheeks where more would be added.

He looked terrified.

Valiel let a ripple of sapphire pass down his blade.

*Kill*, he ordered psychically.

The warriors sprang towards the human. Two kept low, sending a stream of metal from their mandiblasters. Two more leapt into the air, chainswords whirling. The exarch took the direct route, firing from his shuriken pistol as he swung his claw into position.

It all happened in a single heartbeat, and yet the human reacted. That should have been impossible.

Mandiblaster darts homed in and folded out of existence. Shuriken bolts disappeared, winking into nothingness. The man raised his hand and the warriors crumpled into agony. Valiel felt their psychic screams as their souls were ripped from their bodies and sucked, howling, into the box. Dark tongues of matter like strings of ink shot out from the box. They clamped on to the exarch, tearing his spirit from his body. His broken husk fell to the floor, his faceplate distorted into a many-dimensioned mess.

So quick. Valiel remained calm, feeding his blade energy. Tendrils of aether-born plasma curled round his armour like the tails of cats.

'So you've learned some of its tricks,' he said in heavily-accented Gothic. 'That won't help you. If you keep using it, they'll find you.'

Logis Alsmo Charis walked forwards. As he did so the box folded up and switched aspect in his hand. At times it resembled a cube, at others a pyramid, others a rhomboid. Every heartbeat, a new shape. Valiel knew, as the human could not, that it was folding across many dimensions as well. It was an abomination, the product of a mind beyond the imagination of a mon-keigh, and its power had been proscribed on the craftworlds for millennia. Despite his long training, Valiel felt his gaze drawn to it.

So terrible. So beautiful.

'You think I came here to use it?' the logis said, his voice growing in confidence. His fear was fading. 'I came here to hide it. The trail will die.'

'Then so will you.'

Charis flexed his fingers, already laced with steel slivers of augmetic technology.

'I'll find a way.'

He launched a lashing column of black fire from the box.

Valiel sprang clear, kindling the witchblade as he rose. He somersaulted clear of the box's blast, landing lightly on a cogitator bank. His blade shot out, spitting a flurry of brilliant silver stars towards the human. The man evaded the strikes and leapt back towards the warlock.

His outline shimmered like a Warp Spider's. The box was shifting him.

Charis twisted the box. A black mirror flew into being, rotating across the chamber, reflecting thousands of possible states on its shimmering surface. Valiel knew what it was instantly. He twisted away, but the glass enveloped him. As it passed through him, bulging like water across his body, he felt his soul dragged from his body, folded into miniscule shards of pain-filled insignificance. He was pulled from the bank and crashed to the floor.

The surface of the warped glass shattered. Valiel came to a halt, prone, locked down. His sword clattered away. He felt his essence dissipated. There was no physical pain, but the psychic agony was unbearable. He stifled his screams as the human loomed over him. The box was still in his hand, and was changing shape quickly now.

'Unwise, to try and prevent me.'

Valiel let his eyes flicker to the roof.

*Too powerful. Why was I led here?*

He opened his tormented mind, bent all his fading power towards the multiple paths stretching away from this moment. The structure of the universe always gave you options.

*I am only a part of this.*

Valiel felt the humming malevolence of the box grow. With all the strength that remained in him, he locked away everything he knew about the device, its origins, his mission. History, time itself, condensed into a single form. A glyph. A key. One with the right power would know how to use it.

With a cry of agonised effort, a final blast of witch-fire streaked from his clenched fingers, tugging at those strands of his soul still gathered together, tearing the psychic sinews of his inner self.

Charis moved quickly, trying to deflect it with the box, but the bolt flew clear, striking the metal rim of the hatch above, cracking it and careering across the roof. As the flame burned out it left a trail behind it on the stone. An intricate trail.

Charis ignored it. The last traces of terror had left his eyes, and flickers of a confident hatred distorted his features.

'A waste,' he spat, spinning the box-forms on his palm idly. 'You're no different from the rest. Think carefully on that, alien filth. *Your* people started this. *I* will finish it.'

Valiel tried to speak, but his mouth no longer obeyed him. The mon-keigh was mistaken about that, like so much else. He knew nothing of the varied allegiances of Valiel's ancient kind. The mon-keigh were so crude, so *simple*.

The box opened. Defenceless, Valiel felt his soul dragged into isolation, his remaining essence torn from his material form and sucked within the shifting walls of the device. For an instant, while his eyes still worked, he caught a glimpse of what was inside. Part of him understood what was in there, knew it from myths and scraps of legend. He could see movement, layers, shifting upon shifting, the dark heart revolving before a...

He tried to scream, but his vocal chords were no longer his own.

The box clicked shut.

Charis looked down at the burnt-out corpse of the warlock. Not as powerful as he'd been led to fear. The dark ones had been worse.

He hurried over to the altar and placed the box in the receptacle he'd made for it. Leaving it was hard, but he had to master the secrets of it, and *they* were coming. He withdrew his hand and his armoured gauntlet extended over the exposed flesh, sealing him in against the acid. He depressed a rune on the nearby panel and the cogitators clicked into life, feeding the containment field, keeping it safe. A whiff of ozone burst across the chamber, and the air began to crackle with bounded energies.

The tides were returning. The xenos had delayed but not defeated him. With a final glance across the chamber, Charsis let the dome close over his head. He had to leave – they'd be tearing space apart to find him. Once he was safely away, there was work to be done. Lore to be studied. Secrets to be uncovered. And then the long years of stasis while he waited for Riapax to uncover the shaft again.

So much to do before he'd be back. But then there was so much to learn.

RAVENBLADE'S STAFF BURST into flame, kindling on the angular incisions inscribed along the shaft, and the dark wolf's hackles raised. The box held by Charis was shedding psychic energy. *Incredible* amounts. It was opening and closing in on itself with dizzying speed.

Svelok and Varek moved instantly.

'Lokjr!' Svelok barked into the comm-link. 'Down here. Now!'

The sergeant barrelled across the chamber, power fist crackling. Varek let fly a stream of rounds, each aimed with exact precision: head, neck, armour joints. As they hit, they folded out of existence. Nothing left as much as a mark.

Then Svelok was in range. He hurled a heavy blow with the power fist, aiming for the gap between shoulder and helmet. Charis fell back astonishingly quickly, but the fist still caught him, sinking into the armour. It disappeared. The ceramite crumpled and distorted, and the disruption field flew wildly out of frequency.

Svelok fell back with a snarl and snapped up his storm bolter. Before he could get a round away Charis's gauntlet punched him heavily in the face. As the fist impacted, black flames exploded from the blow, spiralling out like seeker flares. Svelok was hurled backwards, feet flung from the ground before crashing into a bank of cogitators. The muzzle of his wolf-helm had been folded in on itself.

'Death, traitor!' roared Varek, tearing straight at Charis, discarding his bolter for his fists. He smashed into the logis, closing his gauntlet over the box, aiming to tear it away.

'No!' cried Ravenblade, swinging his staff into position.

Varek bellowed in agony as his arm was sucked from real space, dragging him after it. The limb was ripped into a vortex of distortion, blood flying in concentric spirals, armour cracking and flesh tearing.

Ravenblade let fly with a searing ball of lightning, engulfing Charis's breastplate and ramming him against the altar. What was left of Varek slumped against the floor, gurgling in a froth of blood, half of his body ripped away. Ravenblade swung round for a second strike, and his staff crackled with storm-pulled fury.

He didn't even see the blast from the box. All he felt was the pain as it hit him. The rending, mind-unlocking pain. That was what the device was for, its only purpose. It had been made by a master of technology so advanced that it looked like sorcery. In that moment, exposed to its searching mind, Ravenblade knew its name. In the ancient xenos language now only spoken in one city in the galaxy, it was the *Ayex Commorragh*. The Heart of Agony.

Black fire shattered his defences, tore through his psychic wards. He felt himself being lifted backwards, armour aflame. He hit the wall with a crack, crashing into the rock. The fire kept coming. Blood trickled down the inside of his helmet. He felt his breastplate rip away, exposing the flesh beneath. The black carapace bubbled and split, shredding the skin, tearing up the muscle.

'For the Allfather!'

Ravenblade half-heard Lokjr's charge into the chamber, his frost axe pulsating with energy. Charis whirled to deal with him, but Svelok was back on his feet too, his bolter spitting. Ravenblade felt consciousness slipping away, and fought to hold on to it.

He was collapsing into shock. He needed to fix on something. Anything.

He let his head fall back. His eyes flicked to the roof. That was when he saw it. Blasted into the ceiling of the chamber, scored in witchfire, was the thing that had drawn him. The rune. It had been in his dreams for months, deep in the void, out on the strike cruiser. It was the key.

It was enough. His mind unlocked.

Deep within him, crippled and bloody, the dark wolf opened its yellow eyes. A succession of images raced through his consciousness, overlapping with each other as they crowded into his mind. He sensed the souls thronging around him, impossibly old, long-dead. There was a warlock in a white mask and black armour. He'd been here, five thousand years ago.

More images rushed into his mind. Another planet, covered in Adeptus Mechanicus complexes, hells of industry. Dark shapes streaked across the burning skies, jagged-winged flyers, crewed by nightmares. There were men and women running, faces contorted with terror. Among them strode thin-limbed corsairs. Eldar they were too, but of a different kind. In the midst was the architect of the Heart, the haemonculus, hunched over his machinery of terror, watching the slaves being herded through the webway portal. His skin was grey, riddled with black veins. The eyes were pitiless wells of ennui, windows on to a heart driven cold by centuries of horror. There was a terrible intelligence there, a mastery of forbidden arts. He'd used the box to create pain from outside the bounds of the universe. That, and that alone, was why it had been made.

The vision shifted. There was fighting, ranks of human troops moving through the shattered cityscape. The corsairs were driven back. The haemonculus had lingered too long, and soldiers in carapace armour, skitarii, ordinatus, all piled into the vision. There were crippling explosions, massed volleys of las-fire, a retreat. The webway portal closed. The nightmares were gone.

It shifted again. In the midst of the ruination, surrounded by weeping survivors and smouldering rubble, a young logis came. He looked handsome, his flesh as yet unmarked by the touch of the Machine-God. He bent down, drawn by a strange black box. It had a certain pleasing construction. He took it, covering it in his robes. He'd keep it secret, learn how to use it.

But the nightmares knew how to find the box. They came back, pursuing him across the stars. While he had it, they could find him. He could never rest long enough to master it. It had to be hidden. Somewhere far away. Safe while he learned what it was. Safe until the trail died and he could come back to collect it.

Ravenblade snapped back into consciousness. The visions shuddered into nothing. He hadn't been summoned here by the box. He'd been summoned here by the witchfire rune, left by the xenos whose presence he still sensed. The real world rushed into focus around him. All that remained of the mind-transfer were five words.

*I have weakened the portal.*

Ravenblade tried to pull himself up. Even his superhuman constitution was near collapse. Blood, half-coagulated, pumped from his exposed chest. Lokjr and Svelok fought on. They were being ripped apart. None of their weapons bit. They ducked around the vicious blasts of black fire with all their skill, but the end was only a matter of time. Even as he watched, Ravenblade saw Lokjr's frost axe suddenly pulled across dimensions and smashed into scraps of metal by the Heart.

He dragged himself into a half-seated position, lungs burning. Charis had closed the hatch above them, sealing them in. He had control over every device in the room and had ensured that none of them would escape.

But Ravenblade was a son of Fenris, and escape was the last thing on his mind. Just like Svelok, he was a dealer in death, a predator, a hunting beast of the endless war. Only the manner of the kill differed.

Ravenblade closed his charred eyes and opened his mind to the immaterium. The dark wolf growled with pleasure. The runes on his armour went black as Ravenblade pulled all his remaining power to himself. He went back to the essence of his Rune Priest training, the primal tools of his art.

The elements. And this was a world of storms.

'Unleash.'

Ravenblade screamed as the pain coursed through his body and mind. Far above, he could sense the torrent answer his call. Clouds boiled and raced, hurtling to the source of the summons. Acid oceans, already close, surged across the blasted land, swollen unnaturally by the power at Ravenblade's command.

The rain increased. It became a deluge, hammering against the rocks. Even shielded by twenty metres of stone, Ravenblade could feel the breaking fury. Corrosive fluid rushed across the valley floor and down the shaft above the chamber, bubbling and churning. He piled on more energy, ignoring the warnings of terminal stress from his body. He felt his primary heart give out, but still the maelstrom responded to the call. He could sense the weight of the acid as it pressed against the hatch. The metal began to steam.

He opened his eyes. Lokjr had been cast aside, his face half-dissolved by the Heart. Even as he watched, Svelok was thrown backwards, a two-metre tall giant in full power armour hurled like a doll across the chamber, shattering machines as he skidded along the floor. Then Charis came for him.

'Russ guide me,' whispered Ravenblade, seizing his bolt pistol from its holster, swinging it upwards and firing at the hatch.

The metal exploded instantly, blowing shards across the chamber, unleashing the torrent. Acid sheeted down. The cogitators fizzed and exploded, sending blooms of sparks skittering across the floor. Ravenblade went into spasms of fresh agony as the searing liquid ran across his open wounds. His back arched as he cried out, doused in gouts of boiling liquid pain.

Too slow, Charis's naked hand was snatched back into its gauntlet. The acid tore through the exposed flesh, eating through skin, bone and metal. The logis shrieked in his turn, his fear unfiltered by the vox-distorter. He tried to clutch the box, but his fingers were gone, washed into the slew of ankle-deep acid bubbling at his feet. It tumbled from his grip, dropping into the seething, corroding mass.

As it hit the liquid, it flipped into a dizzying array of shapes. For a moment it span desperately, its walls folding impossibly fast. Then, feeling even its infinite malignance threatened, the spinning stopped. There was a shudder, and the air around it burned away in a sudden blaze of ozone. The acid bath surged into a boiling sphere, furious and infused with black fire. The box emitted a deafening scream, as if a million tortured voices had been sucked back into the mortal plane for an instant.

Then the acid ball exploded in a blinding, whirling inferno. At its core, the box folded itself out of existence and the psychic backwash from its departure tore out from the epicentre.

Ravenblade cried aloud as the warp echo scored his exposed soul. Eyes bleeding, lungs burning, he hauled himself to his knees, trying to shelter his open chest cavity from the tumbling rain. Every move was a symphony of agony, physical and psychic.

'You... *killed* it!'

Charis stumbled towards him, his remaining gauntlet clutching impotently. Freed from the protection of the box, his armour was corroding fast. Mechadendrites extended, blades whirring. The Rune Priest, chest ripped open, psychic senses seared away, had no defences left. He snatched the bolt pistol into position, but it slipped through his broken fingers.

'For Russ!'

His voice ringing with rage, Svelok burst from the acid like a leviathan rising from the ocean, armour streaming with fluid. He staggered into range and smashed his fist straight through Charis's visor. The glass shattered, cracking the logis back against the altar and snapping his spine. For a moment, Ravenblade caught a glimpse of a hideously ruined face within, riddled with augmetics. Then it was gone, consumed by the foaming deluge.

RAVENBLADE'S VISION WAVERED. He was close to passing out. The acid burned against his chest, eating its way into his core. The liquid was now knee-deep around him.

'We have to go, priest,' Svelok rasped, his battle-plate pitted and steaming. The combat-fury was gone from his voice, replaced by grim resolve. He dragged Ravenblade to his feet, sending fresh needles of pain shooting through his body.

'The staff,' gasped the Rune Priest.

'No time.'

Svelok hauled Ravenblade to the footholds, shouldering the Rune Priest's massive armoured weight. Fluid showered down from the portal, sluicing over Ravenblade's breastplate, snaking under the ruined carapace, worming into his wounds. His organs were failing.

He gritted his teeth. Not yet.

Svelok went first up the ladder, pulling Ravenblade after him. His strength was incredible. It was all

Ravenblade could do to hang on, keep his feet on the holds, stay conscious.

The ascent up the rock was a nightmare. Falling acid burned through the armour plate with horrifying speed. Every agonising step saw their protection thinned a little more. Ravenblade watched the runes on his vambrace blaze red as the liquid sank into the impressions. The runes he'd carved himself, now smoking into oblivion.

They reached the top of the shaft. Shouldering his bulk against the torrent, Svelok pulled himself back onto the valley floor. With an almighty heave, he dragged Ravenblade up behind him.

The fury of the heavens had been unleashed. Lightning streaked across the angry sky. Rain fell in swathes. Acid swilled across the full width of the valley floor, bubbling and foaming. To the south, there were white-topped waves. Riapax was heading back into the void, and the ocean was reclaiming its own. They were out of time.

Ravenblade's helm lenses flickered and went dark. Acid must have got into the mechanism.

'Nearly as... bad as... Fenris,' he gasped, feeling the tightness in his throat grow.

Svelok dragged Ravenblade to his feet, pulling the Rune Priest's arm over his shoulder. Despite his wounds, he was still a furnace of energy and determination. For the first time, Ravenblade began to see his true value to the pack. He was everything a Son of Russ should be.

'Nearly as,' Svelok agreed grimly, dragging them both to higher ground. They reached a flat-topped outcrop, jutting from the rising acid around them. It wouldn't last long. Even now the liquid at its foot was knee-deep. It would soon be waist-deep.

The two of them clambered onto the rock shelf. Ravenblade collapsed against the stone, his breath ragged. Far above them, thunder rolled across the valley. The torrent surged by, washing against the edges of their little island.

Svelok bent over Ravenblade, trying to shield the stricken Rune Priest from the downpour.

'Hold on, prophet,' he said, then corrected himself. '*Brother*. We're not dead yet.'

The Wolf Guard hid his emotions poorly. Ravenblade could sense the full range of frustration and regret. They were far from the pick-up location. Better to prepare for the end, to meet the Allfather with honour. Battle-rage had its place, but not now.

As for himself, he could no longer feel anything in his limbs. His torso was lost in a dull ache, the nerve-endings burned away. A task had been achieved on Gath Rimmon, even if it wasn't the one he'd expected.

'They were blank,' coughed Ravenblade, tasting the blood in his mouth.

'What were?' Svelok's voice was no longer coloured with suspicion. Two battle-brothers had gone. Two pack-members. The bond between them was severed. Now a third strand would be cut.

The roar above them got louder. It wasn't just thunder. There were lights in the clouds, and the whine of engines.

'The runes,' said Ravenblade. He saw the huge

shadow of a Thunderhawk descend from above, searchlights whirling. That was good. Svelok would live to tell the saga.

'Don't speak, brother.'

The pain went. The Allfather had granted him that, at least.

'I will speak,' Ravenblade croaked, letting the last of the air in his lungs bleed away. 'You must learn from this, Wolf Guard. We were part of a greater pattern here. There is always a pattern.'

His vision faded to black.

'Your fury gives you strength, but it is fate that guides you. Remember it.'

The dark wolf gave him a final, mournful look, then loped into the shadows. Ravenblade was truly alone then, just as he had been before taking the Canis Helix.

'Even across so much time and space,' he rasped, feeling Morkai steal upon him. 'The runes never lie.'

# THE REWARDS OF TOLERANCE

## by Gav Thorpe

ENCASED IN A flickering Geller field, the *Vengeful* slid through the psychic tides of the warp. The field flared intermittently as it crossed the path of itinerant warp denizens, becoming a shell of writhing, fanged faces and swirling colours. In the turmoil of its wake, dark shapes gathered in a flitting shoal; occasionally a creature would speed forwards and hurl itself at the strike cruiser, seeking the life force of those within. Each time the unreal predators were hurled back by a flash of psychic force.

Sitting in the Navigator's cockpit Zacherys, former Librarian of the Avenging Sons, gazed out into the warp through eyes ablaze with blue energy. Sparks crackled from the pinpricks of his pupils and thick beads of sweat rolled down his cheeks. With a trembling hand, he reached out to the comm-unit and switched to the command frequency.

'I can hear them whispering,' he growled.

There was a hiss of static before the reply came through the speakers.

'Hold them as long as you can,' said Gessart, the ship's captain. Once master of an Avenging Sons company, he now led a small renegade band only two dozen strong. 'We'll reach safe exit distance in less than an hour.'

The comm buzzed for a few seconds more and fell silent. Left alone in the quiet, Zacherys could not help but listen to the voices pawing at the edge of his hearing. Most were gibberish, some snarled threats, others begged Zacherys to let down his guard. A mellifluous voice cut through, silencing them with its authority.

*I can take you to safety*, it said. *Listen to me, Zacherys. I can protect you. All I ask is a small favour. Just let me help you. Open your thoughts to me. Let me see your mind and I will grant your desires.*

The sensation of claws prising at the sides of Zacherys's thoughts suddenly disappeared, like a great pressure released by an opening airlock. The chittering stopped and the Geller field stabilised, becoming a placid oily-sheened bubble once more.

Zacherys relaxed his fingers, loosening his fist on the arm of the Navigator's chair, indentations left in the metal from his fierce grip. He took a deep breath and closed his eyes. When he opened them, they had returned to normal, the burst of psychic energy drawn back into his mind.

Thank you, he thought.

*You are welcome*, replied the voice.

What do I call you? Zacherys asked.

*Call me Messenger*, it said.

What are you? A daemon?

*I am Messenger. I am the one that will open your mind to your true power. I will show you the full scope of your abilities. Together we will grow stronger. We will both be pupil and teacher.*

We need to break out of warp space, thought Zacherys. I cannot resist another attack.

*Allow me*, said Messenger. *Call to me when you return. I will be waiting.*

The streaming rivers of psychic energy surrounding the *Vengeful* bucked and spiralled, turning upon themselves until they split into an immaterial whirlpool. Through the widening hole, Zacherys could see the blue glow of a star.

Fingers moving gently across the steering panel, he guided the *Vengeful* towards the opening. The strike cruiser burst out of the immaterium with a flash of multi-coloured light. The rift behind fluttered for a moment and disappeared. Silence followed; the emptiness of space. Zacherys looked around and saw a dense swathe of stars: the northern arm of the galactic spiral spread out before him. He smiled with relief and prodded the automatic telemetry systems into action. It was time to find out where they were.

THE RENEGADE SPACE Marines gathered in the briefing hall. The twenty-four warriors barely filled a quarter of the large chamber, which was designed to house a whole Space Marine company. Gessart looked down from the briefing podium and marvelled at how quickly his followers had asserted their individuality. After decades of loyal service to their Chapter – centuries in the case of some – the Space Marines were rediscovering their true selves, throwing off millennia of tradition and dogma.

All of them wore armour blackened with thick paint, their old livery and symbols obliterated. Some had gone further, taking their gear down to the armoury to chisel off Imperial insignia and weld plates over aquilas and other icons of the Imperium. A few had painted new mottos across the black to replace the devotional texts that had been removed. In a neat script, Willusch had written 'The Peace of Death' along the rim of his left shoulder pad. Lehen-hart, with his customary humour, had daubed a white skull across the face of his helm, a ragged bul-let hole painted in the centre of its forehead. Nicz, Gessart's self-appointed second-in-command, sat with a chainsword across his lap, a thin brush in his left hand, putting the finishing touches to his own design: 'The Truth Hurts', written in red paint to resemble smeared blood.

Zacherys was the last to attend. The psyker nodded to Gessart as he sat down, confirming the location estimate he had passed on earlier. Gessart smiled.

'It seems that though the Emperor looks over us no more, we have not yet been abandoned by the galaxy,' he announced. 'Helmabad is more than a dozen light years behind us. That's the only good news. We are dangerously low on supplies, despite what we sal-vaged from Helmabad. We are six thousand light years away from safety; a considerable distance. If we are to complete our journey to sanctuary in the Eye of Terror, we will need more weapons and equipment, as well as food.'

Gessart rasped a hand across the thick stubble on his chin. The Space Marines all looked at him attentively, faces impassive as they received this news. Some habits were harder to break than others and they waited in silence for their leader to continue.

'Whether by luck, fate or some other power, our half-blind flight through the warp has brought us within a hundred light years of the Geddan system. The system is virtually lifeless, but it's a chartist captains' convoy meeting point; merchant ships from across the sector converge there to make the run down past the ork territories towards Rhodus. We'll take what we need from the merchantmen.'

'Those convoys have Imperial Navy escorts,' said Heynke.

'Usually nothing more than a few frigates and destroyers,' said Nicz before Gessart could answer. 'Not too much for a strike cruiser to overcome.'

'If this were a fully-manned ship, I'd agree,' said Gessart. 'But it isn't. If there's a light escort we'll try to cut out a cargo ship or two and avoid confrontation. If there's a more sizeable Imperial Navy presence we cannot risk an open battle. The task is to gather more supplies, not expend what little we have.'

Nicz conceded the point with a shrug.

'You're in charge,' the Space Marine muttered.

Gessart ignored the slight and turned his attention to Zacherys.

'Can you guide us to Geddan in a single jump?'

The psyker looked away for a moment, obviously unsure.

'I think I can manage that,' he said eventually.

'Can you, or can't you?' snapped Gessart. 'I don't want to drop into the middle of something we aren't expecting.'

Zacherys nodded, uncertainly at first and then with greater conviction.

'Yes, I have a way to do it,' the psyker said. 'I can take us to Geddan.'

'Good. There is another issue that needs to be resolved before we leave,' said Gessart. He looked directly at Nicz, who glanced to either side, surprised by his commander's attention.

'Something I've done?' said Nicz.

'Not yet,' replied Gessart. 'The menial crew are still loyal to us, but they do not know the full facts of what happened on Helmabad. If we have to fight at Geddan, there can be no hesitation. I want you to ensure that they will open fire on command, even against an Imperial vessel. I want every weapon system overseen by one of us, and dispose of any crew that may prove problematic.'

'Dispose?' said Nicz. 'You mean kill?'

'Don't get carried away, we cannot run the ship without them. But leave them with no doubt that we are still their masters and they will follow our instructions without question.'

'I'll see that it is done,' said Nicz, patting his chainsword.

'Are there any questions?' Gessart asked the rest of the Space Marines. They exchanged glances and shook their heads until Lehenhart stood up.

'What happens when we reach the Eye of Terror?' he asked.

Gessart considered his reply carefully.

'I don't know. We'll have to go there and find out. At the moment, nobody knows what we have done. I'd rather keep it that way.'

'What if Rykhel somehow survived on Helmabad?' asked Heynke. 'What if he contacts the rest of the Avenging Sons?'

'Between the rebels and the daemons, Rykhel is dead,' said Nicz.

'But what if he isn't?' insisted Heynke.

'Then our former battle-brothers will attempt to live up to their name,' said Gessart. 'That's why we're going to the Eye of Terror. Nobody would dare follow us into that nightmare. Once we attack the convoy word will spread about what we have done. We have one chance to do this right. If we fail, the Emperor's servants will be looking for us, and getting to the Cadian Gate will be all the harder for it.'

'So let's not mess it up,' said Lehenhart.

ZACHERYS'S HAND HESITATED over the warp engine activation rune on the console beside his Navigator's chair. He glanced at the panel above it, looking at the fluctuating lines of green fading into orange and then surging with power into green again. Although the warp engine was not fully active, the psyker could feel the boundaries of reality thinning around the *Vengeful*. Through the canopy around him, he saw the stars wavering, the darkness between them glowing occasionally with rainbows of psychic energy.

He had promised Gessart that he would get the ship to Geddan, thinking he would use the daemon Messenger to do so. He was having second thoughts, but could not back down. Not only would Zacherys face the scorn of the others, the ship was stranded in wilderness space. At some point they would have to re-enter the warp or simply stay here and eventually die from starvation – a prospect even more harrowing for a Space Marine than a normal man. Doubtless they would kill each other before that fate overtook them.

Taking a deep breath, Zacherys touched the rune. From the *Vengeful's* innards a deep rumbling reverberated through the ship, increasing to a rapid vibration that whined in Zacherys's ears.

The starfield around the *Vengeful* wavered and spun, engulfing the starship with a whirl of colours: the eye of a kaleidoscopic storm of the material and immaterial. Zacherys engaged the drive and the strike cruiser lurched into the warp; not a physical strain of inertia but a stretching of the mind, filled with momentary flashes of memory and dizziness. For the psyker, the transition welled up at the base of his skull, suffusing his thoughts with pressure as synapses flared randomly for a heartbeat.

It was over in a moment. The *Vengeful* was sliding along the psychic current, Geller field sparkling around it. Zacherys opened his mind up to the power of the warp and felt the shifting energies around him. He could sense the ebb and flow of the immaterium, but he was no Navigator; he lacked true warp-sight. Though he could feel the titanic psychic power surging around the ship, he could see only a little along their route, enough to avoid the swirls and plunging currents that would hurl them off-course, but little more.

Messenger? he thought. There was no reply and Zacherys became fearful that the creature had tricked him back into warp space, to drift on the tides until the Geller field finally failed and they were set upon by the daemons and other denizens that hungered after their souls.

'Foolish,' Zacherys muttered to himself.

The ship was buffeted by a wave of energy and Zacherys's focus turned to the steering controls as he attempted to ride the surge. As with the warp jump itself, he felt this not in the pit of his stomach like a man upon an ordinary sea, but as crests and troughs of sensation behind his eyes, along every nerve.

He regained some control, moving the *Vengeful* into a calmer stream of power. He was making a huge mistake.

Zacherys's hand hovered over the emergency disengage rune, which would rip open the fabric of real/warp space and dump the *Vengeful* back into the material galaxy. There was no telling what damage would be done to the warp engines, or those on board, and Zacherys would have to confess all to Gessart.

It seemed such an ignominious end. So soon after taking the first steps on the road to freedom. It made a mockery of Zacherys's aspirations; his hopes to understand the nature of his abilities and his place between the real and unreal. The bright path leading from Helmabad he had seen in his visions was guttering and dying, swallowed by the formless energy of the void.

*I am here.*

Zacherys let out an explosive breath of relief.

I need your help, he thought.

*Of course you do*, replied Messenger. *Look how perilous your situation has become, flinging yourselves into our domain without heed to the dangers.*

I need a guide, thought Zacherys. Can you show me the way ahead?

*As I told you before, you must lower your defences and allow me to enter your mind. I must see with your eyes to guide you. Do not worry; I will protect you from the others.*

Zacherys's hand was shaking as he leaned over towards the Geller field controls. It would be a rash act, dooming not just the psyker but every soul on board the *Vengeful*. What option did he have?

*Indeed*, said Messenger. *You have cast yourselves upon the whims of cruel fate. Yet, there is no need to succumb to despair. You can still control your destiny, with me beside you.*

What do you get as you part of the bargain? asked Zacherys. Why should I trust you?

*I get your mind, my friend. And your loyalty. We need each other, you and I. In this world you are at my mercy; but I have no reach into your world other than with your hands. We shall help each other, and both shall benefit.*

You could destroy the ship, thought Zacherys.

*What would I gain? A momentary gratification, a brief peak of power and nothing more. Do not mistake me for the mindless soul-eaters that flock after your ship. I too have my ambitions and desires, and a mind and body such as yours can take me closer to them.*

You will possess me, drive me from my own flesh!

*You know that I cannot. Your armour against me is your will, strengthened over your whole life. We would wage war against each other constantly, neither victorious. You are no normal mortal; you are a Space Marine still, with all the power that entails.*

Klaxons screeched across the *Vengeful* as Zacherys punched in the first cipher to unlock the Geller field controls. Within moments, Gessart was on the comm.

'What is it? Warp breach?' the warband leader demanded.

'There is nothing to fear,' said Zacherys, convincing himself as much as the commander. The blaring was joined by a host of flashing red lights on the display board as Zacherys keyed in the next sequence. 'Everything is under control.'

He tapped out the last digits and pressed the deactivation rune. With a screech that could only be heard inside his head, Zacherys cut the Geller field. The bubble of psychic energy around the starship imploded, the full pressure of the warp rushing into and through the *Vengeful*.

Zacherys felt cold, a freezing chill of the void that encrusted every cell of his being. With gritted teeth, he put his head back against the chair.

'The moment of truth,' he whispered. 'I am at your

mercy, Messenger. Prove me right or wrong.'

The bitter cold vanished, replaced by warmth that glowed through Zacherys's limbs. He felt the heat expanding outwards, engulfing the rest of the ship. The energy of the warp remained, not pushed back like it was with the Geller field, but the *Vengeful* settled in an oasis of calm, resting gently upon the stilled psychic tide.

Zacherys opened his eyes. Other than the tingling in his nerves, the psyker felt no different. He flexed his fingers and looked around until he was confident that he was in full control of his faculties. He laughed, buoyed up by a sudden feeling of ecstasy that suffused his body.

And then he felt it.

It was indistinct, like the tendrils of a light fog, spreading through his mind, dribbling along the course of his thoughts. It was a dark web, an alien cancer latching on to all of his emotions, every hope and fear, dream and disappointment, suckling upon his centuries of experience. Zacherys sensed satisfaction seeping through him, leeched from his new companion.

*Such delights we have to offer one another. But for another time. Tell me, my friend: where do you wish to go?*

GESSART PACED THE command bridge as he waited for the results of the initial sensor sweep. Zacherys had done an admirable job, dropping the ship out of warp space just outside the orbit of Geddan's fourth world. Gessart wondered how the psyker had overcome the graviometric problems that normally prevented ships from emerging so close to a celestial body, but decided against asking for details; the former Librarian's strangely contented expression and the incident with the collapsing Geller field warned Gessart that there was something odd happening, but he could not afford the distraction for the moment.

'Seven signatures on response, captain,' announced Kholich Beyne, the head of the *Vengeful*'s non-Space Marine crew. The young man checked something on the data-slab in his hands. 'No military channels in use.'

'Confirm that,' said Gessart. 'Are there any Imperial Navy vessels?'

Kholich headed over to the sensor technicians and conferred briefly with each. He turned back to Gessart with a solemn expression.

'Confirm that there are no Imperial Navy vessels in the system, captain. The convoy is assembling around the fifth planet. From their comms chatter, they are expecting to receive their escort in the next day or two.'

'Defences in that grid?' Gessart stopped his pacing and knotted his hands behind his back, trying to stay calm.

'We're not picking up any orbital defences, captain. It seems unlikely that the convoy would gather without some form of protection.'

'Surface-to-orbit weapons, most likely,' said Gessart. 'Nothing that can attack us if we get amongst the convoy before they start opening fire.'

He rounded on the comms team.

'Transmit our identifier to the convoy ships. Tell them we will be approaching.'

'If they require an explanation, captain?' asked Kholich. 'What do we tell them?'

'Nothing,' replied Gessart, heading towards the bridge doors. 'Find out who the civilian convoy captain is and inform him that I'll be boarding his vessel and speaking to him in person.'

'Very well, captain,' said Kholich as the armoured doors slid open with a rumble. 'I'll inform you of any developments.'

THOUGH NOT CONSIDERED a large vessel by Imperial standards, the *Vengeful* dwarfed the merchantman carrying Sebanius Loil; the man who had identified himself as the merchant commander of the convoy. Following a terse conversation, during which Gessart had done most of the talking, the trader had acquiesced to the Space Marine's demand to be allowed on board. Now Gessart and his warriors were fully armoured and crossing the few hundred kilometres between the strike cruiser and the *Lady Bountiful* aboard their last surviving Thunderhawk gunship.

Gessart looked at the merchantman through the cockpit canopy, noticing the three defence turrets clustered around her midsection: short-ranged weapons that might fend off a lone pirate but which would be hard-pressed to overload even one of the *Vengeful*'s void shields. Beyond the *Lady Bountiful* was the rest of the convoy, visible only as returns on the Thunderhawk's scanners, separated from each other by several thousand kilometres of vacuum. Four were of similar size, but two of the ships were immense transports, three times the size of the *Vengeful*. Fortunately they were empty, destined to pick up their cargo of an Imperial Guard regiment en route to the warzone in Rhodus.

Bright light streamed from an opening that stretched a quarter of the length of the *Lady Bountiful* as the ship slid back its loading bay doors to allow the Thunderhawk to land. Nicz eased the gunship into a course and speed parallel with the merchantship and then fired the landing thrusters to guide them into the bay.

A lone man waited for Gessart as the Thunderhawk's ramp lowered to the deck, smoke and steam billowing across the bare rockcrete floor. He was stocky, clad in a heavy fur-lined coat with puffed shoulders slashed with red. Sebanius Loil warily watched the Space Marines with one good eye and an augmetic device riveted into his face in place of the other. Lenses clacked as the merchant focussed on Gessart. A servo whined as Loil lifted his right hand in welcome, the sleeve of the coat falling back to reveal a three-clawed metal hand.

'Welcome aboard the *Lady Bountiful*, captain,' said Loil. His voice was a hoarse whisper and through the ruff of the coat Gessart could see more bionics; an artificial larynx bobbed up and down at Loil's throat.

Gessart did not return the greeting. He looked at his warriors over his shoulder and signalled them to spread out around the docking bay.

'I'm taking your cargo,' he said.

Loil did not seem surprised by this pronouncement. He lowered his cybernetic arm with a whirr and held out his good hand towards Gessart.

'You know that I cannot allow that, captain,' said the merchant. 'My cargo is destined for Imperial forces fighting at Rhodus. I have an agreement with the Departmento Munitorum.'

The bionic hand delved into a deep pocket and produced a data-crystal. Loil offered it towards Gessart as proof of his contract.

'You have no choice in the matter,' said Gessart as he thrust Loil aside. 'Your compliance will be for your own good.'

'You cannot seriously threaten us with force,' said Loil, following Gessart as the Space Marine stalked across the bay towards the main doors. Gessart darted the man a look that confirmed he could very well make such a threat. Loil paled and his artificial eye buzzed erratically. 'This is intolerable! I will...'

The trader's words petered away as Zacherys thudded down the ramp. The psyker's eyes were orbs of golden energy. Zacherys turned that infernal gaze upon Loil, who recoiled in horror, holding up his hands in front of his ravaged face. The merchant whimpered and fell to his knees, tears coursing down his scarred cheeks. Zacherys stood over the man for a moment, looking down, lips pursed in contemplation.

'Where is the main cargo hold?' asked Gessart.

Zacherys looked up, broken from his thoughts by Gessart's questions.

'Aft,' said the former Librarian. 'Four bays, all filled

with crates. Too much for the Thunderhawk, we will have to bring the *Vengeful* alongside and dock directly.'

Zacherys held out a hand above Loil's head. He twitched his armoured fingers and the merchant looked up, meeting the psyker's gaze. The gold of Zacherys's eyes spread down his right arm and engulfed the head of the merchant before disappearing. Zacherys smiled and lifted his hand further. The ship's captain rose jerkily to his feet, swaying slightly.

'Lead me to the bridge,' said Zacherys.

Loil's first steps were faltering as he resisted the control of the psyker, scraping his feet across the floor. Zacherys twisted his wrist a fraction and Loil mewled like a wounded animal, knees buckling. The merchant righted himself and stumbled on, Zacherys following with long, slow strides.

The double doors hissed open, revealing a cluster of crew members holding an assortment of weapons: shotguns, autoguns, lasrifles. They stared in disbelief as their captain shuffled through the open doors, Zacherys and Gessart close behind. On their heels, the rest of the Space Marines hefted their bolters meaningfully.

'What do we do, Captain Loil?' asked one of the men, lasgun trembling in his grip.

'Wh-whatever they say,' hissed the merchant. 'Do whatever they say.'

The men looked uncertain. Gessart towered over them, fists clenched.

'Make ready to unload your cargo to our vessel,' he said slowly. 'Comply and no harm will come to you.

Disobey and you will be killed. Put down your weapons.'

All but one of them did as they were told, their guns clattering on the deck. One, face twisted with indignation, raised his shotgun. He didn't have time to pull the trigger. Gessart's fist slammed into his face, snapping the crewman's neck and hurling him across the corridor.

'Pass the word to your crewmates,' said Gessart. 'Unloading will begin in ten minutes.'

ZACHERYS MADE LOIL cut the comm-link and then released his psychic grip on the merchant. The man swooned to the floor, head banging loudly against the deck. Blood oozed from a gash in the captain's scalp. It didn't matter; he had served his purpose. The rest of the convoy would be gathering on the *Lady Bountiful* to await boarding and 'inspection' by the Space Marines.

I think I pushed him too far, thought Zacherys as he noticed blood leaking from Loil's ears and nose.

*It does not matter*, replied Messenger. *There are more of his kind, weak and pathetic, than there are stars in your galaxy. Did you feel how easy it was to control his feeble mind?*

I did, replied Zacherys. The thrill of using the man as a puppet ebbed away, leaving Zacherys strangely empty. What else can I do?

*Whatever you desire. You power will no longer be chained by the dogma of weaklings. The full force of y–Wait! Did you feel that?*

I felt nothing, thought Zacherys. What is it?

*Let me show you.*

Zacherys felt the daemon shifting inside him, pulling back it tendrils from his limbs, coalescing its power in his brain. His witchsight flared into life – the psychic sense that allowed Zacherys to feel the thoughts of others, sense their emotions and locate the spark of their minds in the warp. Zacherys's golden eyes did not see the cramped bridge of the merchantman or the bloodied bodies of the three officers lying crumpled by the door. His thoughts expanded through the ship and beyond, touching on the moon below, sensing the minds of the crew aboard the *Vengeful* alongside. Out and out his mind stretched, reaching through the veil that separated reality from the warp.

And then he felt them.

They were indistinct, faint reflections of presence like shadows in darkness. They were not in the warp; even before his pact with Messenger, Zacherys could tell the approach of a ship by its wake in the immaterium. They were somewhere else.

What are they, he asked? Where are they?

*Between here and there, in their little tunnels burrowed through dimensions. The children of the Dark Prince; you call them eldar.*

Zacherys strained to focus on their location, but could not fix upon them. They were close, within the system. He broke off the search and forced himself back to his mortal senses.

'Gessart, we might have a problem,' he barked over the comm.

* * *

OUT OF GLIMMERING stars of silver, the eldar ships emerged into real space, a little over twenty thousand kilometres away on the starboard bow. Gessart cursed the rudimentary scanner arrays of the *Lady Bountiful*, which were painfully short-ranged and slow. He opened up a channel to the *Vengeful*.

'Kholich, I'm transmitting coordinates. Give me a full augur sweep of that area. Three eldar ships detected. I want to know course, speed and type in two minutes.'

Gessart's fingers danced over the transmitter controls as he sent the information to the strike cruiser.

'We have to assume they are hostile,' he said as he stabbed the transmit rune. Zacherys, Nicz, Lehenhart and Ustrekh were with him in the bridge while the others oversaw the transfer of the cargo containers from the hold to the bays of the *Vengeful*. 'How much longer until we have what we need?'

'Not long enough,' replied Nicz. 'Assuming they come for us as quick as they can.'

'They will,' said Zacherys. 'They are predators and they are hunting. I feel their desire for the kill.'

Gessart flexed his gauntleted fingers with agitation.

'If we cut and run now, we might get away,' he muttered, more to himself than his companions. 'But then we will have to find more supplies before we reach the Eye. Yet, we have no idea of their strength or intent. A stiff warning may force them to break off. They cannot know our numbers either.'

'I say we fight,' said Ustrekh. 'They've come here looking for easy pickings. They'll have little stomach for a real battle.'

Gessart turned to Lehenhart, knowing the veteran would have his own thoughts on the matter.

'It won't take them long to get here,' said Lehenhart. 'Whatever we're going to do, we have to decide quickly. If we leave it too late to run, their ships can easily overhaul a strike cruiser. If we're going to fight, we had best start preparing our defences.'

Gessart sighed. That observation didn't make the choice any easier. The comm chimed in his ear before he could say anything else.

'This is *Vengeful*,' came Kholich's tinny voice. 'Confirm three vessels on a closing course. Warships, cruiser-class. We're beating to orders, arming weapon batteries and setting plasma reactors to battle readiness. Do you wish us to break from docking?'

Gessart glared at the main screen, searching for a sign of the attackers but they were still too far away to be seen against the darkness of space. On the scanner, he could see the merchant ships closest to the eldar turning away, scattering in all directions like sheep before wolves.

'Remain docked,' said Gessart.

'Captain, we will not have battle manoeuvrability whilst attached to the *Lady Bountiful*.'

'Do not question my orders! Continue loading until the enemy are ten thousand kilometres away and then break docking. Take up escort position on the *Lady Bountiful*. We will remain aboard the trader. Signal the civilian fleet to maintain formation and make best speed to our location.'

'Understood, captain.'

The link crackled and fell silent. With a sub-vocal

order, he switched the comm to his command channel, addressing the Space Marines of his force.

'Arm the crew,' he said. 'Let them fight for their vessel alongside us. If nothing else, they will be a distraction to the enemy. Remember that we do not fight for the Emperor, nor to protect these people and their ships. This is a battle we must win because our survival depends upon it. Fail here and we are doomed. Better to die in battle now than to eke out a worthless existence drifting the stars. Our destiny is in our hands and though we are no longer slaves to the Imperium, we are still Space Marines!'

THE ELDAR WERE not dissuaded from their attack by the presence of the *Vengeful*. The three warships swooped in for the kill, sleek, fast and deadly. On the *Lady Bountiful's* flickering scanner, Gessart watched the pirates circling around one of the other merchantmen.

'Detect laser weaponry fire,' Kholich reported from the strike cruiser. 'They are targeting the engines of the *Valdiatius Five*. Shall we move to intercept, captain?'

Gessart quickly assessed the situation on the scanner. As well as the *Lady Bountiful*, three other ships were already within range of the *Vengeful's* batteries. The rest of the convoy were making slow progress and the eldar would fall upon each in turn without having to risk a confrontation with the strike cruiser if it maintained its current position.

'Put yourself between the raiders and the rest of the convoy,' he told Kholich. 'Force them towards our position.'

'Affirmative, captain, moving to intercept,' replied Kholich.

'Engage at long range only,' Gessart added. It was unlikely the eldar would risk boarding a Space Marine vessel, but he didn't want to risk losing the strike cruiser. He turned to Nicz, who was at the helm and engine controls. 'Can you manoeuvre this piece of scrap?'

'Engines and control systems responding well,' replied Nicz without looking up. 'The ship's a mess on the outside, but Loil kept the important functions well maintained.'

'Can you simulate thruster difficulties?'

Nicz glanced at Gessart, guessing his intent.

'I can set them up with intermittent firing,' he said. 'We'll fall behind the rest of the ships and make ourselves an easy target.'

'Do it,' said Gessart, returning his attention to the scanner screen.

As he had hoped, the eldar were unwilling to tackle the strike cruiser directly, despite having more ships. As the *Vengeful* cut through the scattered ships of the convoy, the pirates broke away from their attack and retreated, putting several thousand kilometres between themselves and the escort.

The *Lady Bountiful* trembled violently as Nicz misfired the engines. His armour was bathed with an orange glow as warning lights flickered across the panel in front of him.

'Venting plasma,' he announced.

The ship shook again and rocked to starboard as a plume of superheated gas exploded from emergency exhausts along the portside stern. Nicz was deliberately clumsy in his attempts to correct their course, causing the ship to list sideways for several minutes while the main engines stuttered with flaring blasts of fire. Another glance at the scanner confirmed to Gessart that the three other merchant ships close to the *Lady Bountiful* were pulling away, heading directly from the eldar attack.

'Come on, take the bait,' Gessart muttered. 'Look at us, we're crippled. Come and get us!'

His attention was fixed on the scanner display, but the vague blobs of green that represented the eldar ships were too inaccurate to track any heading changes. He growled with frustration and fought the urge to slam his fist through the useless piece of equipment.

'Kholich, report!' he snapped. 'What are the enemy doing?'

'They've altered course towards you, captain,' Kholich reported. 'Not at full speed. They seem cautious.'

'They're waiting to see what you are going to do,' Nicz cut in across the comm. 'Move further away from our position.'

'Captain?' Kholich was uncertain, surprised by the break in protocol.

'Move out of weapons range of the *Lady Bountiful*,' Gessart said. 'But stand ready to come about and make full speed to our position if needed. Keep me informed of the eldar's movement, these scanners are worthless.'

'Affirmative, captain.'

Gessart broke the link and rounded on Nicz, stalking across the bridge to slam an open hand into the Space Marine's armoured chest.

'Stay off the command channel!' Gessart growled. 'I am still in charge.'

Nicz knocked away his leader's hand and stepped forwards, the grille of his helm a few centimetres from Gessart's.

'You're just guessing,' Nicz replied calmly. 'You haven't any more idea what to do than the rest of us. We should be aboard the *Vengeful*, chasing down these scum.'

'They would run rings around us, and you know it,' snapped Gessart. 'If they split up, we'll have no chance of catching any of them. We need to draw them in, convince them to board. That's when we'll have the advantage.'

Nicz stepped back and his shock was clear in his voice.

'You intend to counter-board one of their ships?'

'If possible. We will have to see how badly they want to fight.'

Nicz said nothing but a shake of the head made it clear what he thought of Gessart's plan. Gessart turned away and returned to his place at the command controls. His fingers drummed the side of the scanner display as he waited to find out what the eldar would do next.


'THEY'RE USING CUTTERS on the starboard bow!' Lehenhart reported. 'Decks six and seven.'

'Meet me at Lehenhart's position,' Gessart told his

warriors. One of the eldar warships had snared the *Lady Bountiful* in a gravity net and had pulled her alongside to board. The other two raiders had taken up a position a few thousand kilometres away to block the path of the *Vengeful* if it tried to intervene.

Gessart swung around to face Nicz. 'Can I trust you to keep an eye on the other two ships?'

'I'll tell you if either of them tries to board,' the Space Marine replied.

Gessart nodded and ran out of the bridge. He pounded along the uppermost deck until he came to a stairwell. Ducking sideways to fit his bulk through the low door, he hurled himself down the metal steps three at a time, the mesh buckling slightly under the impact of his boots. Three decks down, he squeezed into a narrow passageway flanked by rows of small cabins. Turning to his left he headed towards the bow of the ship. After a few hundred metres the corridor split to the left and right. Bolter fire ran along the bare metal walls from starboard.

Unslinging his storm bolter, Gessart slowed to a jog, eyes scanning the open doorways ahead. He saw nothing until Lehenhart advanced into view along the gallery at the end of the passage, his bionic right hand holding his bolter in a firing position, serrated combat knife in the left. Bright blue lances of laser light erupted from ahead of the Space Marine, zipping past him as he shifted to his left and returned fire, his bolter blazing three times, the roar of each round echoing along the corridor around Gessart.

Glancing over his shoulder at the thump of booted feet, Gessart saw Willusch, Gerhart and Johun a few dozen strides behind him. Over the comm, he heard the reports of others closing in from aft.

Lehenhart had moved out of sight; as Gessart turned into the starboard gallery he saw the Space Marine holding a landing ahead, firing down the stairwell. Five eldar bodies lay sprawled on the decking. Gessart paused for a moment to examine the dead aliens.

Each was as tall as a Space Marine, though far slighter of build. They had thin, angular faces, their almond-shaped eyes wide with the gaze of the dead, ears slightly pointed, brows high and arched. They appeared to have no uniform, though all five wore close-fitting tunics of iridescent scales. One was swathed in the ragged remains of a long red cloak, half his chest missing from a bolt detonation; another was sprawled across the corridor face-down, two holes in the back of his high-collared, dark blue coat. Two of the others were female, their hair wound in elaborate blonde braids spattered with bright red blood, skin-tight suits of black and white beneath their mesh armour; the last half-sat against the wall, narrow chin on chest, head shaven but for a blue scalplock, wearing a broad-shouldered black jacket studded with glistening gems, his legs naked but for knee-high boots.

Long-barrelled lasrifles lay on the floor next to each body, of similar design but each decorated with different coloured gemstones and swirling golden filigrees. Gessart picked up one of the weapons and examined it. It was elegant, powered by some form of crystal cell in the thin stock of the weapon. It crumpled easily as he tightened his grip, no sturdier than the creature that had wielded it.

Reaching Lehenhart, Gessart leaned over the balustrade and saw lithe figures darting from cover to cover on the landing below. He snatched two fragmentation grenades from his belt, thumbed the activation studs and dropped them over the edge. The stairwell rang with twin detonations; shrapnel and smoke filled the enclosed space, a lingering scream signalling that he had found at least one target.

'Do we wait, or go to them?' asked Lehenhart.

Gessart dragged up his memory of the ship's layout; he had to assume the eldar had scanned the vessel and knew something of its configuration as well. The upper four decks only extended for a third of the ship and did not connect to the hold directly. If the eldar were after the cargo – which was no longer aboard – they would have to go down to the lower six decks. With only twenty-five Space Marines to cover the hold, loading bays, docking areas and crew quarters, it would be hard to concentrate any resistance.

'Counter-attack!' Gessart told his warriors. 'Make them pay in blood for ever setting foot on this ship!'

A fusillade of bright blasts and blurring discs filled the stairwell. Gessart recognised shuriken catapult fire amongst the laser shots. He leaned over the railing and unleashed a hail of fire from his storm bolter, the explosive ammunition ripping a trail of splintering metal across the landing below. Slender shapes darted from the shadows and he was engulfed by a hail of razor-sharp projectiles. Pushing himself back, he glanced down at his armour and saw a row of barbed discs embedded across his chest plastron.

'With me,' he growled, pounding down the steps. He heard Lehenhart and the others close behind.

The railing buckled as Gessart grabbed a hold to swing around a turn in the steps. Enemy fire stormed up to meet him; las-bolts seared the paint from his armour while more shurikens sliced through his left arm and leg.

With a leap, he crashed to the landing. There were more than a dozen eldar taking cover in the two doorways; they were dressed in the same strange mix of coats, cloaks and armour he had seen on the bodies above. Quicker than a heartbeat, some of the alien warriors leapt to attack, wielding chainswords with glittering teeth and long blades that gleamed with energy.

Gessart let loose with another burst of fire, shredding an eldar directly in front of him. Before he could adjust his aim, two more were upon him, the teeth of their chainswords shrieking as they skittered across his right shoulder pad and backpack. He swung the storm bolter like a club, aiming for the head of one of his attackers. The eldar dropped cat-like to all fours and then leapt past, dragging her chainsword across the side of Gessart's helm. He took a step back, trying to keep both assailants in view.

Lehenhart arrived at a run, smashing his fist into the back of one of the eldar. The alien bent awkwardly and flopped to the ground, limbs twitching.

Gessart had no time to spare a further glance for his warriors coming in behind him as more eldar appeared at the doorway ahead, pistols and swords gripped by slender fingers.

Gessart turned his right shoulder towards them and charged with a roar. Most of the eldar scattered quickly from his path but one was caught with nowhere to go; he was smashed bloodily into the wall by the headlong rush. A warning siren sounded in Gessart's ears as blades bit deep into his backpack and legs, the eldar like a swarm of wasps, darting in to strike before swiftly retreating out of reach.

The Space Marine swung a booted foot at the closest, looking to sweep away the pirate's legs. The eldar nimbly somersaulted over Gessart's attack and landed with sure-footed grace to fire his pistol directly into Gessart's face.

Gessart's finger tightened instinctively on the trigger as he reeled back. Through the cracked lenses of his helm he saw the alien bisected by bolts, sheared through by detonations across his scale-armoured stomach.

Detecting the patter of feet behind him, Gessart swung around to confront a new attacker, but found only empty air. The eldar were falling back, disappearing quickly along both passageways. Willusch and Lehenhart set off after them but Gessart called them back.

'They'll pick each of us off if we split up,' he said. 'Let's not run into an ambush.'

He quickly took stock of the scene. Two of his warriors lay still on the steps, their armour and flesh cut through to the bone in dozens of places. Another three were bleeding heavily from wounds to their arms and legs.

'Report in!' he barked over the comm.

The replies painted a complicated picture. Some of his Space Marines had fended off an eldar advance along the portside, causing significant casualties for no losses. Another group had been caught out on their way to support Gessart and two of their number had fallen in moments before the eldar had swiftly withdrawn. Those who had been stationed by the aft holds were still making their way towards the bow and had yet to encounter any foes.

Unfortunately the *Lady Bountiful* had no internal scanners to keep track of the pirates. Gessart looked for Heynke, who had the force's only functional auspex. The Space Marine was at the top of the flight of steps, bolter in his hands, guarding the approach from above. His armour appeared undamaged, in stark contrast to the others, who all showed signs of the brief but fierce fight.

'Heynke, use the auspex,' Gessart said, checking the ammunition counter on his storm bolter. Seventeen rounds left. He had two more magazines at his belt. More than enough for the moment.

Heynke hooked his bolter to his belt and unslung the scanning device. His armoured fingers coaxed the machine into life, his helm reflecting the pale yellow of the display. Heynke moved the auspex around, trying to get a fix on the lifesigns of the eldar.

'Most have reached the upper decks,' he reported. 'Too much interference from the superstructure for an accura... Hold on, something strange.'

'What is it?' demanded Gessart leaping up the steps to stand beside Heynke.

'Look for yourself,' the Space Marine said, holding the auspex towards Gessart.

The semi-circular screen was filled with bright lines – the power conduits running through the walls of the ship. The eldar showed as fainter traces, little more than pale yellow smudges. The largest concentration was two decks above in the crew mess hall. They were not moving.

'What do you think they are up to?' asked Heynke.

Gessart did not know and any speculation he might offer was abruptly stopped by a buzzing over the comm. The static lasted for a few moments, scaling higher in pitch, and then stopped. There was a pause before he heard a voice, the words slightly stilted with a mechanical edge to them.

'Commander of the Space Marines,' it said. 'I have found the air upon which you speak. Heed the wisdom of my words. This loss of life is senseless and is not of benefit to myself or to you. I have become aware that we should not be adversaries. I detect the eyes that see far and know that you are aware of where I am. I have knowledge that you would wish I share with you. Meet me where we can hold conference and we will discuss this matter like civilised creatures.'

The link crackled again and fell silent.

'Was that…?' said Lehenhart. 'Did that bastard override our comm-frequency?'

'How?' said Heynke.

'Forget how, did you hear what he said?' This was from Freichz. 'He wants a truce!'

Gessart's comm chimed again, signalling a switch to the private channel. He bit back a snarl of frustration at this fresh interruption.

'Yes?' he snapped.

'Gessart, we have a serious problem,' replied Zacherys. 'Ships have broken through the warp boundary. I believe it is the Imperial Navy escort for the convoy.'

'Did you hear the pirate commander?'

'I did. I believe this is the information he wished to pass to us. Somehow he knows that we are protecting the fleet for ourselves. I would recommend that you hear what he has to say.'

'Agreed. Meet me at the aft entrance to the mess hall.' Gessart switched to general transmission. 'Take up guard positions around the mess hall but do not enter. This may be some kind of trick, so stay alert.'

He snapped off more precise orders and instructed Tylo, the Apothecary, to set up an aid station in one of the holds so that the wounded could be tended. With these preparations made, Gessart headed up the stairwell, uncertain what to expect.

ZACHERYS MET GESSART outside the mess hall. There was bright eldar blood splashed across the psyker's armour, some of it still steaming and bubbling. Gessart decided it would be better not to ask. The main doors of the mess hall slid open in front of them and they stepped inside, weapons in hand.

The mess hall was a wide open space, divided by long tables and benches riveted to the floor. At the centre several dozen eldar waited, some of them with weapons ready, most of them lounging across the tables and seats. Gessart's eye was immediately drawn to the one at the centre of the group, who leaned against the end of a table with his legs casually crossed, arms folded. He was dressed in a long coat of green and red diamond patches, which reached to his booted ankles. A ruff of white and blue feathers jutted from the high collar, acting as a wispy halo for his narrow, sharp-cheeked face. His skin was almost white, his hair black and pulled back in a single braid plaited with shining thread. Dark eyes fixed on Gessart as the Space Marine stomped across the metal floor and stopped about ten metres away.

The eldar straightened and his lips moved faintly. The words that echoed across the hall came not from his mouth, but from a brooch upon his lapel, shaped like a thin, stylised skull.

'What is the name of he who has the honour of addressing Aradryan, Admiral of the Winter Gulf?'

'Gessart. Is that a translator?'

'I understand your crude language, but will not sully my lips with its barbaric grunts,' came the metallic reply.

Zacherys moved up next to Gessart and Aradryan's eyes widened with shock and fear. He looked at Gessart with a furrowed brow.

'That you consort with this sort of creature is ample evidence that you are no longer in service to the Emperor of Mankind. We have encountered other renegades like yourselves in the past. My assumptions are proven correct.'

'Zacherys is one of us,' said Gessart with a glance towards the psyker. 'What do you mean?'

'Can you not see that which dwells within him?' The machine spoke in a flat tone but Aradryan's incredulity was clear.

'What do you want?' demanded Gessart.

'To save needless loss for both of us,' Aradryan replied, opening his hands in a placating gesture. 'You will soon be aware that those whose duty it is to protect these vessels are close at hand. If we engage in this pointless fighting they will come upon us both. This does not serve my purpose or yours. I propose that we settle our differences in a peaceful way. I am certain that we can come to an agreement that accommodates the desires of both parties.'

'A truce? We divide the spoils of the convoy?'

'It brings happiness to my spirit to find that you understand my intent. I feared greatly that you would respond to my entreaty with the blind ignorance that blights so many of your species.'

'I have become a recent acquaintance of compromise,' said Gessart. 'I find it makes better company than the alternatives. What agreement do you propose?'

'There is time enough for us both to take what we wish before these new arrivals can intervene in our affairs. We have no interest in the clumsy weapons and goods these vessels carry. You may take as much as you wish.'

'If you don't want the cargo, what is your half of the deal?'

'Everything else,' said Aradryan with a sly smile.

'He means the crews,' whispered Zacherys.

'That is correct, tainted one,' said Aradryan. The eldar pirate fixed his large eyes on Gessart, the hint of a smile twisting his thin lips. 'Do you accede to these demands, or do you wish that we expend more energy killing one another in a pointless display of pride? You must know that I am aware of how few warriors you have should you choose to fight.'

'How long before the escort arrives?' Gessart asked Zacherys.

'Two days at the most.'

'You have enough time to unload whatever you wish and will not be hampered by my ships or my warriors. You have my assurance that you will be unmolested if you offer me the same.'

Gessart stared at Aradryan for some time, but it was impossible to discern the alien's thoughts from his expression. He knew that he could no more trust an eldar than he could take his eye off Nicz, but there seemed little choice. He suppressed a sigh, wondering what it was that he had done to deserve a succession of impossible decisions lately: between protecting innocents and killing the enemy on Archimedon, between millions of rebels and a host of daemons at Helmabad, and now he had to make a bargain with an alien or risk being destroyed by those he had once fought alongside.

'The terms are agreed,' said Gessart. 'I will order my warriors to suspend fighting. I have no control over the crews of the convoy.'

'We are capable of dealing with such problems in

our own way,' said Aradryan. 'Be thankful that this day you have found me in a generous mood.'

Gessart hefted his storm bolter and fixed the eldar pirate with a cold stare.

'Don't give me an excuse to change my mind.'

ALL AVAILABLE SPACE aboard the *Vengeful* was packed with pillaged supplies. Crates filled the hangars that had berthed lost Thunderhawks; ammunition boxes were piled high in the chapel and Reclusiam; crew quarters that would never again house battle-brothers were used as storage for medical wares and maintenance parts. Gessart was exceptionally pleased with the haul; they had enough to survive for several years if necessary.

He stood on the bridge of the strike cruiser as it broke dock from the civilian transport. It had taken more than a day to ferry everything across, and two of the convoy's ships had been left untouched: there simply wasn't room to take on board anything else. As the *Vengeful* powered away one of the eldar cruisers slipped past, the swirl of its gravity nets hooking onto the cargo hauler. The alien ship glided serenely on, its yellow hull fluctuating with black tiger stripes, its solar sails shimmering gold.

'Are we ready to jump?' Gessart asked Zacherys.

'At your command,' came the reply.

Gessart caught Nicz staring at him.

'Don't tell me that you disapprove,' said Gessart.

'Not at all, quite the opposite,' replied Nicz. 'I wondered if Helmabad was a unique moment, but I see that I might be wrong.'

'Let me convince you,' said Gessart, striding to the gunnery control panel.

The systems had been at full power since their first arrival so he knew the eldar would not detect a spike in power. The lock-on was another matter. His fingers danced over the controls as gun ports slid open along the starboard side of the strike cruiser. The eldar ship was only a few hundred kilometres away and the targeting metriculators found their range within seconds.

'What are you doing?' said Nicz

'Leaving the Imperial Navy something to play with,' Gessart replied with a smile.

Gessart tapped in the command for a single salvo and pressed the firing rune. The *Vengeful* shook as the ship unleashed a full broadside at the eldar cruiser. On the main screen explosions blossomed around the alien ship, snapping the main sail mast and rippling along the hull. Flames billowed from exploding gases, the pressure of their release causing the cruiser to yaw violently.

'Zacherys, take us into the warp.'

# BLACK DAWN

## by C. L. Werner

LABOURERS BUSTLED ABOUT the busy star port of Izo Primaris, capital city of Vulscus. Soldiers of the Merchant Guild observed the workers with a wary eye and a ready grip on the lasguns they carried. Hungry men from across Vulscus were drawn to the walled city of Izo Primaris seeking a better life. What they discovered was a cadre of guilds and cartels who maintained an iron fist upon all commerce in the city. There was work to be had, but only at the wages set by the cadre. The Merchant Guild went to draconian extremes to ensure none of their workers tried to augment their miserable earnings by prying into the crates offloaded from off-world ships.

As a heavy loading servitor trundled away from the steel crates it had unloaded, a different sort of violation of the star port's custom was unfolding. Only minutes before the steel boxes had rested inside the hold of a sleek galiot. The sinister-looking black-hulled freighter had landed upon Vulscus hours before, its master, the rogue trader Zweig Barcelo, having quickly departed the star port to seek an audience with the planetary governor.

Behind him, Zweig had left his cargo, admonishing the Conservator of the port to take special care unloading the crates and keeping people away from them. He had made it clear that the Guilders would be most unhappy if they were denied the chance to bid upon the goods he had brought into the Vulscus system.

Most of the crates the servitors offloaded from the galiot indeed held an exotic menagerie of off-world goods. One, however, held an entirely different cargo.

A small flash of light, a thin wisp of smoke and a round section of the steel crate fell from the side of the metal box. Only a few centimetres in size, the piece of steel struck the tarmac with little more noise than a coin falling from the pocket of a careless labourer. The little hole in the side of the crate was not empty for long. A slender stick-like length of bronze emerged from the opening, bending in half upon a tiny pivot as it cleared the edges of the hole. From the tip of the instrument, an iris slid open, exposing a multifaceted crystalline optic sensor. Held upright against the side of the box, the stick-like instrument slowly pivoted, searching the area for any observers.

Its inspection completed, the compact view scope was withdrawn back into the hole as quickly as it had materialised. Soon the opposite side of the steel crate began to spit sparks and thin streams of smoke. Molten lines of superheated metal disfigured the face of the box as the cargo within cut through the heavy steel. Each precise cut converged upon the others, forming a door-like pattern. Unlike the small round spy hole, the square carved from the opposite side of the crate was not allowed to crash to the ground. Instead, powerful hands gripped the cut section at each corner, fingers encased in ceramite immune to the glowing heat of the burned metal. The section was withdrawn into the crate, vanishing without trace into the shadowy interior.

Almost as soon as the opening was finished, a burly figure stalked away from the crate, his outline obscured by the shifting hues of the camo-cloak draped about his body. The man moved with unsettling grace and military precision despite the heavy carapace armour he wore beneath his cloak. In his hands, he held a thin, narrow-muzzled rifle devoid of either stock or magazine. He kept one finger coiled about the trigger of his rifle as he swept across the tarmac, shifting between the shadows.

Brother-Sergeant Carius paused as a team of labourers and their Guild wardens passed near the stack of crates he had concealed himself behind. The single organic eye remaining in his scarred face locked upon the leader of the wardens, watching him carefully. If any of the workers or their guards spotted him, they would get their orders from this man. Therefore the warden would be the first to die if it came to a fight.

A soft hiss rose from Carius's rifle, long wires

projecting outwards from the back of the gun's scope.
The Scout-sergeant shifted his head slightly so that
the wires could connect with the mechanical optic
that had replaced his missing eye. As the wires
inserted themselves into his head, Carius found his
mind racing with the feed from his rifle's scope, a
constantly updating sequence indicating potential
targets, distance, obstructions and estimated velocity.

Carius ignored the feed from his rifle and concentrated upon his own senses instead. The rifle could
tell him how to shoot, but it couldn't calculate when.
The Scout-sergeant would need to watch for that
moment when stealth would give way to violence.
There were ten targets in all. He estimated he could
put them down in three seconds. He didn't want it to
come to that. There was just a chance one of them
might be able to scream before death silenced him.

The work crew rounded a corner and Carius shook
his head to one side, ending the feed from his rifle
and inducing the wires to retract back into the scope.
He rose from the crouch he had assumed and gestured with his fingers to the shadows around him.
Other Scouts rushed from the darkness, following
the unspoken commands their sergeant had given
them. Three of them formed a defensive perimeter,
watching for any other workers who might stray into
this quadrant of the star port. The other six assaulted
the ferrocrete wall of the storage facility, employing
the lowest setting of the melta-axes they had used to
silently cut through the side of the cargo crate.

Carius watched his men work. The ferrocrete
would take longer to cut through than the steel crate,

but the knife-like melta-blades would eventually open the wall as easily as the box. The Scout Marines would then be loosed upon Izo Primaris proper.

Then their real work would begin.

MATTIAS HELD A gloved hand to his chin and watched through lidded eyes as the flamboyant off-worlder was led into the conference hall. The governor of Vulscus and the satellite settlements scattered throughout the Boras system adopted a manner of aloof disdain mixed with amused tolerance. He felt it was the proper display of emotion for a man entrusted with the stewardship of seven billion souls and the industry of an entire world.

Governor Mattias didn't feel either aloof or amused, however. The off-worlder wasn't some simple tramp merchant looking to establish trade on Vulscus or a wealthy pilgrim come to pay homage to the relic enshrined within the chapel of the governor's palace.

Zweig, the man called himself, a rogue trader with a charter going back almost to the days of the Heresy itself. The man's charter put him above all authority short of the Inquisition and the High Lords of Terra themselves. For most of his adult life, Mattias had been absolute ruler of Vulscus and her outlying satellites. It upset him greatly to know a man whose execution he couldn't order was at large upon his world.

The rogue trader made a garish sight in the dark, gothic atmosphere of the conference hall. Zweig's tunic was fashioned from a bolt of cloth so vibrant it seemed to glow with an inner light of its own, like the radioactive grin of a mutant sump-ghoul. His vest was a gaudy swirl of crimson velvet, vented by crosswise slashes in a seemingly random pattern. The hologlobes levitating beneath the hall's vaulted ceiling reflected wildly from the synthetic diamonds that marched along the breast of the trader's vest. Zweig's breeches were of chuff-silk, of nearly transparent thinness and clinging to his body more tightly than the gloves Mattias wore. Rough, grox-hide boots completed the gauche exhibition, looking like something that might have been confiscated from an ork pirate. The governor winced every time the ugly boots stepped upon the rich ihl-rugs which covered the marble floors of his hall. He could almost see the psycho-reactive cloth sickening from the crude footwear grinding into its fibres.

Zweig strode boldly between the polished obsidian columns and the hanging nests of niktiro birds that flanked the conference hall, ignoring the crimson-clad Vulscun excubitors who glowered at him as he passed. Mattias was tempted to have one of his soldiers put a shaft of las-light through the pompous off-worlder's knee, but the very air of arrogance the rogue trader displayed made him reconsider the wisdom of such action. It would be best to learn the reason for Zweig's bravado. A rogue trader didn't live long trusting that his charter would shield him from harm on every backwater world he visited. The Imperium was a big place and it might take a long time for news of his demise to reach anyone with the authority to do anything about it.

The rogue trader bowed deeply before Mattias's table, the blue mohawk into which his hair had been waxed nearly brushing across the ihl-rugs. When he rose from his bow, the vacuous grin was back on his face, pearly teeth gleaming behind his dusky lips.

'The Emperor's holy blessing upon the House of Mattias and all his fortune, may his herds be fruitful and his children prodigious. May his enterprise flourish and his fields never fall before the waning star,' Zweig said, continuing the stilted, antiquated form of address that was still practised in only the most remote and forgotten corners of the segmentum. The governor bristled under the formal salutation, unable to decide if Zweig was using the archaic greeting because he thought Vulscus was such an isolated backwater as to still employ it or because he wanted to subtly insult Mattias.

'You may dispense with the formality,' Mattias cut off Zweig's address with an annoyed flick of his hand. 'I know who you are, and you know who I am. More importantly, we each know what the other is.' Mattias's sharp, mask-like face pulled back in a thin smile. 'I am a busy man, with little time for idle chatter. Your charter ensures you an audience with the governor of any world upon which your custom takes you.' He spat the words from his tongue as though each had the taste of sour-glass upon them. 'I, however, will decide how long that audience will be.'

Zweig bowed again, a bit more shallowly than his first obeisance before the governor. 'I shall ensure that I do not waste his lordship's time,' he said. He glanced about the conference hall, his eyes lingering on the twin ranks of excubitors. He stared more closely at the fat-faced ministers seated around Mattias at the table. 'However, I do wonder if what I have to say should be shared with other ears.'

Mattias's face turned a little pale when he heard Zweig speak. Of course the rogue trader had been scanned for weapons before being allowed into the governor's palace, but there was always the chance of something too exotic for the scanners to recognise. He had heard stories about jokaero digi-weapons that were small enough to be concealed in a synthetic finger and deadly enough to burn through armaplas in the blink of an eye.

'I run an impeccable administration,' Mattias said, trying to keep any hint of suspicion out of his tone. 'I have no secrets from my ministers, or my people.'

Zweig shrugged as he heard the outrageous claim, but didn't challenge Mattias's claim of transparency. 'News of the recent... fortunes... of Vulscus has travelled far. Perhaps farther than even you intended, your lordship.'

An excited murmur spread among the ministers, but a gesture from Mattias silenced his functionaries.

'Both the Adeptus Mechanicus and the Ecclesiarchy have examined the relic,' Mattias told Zweig. 'They are convinced of its authenticity. Not that their word was needed. You only have to be in the relic's presence to feel the aura of power that surrounds it.'

'The bolt pistol of Roboute Guilliman himself,' Zweig said, a trace of awe slipping past his pompous demeanour. 'A weapon wielded by one of the holy primarchs, son of the God-Emperor Himself!'

'Vulscus is blessed to have such a relic entrusted to her care,' Mattias said. 'The relic was unearthed by labourers laying the foundation for a new promethium refinery in the Hizzak quarter of Izo Secundus, our oldest city. All Vulscuns proudly remember that it was there the primarch led his Adeptus Astartes in the final battle against the heretical Baron Unfirth during the Great Crusade, ending generations of tyranny and bringing our world into the light of the Imperium.'

Zweig nodded his head in sombre acknowledgement of Mattias's statement. 'My… benefactors… are aware of the relic and the prosperity it will surely bestow upon Vulscus. It is for that reason they… contracted me… to serve as their agent.'

The rogue trader reached to his vest, hesitating as some of the excubitors raised their weapons. A nod of the governor's head gave Zweig permission to continue. Carefully he removed a flat disc of adamantium from a pocket inside his vest. Wax seals affixed a riotous array of orisons, declarations and endowments to the disc, but it was the sigil embossed upon the metal itself that instantly arrested the attention of Mattias and his ministers. It was the heraldic symbol of House Heraclius, one of the most powerful of the Navis Nobilite families in the segmentum.

'I am here on behalf of Novator Priskos,' Zweig announced. 'House Heraclius is anxious to strengthen its dominance over the other Great Families sanctioned to transport custom in this sector. The novator has empowered me to treat with the governor of Vulscus to secure exclusive rights to the transportation of pilgrims to view your sacred relic. The agreement would preclude allowing any vessel without a Navigator from House Heraclius to land on your world.'

There was no need for Mattias to silence his ministers this time. The very magnitude of Zweig's announcement had already done that. Every man in the conference hall knew the traffic of pilgrims to their world would be tremendous. Other worlds had built entire cathedral cities to house lesser relics from the Great Crusade and to accommodate the vast numbers of pilgrims who journeyed across the stars to pay homage to such trifles as a cast-off boot worn by the first ecclesiarch and a dented copper flagon once used by the primarch Leman Russ. The multitudes that would descend upon Vulscus to see a relic of such import as the actual weapon of Roboute Guilliman himself would be staggering. To give a single Navigator House a monopoly on that traffic went beyond a simple concession. The phrase 'kingmaker' flashed through the governor's mind.

'I will need to confer with the full Vulscun planetary council,' Mattias said when he was able to find his voice. House Heraclius would be a dangerous enemy to make, but conceding to its request would not sit well with the other Navigators. The governor knew there was no good choice to make, so he would prefer to allow the planetary council to consider the matter – and take blame for the consequences when they came.

Zweig reached into his pocket again, removing an

ancient chronometer. He made a show of sliding its cover away and studying the phased crystal display. Slowly, he nodded his head. 'Assemble the leaders of your world, governor. I can allow you time to discuss your decision. Novator Priskos is a patient… man. He would, however, expect me to be present for your deliberations to ensure that a strong case is made for House Heraclius being granted this concession.'

Mattias scowled as Zweig fixed him with that ingratiating smile of his. The governor didn't appreciate people who could make him squirm.

'THAT WHICH SERVES the glory of the God-Emperor is just and will endure. That which harms the Imperium built by His children is false and shall be purged by flame and sword. With burning hearts and cool heads, we shall overcome that which has offended the Emperor's will. Our victory is ordained. Our victory is ensured by our faith in the Emperor.'

The words rang out through the ancient, ornate chapel, broadcast from the vox-casters built into the skull-like helm of Chaplain Valac, repeated by the speakers built into the stone cherubs and gargoyles that leaned down from the immense basalt columns that supported the stained plexiglass ceiling far overhead. Stars shone through the vibrant roof, casting celestial shadows across the throng gathered within the massive temple.

Each of the men who listened to Valac's words was a giant, even the smallest of their number over two metres in height. Every one of the giants was encased in a heavy suit of ceramite armour. The bulky armour was painted a dull green, dappled with blacks and browns to form a camouflaged pattern. Only the right pauldron was not covered in the patchwork series of splotches or concealed by fabric strips of scrim. The thick plate of armour above the right shoulder of each giant bore a simple field of olive green broken by a pair of crossed swords in black. It was a symbol that had announced doom upon a thousand worlds. It was the mark of the Adeptus Astartes, the heraldry of the Chapter of Space Marines called the Emperor's Warbringers.

'This day I remind the Fifth Company of its duty,' Valac continued, his armoured bulk pacing before the golden aquila looming above the chapel's altar. Unlike the rest of the Warbringers, who had removed their helms when they entered the holy shrine, the Chaplain kept his visage locked behind his skull-like mask of ceramite. He alone had not covered his armour in camouflage, his power armour retaining its grim black colouration.

'The Emperor expects us to do that which will bring honour upon His name. All we have accomplished in the past is dust and shadow. It is the moment before us that is of consequence. We do not want to fail Him. Through our victory, we shall show that we are proud to serve Him and to know that He has chosen us to be His mighty servants.

'The Fifth Company is ready for anything and we shall not be found lacking. Let no doubt enter your mind. We have no right to decide innocence or guilt. We are only the sword. The Emperor will know His own. The Emperor has commanded and we will follow His holy words before all others. In this hour of reflection and contemplation, we see victory before us. We need only deny the temptations of doubt and seize it. That is the duty of this hour!'

At the rear of the chapel, Inquisitor Korm listened to Chaplain Valac preach to his fellow Warbringers. A guest upon the Warbringers' battle-barge, the inquisitor had decided to keep himself as inconspicuous as possible. Even Korm felt a trickle of fear in his heart as he heard Valac's fiery words, as he watched the Chaplain instil upon the armoured giants kneeling before him a cold, vicious determination to descend upon their enemies without mercy or quarter. Korm knew he was hearing the death of an entire city echoing through the vaulted hall of the chapel. A twinge of guilt flickered through his mind as he considered how many innocent people were going to die in a few hours.

Korm quickly suppressed the annoying emotion. He'd done too many things over his life to listen to his conscience now. Ten thousand, even a million hapless citizens of the Imperium were a small price to pay for the knowledge he sought. Knowledge he alone would possess because only he knew the secret of the relic that Governor Mattias had unearthed.

Unleashing the Warbringers upon Vulscus was a brutal solution to Korm's problem, but the inquisitor had learned long ago that the surest way to victory was through excessive force.

If there was one thing the Warbringers did better than anyone, it was excessive force. Korm smiled grimly as he listened to the Chaplain's closing words.

'Now, brothers, rise up and let the Emperor's enemies discover the price of heresy! Let the storm of judgement be set loose!'

THE FACTORY WORKER crumpled into a lifeless heap as the vibro-knife punctured his neck and slashed the carotid artery. Carius lowered the grimy corpse to the peeling linoleum tiles that covered the floor. The Scout-sergeant pressed his armoured body against the filthy wall of the hallway and brought the tip of his boot against the clapboard door the worker had unlocked only a few seconds before. Slowly, Carius nudged the door open. Like a shadow, he slid into the opening, closing the portal behind him.

Scout-Sergeant Carius had been lurking in the dusty archway that marked a long-forgotten garbage chute, biding his time as he waited for the factories of Izo Primaris to disgorge their human inmates. He had watched as workers trudged down the hall, shuffling down the corridor half-dead with fatigue. He had let them all pass, maintaining his vigil until he saw the man he wanted. Carius's victim was just another nameless cog in the economy of the Imperium, a man of no importance or consequence. The only thing that made him remarkable was the room he called home. That minor detail had caused fifteen centimetres of gyrating steel to sink into the back of the man's neck.

Carius paused when he crossed the threshold, his ears trained upon the sounds of the dingy apartment he had invaded. He could hear the mineral-tainted water rumbling through the pipes, could fix the lairs of sump-rats in the plaster walls, could discern the pebbly groan of air rattling through vents. The Scout-sergeant ignored these sounds. It was the slight noise of footsteps that had his attention.

The apartment was a miserable hovel, ramshackle factory-pressed furnishings slowly decaying into their constituent components. A threadbare rug was thrown across the peeling floor in some vain effort to lend a touch of dignity to the place. A narrow bed was crushed against one wall, a scarred wardrobe lodged in a corner. Table, chairs, a mouldering couch, a lopsided shelf supporting a sorry collection of crystal miniatures, these were the contents of the apartment. These, and a wide window looking out upon the boulevard.

Carius followed the sound of footsteps. The main room of the apartment had two lesser ancillary chambers – a pail closet and a galley. It was from the galley that the sounds arose.

The Scout-sergeant edged along the wall until he stood just at the edge of the archway leading into the galley. The pungent smell of boiling vegetables struck his heightened olfactory senses, along with a suggestion of sweat and feminine odour. Carius dug his armoured thumb into the wall, effortlessly ripping a clump of crumbly grey plaster free. Without turning from the archway, he threw the clump of plaster against the apartment door. The impact sounded remarkably like a door slamming shut; the fragments of plaster tumbling across the floor as they exploded away from the impact resembled the sound of footsteps.

'Andreas!' a woman's voice called. 'Dinner is–'

The worker's wife didn't have time to do more than blink as Carius's armoured bulk swung out from the wall and filled the archway as she emerged from the galley to welcome her husband. The vibro-knife stabbed into her throat, stifling any cry she might have made.

Carius depressed the vibro-knife's activation stud, ending the shivering motion of the blade and slid the weapon back into its sheath. Walking away from the body, he shoved furniture out of his way, advancing to the window. The sergeant stared through the glazed glass and admired the view of the boulevard outside. From the instant he had inspected the building from the street below, he had expected this room to offer such a vantage point.

The apartment door opened behind him, but Carius did not look away from the window. He knew the men moving into the room were his own.

'Report,' Carius ordered.

'Melta bombs placed at power plant,' one of the Scouts stated, his voice carrying no inflection, only the precise acknowledgement of a job completed.

'Melta bombs in position at defence turrets nine and seven,' the other Scout said.

Carius nodded his head. The two Scouts had been charged with targets closest to their current position. It would take time for the others to reach their targets and filter back. The sergeant studied the chronometer fixed to the underside of his gauntlet. The attack would not begin for some hours yet. His squad was still ahead of schedule. By the time they were finished, all of Izo Primaris's defence turrets would be sabotaged, leaving the city unable to strike any aerial attackers until it could scramble its own aircraft. Carius shook his head as he considered what value the antiquated PDF fighters would have against a Thunderhawk. The defence turrets had been the only real menace the Space Marines could expect as they made their descent from the orbiting battle-barge, the deadly *Deathmonger*.

Other melta bombs would destroy the city's central communications hub and disable the energy grid. Izo Primaris would be plunged into confusion and despair even before the first Warbringers descended upon the city.

The local planetary defence force was of little concern to the Warbringers. Unable to contact their central command, they would be forced to operate in a disjointed, fragmented fashion, a type of combat for which they were unprepared. There was only one factor within Izo Primaris that might prove resilient enough to react to the havoc preceding the Warbringers' assault.

Carius motioned with his hand, gesturing for the two Scout Marines to occupy rooms to either side of the apartment he had secured. The Scouts slipped back into the hall with the same silence with which they had entered. Carius unslung the needle rifle looped over his shoulder. The back of the scope opened, sending wires slithering into his artificial eye.

Through the prism of the rifle's scope, Carius studied the massive, fortress-like structure of plasteel and ferrocrete that rose from the squalor of the district like an iron castle. A gigantic Imperial aquila was etched in bronze upon each side of the imposing structure, the precinct courthouse of the city's contingent of the Adeptus Arbites.

Brutal enforcers of the *Lex Imperialis*, the Imperial Law every world within the Imperium was bound by, the Arbites had the training, the weapons and the skill to prove a troublesome obstacle if allowed the chance. Carius and his Scouts would ensure the arbitrators did not get that chance. Their mission of sabotage completed, the Scouts would fan out across the perimeter of the courthouse. Sniper fire would keep the arbitrators pinned down inside their fortress. In time, the arbitrators would find a way around the lethal fire of Carius and his men. By then, however, the Warbringers should have accomplished their purpose in Izo Primaris.

Carius watched as armoured arbitrators paced about the perimeter fence separating the courthouse from the slums around it. His finger rested lightly against the trigger of his rifle, the weapon shifting ever so slightly as he maintained contact with the target he had chosen.

When the signal came, Carius and his Scouts would be ready.

It wasn't really surprising that the planetary council of Vulscus met in a section of the governor's palace. Mattias was a ruler who believed in allowing his subjects the illusion of representation, but wasn't foolish enough to allow the council to actually conduct its business outside his own supervision. Even so, there were times when the representatives of the various merchant guilds and industrial combines could be exceedingly opinionated. Occasionally, Mattias had found it necessary to summon his excubitors to maintain order in the council chamber.

The debate over the proposal Zweig had brought to Vulscus was proving to be just such a divisive subject. Lavishly appointed guilders roared at fat promethium barons, the semi-mechanical tech-priests lashing out against the zealous oratory of the robed ecclesiarches. Even the handful of wiry rogues representing the trade unions felt they had to bare their teeth and demand a few concessions to compensate the unwashed masses of workers they supposedly championed. As soon as one of the industrialists or guilders tossed a bribe their way, the union men would shut up. The others would be more difficult to silence.

Arguments arose over the wisdom of defying the other Great Families by honouring the request of House Heraclius. Some felt that the pilgrims should be able to reach Vulscus by whatever means they could, others claimed that by having a single family of Navigators controlling the traffic there would be less confusion and more order. Those guilders and industrialists who already had exclusive contracts with House Heraclius to ship goods through the warp sparred with those who had dealings with other Navigators and worried about how the current situation would impact their own shipping agreements.

Throughout it all, Mattias watched the planetary council shout itself hoarse and wondered if perhaps he should have bypassed them and just made the decision himself. If anyone had been too upset with his decision, he could have always sent the PDF to re-educate them.

He glanced across the tiers of the council chamber to the ornate visitors' gallery. No expense had been spared to make the gallery as opulent and impressive as possible. Visiting dignitaries were surrounded by vivid holo-picts of assorted scenes of Vulscun history and culture, the walls behind them covered in rich tapestries depicting the wonders of Vulscun industry and the extensive resources of the planet and her satellites. If the vicious debates of the planetary council failed to interest a visiting ambassador, the exotic sculptures of Vulscun beauties would usually suffice to keep him entertained.

Zweig, however, didn't even glance at the expensive art all around him in the gallery. He stubbornly kept watching the debate raging below him, despite the tedium of such a vigil. Mattias could tell the rogue trader was bored by the whole affair. He kept looking at his antique chronometer.

The governor chuckled at Zweig's discomfort. The man had asked for this, after all. He'd kept pestering Mattias about when the council could be gathered and if all the leaders of Vulscus would be present to hear him make his case for Novator Priskos. Despite repeated assurances from the governor, Zweig had been most insistent that all of the men who controlled Vulscus should be in attendance when he introduced the Navigator's proposal.

Well, the rogue trader had gotten his wish. He had presented his proposal to the planetary council. Now he could just sit back and wait a few weeks for their answer.

Mattias chuckled again when he saw Zweig fussing about with his chronometer again. The governor wondered if the rogue trader might consider selling the thing. Mattias had never seen a chronometer quite like it. He was sure it would make an interesting addition to his private collection of off-world jewellery and bric-a-brac.

The governor's amusement ended when there was a bright flash from Zweig's chronometer. At first Mattias thought perhaps Zweig's incessant toying with the device had caused some internal relay to explode. It was on his lips to order attendants to see if the rogue trader had been injured, but the words never left his mouth.

Shapes were appearing on the gallery beside Zweig, blurry outlines that somehow seemed far more real than the holo-picts playing around them. With each second, the shapes became more distinct, more solid. They were huge, monstrous figures, twice the height of a man and incredibly broad. Though their outlines were humanoid, they looked more machine than man, great bulky brutes of tempered plasteel and adamantium.

Mattias stared in shock as the strange manifestations began to move, lumbering across the gallery. The giants were painted in a dull olive drab, mottled with splashes of black and brown to help break up their outlines. If not for the confusing blur of colour, the governor might have recognised them for what they were sooner. It was only when one of the giants shifted its arm, raising a hideous rotary autocannon over the railing of the gallery, that the governor saw the ancient stone cruciform bolted to the armoured shoulder. It was then that he knew the armoured giants surrounding Zweig were Space Marines.

The chronometer Zweig had been toying with was actually a homing beacon. The Space Marines had fixed the beacon's location and teleported down into the council chamber. There could be no doubt as to why. For some reason, the rogue trader had brought death to the leaders of Vulscus.

A hush fell upon the chamber as the councillors took notice of the five giants looming above them from the gallery. Arguments and feuds were forgotten in that moment as each man stared up into the waiting jaws of destruction. Some cried out in terror; some fell to their knees and pleaded innocence; others made the sign of the aquila and called upon the Emperor of Mankind.

Whatever their reaction, their end was already decided. In unison, the Warbringers in their heavy Terminator armour opened fire upon the cowering councillors. Five assault cannons tore into the screaming men, bursting their bodies as though they were rotten fruit.

In a matter of seconds, the ornate council chamber became a charnel house.

* * *

SIRENS BLARED THROUGHOUT Izo Primaris. Smoke curled skywards from every quarter, turning the purplish twilight black with soot. Crisis control tractors trundled into the streets, smashing their way through the evening traffic, oblivious to any concern save that of reaching the stricken sections of the city. No industrial accident, no casual arson in a block of filthy tenements, not even the tragic conflagration of the opulent residence of a guilder could have provoked such frantic, brutal reaction. The explosions had engulfed the defence batteries, all five of the massive forts crippled in the blink of an eye by melta bombs.

Even as the crisis tractors smashed a path through the crowded streets, tossing freight trucks and commuter sedans like chaff before a plough, more explosions ripped through the city. Lights winked out, a malignant darkness spreading through the capital. A pillar of fire rising from the heart of the metropolitan sprawl was the only monument to the site of Izo Primaris's central power plant. It would be hours before tech-priests at the substations would be able to redirect the city's energy needs through the battery of back-up plants. They wouldn't even try. To do that, the tech-priests required absolution from their superiors.

The destruction of the communications hub made the earlier explosions seem tame by comparison. Plasteel windows cracked a kilometre and a half away from the cloud of noxious smoke that heralded the silencing of a planet. A skyscraper of ferrocrete and reinforced armaplas, the communications tower had bristled with satellite relays and frequency transmitters, its highest chambers, five hundred metres above the ground, devoted to the psychic exertions of the planet's astropaths. Governor Mattias, always mindful of his own security and power, had caused all communications on Vulscus to be routed through the tower, where his private police could check every message for hints of sedition and discontent.

Now the giant tower had fallen, brought to ruin by the timed blast of seven melta bombs planted in its sub-cellars. With the death of the hub, every vox-caster on Vulscus went silent.

All except those trained upon a different frequency. A frequency being relayed from a sinister vessel in orbit around the world.

Izo Primaris maintained three PDF garrisons within its walled confines. Two infantry barracks and a brigade of armour. Despite the silence of the vox-casters and their inability to raise anyone in central command, the soldiers of the Vulscun Planetary Defence Forces were not idle. Lasguns and flak armour were brought from stores, companies and regiments were quickly mustered into formation.

There was nothing to disturb the hasty muster of soldiers at the two infantry barracks. The tank brigade was not so fortunate. The Scout Marine who had visited them had not placed melta bombs about their headquarters or tried to sabotage the fifty Leman Russ-pattern tanks housed in the base's motor pool. What he had done instead was even more deadly.

A bright flash burst into life at the centre of the

courtyard where the PDF tankmen were scrambling to their vehicles. A survivor of the massacre in the council chamber would have recognised that flash, would have shouted a warning as hulking armoured shapes suddenly appeared. From the orbiting battle-barge, five more Terminators had followed a homing beacon and been teleported with unerring precision to their target.

The olive-drab giants opened fire upon the tankmen, tearing their bodies to pieces with concentrated fire from their storm bolters. One of the Space Marines, his bulky armour further broadened by the box-like weapon system fastened to his shoulders, targeted the tanks themselves. Shrieking as they shot upwards from the cyclone missile launcher, a dozen armour-busting krak missiles streamed towards the PDF tanks. The effect upon the armoured vehicles was much like that of the storm bolters upon the stunned tankmen. Reinforced armour plate crumpled like tin-foil as the missiles slammed home, their shaped warheads punching deep into the tanks' hulls before detonating. The effect was like igniting a plasma grenade inside a steel can. The tanks burst apart from within as the explosives gutted their innards.

In a few minutes, the surviving tankmen retreated back into their barracks, seeking shelter behind the thick ferrocrete walls. The Terminators ignored the sporadic lasgun fire directed on them, knowing there was no chance such small arms fire could penetrate their armoured shells. They turned away from the barracks, maintaining a vigil on the gated entryway to the motor pool.

Despite the carnage they had wrought, the mission the Terminators had been given was not one of slaughter. It was to keep the tanks from mobilising and spreading out into the city where they might interfere with the Warbringers' other operations.

CARIUS FOLLOWED THE read from his scope and opened fire. He aimed thirteen centimetres above the arbitrator he had chosen for his victim, allowing for the pull of gravity upon his shot. The slender sliver-like needle struck home, slicing through the arbitrator's jaw just beneath the brim of his visor. The Enforcer didn't even have time to register pain before the deadly poison upon the needle dropped him. His body twitched and spasmed upon the cobblestones outside the courthouse, drawing in other arbitrators, rushing to investigate their comrade's plight. Three more of the Enforcers were dropped as the other snipers staged around the courthouse opened fire.

The arbitrators fell back into their fortress, employing riot shields to protect themselves as they withdrew. Carius kept his rifle aimed upon the entrance of the courthouse. Experience and the mem-training he had undergone when a neophyte told Carius what to expect next. These arbitrators were especially well trained, the sergeant conceded. They beat his estimate by a full minute when they emerged from the courthouse in a phalanx, employing their riot shields to form a bulwark against the sniper fire.

Emotionlessly, Carius scanned the crude defensive line. He nodded his head slightly when he saw the man he wanted. The Judge wore a stormcloak over his carapace armour and a golden eagle adorned his helmet. Carius aimed at that bit of ostentation, sending a poisoned needle sizzling through one of the riot shields to embed itself in the beak of the eagle. The Judge felt the impact of the shot, ducking his head and reaching to his helmet. The Scout-sergeant wasn't disappointed when he saw the Judge's face go white when his fingers felt the slivers of Carius's bullet embedded in his helmet.

The Judge rose and shouted at the arbitrators. It was again to the credit of the Enforcers that they did not allow the Judge's panic to infect them and their second retreat into the courthouse was made in perfect order, the phalanx never disintegrating into a panicked mob.

Carius leaned back, resting his elbows against the sill of the window. The next thing the arbitrators would try would be to use one of their Rhino armoured transports to affect a breakout. Brother Domitian would be in position with his heavy bolter to thwart that attempt. After that, the Enforcers would have to think about their next move.

Carius was content to let them think. While the arbitrators were thinking they would be safely contained inside the courthouse where they couldn't interfere with the Warbringers.

WITH THE DEFENCE batteries destroyed and communications down, there was no warning for the people of Izo Primaris when five gun-laden assault craft descended upon the city. Two of the powerful

Thunderhawk gunships hurtled into the ferrocrete canyons of the city, guided through the black maze of the darkened metropolis by holo-maps taken by the battle-barge from orbit. As the Thunderhawks progressed only a dozen metres above the streets, their speed gradually slowed. Intermittent bursts of lascannon fire slammed into the sides of buildings or gouged craters from the tarmac. Screams of terror rose from civilians as they streamed from their wounded homes, filling the streets with a mass of frightened humanity.

Coldly, with a callous precision, the Warbringers employed the heavy bolters mounted upon their Thunderhawks to herd the frantic mob through the streets. The objective of this brutal tactic soon showed itself. The infantry regiments were finally marching from their garrisons, trying to restore order to the stricken city. The desperate mob rushed into the face of their marching columns.

The PDF commanders hesitated to give the order to open fire on their own people. The delay could not be recovered. Even as the belated command was given, the civilians were crashing into the soldiers, confusing their ranks, breaking the cohesion of their units.

The Thunderhawks dropped still lower, the ramps set into the rear of their hulls opening. Green-armoured giants jumped from the moving gunships, rolling across the tarmac as they landed. Each of the Warbringers was soon on his feet again, the lethal bulk of a boltgun clenched in his steel gauntlets. While the PDF still fought to free themselves of the civilian herd, the Space Marines moved into position, establishing a strongpoint at the intersection nearest their enemies.

Both Thunderhawks surged forwards with a burst of speed, sweeping over the embattled PDF troops. One soldier managed to send a rocket screaming up at one of the gunships, the warhead impacting against the hull and blackening the armour plate. Any jubilation over the attack was quickly extinguished as the Thunderhawks reached the rear of the PDF columns. Spinning full around, the gunships came back, their lascannons blazing. The withering fire slammed into the PDF regiments, forcing them forwards. It was their turn to be herded through the streets, herded straight into the waiting guns of the Warbringers on the ground.

OF THE REMAINING Thunderhawks, one sped across Izo Primaris to disgorge its cargo of power-armoured giants at the armour base so that they might support the action entrusted to the Terminators. The other two made straight for the governor's palace.

The compound was in a state of siege, frightened citizens hammering at its gates, demanding answers from their leaders. The red-uniformed excubitors held the mob back, employing shock mauls to break the arms of anyone trying to climb over the walls, using laspistols on those few who actually made it over the barrier.

The gunships unleashed the fury of their heavy bolters into both mob and guards, the explosive rounds shearing through the crimson armour of the excubitors as though it were paper. Citizens fled back into the darkened streets, wailing like damned souls as terror pounded through their hearts. The excubitors attempted to fall back to defensive positions, but the punishment being visited on them by the heavy bolters soon caused the guards to abandon that plan and retreat back into the palace itself.

In short order, a landing zone had been cleared. The Thunderhawks descended into the lush gardens fronting Governor Mattias's palace, the backwash of their powerful engines crushing priceless blooms imported from Terra into a mess of mangled vegetation. Armoured ramps dropped open at the rear of each gunship, ceramite-encased giants rushing to assume a perimeter around the garden. Two gigantic machines, lumbering monstrosities twice as tall as even the gigantic Space Marines, emerged from the Thunderhawks behind the Warbringers. Vaguely cast in a humanoid form, the torso of each machine encased the armoured sarcophagus of a crippled Warbringer, his mind fused to the adamantium body which now housed it. The Dreadnoughts were revered battle-brothers of the Warbringers, ancient warriors who fought on through the millennia in their ageless metal tombs.

The two Dreadnoughts fanned out across the gardens, one training its deadly weapons on the wall at the front of the compound, the other facing towards the palace itself. Almost immediately the huge machine was spurred into action as solid shot from a heavy stubber mounted in an ornate cupola began firing upon it. The bullets glanced off the Dreadnought's thick hull, barely scratching the olive drab paint that coated it. Power hissed through the over-sized energy coils of the immense weapon that was fitted to the machine's left arm. When the coils began to glow with the intensity of a supernova, the Dreadnought pivoted at its waist and raised the arm towards the cupola.

A blinding burst of light erupted from the nozzle that fronted the Dreadnought's cumbersome weapon. The blazing ball of gas sizzled across the gardens, striking the cupola at its centre. Instantly the structure vanished in a great cloud of boiling nuclear malignance as the charged plasma reacted with the solid composition of the cupola. The sun gun immolated the excubitors who had fired upon the Dreadnought, reduced their heavy stubber to a molten smear and fused the cupola into something resembling a charred brick.

After that, an eerie silence fell across the compound. The governor's guards were not about to provoke the wrath of the Dreadnoughts a second time.

With the Dreadnoughts in command of the exterior, the twenty Warbringers left the defence of the perimeter to their ancient brethren and rushed the palace itself. Gilded doors designed to withstand the impact of a freight tractor were quickly shattered by the chainswords of the Space Marines, the diamond-edged blades tearing through the heavy oorl-wood panels and the plasteel supports.

As the first Warbringers breeched the doors and entered the palace itself, Inquisitor Korm emerged from one of the Thunderhawks, his imposing figure dwarfed by the huge armoured warriors who flanked him. Captain Phazas held his helmet in the crook of his arm, exposing a leathery face and a forehead bristling with steel service studs. Chaplain Valac, as ever, kept his countenance locked behind the death's head mask of his helm.

Phazas pressed a finger against his ear, closing one eye as he digested the vox-cast being relayed to him. 'Squad Boethius has secured the council building,' he told Korm. The captain's grim face twisted in a scowl. 'Zweig reports that Governor Mattias escaped before the operation was complete. Some kind of personal force field.'

'We will track down the heretic,' Korm assured the fearsome Phazas. 'There is no escape for him. With his regime broken, he will try to flee Vulscus.' The inquisitor's eyes burned with a fanatical light, his lip curling in disgust. 'First he will try to secure his most precious treasure.'

'The obscene shall be cast low in the midst of their obscenity,' Chaplain Valac's stern voice intoned. 'For them, death is but the doorway to damnation.'

Korm turned away from Valac and directed his attention back to Phazas. 'Have your men search the palace, sweep through it room by room. Mattias must not leave the compound with the relic.'

'The Warbringers know their duty,' Phazas answered, annoyance in his tone. 'The heretic will be found. The relic will be recovered.' He spoke as though both tasks had already been accomplished, statement rather than speculation. Korm knew better than to question the captain's belief in his men.

A man didn't live long enough to become an inquisitor if he were a fool.

GOVERNOR MATTIAS HAD retreated to a fortified bunker deep beneath his palace. The Warbringers had intercepted the governor before he could reach his escape route: a private tunnel connecting the complex to the underrail network beneath Izo Primaris. Twenty excubitors had been killed in the ensuing firefight. Mattias and his ten surviving guards had fallen back to the bunker.

Designed to be proof against rebellion and civil unrest, the governor's bunker proved no obstacle to the Warbringers, warriors used to breaching the bulkheads of renegade starships and assaulting the citadels of xenos armies. The huge steel doors that blocked the entrance to the bunker were quickly reduced to slag by a concentrated blast from a plasma cannon. The Warbringers rushed through the opening while molten metal still dripped from the frame.

One of the power-armoured giants vanished in a burst of light, flesh and ceramite liquefied by the searing energy that smashed into him. Instantly the other Warbringers flattened against the walls, voxing warnings to their comrades. Mattias only had a few guards left to him, but these last excubitors had something the others didn't. They had a multi-melta.

The crimson-armoured excubitors swung the heavy weapon around on its tripod. Nestled behind a ferrocrete pillbox, the guards tried to bring their deadly weapon to bear on the Warbringers already in the corridor. The armoured giants could see the barrels of the multi-melta pivoting within the narrow loop-hole. One of the Warbringers racked his boltgun and emptied a clip into the pillbox, the explosive rounds digging little craters in the thick surface, drawing the attention of the gun crew.

As the multi-melta swung around to fire on the shooter, he threw himself flat to the floor. The super-heated beam of light flashed through the air above him, melting the stabiliser jets and air purification intakes on the Warbringer's backpack, but doing no harm to the Space Marine himself.

Instantly, the other Warbringers in the corridor charged the pillbox. It would take three seconds for the multi-melta to cool down enough to be fired again. The Space Marines intended to have the strongpoint disabled before then. The foremost of the armoured giants reached to his belt, removing a narrow disc of metal. He flung this against the face of the pillbox, black smoke filling the corridor as the blind grenade exploded. The optical sensors built into the War-bringers' helmets allowed them to pierce the dense cloud of inky smoke. The excubitors inside the pillbox were not so fortunate. Frantically they tried to fire the multi-melta into the darkness, the blazing beam of light striking only the ferrocrete wall of the bunker.

Pressed against the face of the pillbox, two of the Warbringers pushed tiny discs through the loophole, then turned away as the frag grenades detonated inside the strongpoint. The menace of the multi-melta was over.

The Warbringers swept around the now silent pillbox, pressing on down the corridor. Las-bolts cracked against their power armour as they converged upon an armaplas barricade thrown across the middle of the hallway, the governor and the last of his guards mounting a hopeless last-ditch effort to defy the oncoming Space Marines.

'This is an unjust act!' Mattias shrieked. 'I have paid the Imperial tithe, I have exceeded the conscription levels for the Imperial Guard! You have no right here! Vulscus is loyal!'

The governor's desperate plea went unanswered by the Space Marines sweeping down the hall. Precise shots from the huge boltguns the Warbringers bore brought death to two of the remaining excubitors. A third threw down his weapon, climbing over the barricade in an effort to surrender. A bolt-round tore through his chest, splattering his organs across the armaplas fortification. The orders the Warbringers were under had been explicit: no prisoners.

'Surrender the relic,' the sepulchral voice of Chaplain Valac boomed through the bunker, magnified by the vox-amplifiers built into his skull-faced helm. The black-armoured Warbringer marched down the corridor, the winged crozius clenched in his fist glowing with power as he approached the barricade. 'Atone for your faithlessness and be returned to the Emperor's grace in death.'

The governor cringed as he heard Valac's words, but quickly recovered. His face pulled back in a sneer of contempt. 'The relic? That is why you have destroyed my city?' Bitter laughter choked Mattias's voice. 'The noble Adeptus Astartes, sons of the Emperor! Common thieves!'

Perhaps the governor might have said more, but his tirade had focussed every bolter in the corridor upon him. Mattias was thrown back as the concentrated fusillade struck him, tossing his body back from the edge of the barricade. The last two excubitors, their reason broken by the hopelessness of their situation, broke from cover and charged straight towards the Warbringers, their lasguns firing harmlessly at the power-armoured giants.

Chaplain Valac pressed forwards, climbing over the barricade and walking towards the crumpled body of Governor Mattias. The governor's reductor field had prevented the fusillade from ripping apart his body, but hadn't been equal to the momentum of the shots. The impact had hurled him across the corridor to crash against the unyielding ferrocrete wall.

There was no sympathy as Valac stared down at the broken governor. Even with half his bones shattered, Mattias tried to defend the object cradled against his chest. Wrapped tightly in a prayer rug soaked in sacred unguents and adorned with waxen purity seals and parchment benedictions, even now the governor could feel the supernatural power of the relic giving him strength.

'You have no right,' Mattias snarled at Valac. 'Roboute Guilliman left it here, left it for Vulscus!'

'No,' Valac's pitiless voice growled. He raised the heavy crozius he carried, energy bristling about the club-like baton. 'He didn't leave it.' The Chaplain brought his staff smashing down, its power field easily bypassing the reductor field that protected the governor. Mattias's head was reduced to pulp beneath Valac's blow.

Grimly, Valac removed the relic from the bloodied corpse. Turning away from Mattias's body, the Chaplain began stripping away the pious adornments that surrounded the relic, flinging them aside as though they were unclean filth. Soon he exposed a bolt pistol of ancient pattern, its surface encrusted by millennia of decay and corrosion.

'You have secured the relic,' Inquisitor Korm beamed as he marched down the corridor, Captain Phazas beside him. A triumphant smile was on Korm's lean face. 'We must get it to the fortress on Titan so that the Ordo Malleus may study it.'

Valac shook his head. 'No,' he intoned. His fist clenched tighter about the bolt pistol, the pressure causing some of the corrosion to flake away, exposing the symbol of an eye engraved into the grip of the gun. 'It is an abomination and must be purged. You have brought us here to do the Emperor's work, and it shall be done.'

Korm stared in disbelief at the grim Warbringer Chaplain. The inquisitor had been the one who had uncovered the truth about the relic so recently discovered on Vulscus, a truth locked away in the archives on Titan. Roboute Guilliman had indeed been on Vulscus, but it had not been the Ultramarines or their primarch who had brought the planet into the Imperium, though such was the official version preached by the Ecclesiarchy and taught in sanctioned histories of the world. The real liberators had been the Lunar Wolves. If a primarch had left a relic upon a Vulscun battlefield, it had been left by that of the Lunar Wolves. It had been left by the arch-traitor, Warmaster Horus.

The fearsome Chaplain marched across the bunker to the shambles that had been left of the pillbox. Clenching the relic in one hand, Valac ripped the damaged multi-melta from the emplacement. Korm gasped in alarm as he understood the Chaplain's purpose. The relic was tainted, a thing of heresy and evil to be sure, corrupting even the innocent by pretending to be something holy. But it was more important that it be studied, not destroyed!

Phazas laid a restraining hand upon Korm's shoulder before the inquisitor could interfere. 'Two fates present themselves,' the captain told him. 'You can return to Titan a hero who has brought about the destruction of an unholy thing. Or you can be denounced as a Horusian radical and perish with the relic. Make your choice, inquisitor.'

Sweat beaded Korm's brow as he watched Chaplain Valac throw the relic onto the ground and aim the heavy multi-melta at it. At such range, the bolt pistol would be reduced to vapour, annihilated more completely than if it had been cast into the centre of a sun.

Korm knew he would share the same annihilation if he broke faith with the Warbringers. The Adeptus Astartes had a very narrow definition of duty and honour. Anything tainted by contact with heresy was a thing to be destroyed.

As he watched Valac obliterate the relic, Korm decided to keep quiet. He'd been an inquisitor for a long time. A man didn't last that long if he were a fool.

# THE LONG GAMES AT CARCHARIAS

## By Rob Sanders

THE END BEGAN with the *Revenant Rex*.

An interstellar beast. Bad omen of omens. A wanderer: she was a regular visitor to this part of the segmentum. The hulk was a drifting gravity well of twisted rock and metal. Vessels from disparate and distant races nestled, broken-backed amongst mineral deposits from beyond the galaxy's borders and ice frozen from before the beginning of time. A demented logic engine at the heart of the hulk – like a tormented dreamer – guided the nightmare path of the beast through the dark void of Imperial sectors, alien empires of the Eastern Fringe and the riftspace of erupting maelstroms. Then, as if suddenly awoken from a fevered sleep, the daemon cogitator would initiate the countdown sequence of an ancient and weary warp drive. The planetkiller would disappear with the expediency of an answered prayer, destined to drift up upon the shores of some other bedevilled sector, hundreds of light years away.

The *Revenant Rex* beat the Aurora Chapter at Schindelgheist, the Angels Eradicant over at Theta Reticuli and the White Scars at the Martyrpeake. Unfortunately the hulk was too colossal and the timeframes too erratic for the cleanse-and-burn efforts of the Adeptus Astartes to succeed: but Chapter pride and zealotry ensured their superhuman efforts regardless. The behemoth was infested with greenskins of the Iron Klaw Clan – that had spent the past millennia visiting hit-and-run mayhem on systems across the segmentum, with abandoned warbands colonising planetary badlands like a green, galactic plague. The Warfleet Ultima, where it could gather craft in sufficient time and numbers, had twice attempted to destroy the gargantuan hulk. The combined firepower of hundreds of Navy vessels had also failed to destroy the beast, simply serving to enhance its hideous melange further.

All these things and more had preyed upon Elias Artegall's conscience when the *Revenant Rex* tumbled into the Gilead Sector. Arch-Deacon Urbanto. Rear Admiral Darracq. Overlord Gordius. Zimner, the High Magos Retroenginericus. Grand Master Karmyne of the Angels Eradicant. Artegall had either received them or received astrotelepathic messages from them all.

'Chapter Master, the xenos threat cannot be tolerated…'

'The Mercantile Gilead have reported the loss of thirty bulk freighters…'

'Master Artegall, the greenskins are already out of control in the Despot Stars…'

'That vessel could harbour ancient technological secrets that could benefit the future of mankind…'

'You must avenge us, brother…'

The spirehalls of the Slaughterhorn had echoed with their demands and insistence. But to war was a Space Marine's prerogative. Did not Lord Guilliman state on the steps of the Plaza Ptolemy: 'There is but one of the Emperor's Angels for every world in the Imperium; but one drop of Adeptus Astartes blood for every Imperial citizen. Judge the necessity to spill such a precious commodity with care and if it must be spilt, spill it wisely, my battle-brothers.'

Unlike the Scars or the Auroras, Artegall's Crimson Consuls were not given to competitive rivalry. Artegall did not desire success because others had failed. Serving at the pleasure of the primarch was not a tournament spectacle and the *Revenant Rex* was not an opportunistic arena. In the end, Artegall let his battered copy of the *Codex Astartes* decide. In those much-thumbed pages lay the wisdom of greater men than he: as ever, Artegall put his trust in their skill and experience. He chose a passage that reflected his final judgement and included it in both his correspondence to his far-flung petitioners and his address to the Crimson Consuls, First Company on board the battle-barge *Incarnadine Ecliptic*.

'From *Codicil CC-LXXX-IV.ii: The Coda of Balthus Dardanus, 17th Lord of Macragge* – entitled *Staunch Supremacies.* "For our enemies will bring us to battle on the caprice of chance. The alien and the renegade are the vagaries of the galaxy incarnate. What can we truly know or would want to of their ways or motivations? They are to us as the rabid wolf at the closed door that knows not even its own mind. Be that door. Be the simplicity of the steadfast and unchanging: the barrier between what is known and the unknowable. Let the Imperium of Man realise its manifold destiny within while without its mindless foes dash themselves against the constancy of our adamantium. In such uniformity of practice and purpose lies the perpetuity of mankind." May Guilliman be with you.'

'And with you,' Captain Bolinvar and his crimson-clad 1st Company Terminator Marines had returned. But the primarch had not been with them and Bolinvar and one hundred veteran sons of Carcharias had been forsaken.

Artegall sat alone in his private Tactical Chancelorium, among the cold ivory of his throne. The Chancelorium formed the very pinnacle of the Slaughterhorn – the Crimson Consuls fortress-monastery – which in turn formed the spirepeak of Hive Niveous, the Carcharian capital city. The throne was constructed from the colossal bones of shaggy, shovel-tusk Stegodonts, hunted by Carcharian ancestors, out on the Dry-blind. Without his armour the Chapter Master felt small and vulnerable in the huge throne – a sensation usually alien to an Adeptus Astartes' very being. The chamber was comfortably gelid and Artegall sat in his woollen robes, elbow to knee and fist to chin, like some crumbling statue from Terran antiquity.

The Chancelorium began to rumble and this startled the troubled Chapter Master. The crimson-darkness swirl of the marble floor began to part in front of him and the trapdoor admitted a rising platform upon which juddered two Chapter serfs in their own zoster robes. They flanked a huge brass pict-caster that squatted dormant between them. The serfs were purebred Carcharians with their fat, projecting noses, wide nostrils and thick brows. These on top of stocky, muscular frames, barrel torsos and thick arms decorated with crude tattoos and scar-markings. Perfectly adapted for life in the frozen underhive.

'Where is your master, the Chamber Castellan?' Artegall demanded of the bondsmen. The first hailed his Chapter Master with a fist to the aquila represented on the Crimson Consuls crest of his robes.

'Returned presently from the underhive, my lord – at your request – with the Lord Apothecary,' the serf answered solemnly. The second activated the pict-caster, bringing forth the crystal screen's grainy picture.

'We have word from the Master of the Fleet, Master Artegall,' the serf informed him.

Standing before Artegall was an image of Hecton Lambert, Master of the Crimson Consuls fleet. The Space Marine commander was on the bridge of the strike cruiser *Anno Tenebris*, high above the gleaming, glacial world of Carcharias.

'Hecton, what news?' Artegall put to him without the usual formality of a greeting.

'My master: nothing but the gravest news,' the Crimson Consul told him. 'As you know, we have been out of contact with Captain Bolinvar and the *Incarnadine Ecliptic* for days. A brief flash on one of our scopes prompted me to despatch the frigate *Herald Angel* with orders to locate the *Ecliptic* and report back. Twelve hours into their search they intercepted the following pict-cast, which they transmitted to the *Anno Tenebris*, and which I now dutifully transmit to you. My lord, with this every man on board sends his deepest sympathies. May Guilliman be with you.'

'And with you,' Artegall mouthed absently, rising out of the throne. He took a disbelieving step towards the broad screen of the pict-caster. Brother Lambert disappeared and was replaced by a static-laced image, harsh light and excruciating noise. The vague outline of a Crimson Consuls Space Marine could be made out. There were sparks and fires in the background, as well as the silhouettes of injured Space Marines and Chapter serfs stumbling blind and injured through the smoke and bedlam. The Astartes identified himself but his name and rank were garbled in the intruding static of the transmission.

'...this is the battle-barge *Incarnadine Ecliptic*, two days out of Morriga. I am now ranking battle-brother. We have sustained critical damage...' The screen erupted with light and interference.

Then: 'Captain Bolinvar went in with the first wave. Xenos resistance was heavy. Primitive booby traps. Explosives. Wall-to-wall green flesh and small arms. By the primarch, losses were minimal; my injuries, though, necessitated my return to the *Ecliptic*. The captain was brave and through the use of squad rotations, heavy flamers and teleporters our Consul Terminators managed to punch through to an enginarium with a power signature. We could all hear the countdown, even over the vox. Fearing that the *Revenant Rex* was about to make a warp jump I begged the captain to return. I begged him, but he transmitted that the only way to end the hulk and stop the madness was to sabotage the warp drive.'

Once again the lone Space Marine became enveloped in an ominous, growing brightness. 'His final transmission identified the warp engine as active but already sabotaged. He said the logic engine wasn't counting down to a jump... Then, the *Revenant Rex*, it – it just, exploded. The sentry ships were caught in the blast wave and the *Ecliptic* wrecked.'

A serf clutching some heinous wound to his face staggered into the reporting Space Marine. 'Go! To the pods,' he roared at him. Then he returned his attention to the transmission. 'We saw it all. Detonation of the warp engines must have caused some kind of immaterium anomaly. Moments after the hulk blew apart, fragments and debris from the explosion – including our sentry ships – were sucked back through a collapsing empyrean vortex before disappearing altogether. We managed to haul off but are losing power and have been caught in the gravitational pull of a nearby star. Techmarine Hereward has declared the battle-barge unsalvageable. With our orbit decaying I have ordered all surviving Adeptus Astartes and Chapter serfs to the saviour pods. Perhaps some may break free. I fear our chances are slim... May Guilliman be with us...'

As the screen glared with light from the damning star and clouded over with static, Artegall felt like he'd been speared through the gut. He could taste blood in his mouth: the copper tang of lives lost. One hundred Crimson Consuls. The Emperor's Angels under his command. The Chapter's best fighting supermen, gone with the irreplaceable seed of their genetic heritage. Thousands of years of combined battle experience lost to the Imperium. The Chapter's entire inheritance of Tactical Dreadnought Armour: every suit a priceless relic in its own right. The venerable *Ecliptic*. A veteran battle-barge of countless engagements and a piece of Caracharias among the stars. All gone. All claimed by the oblivion of the warp or cremated across the blazing surface of a nearby sun.

'You must avenge us, brother–'

Artegall reached back for his throne but missed and staggered. Someone caught him, slipping their shoulders underneath one of his huge arms. It was Baldwin. He'd been standing behind Artegall, soaking up the tragedy like his Chapter Master. The Space Marine's weight alone should have crushed the Chamber Castellan, but Baldwin was little more than a mind and a grafted, grizzled face on a robe-swathed brass chassis. The serf's hydraulics sighed as he took his master's bulk.

'My lord,' Baldwin began in his metallic burr.

'Baldwin, I lost them…' Artegall managed, his face a mask of stricken denial. With a clockwork clunk of gears and pistons the Chamber Castellan turned on the two serfs flanking the pict-caster.

'Begone!' he told them, his savage command echoing around the bronze walls of the Chancelorium. As the bondsmen thumped their fists into their aquilas and left, Baldwin helped his master to the cool bone of his throne. Artegall stared at the serf with unseeing eyes. They had been recruited together as savage underhivers and netted, kicking and pounding, from the fighting pits and tribal stomping grounds of the abhuman-haunted catacombs of Hive Niveous. But whereas Artegall had passed tissue compatibility and become a Neophyte, Baldwin had fallen at the first hurdle. Deemed unsuitable for surgical enhancement, the young hiver was inducted as a Chapter serf and had served the Crimson Consuls ever since. As personal servant, Baldwin had travelled the galaxy with his superhuman master.

As the decades passed, Artegall's engineered immortality and fighting prowess brought him promotion, while Baldwin's all-too-human body brought him the pain and limitation of old age. When Elias Artegall became the Crimson Consuls' Chapter Master, Baldwin wanted to serve on as his Chamber Castellan. As one century became the next, the underhiver exchanged his wasted frame for an engineered immortality of his own: the brass bulk of cylinders, hydraulics and exo-skeletal appendages that whirred and droned before the throne. Only the serf's kindly face and sharp mind remained.

Baldwin stood by as Artegall's body sagged against the cathedra arm and his face contorted with silent rage. It fell with futility before screwing up again with the bottomless fury only an Adeptus Astartes could feel for his foes and himself. Before him the Crimson Consul could see the faces of men with whom he'd served. Battle-brothers who had been his parrying arm when his own had been employed in death-dealing; Space Marines who had shared with him the small eternities of deep space patrol and deathworld ambush; friends and loyal brethren.

'I sent them,' he hissed through the perfection of his gritted teeth.

'It is as you said to them, my lord. As the *Codex* commanded.'

'Condemned them...'

'They were the door that kept the rabid wolf at bay. The adamantium upon which our enemies must be dashed.'

Artegall didn't seem to hear him: 'I walked them into a trap.'

'What is a space hulk if it not be such a thing? The sector is safe. The Imperium lives on. Such an honour is not without cost. Even Guilliman recognises that. Let me bring you the comfort of his words, my master. Let the primarch show us his way.'

Artegall nodded and Baldwin hydraulically stomped across the chamber to where a lectern waited on a gravitic base. The top of the lectern formed a crystal case that the Castellan opened, allowing the preservative poison of argon gas to escape. Inside, Artegall's tattered copy of the *Codex Astartes* lay open as it had done since the Chapter Master had selected his reading for the 1st Company's departure. Baldwin drifted the lectern across the crimson marble of the Chancelorium floor to the throne's side. Artegall was on his feet. Recovered. A Space Marine again. A Chapter Master with the weight of history and the burden of future expectation on his mighty Astartes' shoulders.

'Baldwin,' he rumbled with a steely-eyed determination. 'Were your recruitment forays into the underhive with the Lord Apothecary fruitful?'

'I believe so, my lord.'

'Good. The Chapter will need Carcharias to offer up its finest flesh, on this dark day. You will need to organise further recruitment sweeps. Go deep. We need the finest savages the hive can offer. Inform Lord Fabian that I have authorised cultivation of our remaining seed. Tell him I need one hundred Crimson sons. Demi gods all, to honour the sacrifice of their fallen brethren.'

'Yes, Chapter Master.'

'And Baldwin.'

'My master?'

'Send for the Reclusiarch.'

'High Chaplain Enobarbus is attached to the 10th Company,' Baldwin informed Artegall with gentle, metallic inflection. 'On training manoeuvres in the Dry-blind.'

'I don't care if he's visiting Holy Terra. Get him here. Now. There are services to organise. Commemorations. Obsequies. The like this Chapter has never known. See to it.'

'Yes, my master,' Baldwin answered and left his lord to his feverish guilt and the cold words of Guilliman.

\* \* \*

'BY NOW YOUR lids are probably frozen to your eye-balls,' growled High Chaplain Enobarbus over the vox-link. 'Your body no longer feels like your own.'

The Crimson Consuls Chaplain leant against the crumbling architecture of the Archaphrael Hive and drank in the spectacular bleakness of his home world. The Dry-blind extended forever in all directions: the white swirl, like a smazeous blanket of white, moulded from the ice pack. By day, with the planet's equally bleak stars turning their attentions on Carcharias, the dry ice that caked everything in a rime of frozen carbon dioxide bled a ghostly vapour. The Dry-blind, as it was called, hid the true lethality of the Carcharian surface, however. A maze of bottomless crevasses, fissures and fractures that riddled the ice beneath and could only be witnessed during the short, temperature-plummeting nights, when the nebulous thunderhead of dry ice sank and re-froze.

'Your fingers are back in your cells, because they sure as Balthus Dardanus aren't part of your hands any more. Hopes of pulling the trigger on your weapon are a distant memory,' the High Chaplain voxed across the open channel.

The Chaplain ran a gauntlet across the top of his head, clearing the settled frost from his tight dread-locks and flicking the slush at the floor. With a ceramite knuckle, he rubbed at the socket of the eye he'd lost on New Davalos. Now stapled shut, a livid scar ran down one side of his brutal face, from the eyelid to his jaw, where tears constantly trickled in the cold air and froze to his face.

'Skin is raw: like radiation burns – agony both inside and out.'

From his position in the twisted, frost-shattered shell that had been the Archaphrael Hive, Enobarbus could hear fang-face shredders. He fancied he could even spot the tell-tale vapour wakes of the shredders' dorsal fins cutting through the Dry-blind. Archaphrael Hive made up a triumvirate of cities called the Pale Maidens that stood like ancient monuments to the fickle nature of Carcharian meteorology. A thousand years before the three cities had been devastated by a freak polar cyclone colloquially referred to as 'The Big One' by the hivers. Now the ghost hives were used by the Crimson Consuls as an impromptu training ground.

'And those are the benefits,' Enobarbus continued, the High Chaplain's oratory sailing out across the vox waves. 'It's the bits you can't feel that you should worry about. Limbs that died hours ago. Dead meat that you're dragging around. Organs choking on the slush you're barely beating around your numb bodies.'

He had brought the 10th Company's 2nd and 7th Scout sniper squads out to the Pale Maidens for stealth training and spiritual instruction. As a test of their worth and spirit, Enobarbus had had the Space Marine Scouts establish and hold ambush positions with their sniper rifles in the deep Carcharian freeze for three days. He had bombarded them endlessly with remembered readings from the *Codex Astartes*, faith instruction and training rhetoric across the open channels of the vox.

Behind him Scout-Sergeant Caradoc was adjusting his snow cloak over the giveaway crimson of his carapace armour plating and priming his shotgun. Enobarbus nodded and the Scout-sergeant melted into the misty, frost-shattered archways of the Archaphrael Hive.

While the Scouts held their agonising positions, caked and swathed in dry ice, Enobarbus and the Scout-sergeants had amused themselves by trapping fang-face shredders. Packs of the beasts roamed the Dry-blind, making the environment an ever more perilous prospect for travellers. The shredders had flat, shovel-shaped maws spilling over with needle-like fangs. They carried their bodies close to the ground and were flat but for the razored dorsal fin protruding from their knobbly spines. They used their long tails for balance and changing direction on the ice. Like their dorsals, the tails were the razor-edged whiplash that gave them their name. Their sharp bones were wrapped in an elastic skin-sheen that felt almost amphibious and gave the beasts the ability to slide downhill and toboggan their prey. Then they would turn their crystal-tip talons on their unfortunate victims: shredding grapnels that the creatures used to climb up and along the labyrinthine crevasses that fractured the ice shelf.

'This is nothing. Lips are sealed with rime. Thought is slow. It's painful. It's agony. Even listening to this feels like more than you can bear.'

Enobarbus pulled his own cape tight about his power armour. Like many of his calling the High Chaplain's plate was ancient and distinct, befitting an Adeptus Astartes of his status, experience and wisdom. Beyond the heraldry and honorifica decorating his midnight adamantium shell and the skullface helmet hanging from his belt, Enobarbus sported the trappings of his home world. The shredder-skin cape hung over his pack, with its razor dorsal and flaps that extended down his arms and terminated in the skinned creature's bestial claws: one decorating each of the High Chaplain's gauntlets.

'But bear it you must, you worthless souls. This is the moment your Emperor will need you. When you feel you have the least to give: that's when your primarch demands the most from you. When your battle-brother is under the knife or in another's sights – this is when you must be able to act,' the High Chaplain grizzled down the vox with gravity. Switching to a secure channel Enobarbus added, 'Sergeant Notus: now, if you will.'

Storeys and storeys below, down in the Dry-blind where Enobarbus and the Scout-sergeants had penned their captured prey, Notus would be waiting for the signal. A signal the Chaplain knew he'd received because of the high-pitched screeches of the released pack of shredders echoing up the shattered chambers and frost-bored ruins of the hive interior. The *Codex Astartes* taught of the nobility of aeon-honoured combat tactics and battle manoeuvres perfectly realised. It was Guilliman's way. The Rules of Engagement. The way in which Enobarbus was instructing his Scouts. But in their war games about the Pale Maidens, Enobarbus wasn't playing the role of the noble Space Marine. He was everything else the galaxy might throw at them: and the enemies of the Astartes did not play by the rules.

With the Scout Marines undoubtedly making excellent use of the hive's elevation and dilapidated exterior – as scores of previous Neophytes had – Enobarbus decided to engage them on multiple fronts at once. While the starving shredders clawed their way up through the ruined hive, intent on ripping the frozen Scouts to pieces, Scout-Sergeant Caradoc was working his way silently down through the derelict stairwells and halls of the hive interior with his shotgun. The High Chaplain decided to come at his Scouts from an entirely different angle.

Slipping his crozius arcanum – the High Chaplain's sacred staff of office – from his belt and extending the shredder talons on the backs of his gauntlets, Enobarbus swung out onto the crumbling hive wall exterior and began a perilous climb skywards. The shell of the hive wall had long been undermined by the daily freeze-thaw action of Caracharian night and day. Using the sharpened point of the aquila's wings at the end of his crozius like an ice pick and the crystal-tip claws of the shredder, the High Chaplain made swift work of the frozen cliff-face of the dilapidated hive.

'There is nothing convenient about your enemy's desires. He will come for you precisely in the moment you have set aside for some corporal indulgence,' Enobarbus told the Scouts, trying hard not to let his exertions betray him over the vox. 'Exhaustion, fear, pain, sickness, injury, necessities of the body and as an extension of your bodies, the necessities of your weapons. Keep your blade keen and your sidearm clean. Guilliman protect you on the reload: the most necessary of indulgences – a mechanical funeral rite.'

Heaving himself up through the shattered floor of a gargoyle-encrusted overhang, the High Chaplain drew his bolt pistol and crept through to a balcony. The tier-terrace was barely stable but commanded an excellent view: too much temptation for a sniper Scout. But as Enobarbus stalked out across the fragile space he found it deserted. The first time in years of such training exercises he'd discovered it as such.

The High Chaplain nodded to himself. Perhaps this cohort of Neophytes was better. Perhaps they were learning faster: soaking up the wisdom of Guilliman and growing into their role. Perhaps they were ready for their Black Carapace and hallowed suits of power armour. Emperor knows they were needed. Chapter Master Artegall had insisted that Enobarbus concentrate his efforts on the 10th Company. The Crimson Consuls had had their share of past tragedies.

The Chapter had inherited the terrible misfortune of a garrison rotation on the industrial world of Phaethon IV when the Celebrant Chapter could not meet their commitments. Word was sent that the Celebrants were required to remain on Nedicta Secundus and protect the priceless holy relics of the cardinal world from the ravages of Hive Fleet Kraken and its splintered tyranid forces. Phaethon IV, on the other hand, bordered the Despot Stars and had long been coveted by Dregz Wuzghal, Arch-Mogul of

Gunza Major. The Crimson Consuls fought bravely on Phaethon IV, and would have halted the beginnings of Waaagh! Wuzghal in its tracks: something stirred under the factories and power plants of the planet, however. Something awoken by the nightly bombing raids of the Arch-Mogul's 'Green Wing'. Something twice as alien as the degenerate greenskins: unfeeling, unbound and unstoppable. An ancient enemy, long forgotten by the galaxy and entombed below the assembly lines and Imperial manufacturing works of Phaethon, skeletal nightmares of living silver: the necrons. Between greenskin death from above and tomb warriors crawling out of their stasis chambers below, the industrial worlders and their Crimson Consuls guardians hadn't stood a chance and the Chapter lost two highly-decorated companies. As far as Enobarbus knew, the necron and the Arch-Mogul fought for Phaethon still.

The High Chaplain held his position. The still air seared the architecture around him with its caustic frigidity. Enobarbus closed his eyes and allowed his ears to do the work. He filtered out the freeze-thaw expansion of the masonry under his boots, the spiritual hum of the sacred armour about his body and the creak of his own aged bones. There it was. The tell-tale scrape of movement, the tiniest displacement of weight on the balcony expanse above. Back-tracking, the High Chaplain found a craterous hole in the ceiling. Hooking his crozius into the ruined stone and corroded metal, the Crimson Consul heaved himself noiselessly up through the floor of the level above.

Patient, like a rogue shredder on ambush in the Dry-blind – masked by the mist and hidden in some ice floor fissure – Enobarbus advanced with agonising care across the dilapidated balcony. There he was. One of the 10th Company Scouts. Flat to the steaming floor, form buried in his snow cloak, helmet down at the scope of his sniper rifle: a position the Neophyte had undoubtedly held for days. The balcony was an excellent spot. Despite some obstructive masonry, it commanded a view of the Dry-blind with almost the same breathtaking grandeur of the platform below. Without a sound, Enobarbus was above the sniper Scout, the aquila-wing blade-edge of his crozius resting on the back of the Scout's neck, between the helmet and the snow cloak.

'The cold is not the enemy,' the High Chaplain voxed across the open channel. 'The enemy is not even the enemy. You are the enemy. Ultimately you will betray yourself.'

When the Scout didn't move, the Chaplain's lip curled with annoyance. He locked his suit vox-channels and hooked the Scout's shoulder with the wing-tip of the crozius.

'It's over, Consul,' Enobarbus told the prone form. 'The enemy has you.'

Flipping the Scout over, Enobarbus stood there in silent shock. Cloak, helmet and rifle were there but the Scout was not. Instead, the butchered body of a Shredder lay beneath, with the hilt of a gladius buried in its fang-faced maw. Enobarbus shook his head. Anger turned to admiration. These Scouts would truly test him.

Enobarbus switched to the private channel he shared with Scout-Sergeant Notus to offer him brief congratulations on his Scouts and to direct him up into the ruined hive.

'What in Guilliman's name are–' Enobarbus heard upon the transferring frequency. Then the unmistakable whoosh of las-fire. The High Chaplain heard the Scout-sergeant roar defiance over the vox and looking out over the Dry-blind, Enobarbus saw the light show, diffused in the swirling miasma, like sheet lightning across a stormy sky. Something cold took hold of the High Chaplain's heart. Enobarbus had heard thousands of men die. Notus was dead.

Transferring channels, Enobarbus hissed, 'Override Obsidian: we are under attack. This is not a drill. 2nd and 7th, you are cleared to fire. Sergeant Caradoc, meet me at the–'

Shotgun blasts. Rapid and rushed. Caradoc pressed by multiple targets. The crash of the weapon bounced around the maze of masonry and wormholed architecture.

'Somebody get me a visual,' the High Chaplain growled over the vox before slipping the crozius into his belt. Leading with his bolt pistol, Enobarbus raced for the fading echo of the sergeant's weapon. Short sprints punctuated with skips and drops through holes and stairwells.

'Caradoc, where are you?' Enobarbus voxed as he threaded his way through the crumbling hive. The shotgun fire had died away but the Scout-sergeant wasn't replying. '2nd squad, 7th squad, I want a visual on Sergeant Caradoc, now!'

But there was nothing: only an eerie static across the channel. Rotating through the frequencies, Enobarbus vaulted cracks and chasms and thundered across frost-hazed chambers.

'Ritter, Lennox, Beade…' the High Chaplain cycled but the channels were dead. Sliding down into a skid, the shredder-skin cape and the greave plates of his armour carrying him across the chamber floor, Enobarbus dropped down through a hole and landed in a crouch. His pistol was everywhere, pivoting around and taking in the chamber below. An Astartes shotgun lay spent and smoking nearby and a large body swung from a creaking strut in the exposed ceiling. Caradoc.

The Scout-sergeant was hanging from his own snow cloak, framed in a gaping hole in the exterior hive wall, swinging amongst the brilliance of the Dry-blind beyond. The cloak, wrapped around his neck as it was, had been tied off around the strut like a noose. This wouldn't have been enough to kill the Space Marine. The dozen gladius blades stabbed through his butchered body up to their hilts had done that. The sickening curiosity of such a vision would have been enough to stun most battle-brothers but Enobarbus took immediate comfort and instruction from his memorised *Codex*. There was protocol to follow. Counsel to heed.

Snatching his skull-face helmet from his belt, Enobarbus slapped it on and secured the seals. With pistol still outstretched in one gauntlet, the High Chaplain felt for the rosarius hanging around his neck. He would have activated the powerful force field generator but an enemy was already upon him. The haze of the chamber was suddenly whipped up in a rush of movement. Shredders. Lots of them. They came out of the floor. Out of the roof. Up the exterior wall, as the High Chaplain had. Snapping at him with crystal claws and maws of needle-tip teeth. Enobarbus felt their razored tails slash against his adamantium shell and the vice-like grip of their crushing, shovel-head jaws on his knees, his shoulder, at his elbows and on his helmet.

Bellowing shock and frustration, Enobarbus threw his arm around, dislodging two of the monsters. As they scrambled about on the floor, ready to pounce straight back at him, the High Chaplain ended them with his bolt pistol. Another death-dealer tore at him from behind and swallowed his pistol and gauntlet whole. Again, Enobarbus fired, his bolt-rounds riddling the creature from within. The thing died with ease but its dagger-fang jaws locked around his hand and weapon, refusing to release. The darkness of holes and fractured doorways continued to give birth to the Carcharian predators. They bounded at him with their merciless, ice-hook talons, vaulting off the walls, floor and ceiling, even off Caradoc's dangling corpse.

Snatching the crozius arcanum from his belt the High Chaplain thumbed the power weapon to life. Swinging it about him in cold fury, Enobarbus cleaved shredders in two, slicing the monsters through the head and chopping limbs and tails from the beasts.

The floor erupted in front of the Space Marine and

a hideously emaciated shredder – big, even for its kind – came up through the frost-shattered masonry. It leapt at Enobarbus, jaws snapping shut around his neck and wicked talons hooking themselves around the edges of his chest plate. The force of the impact sent the High Chaplain flailing backwards, off balance and with shredders hanging from every appendage.

Enobarbus roared as his armoured form smashed through part of a ruined wall and out through the gap in the hive exterior. The Crimson Consul felt himself falling. Survival instinct causing his fist to open, allowing the crozius to be torn from him by a savage little shredder. Snatching at the rapidly disappearing masonry, Enobarbus elongated his own shredder claw and buried the crystal-tip talon in the ancient rockcrete. The High Chaplain hung from two monstrous digits, shredders in turn hanging from his armour. With the dead-weight and locked jaw of the pistol-swallowing shredder on the other arm and the huge beast now hanging down his back from a jaw-hold on his neck, Enobarbus had little hope of improving his prospects. Below lay thousands of metres of open drop, a ragged cliff-face of hive masonry to bounce off and shredder-infested, bottomless chasms of ice waiting below the white blanket of the Dry-blind. Even the superhuman frame of the High Chaplain could not hope to survive such a fall.

Above the shrieking and gnawing of the beasts and his own exertions, Enobarbus heard the hammer of disciplined sniper fire. Shredder bodies cascaded over the edge past the High Chaplain, either blasted apart by the accurate las-fire or leaping wildly out of its path. Enobarbus looked up. The two talons from which he hung scraped through the rockcrete with every purchase-snapping swing of the monsters hanging from the Crimson Consul. There were figures looking down at him from the edge. Figures in helmets and crimson carapace, swathed in snow cloaks and clutching sniper rifles. On the level above was a further collection looking down at him and the same on the storey after that.

Enobarbus recognised the Scout standing above him.

'Beade...' the High Chaplain managed, but there was nothing in the blank stare or soulless eyes of the Neophyte to lead Enobarbus to believe that he was going to live. As the barrel of Beade's rifle came down in unison with his Space Marine Scout compatriots, the High Chaplain's thoughts raced through a lifetime of combat experience and the primarch's teaching. But Roboute Guilliman and his *Codex* had nothing for him and, with synchronous trigger-pulls that would have been worthy of a firing squad, High Chaplain Enobarbus's las-slashed corpse tumbled into the whiteness below.

THE ORATORIUM WAS crowded with hulking forms, their shadows cutting through the hololithic graphics of the chamber. Each Crimson Consul was a sculpture in muscle, wrapped in zoster robes and the colour of their calling. Only the two Astartes on the Oratorium door stood in full cream and crimson ceremonial armour, Sergeants Ravenscar and Bohemond watching silently over their brothers at the circular runeslab that dominated the chamber. The doors parted and Baldwin stomped in with the hiss of hydraulic urgency, accompanied by a serf attendant of his own. The supermen turned.

'The Reclusiarch has not returned as ordered, master,' Baldwin reported. 'Neither have two full Scout squads of the 10th Company and their sergeants.'

'It's the time of year I tell you,' the Master of the Forge maintained through his conical faceplate. Without his armour and colossal servo-claw, Maximagne Ferro cut a very different figure. Ferro wheezed a further intake of breath through his grilles before insisting: 'Our relay stations on De Vere and Thusa Minor experience communication disruption from starquakes every year around the Antilochal Feast day.'

The Slaughterhorn's Master of Ordnance, Talbot Faulks, gave Artegall the intensity of his magnobionic eyes, their telescrew mountings whirring to projection. 'Elias. It's highly irregular: and you know it.'

'Perhaps the High Chaplain and his men have been beset by difficulties of a very natural kind,' Lord Apothecary Fabian suggested. 'Reports suggest carbonic cyclones sweeping in on the Pale Maidens from the east. They could just be waiting out the poor conditions.'

'Enjoying them, more like,' Chaplain Mercimund told the Apothecary. 'The Reclusiarch would loathe missing an opportunity to test his pupils to their limits. I remember once, out on the–'

'Forgive me, Brother-Chaplain. After the Chapter Master's recall?' the Master of Ordnance put to him. 'Not exactly in keeping with the *Codex*.'

'Brothers, please,' Artegall said, leaning thoughtfully against the runeslab on his fingertips. Hololithics danced across his grim face, glinting off the neat rows of service studs running above each eyebrow. He looked at Baldwin. 'Send the 10th's Thunderhawks for them with two further squads for a search, if one is required.'

Baldwin nodded and despatched his attendant. 'Chaplain,' Artegall added, turning on Mercimund. 'If you would be so good as to start organising the commemorations, in the High Chaplain's absence.'

'It would be an honour, Chapter Master,' Mercimund acknowledged, thumping his fist into the Chapter signature on his robes earnestly before following the Chamber Castellan's serf out of the Oratorium. Baldwin remained.

'Yes?' Artegall asked.

Baldwin looked uncomfortably at Lord Fabian, prompting him to clear his throat. Artegall changed his focus to the Apothecary. 'Speak.'

'The recruitment party is long returned from the underhive. Your Chamber Castellan and I returned together – at your request – with the other party members and the potential aspirants. Since they were not requested, Navarre and his novice remained on some matter of significance: the Chief Librarian did not share it with me. I had the Chamber Castellan check with the Librarium…'

'They are as yet to return, Master Artegall,' Baldwin inserted.

'Communications?'

'We're having some difficulty reaching them,' Baldwin admitted.

Faulks's telescopic eyes retracted. 'Enobarbus, the *Crimson Tithe*, the Chief Librarian...'

'Communication difficulties, all caused by seasonal starquakes, I tell you,' Maximagne Ferro maintained, his conical faceplate swinging around to each of them with exasperation. 'The entire hive is probably experiencing the same.'

'And yet we can reach Lambert,' Faulks argued.

Artegall pursed his lips: 'I want confirmation of the nature of the communication difficulties,' he put to the Master of the Forge, prompting the Techmarine to nod slowly. 'How long have Captain Baptista and the *Crimson Tithe* been out of contact?'

'Six hours,' Faulks reported.

Artegall looked down at the runeslab. With the loss of the Chapter's only other battle-barge, Artegall wasn't comfortable with static from the *Crimson Tithe*.

'Where is she? Precisely.'

'Over the moon of Rubessa: quadrant four-gamma, equatorial west.'

Artegall fixed his Chamber Castellan with cold, certain eyes.

'Baldwin, arrange a pict-link with Master Lambert. I wish to speak with him again.'

'You're going to send Lambert over to investigate?' Faulks enquired.

'Calm yourself, brother,' Artegall instructed the Master of Ordnance. 'I'm sure it is as Ferro indicates.

I'll have the Master of the Fleet take the *Anno Tenebris* to rendezvous with the battle-barge over Rubessa. There Lambert and Baptista can have their enginseers and the Sixth Reserve Company's Techmarines work on the problem from their end.'

Baldwin bowed his head. The sigh of hydraulics announced his intention to leave. 'Baldwin,' Artegall called, his eyes still on Faulks. 'On your way, return to the Librarium. Have our astropaths and Navarre's senior Epistolary attempt to reach the Chief Librarian and the *Crimson Tithe* by psychic means.'

'My lord,' Baldwin confirmed and left the Oratorium with the Master of the Forge.

'Elias,' Faulks insisted as he had done earlier. 'You must let me take the Slaughterhorn to Status Vermillion.'

'That seems unnecessary,' the Lord Apothecary shook his head.

'We have two of our most senior leaders unaccounted for and a Chapter battle-barge in a communications black-out,' Faulks listed with emphasis. 'All following the loss of one hundred of our most experienced and decorated battle-brothers? I believe that we must face the possibility that we are under some kind of attack.'

'Attack?' Fabian carped incredulously. 'From whom? Sector greenskins? Elias, you're not entertaining this?'

Artegall remained silent, his eyes following the path of hololithic representations tracking their way across the still air of the chamber.

'You have started preparing the Chapter's remaining

gene-seed?' Artegall put to the Lord Apothecary.

'As you ordered, my master,' Fabian replied coolly. 'Further recruiting sweeps will need to be made. I know the loss of the First Company was a shock and this on top of the tragedies of Phaethon IV. But, this is our Chapter's entire stored genetic heritage we are talking about here. You have heard my entreaties for caution with this course of action.'

'Caution,' Artegall nodded.

'Elias,' Faulks pressed.

'As in all things,' Artegall put to his Master of Ordnance and the Apothecary, 'we shall be guided by Guilliman. The *Codex* advises caution in the face of the unknown – *Codicil MX-VII-IX.i: The Wisdoms of Hera*, "Gather your wits, as the traveller gauges the depth of the river crossing with the fallen branch, before wading into waters wary." Master Faulks, what would you advise?'

'I would order all Crimson Consuls to arms and armour,' the Master of Ordnance reeled off. 'Thunderhawks fuelled and prepped in the hangers. Penitorium secured. Vox-checks doubled and the defence lasers charged for ground to orbit assault. I would also recall Roderick and the Seventh Company from urban pacification and double the fortress-monastery garrison.'

'Anything else?'

'I would advise Master Lambert to move all Crimson Consuls vessels to a similarly high alert status.'

'That is a matter for Master of the Fleet. I will apprise him of your recommendations.'

'So?'

Artegall gave his grim consent, 'Slaughterhorn so ordered to Status Vermillion.'

'I CAN'T RAISE the Slaughterhorn,' Lexicanum Raughan Stellan complained to his Librarian Master.

'We are far below the hive, my novice,' the Chief Librarian replied, his power armour boots crunching through the darkness. 'There are a billion tonnes of plasteel and rockcrete between us and the spire monastery. You would expect even our equipment to have some problems negotiating that. Besides, it's the season for starquakes.'

'Still...' the Lexicanum mused.

The psykers had entered the catacombs: the lightless labyrinth of tunnels, cave systems and caverns that threaded their torturous way through the pulverised rock and rust of the original hive. Thousands of storeys had since been erected on top of the ancient structures, crushing them into the bottomless network of grottos from which the Crimson Consuls procured their most savage potential recruits. The sub-zero stillness was routinely shattered by murderous screams of tribal barbarism.

Far below the aristocratic indifference of the spire and the slavish poverty of the habs and industrial districts lay the gang savagery of the underhive. Collections of killers and their Carcharian kin, gathered for security or mass slaughter, blasting across the subterranean badlands for scraps and criminal honour. Below this kingdom of desperados and petty despots extended the catacombs, where tribes of barbaric brutes ruled almost as they had at the planet's feral dawn. Here, young Carcharian bodies were crafted by necessity: shaped by circumstance into small mountains of muscle and sinew. Minds were sharpened to keenness by animal instinct and souls remained empty and pure. Perfect for cult indoctrination and the teachings of Guilliman.

Navarre held up his force sword, *Chrysaor*, the unnatural blade bleeding immaterial illumination into the darkness. It was short, like the traditional gladius of his Chapter and its twin, *Chrysaen*, sat in the inverse criss-cross of scabbards that decorated the Chief Librarian's blue and gold chest plate. The denizens of the catacombs retreated into the alcoves and shadows at the abnormal glare of the blade and the towering presence of the armoured Adeptus Astartes.

'Stellan, keep up,' Navarre instructed. They had both been recruited from this tribal underworld – although hundreds of years apart. This familiarity should have filled the Carcharians with ease and acquaintance. Their Astartes instruction and training had realised in both supermen, however, an understanding of the untamed dangers of the place.

Not only would their kith and kin dash out their brains for the rich marrow in their bones, their degenerate brothers shared their dark kingdom with abhumans, mutants and wyrds, driven from the upper levels of the hive for the unsightly danger they posed. Navarre and Stellan had already despatched a shaggy, cyclopean monstrosity that had come at them on its knuckles with brute fury and bloodhunger.

Navarre and Stellan, however, were Adeptus Astartes: the Emperor's Angels of Death and demigods among men. They came with dangers of their own. This alone would be enough to ensure their survival in such a lethal place. The Crimson Consuls were also powerful psykers: wielders of powers unnatural and warp-tapped. Without the techno-spectacle of their arms, the magnificence of their blue and gold plating, their superhuman forms and murderous training, Navarre and Stellan would still be the deadliest presence in the catacombs for kilometres in any direction.

The tight tunnels opened out into a cavernous space. Lifting *Chrysaor* higher, the Chief Librarian allowed more of his potential to flood the unnatural blade of the weapon, throwing light up at the cave ceiling. Something colossal and twisted through with corrosion and stalactitular icicles formed the top of the cavern: some huge structure that had descended through the hive interior during some forgotten, cataclysmic collapse. Irregular columns of resistant-gauge rockcrete and strata structural supports held up the roof at precarious angles. This accidental architecture had allowed the abnormality of the open space to exist below and during the daily thaw had created, drop by drop, the frozen chemical lake that steamed beneath it.

A primitive walkway of scavenged plasteel, rock-ice and girders crossed the vast space and, as the Space Marines made their tentative crossing, Navarre's warplight spooked a flock of gliding netherworms. Uncoiling themselves from their icicle bases they flattened their bodies and slithered through the air, angling the drag of their serpentine descent down past the Space Marines and at the crags and ledges of the cavern where they would make a fresh ascent. As the flock of black worms spiralled by, one crossed Stellan's path. The novice struck out with his gauntlet in disgust but the thing latched onto him with its unparalleled prehensility. It weaved its way up through his armoured digits and corkscrewed up his thrashing arm at his helmetless face.

Light flashed before the Lexicanum's eyes. Just as the netherworm retracted its fleshy collar and prepared to sink its venomous beak hooks into the Astartes' young face, Navarre clipped the horror in half with the blazing tip of *Chrysaor*. As the worm fell down the side of the walkway in two writhing pieces, Stellan mumbled his thanks.

'Why didn't you use your powers?' the Chief Librarian boomed around the cavern.

'It surprised me,' was all the Lexicanum could manage.

'You've been out of the depths mere moments and you've already forgotten its dangers,' Navarre remonstrated gently. 'What of the galaxy's dangers? There's a myriad of lethality waiting for you out there. Be mindful, my novice.'

'Yes, master.'

'Did it come to you again?' Navarre asked pointedly.

'Why do you ask, master?'

'You seem, distracted: not yourself. Was your sleep disturbed?'

'Yes, master.'

'Your dreams?'

'Yes, master.'

'The empyreal realm seems a dark and distant place,' Navarre told his apprentice sagely. 'But it is everywhere. How do you think we can draw on it so? Its rawness feeds our power: the blessings our God-Emperor gave us and through which we give back in His name. We are not the only ones to draw from this wellspring of power and we need our faith and constant vigilance to shield us from the predations of these immaterial others.'

'Yes, master.'

'Behind a wall of mirrored-plas the warp hides, reflecting back to us our realities. In some places it's thick; in others a mere wafer of truth separates us from its unnatural influence. Your dreams are one such window: a place where one may submerge one's head in the Sea of Souls.'

'Yes, master.'

'Tell me, then.'

Stellan seemed uncomfortable, but as the two Space Marines continued their careful trudge across the cavern walkway, the novice unburdened himself.

'It called itself Ghidorquiel.'

'You conversed with this thing of confusion and darkness?'

'No, my master. It spoke only to me: in my cell.'

'You said you were dreaming,' Navarre reminded the novice.

'Of being awake,' Stellan informed him, 'in my cell. It spoke. What I took to be lips moved but the voice was in my head.'

'And what lies did this living lie tell you?'

'A host of obscenities, my lord,' Stellan confirmed. 'It spoke in languages unknown to me. Hissed and spat its impatience. It claimed my soul as its own. It said my weakness was the light in its darkness.'

'This disturbed you.'

'Of course,' the Lexicanum admitted. 'Its attentions disgust me. But this creature called out to me across the expanse of time and space. Am I marked? Am I afflicted?'

'No more than you ever were,' Navarre reassured the novice. 'Stellan, all those who bear the burden of powers manifest – the Emperor's sacred gift – of which he was gifted himself – dream themselves face to face with the daemonscape from time to time. Entities trawl the warp for souls to torment for their wretched entertainment. Our years of training and the mental fortitude that comes of being the Emperor's chosen protects us from their direct influence. The unbound, the warp-rampant and the witch are all easy prey for such beasts and through them the daemon worms its way into our world. Thank the primarch we need face such things for real with blessed infrequency.'

'Yes, my lord,' Stellan agreed.

'The warp sometimes calls to us: demands our attention. It's why we did not return to the Slaughterhorn with the others. Such a demand led me beyond the scope of the Lord Apothecary's recruitment party and down into the frozen bowels of Carcharias. Here.'

Reaching the other side of the cavern, Navarre and

Stellan stood on the far end of the walkway, where it led back into the rock face of pulverised masonry. Over the top of the tunnel opening was a single phrase in slap-dash white paint. It was all glyph symbols and runic consonants of ancient Carcharian.

'It's recent,' Navarre said half to himself. Stellan simply stared at the oddness of the lettering. 'Yet its meaning is very old. A phrase that predates the hives, at least. It means, "From the single flake of snow – the avalanche".'

Venturing into the tunnel with force sword held high, Navarre was struck by the patterns on the walls. Graffiti was endemic to the underhive: it was not mere defacement or criminal damage. In the ganglands above it advertised the presence of dangerous individuals and marked the jealously guarded territories of House-sponsored outfits, organisations and posses. It covered every empty space: the walls, the floor and ceiling, and was simply part of the underworld's texture. Below that, the graffiti was no less pervasive or lacking in purpose. Tribal totems and primitive paintings performed much the same purpose for the barbarians of the catacombs. Handprints in blood; primordial representations of subterranean mega-vermin in campfire charcoal; symbolic warnings splashed across walls in the phosphorescent, radioactive chemicals that leaked down from the industrial sectors above. The Carcharian savages that haunted the catacombs had little use for words, yet this was all Navarre could see.

The Chief Librarian had been drawn to this place, deep under Hive Niveous, by the stink of psychic intrusion. Emanations. Something large and invasive: something that had wormed its way through the very core of the Carcharian capital. The ghostly glow of *Chrysaor* revealed it to Navarre in all its mesmerising glory. Graffiti upon graffiti, primitive paintings upon symbols upon markings upon blood splatter. Words. The same words, over and over again, in all orientations, spelt out in letters created in the layered spaces of the hive cacography. Repetitions that ran for kilometres through the arterial maze of tunnels. Like a chant or incantation in ancient Carcharian: they blazed with psychic significance to the Chief Librarian, where to the eyes of the ordinary and untouched, among the background scrawl of the hive underworld, they would not appear to be there at all.

'Stellan! You must see this,' Navarre murmured as he advanced down the winding passage. The Librarian continued: 'Psycho-sensitive words, spelt out on the walls, a conditioned instruction of some kind, imprinting itself on the minds of the underhivers. Stellan: we must get word back to the Slaughterhorn – to Fabian – to the Chapter Master. The recruits could be compromised…'

The Chief Librarian turned to find that his novice wasn't there. Marching back up the passage in the halo of his shimmering force weapon, Navarre found the Lexicanum still standing on the cavern walkway, staring up at the wall above the tunnel entrance with a terrible blankness. 'Stellan? Stellan, talk to me.'

At first Navarre thought that one of the deadly gliding worms had got him, infecting the young Space Marine with its toxin. The reality was much worse.

Following the novice's line of sight, Navarre settled on the white painted scrawl above the tunnel. The ancient insistence, 'From the single flake of snow – the avalanche' in fresh paint. Looking back at the Lexicanum, Navarre came to realise that his own novice had succumbed to the psycho-sensitive indoctrination of his recruiting grounds. All the wordsmith had needed was to introduce his subjects to the trigger. A phrase they were unlikely to come across anywhere else. The timing intentional; the brainwashing complete.

Stellan dribbled. He tried to mumble the words on the wall. Then he tried to get his palsied mouth around his master's name. He failed. The young Space Marine's mind was no longer his own. He belonged to someone else: to the will of the wordsmith – whoever they were. And not only the novice: countless other recruits over the years, for whom indoctrination hid in the very fabric of their worlds and now in the backs of their afflicted minds. All ready to be activated at a single phrase.

Navarre readied himself. Opened his being to the warp's dark promise. Allowed its fire to burn within. Slipping *Chrysaen* from its chest scabbard, the Chief Librarian held both force blades out in front of him. Each master-crafted gladius smoked with immaterial vengeance.

For Stellan, the dangers were much more immediate than brainwashing. Stripped of his years of training and the mental fortitude that shielded an Astartes Librarian from the dangers of the warp, Stellan succumbed to the monster stalking his soul.

Something like shock took the Crimson Consul's face hostage. The novice looked like he had been seized from below. Somehow, horribly, he had. The Librarian's head suddenly disappeared down into the trunk of his blue and gold power armour. An oily, green ichor erupted from the neck of the suit.

'Ghidorquiel...' Navarre spat. The Chief Librarian thrust himself at the quivering suit of armour, spearing his Lexicanum through the chest with *Chrysaor*. The stink of warp-corruption poured from the adamantium shell and stung the psyker's nostrils. Spinning and kicking the body back along the treacherous walkway, Navarre's blades trailed ethereal afterglow as they arced and cleaved through the sacred suit.

Howling fury at the materialising beast within the armour, the Chief Librarian unleashed a blast wave of raw warp energy from his chest that lit up the cavern interior and hit the suit like the God-Emperor's own fist.

The suit tumbled backwards, wrenching and cracking along the walkway until it came to rest, a broken-backed heap. Even then, the armour continued to quiver and snap, rearranging the splintered ceramite plating and moulding itself into something new. On the walkway, Navarre came to behold an adamantium shell, like that of a mollusc, from which slithered an explosion of tentacles. Navarre ran full speed at the daemon while appendages shot for him like guided missiles. Twisting this way and that, but without sacrificing any of his rage-fuelled speed, the Chief Librarian slashed at the beast, his blinding blades shearing off tentacular length and the warp-dribbling tips of the monster feelers.

As the psyker closed with the daemon nautiloid, the warp beast shot its appendages into the fragile walkway's architecture. Hugging the snapping struts and supports to it, the creature demolished the structure beneath the Crimson Consul's feet.

Navarre plummeted through the cavern space before smashing down through the frozen surface of the chemical lake below. The industrial waste plunge immediately went to work on the blue and gold of the Librarian's armour and blistered the psyker's exposed and freezing flesh. Navarre's force blades glowed spectroscopic eeriness under the surface and it took precious moments for the Space Marine to orientate himself and kick for the surface. As his steaming head broke from the frozen acid depths of the lake, Navarre's burn-blurry eyes saw the rest of the walkway collapsing towards him. Ghidorquiel had reached for the cavern wall and, pulling with its unnatural might, had toppled the remainder of the structure.

Again Navarre was hammered to the darkness of the lake bottom, sinking wreckage raining all about the dazed psyker. Somewhere in the chaos *Chrysaen* slipped from Navarre's grip. Vaulting upwards, the Space Marine hit the thick ice of the lake surface further across. Clawing uselessly with his gauntlet, skin aflame and armour freezing up, Navarre stared through the ice and saw something slither overhead. Roaring pain and frustration into the chemical darkness, the Chief Librarian thrust *Chrysaor* through the frozen effluence. Warpflame bled from the blade and across the ice, rapidly melting the crust of the acid bath and allowing the Crimson Consul a moment to suck in a foetid breath and drag himself up the shoreline of shattered masonry.

Ghidorquiel was there, launching tentacles at the psyker. Hairless and with flesh melting from his skull the Librarian mindlessly slashed the appendages to pieces. All the Space Marine wanted was the daemon. The thing dragged its obscene adamantium shell sluggishly away from the lake and the enraged Astartes. Navarre bounded up and off a heap of walkway wreckage, dodging the creature's remaining tentacles and landing on ceramite. Drawing on everything he had, the Chief Librarian became a conduit of the warp. The raw, scalding essence of immaterial energy poured from his being and down through the descending tip of his force sword. *Chrysaor* slammed through the twisted shell of Stellan's armour and buried itself in the daemon's core. Like a lightning rod, the gladius roasted the beast from the inside out.

Armour steamed. Tentacles dropped and trembled to stillness. The daemon caught light. Leaving the force blade in the monstrous body, Navarre stumbled down from the creature and crashed to the cavern floor himself. The psyker was spent: in every way conceivable. He could do little more than lie there in his own palsy, staring at the daemon corpse lit by *Chrysaor*'s still gleaming blade. The slack, horrible face of the creature had slipped down out of the malformed armour shell: the same horrific face that the novice Stellan had confronted in his dreams.

Looking up into the inky, cavern blackness, Navarre wrangled with the reality that somehow he had to get out of the catacombs and warn the Slaughterhorn of impending disaster. A *slurp* drew his face back to the creature; sickeningly it began to rumble with daemonic life and throttled laughter. Fresh tentacles erupted from its flaming sides and wrapped themselves around two of the crooked pillars of rockcrete and metal that were supporting the chamber ceiling and the underhive levels above.

All Navarre could do was watch the monster pull the columns towards its warp-scorched body and roar his frustration as the cavern ceiling quaked and thundered down towards him, with the weight of Hive Niveous behind it.

THE ORATORIUM SWARMED with armoured command staff and their attendants. Clarifications and communications shot back and forth across the chamber amongst a hololithic representation of the Slaughterhorn fortress-monastery that crackled disturbance every time an officer or Crimson Consuls serf walked through it.

'They discovered nothing, my lord,' Baldwin informed Artegall in mid-report. 'No High Chaplain; no Scout squads; nothing. They've scoured the Dry-blind around the Pale Maidens. They're requesting permission to bring the Thunderhawks back to base.'

'What about Chief Librarian Navarre?' Artegall called across the Oratorium.

'Nothing, sir,' Lord Apothecary Fabian confirmed. 'On the vox or from the Librarium.'

'Planetary Defence Force channels and on-scene Enforcers report seismic shift and hive tremors in the capital lower levels,' the Master of the Forge reported, his huge servo-claw swinging about over the heads of the gathering.

'What about the *Crimson Tithe*?'

'Patching you through to Master Lambert now,' Maximagne Ferro added, giving directions to a communications servitor. The hololithic representation of the Slaughterhorn disappeared and was replaced with the phantasmal static of a dead pict-feed that danced around the assembled Crimson Consuls.

'What the hell is happening up there, Maximagne?' Artegall demanded, but the Master of the Forge was working furiously on the servitor and the brass control station of the runeslab. The static disappeared before briefly being replaced by the Slaughterhorn and then a three-dimensional hololith of the Carcharian system. Artegall immediately picked out their system star and their icebound home world: numerous defence monitors and small frigates were stationed in high orbit. Circling Carcharias were the moons of De Vere, Thusa Major and Thusa Minor between which two strike cruisers sat at anchor. Most distant was Rubessa; the Oratorium could see the battle-barge *Crimson Tithe* beneath it. Approaching was Hecton Lambert's strike cruiser, *Anno Tenebris*. The hololithic image of the Adeptus Astartes strike cruiser suddenly crackled and then disappeared.

The Oratorium fell to a deathly silence.

'Master Maximagne…' Artegall began. The Master of the Forge had a vox-headset to one ear.

'Confirmed, my lord. The *Anno Tenebris* has been destroyed with all on board.' The silence prevailed. 'Sir, the *Crimson Tithe* fired upon her.'

The gathered Adeptus Astartes looked to their Chapter Master, who, like his compatriots, could not believe what he was hearing.

'Master Faulks,' Artegall began. 'It seems you were correct. We are under attack. Status report: fortress-monastery.'

'In lockdown as ordered, sir,' the Master of Ordnance reported with grim pride. 'All Crimson Consuls are prepped for combat. All sentry guns manned. Thunderhawks ready for launch on your order. Defence lasers powered to full.'

Captain Roderick presented himself to his Chapter Master: 'My lord, the Seventh Company has fortified the Slaughterhorn at the Master of Ordnance's instruction. Nothing will get through – you can be sure of that.'

'Sir,' Master Maximagne alerted the chamber: '*Crimson Tithe* is on the move, Carcharias bound, my lord.'

Artegall's lip curled into a snarl. 'Who the hell are they?' he muttered to himself. 'What about our remaining cruisers?'

Faulks stepped forwards indicating the cruisers at anchor between the hololithic moons of Thusa Major and Thusa Minor. 'At full alert as I advised. The *Caliburn* and *Honour of Hera* could plot an intercept course and attempt an ambush…'

'Out of the question,' Artegall stopped Faulks. 'Bring

the strike cruisers in above the Slaughterhorn at low orbit. I want our defence lasers to have their backs.'

'Yes, my master,' Faulks obeyed.

'Baldwin…'

'Lord?'

'Ready my weapons and armour.'

The Chamber Castellan nodded slowly, 'It would be my honour, master.' The Crimson Consuls watched the serf exit, knowing what this meant. Artegall was already standing at the head of the runeslab in a functional suit of crimson and cream power armour and his mantle. He was asking for the hallowed suit of artificer armour and master-crafted bolter that resided in the Chapter Master's private armoury. The gleaming suit of crimson and gold upon which the honourable history of the Crimson Consuls Chapter was inscribed and inlaid in gemstone ripped from the frozen earth of Carcharias itself. The armour that past Masters had worn when leading the Chapter to war in its entirety: Aldebaran; the Fall of Volsungard; the Termagant Wars.

'Narke.'

'Master Artegall,' the Slaughterhorn's chief astropath replied from near the Oratorium doors.

'Have you been successful in contacting the Third, Fifth or Eighth Companies?'

'Captain Neath has not responded, lord,' the blind Narke reported, clutching his staff.

Artegall and Talbot Faulks exchanged grim glances. Neath and the 8th Company were only two systems away hunting Black Legion Traitor Marine degenerates in the Sarcus Reaches.

'And Captain Borachio?'

Artegall had received monthly astrotelepathic reports from Captain Albrecht Borachio stationed in the Damocles Gulf. Borachio had overseen the Crimson Consuls contribution to the Damocles Crusade in the form of the 3rd and 5th Companies and had present responsibility for bringing the Tau commander, O'Shovah, to battle in the Farsight Enclaves. Artegall and Borachio had served together in the same squad as battle-brothers and Borachio beyond Baldwin, was what the Chapter Master might have counted as the closest thing he had to a friend.

'Three days ago, my lord,' Narke returned. 'You returned in kind, Master Artegall.'

'Read back the message.'

The astropath's knuckles whitened around his staff as he recalled the message: '… encountered a convoy of heavy cruisers out of Fi'Rios – a lesser sept, the Xenobiologis assure me, attempting to contact Commander Farsight. We took a trailing vessel with little difficulty but at the loss of one Carcharian son: Crimson Consul Battle-Brother Theodoric of the First Squad: Fifth Company. I commend Brother Theodoric's service to you and recommend his name be added to the Shrine of Hera in the Company Chapel as a posthumous recipient of the Iron Laurel…'

'And the end?' Artegall pushed.

'An algebraic notation in three dimensions, my lord: $Kn\ \Omega\ iii - \pi\ iX\ (Z\text{-}) - \boxtimes\ v.R\ (!?)\ 0\text{-}1.$'

'Coordinates? Battle manoeuvres?' Talbot Faulks hypothesised.

'Regicide notations,' Artegall informed him, his mind elsewhere. For years, the Chapter Master and Albrecht Borachio had maintained a game of regicide across the stars, moves detailed back and forth with their astropathic communiqués. Each had a board and pieces upon which the same game had been played out; Artegall's was an ancient set carved from lacquered megafelis sabres on a burnished bronze board. Artegall moved the pieces in his mind, recalling the board as it was set up on a rostra by his throne in the Chancelorium. Borachio had beaten him: 'Blind Man's Mate...' the Chapter Master mouthed.

'Excuse me, my lord?' Narke asked.

'No disrespect intended,' Artegall told the astropath. 'It's a form of victory in regicide, so called because you do not see it coming.'

The corridor outside the Oratorium suddenly echoed with the sharp crack of bolter fire. Shocked glances between Artegall and his Astartes officers were swiftly replaced by the assumption of cover positions. The armoured forms took advantage of the runeslab and the walls either side of the Oratorium door.

'That's inside the perimeter,' Faulks called in disbelief, slapping on his helmet.

'Well inside,' Artegall agreed grimly. Many of the Space Marines had drawn either their bolt pistols or their gladius swords. Only Captain Roderick and the Oratorium sentry sergeants, Bohemond and Ravenscar, were equipped for full combat with bolters, spare ammunition and grenades.

With the muzzle of his squat Fornax-pattern bolt pistol resting on the slab, the Master of Ordnance brought up the hololithic representation of the Slaughterhorn once more. The fortress-monastery was a tessellation of flashing wings, towers, hangars and sections.

'Impossible…' Faulks mumbled.

'The fortress-monastery is completely compromised,' Master Maximagne informed the chamber, cycling through the vox-channels.

Bolt shells pounded the thick doors of the Oratorium. The 7th Company captain held a gauntleted finger to the vox-bead in his ear.

'Roderick,' Artegall called. 'What's happening?'

'My men are being fired upon from the inside of the Slaughterhorn, my lord,' the captain reported bleakly. 'By fellow Astartes – by Crimson Consuls, Master Artegall!'

'What has happened to us?' the Chapter Master bawled in dire amazement.

'Later, sir. We have to get you out of here,' Faulks insisted.

'What sections do we hold?' Artegall demanded.

'Elias, we have to go, now!'

'Master Faulks, what do we hold?'

'Sir, small groups of my men hold the Apothecarion and the north-east hangar,' Roderick reported. 'The Barbican, some Foundry sections and Cell Block Sigma.'

'The Apothecarion?' Fabian clarified.

'The gene-seed,' Artegall heard himself mutter.

'The Command Tower is clear,' Faulks announced,

reading details off the hololith schematic of the monastery. Bolt-rounds tore through the metal of the Oratorium door and drummed into the runeslab column. The hololith promptly died. Ravenscar pushed Narke, the blind astropath, out of his way and poked the muzzle of his weapon through the rent in the door. He started plugging the corridor with ammunition-conserving boltfire.

'We must get the Chapter Master to the Tactical Chancelorium,' Faulks put to Roderick, Maximagne and the sentry sergeants.

'No,' Artegall barked back. 'We must take back the Slaughterhorn.'

'Which we can do best from your Tactical Chancelorium, my lord,' Faulks insisted with strategic logic. 'From there we have our own vox-relays, tactical feeds and your private armoury: it's elevated for a Thunderhawk evacuation – it's simply the most secure location in the fortress-monastery,' Faulks told his master. 'The best place from which to coordinate and rally our forces.'

'When we determine who they are,' Fabian added miserably. Artegall and the Master of Ordnance stared at one another.

'Sir!' Ravenscar called from the door. 'Coming up on a reload.'

'Agreed,' Artegall told Faulks. 'Captain Roderick shall accompany Master Maximagne and Lord Fabian to secure the Apothecarion; the gene-seed must be saved. Serfs with your masters. Sergeants Ravenscar and Bohemond, escort the Master of Ordnance and myself to the Tactical Chancelorium.

Narke, you will accompany us. All understood?'

'Yes, Chapter Master,' the chorus came back.

'Sergeant, on three,' Artegall instructed. 'One.' Bohemond nodded and primed a pair of grenades from his belt. 'Two.' Faulks took position by the door stud. 'Three'. Roderick nestled his bolter snug into his shoulder as Faulks activated the door mechanism.

As the door rolled open, Ravenscar pulled away and went about reloading his boltgun. Bohemond's grenades were then followed by replacement suppression fire from Captain Roderick's bolter.

The brief impression of crimson and cream armour working up the corridor was suddenly replaced with the thunder and flash of grenades. Roderick was swiftly joined by Bohemond and then Ravenscar, the three Space Marines maintaining a withering arc of fire. The command group filed out of the Oratorium with their Chapter serf attendants, the singular crash of their Fornax-pattern pistols joining in the cacophony.

With Roderick's precision fire leading the Lord Apothecary and the Master of the Forge down a side passage, Bohemond slammed his shoulder through a stairwell door to lead the other group up onto the next level. The Crimson Consuls soon fell into the surgical-style battle rotation so beloved of Guilliman: battle-brother covering battle-brother; arc-pivoting and rapid advance suppression fire. Ravenscar and Bohemond orchestrated the tactical dance from the front, with Artegall's pistol crashing support from behind and the Master of Ordnance covering the rear with his own, while half dragging the blind Narke behind him.

Advancing up through the stairwell, spiralling up through the storeys, the Astartes walked up into a storm of iron: armoured, renegade Crimson Consuls funnelled their firepower down at them from a gauntlet above. Unclipping a grenade, Ravenscar tossed it to his brother-sergeant. Bohemond then held the explosive, counting away the precious seconds before launching the thing directly up through the space between the spiral stair rails. The grenade detonated above, silencing the gunfire. A cream and crimson body fell down past the group in a shower of grit. The sergeants didn't wait, however, bounding up the stairs and into the maelstrom above.

Dead Crimson Consuls lay mangled amongst the rail and rockcrete. One young Space Marine lay without his legs, his helmet half blasted from his face. As blood frothed between the Adeptus Astartes' gritted teeth the Space Marine stared at the passing group. For Artegall it was too much. Crimson Consuls spilling each other's sacred blood. Guilliman's dream in tatters. He seized the grievously wounded Space Marine by his shattered breastplate and shook him violently.

'What the hell are you doing, boy?' Artegall roared, but there was no time. Scouts in light carapace armour were spilling from a doorway above, bouncing down one storey to the next on their boot tips, bathing the landings with scattershot from their shotguns. Bolt-rounds sailed past Faulks from below, where renegade Crimson Consuls had followed in the footsteps of their escape. The shells thudded into the wall above the kneeling Artegall and punched through the stumbling astropath, causing the Master of Ordnance to abandon his handicap and force back their assailants with blasts from a recovered bolter.

'Through there!' Faulks bawled above the bolt chatter, indicating the nearest door on the stairwell. Again Bohemond led with his shoulder, blasting through the door into a dormitory hall. The space was plain and provided living quarters for some of the Slaughterhorn's Chapter serfs. Bright, white light was admitted from the icescape outside through towering arches of plain glass, each depicting a bleached scene from the Chapter's illustrious history, picked out in lead strips.

Ravenscar handed Artegall his bolter and took a blood-splattered replacement from the stairwell for himself.

'There's a bondsman's entrance to the Chancelorium through the dormitories,' Artegall pointed, priming the bolter. Their advance along the window-lined hall had already been ensured by the bolt-riddled door being blasted off its hinges behind them.

'Go!' Faulks roared. The four Space Marines stormed along the open space towards the far end of the hall. The searing light from the windows was suddenly eclipsed, causing the Astrartes to turn as they ran. Drifting up alongside the wall, directed in on their position by the renegade Astartes, was the sinister outline of a Crimson Consuls Thunderhawk. As the monstrous aircraft hovered immediately outside, the heavy bolters adorning its carrier compartment unleashed their fury.

All the Space Marines could do was run as the great accomplishments of the Chapter shattered behind them. One by one the windows imploded with anti-personnel fire and fragmentation shells, the Thunderhawk gently gliding along the wall. The rampage caught up with Ravenscar who, lost in the maelstrom of smashed glass and lead, soaked up the heavy bolter's punishment and in turn became a metal storm of pulped flesh and fragmented armour. At the next window, Artegall felt the whoosh of the heavy bolter rounds streak across his back. Detonating about him like tiny frag grenades, the rounds shredded through his pack and tore up the ceramite plating of his armoured suit. Falling through the shrapnel hurricane, Artegall tumbled to the floor before hitting the far wall.

Gauntlets were suddenly all over him, hauling the Chapter Master in through an open security bulkhead, before slamming the door on the chaos beyond.

By comparison the command tower was silent. Artegall squinted, dazed, through the darkness of the Chancelorium dungeon-antechamber, his power armour steaming and slick with blood, lubricant and hydraulic fluid.

As Artegall came back to his senses, he realised that he'd never seen this part of his fortress-monastery before; traditionally it only admitted Chapter serfs. Getting unsteadily to his feet he joined his battle-brothers in stepping up on the crimson swirl of the marble trapdoor platform. With Sergeant Bohemond and Master Faulks flanking him, the Chapter Master activated the rising floor section and the three Crimson Consuls ascended up through the floor of Artegall's own Tactical Chancelorium.

'Chapter Master, I'll begin–'

Light and sound: simultaneous.

Bohemond and Faulks dropped as the backs of their heads came level with the yawning barrels of waiting bolters and their skulls were blasted through the front of their faceplates. Artegall span around but found that the bolters, all black paint and spiked barrels, were now pressed up against the crimson of his chest.

His assailants were Space Marines: Traitor Astartes. The galaxy's arch-traitors: the Warmaster's own – the Black Legion. Their cracked and filthy power armour was a dusty black, edged with gargoylesque details of dull bronze. Their helmets were barbed and leering and their torsos a tangle of chains and skulls. With the smoking muzzle of the first still resting against him, the second disarmed the grim Chapter Master, removing his bolter and slipping the bolt pistol and gladius from his belt. Weaponless, he was motioned round.

Before him stood two Black Legion officers. The senior was a wild-eyed captain with teeth filed to sharp points and a flea-infested wolf pelt hanging from his spiked armour. The other was an Apothecary whose once-white armour was now streaked with blood and rust and whose face was shrunken and soulless like a zombie.

'At least do me the honour of knowing who I am addressing, traitor filth,' the Chapter Master rumbled.

This, the Black Legion captain seemed to find amusing.

'This is Lord Vladivoss of the Black Legion and his Apothecary Szekle,' a voice bounced around the vaulted roof of the Chancelorium, but it came from neither Chaos Marine. The Black Legion Space Marines parted to reveal the voice's owner, sitting in Artegall's own bone command throne. His armour gleamed a sickening mazarine, embossed with the necks of green serpents that entwined his limbs and whose heads clustered on his chest plate in the fashion of a hydra. The unmistakable iconography of the Alpha Legion. The Space Marine sat thumbing casually through the pages of the *Codex Astartes* on the Chapter Master's lectern.

'I don't reason that there's any point in asking you that question, renegade,' Artegall snarled.

The copper-skinned giant pushed the anti-gravitic lectern to one side, stood and smiled: 'I am Alpharius.'

A grim chuckle surfaced in Artegall. He hawked and spat blood at the Alpha Legionnaire's feet.

'That's what I think of that, Alpha,' the Chapter Master told him. 'Come on, I want to congratulate you on your trademark planning and perfect execution: Alpharius is but a ghost. My Lord Guilliman ended the scourge – as I will end you, monster.'

The Legionnaire's smile never faltered, even in the face of Artegall's threats and insults. It grew as the Space Marine came to a private decision.

"I am Captain Quetzal Carthach, Crimson Consul,' the Alpha Legion Space Marine told him, 'and I have come to accept your unconditional surrender.'

'The only unconditional thing you'll get from me, Captain Carthach, is my unending revulsion and hatred.'

'You talk of ends, Chapter Master,' the Legionnaire said calmly. 'Has Guilliman blinded you so that you cannot see your own. The end of your Chapter. The end of your living custodianship, your shred of that sanctimonious bastard's seed. I wanted to come here and meet you. So you could go to your grave knowing that it was the Alpha Legion that had beaten you; the Alpha Legion who are eradicating Guilliman's legacy one thousand of his sons at a time; the Alpha Legion who are not only superior strategists but also superior Space Marines.'

Artegall's lips curled with cold fury.

'Never...'

'Perhaps, Chapter Master, you think there's a chance for your seed to survive: for future sons of Carcharias to avenge you?' The Alpha Legion giant sat back down in Artegall's throne. 'The Tenth was mine before you even recruited them – as was the Ninth Company before them: you must know that now. I lent you their minds but not their true allegiance: a simple phrase was all that was needed to bring them back to the Alpha Legion fold. The Second and Fourth were easy: that was a mere administrative error, holding the Celebrants over at Nedicta Secundus and drawing the Crimson Consuls to the waiting xenos deathtrap that was Phaethon IV.'

Artegall listened to the Alpha Legionnaire honour himself with the deaths of his Crimson Consul brothers. Listened, while the Black Legion Space Marine looked down the spiked muzzle of his bolter at the back of the Chapter Master's head.

'The Seventh fell fittingly at the hands of their brothers, foolishly defending your colourfully-named fortress-monastery from a threat that was within rather than without. The Eighth, well, Captain Vladivoss took care of those in the Sarcus Reaches – and now the good captain has earned his prize. Szekle,' the Alpha Legion Space Marine addressed the zombified Chaos Space Marine. 'The Apothecarion is now in our hands. You may help yourself to the Crimson Consuls' remaining stocks of gene-seed. Feel free to extract progenoids from loyalists who fought in our name. Fear not, they will not obstruct you. In fact, the completion of the procedure is their signal to turn their weapons on themselves. Captain Vladivoss, you may then return to Lord Abaddon with my respects and your prize – to help replenish the Black Legion's depleted numbers in the Eye of Terror.'

Vladivoss bowed, while Szekle fidgeted with dead-eyed anticipation.

'Oh, and captain,' Carthach instructed as Artegall was pushed forwards towards the throne, 'leave one Legionnaire, please.'

With Captain Vladivoss, his depraved Apothecary and their Chaos Space Marine sentry descending through the trapdoor on the marble platform with Bohemond and Faulk's bodies, Carthach came to regard the Chapter Master once again.

'The *Revenant Rex* was pure genius. That I even

admit to myself. What I couldn't have hoped for was the deployment of your First Company Terminator veterans. That made matters considerably easier down the line. You should receive some credit for that, Chapter Master Artegall,' Carthach grinned nastily.

A rumble like distant thunder rolled through the floor beneath Artegall's feet. Carthach seemed suddenly excited. 'Do you know what that is?' he asked. The monster didn't wait for an answer. Instead he activated the controls in the bone armrest of Artegall's throne. The vaulted ceiling of the Tactical Chancelorium – which formed the pinnacle of the Command Tower – began to turn and unscrew, revealing a circular aperture in the roof that grew with the corkscrew motion of the Tower top.

The Alpha Legionnaire shook his head in what could have been mock disappointment.

'Missed it: that was your Slaughterhorn's defence lasers destroying the strike cruisers you ordered back under their protection. Poetic. Or perhaps just tactically predictable. Ah, now look at this.'

Carthach pointed at the sky and with the Chaos Space Marine's bolter muzzle still buried in the back of his skull, Artegall felt compelled to look up also. To savour the reassuring bleakness of his home world's sky for what might be the last time.

'There they are, see?'

Artegall watched a meteorite shower in the sky above: a lightshow of tiny flashes. 'I brought the *Crimson Tithe* back to finish off any remaining frigates or destroyers. Don't want surviving Crimson Consuls running to the Aurora Chapter with my strategies and secrets; the Auroras and their share of Guilliman's seed may be my next target. Anyway, the beautiful spectacle you see before you is no ordinary celestial phenomenon. This is the Crimson Consuls Sixth Company coming home, expelled from the *Crimson Tithe*'s airlocks and falling to Carcharias. The battle-barge I need – another gift for the Warmaster. It has the facilities on board to safely transport your seed to the Eye of Terror, where it is sorely needed for future Black Crusades. Who knows, perhaps one of your line will have the honour of being the first to bring the Warmaster's justice to Terra itself? In Black Legion armour and under a traitor's banner, of course.'

Artegall quaked silent rage, the Chapter Master's eyes dropping and fixing on a spot on the wall behind the throne.

'I know what you're thinking,' Carthach informed him. 'As I have all along, Crimson Consul. You're pinning your hopes on Captain Borachio. Stationed in the Damocles Gulf with the Third and Fifth Companies… Did you find my reports convincing?'

Artegall's eyes widened.

'Captain Borachio and his men have been dead for two years, Elias.'

Artegall shook his head.

'The Crimson Consuls are ended. I am Borachio,' the Alpha revealed, soaking up the Chapter Master's doom, 'and Carthach … and Alpharius.' The captain bent down to execute the final, astrotelepathically communicated move on Artegall's beautifully carved Regicide board. Blind Man's Mate.

Artegall's legs faltered. As the Crimson Consul fell to his knees before Quetzal Carthach and the throne, Artegall mouthed a disbelieving, 'Why?'

'Because we play the Long Game, Elias…' the Alpha Legionnaire told him.

Artegall hoped that the Black Legion's attention span didn't extend half as far as their Alpha Legion compatriots. The Space Marine threw his head back, cutting his scalp against the bolter's muzzle. The weapon smacked the Chaos Space Marine in the throat – the Black Legion savage still staring up into the sky, watching the Crimson Consuls burn in the upper atmosphere.

Artegall surged away from the stunned Chaos Space Marine and directly at Carthach. The Alpha Legion Marine snarled at the sudden, suicidal surprise of it all, snatching for his pistol.

Artegall awkwardly changed direction, throwing himself around the other side of the throne. The Black Legion Space Marine's bolter fire followed him, mauling the throne and driving the alarmed Carthach even further back. Artegall sprinted for the wall, stopping and feeling for the featureless trigger that activated the door of the Chapter Master's private armoury. As the Chaos Space Marine's bolter chewed up the Chancelorium wall, Artegall activated the trigger and slid the hidden door to one side. He felt hot agony as the Chaos Space Marine's bolter found its mark and two rounds crashed through his ruined armour.

Returned to his knees, the Chapter Master fell in through the darkness of the private armoury and slid the reinforced door shut from the inside. In the disappearing crack of light between the door and wall, Artegall caught sight of Quetzal Carthach's face once more dissolve into a wolfish grin.

Throwing himself across the darkness of the armoury floor, the felled Crimson Consul heaved himself arm over agonising arm through the presentation racks of artificer armour: racks from which serfs would ordinarily select the individual plates and adornments and dress the Chapter Master at his bequest. Artegall didn't have time for such extravagance. Crawling for the rear of the armoury, he searched for the only item that could bring him peace. The only item seemingly designed for the single purpose of ending Quetzal Carthach, the deadliest in the Chapter's long history of deadly enemies. Artegall's master-crafted boltgun.

Reaching for the exquisite weapon, its crimson-painted adamantium finished in gold and decorated with gemstones from Carcharias's rich depths, Artegall faltered. The bolt-rounds had done their worst and the Chapter Master's fingers failed to reach the boltgun in its cradle. Suddenly there was sound and movement in the darkness. The hydraulic sigh of bionic appendages thumping into the cold marble with every step.

'Baldwin!' Artegall cried out. 'My weapon, Baldwin… the boltgun.'

The Chamber Castellan slipped the beautiful bolter from its cradle and stomped around to his master. 'Thank the primarch you're here,' Artegall blurted.

In the oily blackness of the private armoury, the Chapter Master heard the thunk of the priming mechanism. Artegall tensed and then fell limp. He wasn't being handed the weapon: it was being pointed at him through the gloom. Whatever had possessed the minds of his Neophyte recruits in the Carcharian underhive had also had time to worm its way into the Chamber Castellan, whose responsibility it was to accompany the recruitment parties on their expeditions. Without the training or spiritual fortitude of an Astartes, Baldwin's mind had been vulnerable. He had become a Regicide piece on a galactic board, making his small but significant move, guided by an unknown hand. Artegall was suddenly glad of the darkness. Glad that he couldn't see the mask of Baldwin's kindly face frozen in murderous blankness.

Closing his eyes, Elias Artegall, Chapter Master and last of the Crimson Consuls, wished the game to end.

# HEART OF RAGE

## by James Swallow

IN THE BLOOD-WARM gloom, amid the shrouding, cloying thickness of the air, the heart beat on. A clock ticking towards death, a ceaseless rhythm echoing through his body. A cadence that inched him, pulse by throbbing pulse, towards the raging madness of the Thirst.

Engorged with vital fluid, the heart pressed against the inside of his ribcage, trip-hammer impacts growing faster and faster, reaching out, threatening to engulf him. His every sense rang with the force of it, the rushing in his ears, his arrow-sharp sight fogged and hazy, the scent of old rust thick in his nostrils... And the taste.

Oh yes, the taste... Congealing upon his tongue, the heavy meat-tang like burned copper, the wash across his fangs. The aching, delirious need to drink deep.

Clouds of ruby and darkness billowed about him,

surrounded him, dragged him roaring into the void, damned and destined to surrender to it. These were the enemies that he and all his kindred could never defeat, the unslakable Red Thirst and its terrible twin, the berserker fury of the Black Rage. These were the legacy of The Flaw, the foes he would face for eternity, beyond all others, for they were trapped within him. Woven like threads of poison through the tapestry of his DNA, the bane-gift of his lord and master ten thousand years dead.

*Sanguinius.* Primarch and noblest among the Emperor's sons. The Great Angel, the Brightest One. The shockwave of the master's murder, millennia gone yet forever resonant, thundered in his veins. The power of the primarch's angelic splendour and matchless strength filled him... And yet the other face of that golden coin was dark, dark as rage, dark as fury, darker than any hell-spawned curse upon creation.

Their boon and their blight. The malevolent mirror of the beast inside every brother of the Blood Angels Chapter.

BROTHER-CODICIER GARAS NORD knelt upon the chapel's flagstones, the only sound about him the whisper of servo-skulls high overhead, watching the lone Space Marine with indifferent attention.

Hunched forwards in prayer, his broad frame was alone before the simple iron altar. Wan light cast by biolumes cast hollow colour over his face. It glittered across the sullen indigo of his battle armour and the gold chasing of the metal skull upon his chest. The glow caught the deep, rich red of his right shoulder pauldron and the sigil of his Chapter, a winged drop of crimson blood. It glittered upon the matrix of fine crystal about his bowed head, where the frame of a psychic hood rose from his gorget – and it caught in accusing shadows the faint trembling of Nord's gauntleted hands, where they met and crossed in the shape of the Imperial aquila.

Nord's eyes were closed, but his senses were open. His hands tightened into fists. The ominous echoes of the dream still clung to him, defeating his every attempt to banish them.

He released a sigh. Visions were no stranger to him. They were as much a tool to his kind as the hood or the force axe sheathed upon his back. Nord had The Sight, the twisted blessing of psionic power, and with it he fought alongside his brothers in the Adeptus Astartes, to bolster them upon the field of conflict. In his time he had seen many things, great horrors spilling into the world from the mad realms of the warp, forms that pulled at reason with their sheer monstrosity. Darkness and hate... And once in a while, a glimpse of something. A possibility. A future.

It had saved his life on Ixion, when prescience turned his head, a split second before a las-bolt cut through the air. He still wore the burn scar from that near-hit across his cheek, livid against his face.

But this was different. No flash of reflex, just a dream, over and over. He could not help but wonder – was it also a warning?

His kind... They had many names – telekine, witchkin, warp-touched, *psyker* – but beyond it all he was something more. A Son of Sanguinius. A Blood Angel. Whatever visions of fate his mind conjured for him, his duty came before them all.

If the spirit of Sanguinius were to beckon him towards a death, then he prayed that it would be a noble sacrifice; an ending not in the wild madness of the Black Rage, but one forged in honour. A death worthy of his primarch, worthy of one who had perished protecting Holy Terra and the Emperor himself from the blades of arch-traitors.

'Nord.' He sensed the new presence in the chapel, the edges of a hard, disciplined psyche, a thing forged like sword-blade steel.

The Codicier opened his eyes and looked up at the statue of the Emperor behind the altar. The Emperor looked down, impassive and silent. The eyes of the carving seemed to track Nord as he bowed before it. It offered only mute counsel, but that was just and right. For now, whatever troubled the Codicier was his burden to carry.

Nord rose to find Brother-Sergeant Kale approaching, his boots snapping against the stone floor. He sketched a salute and Kale nodded in return.

'Sir,' he began. 'Forgive me. I hoped to take a moment of reflection before we embarked upon the mission proper.'

Kale waved away his explanation. 'Your tone suggests you did not find it, Garas.'

Nord gave his battle-brother a humourless smile. 'Some days peace is more difficult to find than others.'

'I know exactly what you mean.' Kale's hand strayed

to his chin and he rubbed the rasp of white-grey
stubble there with red-armoured fingers. 'I doubt I
have had a moment's quiet since we embarked.' He
gestured towards the chapel doors and Nord walked
with him.

The Codicier studied the other man. They were
contrasts in colour and shade, the warrior and the
psyker.

Sergeant Brenin Kale's wargear was crimson from
head to toe, dressed with honour-chains of black
steel and gold detailing, purity seals and engravings
that listed his combat record. Under one arm he carried his helmet, upon it the white laurel of a veteran.
He wore a chainsword in a scabbard along the line of
his right arm, the tungsten fangs of the blade grey
and sharp. His face was pale and pitted, the mark of
radiation damage, and he sported a queue of wiry
hair from a top-knot; and yet there was a patrician
solidity to his aspect, a strength and nobility that
time and war had not yet diminished.

Nord shared Kale's build and stature, as did every
Son of Sanguinius, the bequest of the gene-seed
implantation process each Adeptus Astartes endured
as an initiate. But there the similarity ended. Where
Kale was sallow of face, Nord's skin was rust-red like
the rad-deserts of Baal Secundus, and the laser scar
was mirrored on his other cheek by the electro-tattoo
of a single blood droplet, caught as if falling from the
corner of his eye. Nord's hairless scalp was bare
except for the faint tracery of a molly-wire matrix just
beneath the flesh, implanted to improve connectivity
with his psychic hood. And his armour was a

uniform blue everywhere except his shoulder, contrasting against the red of the rest of his battle-brothers. The colour set him apart, showed him for what he was beneath the plasteel and ceramite. Witchkin. Psyker. A man without his peace.

WITHIN THE CHAPEL, one might have thought they stood inside a church upon any one of billions of hive-worlds across the Imperium. If not for the banners of the Adeptus Astartes and the Navy, the place would be no different from all those other basilicas: sacred places devoted to the worship of the God-Emperor of Humanity. But this church lay deep in the decks of the frigate *Emathia*, protected by vast iron ribs of hull-metal, nestled between the accelerator cores of the warship's primary and secondary lance cannons.

Nord left the sanctum behind, and – so he hoped – his misgivings, walking in easy lockstep with his sergeant. Half-human servitors and worried crew serfs scattered out of their way, clearing a path for the Space Marines.

'We left the warp a few hours ago,' offered Kale. 'The squad is preparing for deployment.'

'I'll join them,' Nord began, but Kale shook his head.

'I want you with me. I have been summoned to the bridge.' A sourness entered the veteran's tone. 'The tech-priest wishes to address me personally before we proceed.'

'Indeed? Does he think he needs to underline our mission to us once again? Perhaps he believes he has not repeated it enough.' Nord was silent for a moment. 'I may not be the best choice to accompany you. I believe our honoured colleague from the Adeptus Mechanicus finds my presence… discomforting.'

Kale's lip curled. 'That's one reason I want you there. Keep the bastard off balance.'

'And the other?'

'In case I feel the need to kill him.'

Nord allowed himself a smirk. 'If you expect me to dissuade you, brother-sergeant, you have picked the wrong man.'

'Dissuade me?' Kale snorted. 'I expect you to assist!'

The gallows humour of the moment faded; to casually discuss the murder of a High Priest of the Magus Biologis, even in rough jest, courted grave censure. But the eminent magi gathered dislike to him with such effortless ease, it was hard to imagine that the man wanted anything else than to be detested. Scant weeks they had been aboard the *Emathia* on its journey to this light-forsaken part of the galaxy, and in that time the Exalted Tech-Priest Epja Xeren had shown only aloof disrespect for both the Blood Angels and the frigate's hardy officers.

Nord wondered why Xeren had not simply used one of the Mechanicum's own starships for this operation, or employed his cadre's tech-guard. Like many factors surrounding this tasking, it sat uneasily with the Codicier; he sensed the same concern in Kale's emotional aura.

'This duty…' said Kale in a low voice, his thoughts clearly mirroring those of his battle-brother, 'it has the stink of subterfuge about it.'

Nord gave a nod. 'And yet, all the diktats from the Adeptus Terra were in order. Despite his manner, the priest is valued by the Imperial Council.'

'Civilians,' grunted the sergeant. 'Politicians! Sometimes I wonder if arrogance is the grease upon their wheels.'

'They might say the same of us. That we Adeptus Astartes consider ourselves to be *their* betters.'

'Just so,' Kale allowed. 'The difference is, where we are concerned, that fact is true.'

EMATHIA'S ORNATE BRIDGE was a vaulted oval cut from planes of brass and steel, dominated by great lenses of crystal ranging down towards the frigate's bow. Below the deck, in work-pits among the ship's cogitators, hunchbacked servitors hissed to one another, busying themselves with the running of the vessel. Officers in blue-black tunics walked back and forth, overseeing their work.

The ship's commander, resplendent in a red-trimmed duty jacket, turned from a gas-lens viewer and gave the Astartes a bow.

'Sergeant Kale, Brother Nord. We're very close now. Come.' Captain Hyban Gorolev beckoned them towards him.

Nord liked the man; Gorolev had impressed him early on with his grasp of Adeptus Astartes protocol and the careful generosity with which he commanded *Emathia*'s crew. Nord had encountered Navy men who ruled their ships through fear and intimidation. Gorolev was quite unlike that; he had a fatherly way to him, a mixture of sternness tempered by sincerity that bonded his crew through mutual loyalty. Nord saw in the captain the mirror of brotherhood with *his* kindred.

'The derelict is near,' he was saying. Gorolev's sandy-coloured face was fixed in a frown. 'Interference continues to defeat the scrying of our sensors, however. There is wreckage. Evidence of plasma fire…' He trailed off.

Nord sensed the man's apprehension but said nothing, catching sight of a readout thick with lines of text in Gothic script. He saw recitations that suggested organic matter out there in the void. Unbidden, the Codicier's gaze snapped up and he stared out through the viewports. The ghost of a cold, undefined emotion began to gather at the base of his thoughts.

'Adeptus Astartes.' The voice had all the tonality of a command, a summons, a demand to be given fealty.

Filtered and machine-altered, the word emitted from a speaker embedded in a face where a mouth had once been. Eyes of titanium clockwork measured the Blood Angels coldly. Flesh, what there was of it, was subsumed into carbide plates that disappeared beneath a hood. A great gale of black robes hung loose to pool upon the decking, concealing a form that was a collection of sharp angles; the silhouette of a body that bore little resemblance to anything natural-born. Antennae blossomed from tailored holes in the habit, and out of hidden pockets, manipulators and snake-like mechadendrites moved, apparently of independent thought and action.

This thing that stood before them at the edge of the frigate's tacticarium, this not-quite-man seemingly built from human pieces and scrapyard leavings... This was Xeren.

'Your mission will commence momentarily,' said the tech-priest. He shifted slightly, and Nord heard the working of pistons. 'You are ready?'

'We are Adeptus Astartes,' Kale replied, with a grimace. The words were answer enough.

'Quite.' Xeren inclined his head towards the hololithic display, which showed flickers of hazy light. 'This zone is filthy with expended radiation. It may trouble even your iron constitution, Blood Angel.'

'Doubtful.' Kale's annoyance was building. 'Your concern is noted, magi. But now we are here, I am more interested in learning the identity of this hulk you have tasked us to secure for you. We cannot prosecute a mission to the best of our abilities without knowing what we will face.'

'But you are Adeptus Astartes,' said Xeren, making little effort to hide his mocking tone. Before Kale could respond, the tech-priest's head bobbed. 'You are quite right, brother-sergeant,' he demurred, 'I have been secretive with the specifics of this operation. But once you see your target, you will understand the need for such security.'

There was a clicking sound from Xeren's chest; Nord wondered if it might be the Mechanicum cyborg's equivalent of a gasp.

'Sensors are clearing,' noted Gorolev. 'We have a clean return.'

'Show me,' snapped Kale.

Earlier during the voyage, just to satisfy his mild interest, Nord had allowed his psychic senses to brush the surface of Xeren's mind. What he had sensed there was unreadable; not shrouded, but simply *inhuman*. Nothing that he could interpret as emotions, only a coldly logical chain of processes with all the nuance of a cogitator program. And yet, as the hololith stuttered and grew distinct, for the briefest of moments Nord was certain he felt the echo of a covetous thrill from the tech-priest.

'Here is your target,' said Xeren.

'Throne of Terra...' The curse slipped from Gorolev's lips as the image solidified. '*Xenos!*'

It resembled a whorled shell, a tight spiral of shimmering bone curved in on itself. Coils of fibrous matter that suggested sinew webbed it, and from one vast orifice along the ventral plane, a nest of pasty tenticular forms issued outwards, grasping at nothing.

It lay among a drift of broken chitin and flash-frozen fluids, listing. Great scars marked the flanks of the alien construct, and in places there were craters, huge pockmarks that had exploded outwards like city-sized pustules.

There seemed to be no life to it. It was a gargantuan, bilious corpse. A dead horror, there in the starless night.

'This is what you brought us to find?' Kale's voice was loaded with menace. 'A *tyranid* craft?'

'A hive ship,' Xeren corrected. The tech-priest ignored the silence that had descended on the

*Emathia*'s bridge, the mute shock upon the faces of Gorolev's officers.

'A vessel of this tonnage is no match for a tyranid hive,' said Nord. 'Their craft have defeated entire fleets and pillaged the crews for raw bio-mass to feast upon!'

'It is dead,' said the priest. 'Have no fear.'

'I am not afraid,' Nord retorted, 'but neither am I a fool! The tyranids are not known as "the Great Devourer" without reason. They are a plague, organisms that exist solely to consume and replicate. To destroy all life unlike them.'

'You forget yourself.' Xeren's tone hardened. 'The authority here is mine. I have brought you to this place for good reason. Look to the hive. It is dead,' he repeated.

NORD STUDIED THE image. The xenos craft exhibited signs of heavy damage, and its motion and course suggested it was unguided.

'My orders come from the highest echelons of the Magistratum,' continued the tech-priest. 'I am here to oversee the capture of this derelict, in the name of the God-Emperor and Omnissiah!'

'Capture…' Kale echoed the word. Nord saw the veteran's sword-hand twitch as he weighed the command.

'Consider the bounty within that monstrosity,' Xeren addressed them, Adeptus Astartes and officers all. 'Nord is quite correct. The tyranids are a scourge upon the stars, a virus writ large. But like any virus, it must be studied if a cure is to be found.' A spindly machine-arm whirred, moving to point at the image. 'This represents an unparalleled opportunity. This hive ship is a treasure trove of biological data. If we take it, learn its secrets…' He gave a clicking rasp. 'We might turn the xenos against themselves. Perhaps even tame them…'

'How did you know this thing was here?' Nord tore his gaze from the display.

Xeren answered after a moment. 'The first attempt to take the hive was not a success. There were complications.'

'You will tell us what transpired,' said Kale. 'Or we will go no further.'

'Aye,' rasped Gorolev. The captain had turned pale and sweaty, his fingers kneading the grip of his holstered laspistol.

Xeren gave another clicking sigh, and inclined his head on whining motors. 'A scouting party of Archeo-Technologists boarded the craft under the command of an adept named Indus. We believe that a splinter force from a larger hive fleet left this ship behind after it suffered some malfunction. Evidence suggests–'

'This Adept Indus,' Kale broke in. 'Where is he?'

Xeren looked away. 'The scouting party did not return. Their fate is unknown to me.'

'Consumed!' grated Gorolev. 'Throne and Blood! Any man that ventures in there would be torn apart!'

'*Captain,*' warned the brother-sergeant.

The tech-priest paid no attention to the officer's outburst. 'It is my firm belief that the hive ship, although not without hazards, is dormant. For the moment, at least.' He came closer on iron-clawed feet. 'You understand now why the Adeptus Mechanicus wish to move with alacrity, Blood Angel?'

'I understand,' Kale replied, and Nord saw the tightening of his jaw. Without another word, the veteran turned on his heel and strode away. Nord moved with him, and they were into the corridor before the Space Marine felt a hand upon his forearm.

'LORDS.' GOROLEV SHOT a look back towards the bridge as the hatch slammed shut, his eyes narrowing. 'A word?' Suspicion flared black in the man's aura.

'Speak,' Kale replied.

'I've made no secret of my reservations about the esteemed tech-priest's motive and manner,' said the captain. 'I cannot let this pass without comment.' His face took on the cast of anger and old fear. 'By the Emperor's grace, I am a veteran of many conflicts with the xenos, those tyranid abominations among them.' Gorolev's words brimmed with venom. 'Those… *things*. I've seen them rape worlds and leave nothing but ashen husks in their wake.' He leaned closer. 'That hive ship should not be studied like some curiosity. It should be *atomised*!'

Kale held up a hand and Gorolev fell silent. 'There is nothing you have said I disagree with, ship-master. But we are servants of the God-Emperor, Nord and I, you and your crew, even Xeren. And we have our duty.'

For a moment, it seemed as if Gorolev was about to argue; but then he nodded grimly, resigned to fulfilling his orders. 'Duty, then. In the Emperor's name.'

'In the Emperor's name,' said Kale.

Nord opened his mouth to repeat the oath, but he found his voice silenced.

So fleeting, so mercurial and indistinct that it was gone even as he turned his senses towards it, Nord felt… *Something*.

A gloom, stygian-deep and ominous, passing over him as a storm cloud might obscure the sun. There, and gone. A presence. A mind?

The sense of black and red clouds pressed in on the edges of his thoughts and he pushed them away.

'Nord?' He found Kale studying him with a careful gaze.

He cleared his thoughts with a moment's effort. 'Brother-Sergeant,' he replied. 'The mission, then?'

Kale nodded. 'The mission, aye.'

THE BOARDING TORPEDO penetrated the hull of the tyranid vessel high along the dorsal surface. Serrated iron razor-cogs bit into the bony structure and turned, ripping at shell-matter and bunches of necrotic muscle, dragging the pod through layers of decking, into the voids of the hive ship's interior.

Then, at rest, the seals released and the Space Marines deployed into the alien hulk, weapons rising to the ready.

Sergeant Kale led from the front, as he always did. He slipped down from the mouth of the boarding torpedo, playing his bolt pistol back and forth, sweeping the chamber for threats. Nord was next, then Brother Dane, Brother Serun and finally Corae, who moved with care as he cradled his flame-thrower.

The weapon's pilot lamp hissed quietly to itself, dancing there in the wet, stinking murk.

The Codicier felt the floor beneath his boots give under his weight; the decking – if it could be called that – was made up of rough plates of bone atop something that could only be flesh, stretching away in an arching, curved passageway. By degrees, the chamber lightened as Nord's occulobe implant contracted, adjusting the perception range of his eyes.

Great arching walls that resembled flayed meat rose around the Blood Angels, along with fluted spires made of greasy black cartilage that drooled thin fluids. Puckered sphincters lay sagging and open, allowing a slaughterhouse stench to reach them. Here and there were the signs of internal damage, long festering wounds open and caked with xenos blood.

Nord picked out glowing boles upon the walls arranged at random intervals; it took a moment before he realised that they were actually fist-sized beetles, clinging to the skin-walls, antennae waving gently, bodies lit with dull bio-luminescence.

There were more insectile creatures in the shadows, little arachnid things that moved sluggishly, crawling in and out of the raw-edged cuts.

'Damage everywhere,' noted Serun, his gruff voice flattened by the thick air of the tyranid craft. 'But no signs of weapons fire.'

'It appears the tech-priest was right.' Kale examined one of the walls. 'Whatever fate befell this ruin, it was not caused by battle.' He beckoned his men on. 'Serun, do you have a reading?'

Brother Serun studied the sensor runes on the auspex device in his hand. 'A faint trace from the adept's
personal locator.' He pointed in an aftward direction.
'That way.'

Kale's gaze drifted towards Nord. 'Is he alive, this
man Indus?'

The psyker stiffened; warily extending his preternatural senses forwards. He could discern only the
pale glitters of thought-energy from the spider-things
and the lamp-beetles; nothing that might suggest a
reasoning mind, let alone a human one. 'I have no
answer for you, sir,' he said at length.

'With caution, then, brothers.' Kale walked on, and
they followed him, silent and vigilant.

THE CORRIDOR NARROWED into a tube, and Nord imagined it a gullet down which the Adeptus Astartes were
travelling. He had encountered tyranids before, but
only upon the field of battle, and then down the
sights of a missile launcher. He had never ventured
aboard one of their craft, and it was exactly the horror he had expected it to be.

Tyranid vessels were not the product of forges and
shipyards; they were spawned. Hive ships were spun
out of knots of meat and bone, grown on the surface
of captured worlds in teeming vats filled with a broth
of liquefied biomass. They were living things, animals by some vague definition of the term.
Electrochemical processes and nerve ganglions transmitted commands about its flesh; pheremonic
discharges regulated its internal atmosphere;
exothermic chemistry created light and heat. Its hull

was skeletal matter, protecting the crew that swarmed like parasites inside the gut of the craft. Together, the hive was a contained, freakish ecosystem, drifting from world to world driven by the need to feed and feed.

Even in this half-dead state, Nord could taste the echo of that aching, bone-deep craving, as if it were leaking from the twitching walls. The fleshy wattles that dangled from the ceiling, the corpse-grey cilia and phlegmy deposits around his feet, all of it sickened him with its dead stench and the sheer, revolting affront of the tyranids' very existence. This xenos abortion was everything that the Imperium, in all its human glory, was not. A chaotic riot of mutant life, disordered and rapacious, without soul or intellect. The absolute antithesis of the civilisation the Adeptus Astartes had fought to preserve since the days of Old Night.

Nord's hand tightened around his pistol; the urge to kill this thing rose high, and he reined it in, denying the tingle of a building Rage before it had freedom to form.

The chamber broadened into an uneven space, dotted with deep pits of muddy liquid that festered and spat, gaseous discharges chugging into the foetid air. Mounds of fatty deposits lay in uneven heaps, the ejecta from the processes churning in the ponds.

Serun gestured. 'Rendering pools. Bio-mass is brought here to be denatured into a liquid slurry.'

Corae spoke for the first time since they had boarded. 'To what end?'

'To feed the hive,' Serun replied. 'This... gruel is the

raw material of the tyranids. They consume it, shape it. It is where they are born from.'

Kale dropped to his haunches. 'And where they kill,' he added. The sergeant picked something metallic from the spoil heaps and turned it in his fingers. A rank sigil of iron and copper, a disc cut to resemble a cogwheel. Upon it, the design of a skull, the symbol of the Adeptus Mechanicus.

Corae turned his face and spat in disgust. 'Emperor protect me from such a fate.'

'More here,' said Brother Dane. With care, he drew to him a twisted shape afloat on one of the pools. It was a man's ribcage and part of a spine, but the bone was rubbery and distended where acidic fluids had eaten into it. It crumbled like wet sand in the Blood Angel's grip.

'Adept Indus, perhaps, and his scout team...' Kale suggested. He turned to face Nord and saw the psyker glaring into the dimness. 'Brother?'

The question had barely left his lips when the Codicier gave an explosive shout. '*Enemy!*'

The shapes came at them from out of the twisted, sinewy ropes about the walls. Three beasts, bursting from concealment as one, attacking from all sides.

Corae was quick, clutching the trigger bar of his flamer. A bright gout of blazing promethium jetted from the bell-mouth of the weapon and engulfed the closest tyranid in flames, but on it came, falling into the red wave of death.

The second skittered across the ground, low and fast, dragging itself in loping jerks by its taloned limbs and great curved claws. Dane, Serun and the sergeant turned their bolters on it in a hail of punishing steel.

The third found Nord and dove at him, falling from the ceiling, spinning about as it came. He flung himself backwards, his storm bolter crashing, his free hand reaching for the hilt of his force axe.

The tyranid landed hard and rocked off its hooves; Nord got his first good look at the thing and recognition unfolded in his forebrain, the legacy of a hundred hypnogogic combat indoctrination tapes. A lictor.

Humanoid in form, tall and festooned with barbs, they sported massive scything talons and a cobra-head tail. Where a man would have a mouth, the lictors grew a wriggling orchard of feeder tendrils. They were hunter-predator forms, deployed alone or in small packs, stealthy and favoured of ambush attacks. Unless Nord and his brothers killed them quickly, they would spill fresh pheromones into the air and summon more of their kind.

He reversed and met the alien with the flickering crystal edge of the axe, reaching into his heart and finding the reservoir of psychic might lurking within him. As the axe-head bit into the lictor's chest, Nord channelled a quickening from the warp along the weapon's psi-convector and into the xenos's new wound. Its agonised shriek battered at him, and he staggered as it tried to claw through his armour. Nord's bolter crashed again, hot rounds finding purchase in the pasty flesh of its thorax. He withdrew the axe again and struck again, over and over, riding on the battle-anger welling up inside him.

The Blood Angel was dimly aware of a death-wail off to his right, half-glimpsing another lictor fall as it was opened by shellfire and chainblade; but his target still lived.

A talon swept down, barbs screeching as they scored Nord's chest plate; in turn he let the axe fall again, this time severing a monstrous limb at the joint. Gouts of black blood spurted, burning where it landed, and the Codicier threw a wall of psionic pressure outwards, battering at the wounded creature.

The lictor's hooves slipped on the lip of a bio-pool and it stumbled backwards into the lake of stringy muck; instantly the churning acids ate into the tyranid and it collapsed, drowning and melting.

Nord regained his balance and waved a hand in front of his visor as oily smoke wafted past; the third tyranid was also dying, finally succumbing to Corae's flamer and the impacts of krak grenades.

A mechanical voice grated through his vox-link. *'Kale. Respond. This is Xeren. We have detected weapons fire. Report status immediately.'*

Ignoring the buzzing of the tech-priest, the psyker approached the last dying lictor as Corae took aim with his flame-thrower, twisting the nozzle to adjust the dispersal pattern. The force axe still humming in his hand, his psychic power resonating through him, Nord caught the sense of the tyranid's animal mind, trapped in its death throes. He winced, the touch of it more abhorrent to him than anything he had yet witnessed aboard the hive ship.

Yet there, in the mass of its unknowable, alien

thoughts, he glimpsed something. Great swirling clouds of red and black. And men, robed men with skeletal limbs of metal and copper cogs about their necks.

Corae pulled the trigger and laid a snake of fire over the beast, boiling its soft tissues beneath the hard chitin armour. Nord sheathed his axe and heard the voice again. Xeren seemed impatient.

*'Perhaps you should not engage every tyranid you see.'*

Kale was plucking spent flesh hooks from the crevices of his armour with quick, spare motions. 'The xenos did not offer us the choice, priest. And I remind you who it was that told us this ship was dead.'

*'Where the tyranids are concerned, there are degrees of death. The ship is dormant, and so the majority of the swarm aboard should be quiescent. But some may retain a wakeful state... I suggest you avoid further engagements.'*

'I will take that under advisement,' Kale retorted.

Xeren continued. *'You are proceeding too slowly, brother-sergeant, and without efficiency. Indus is the primary objective. Divide your forces to cover a greater area. Find him for me.'*

The sergeant holstered his gun, and any reply he might have made was rendered pointless as the tech-priest cut the vox signal.

Serun's hands closed into fists. 'He dares bray commands as if he were Chapter Master? The scrawny cog has no right–'

'Decorum, kinsman,' said Kale. 'We are the Sons of Sanguinius. A mere tech-priest is not worth our enmity. We'll find Xeren's lost lamb soon enough and be done.'

'If he still lives,' mused Corae, nudging the powdery bones with his boot.

RELUCTANTLY, BROTHER-SERGEANT KALE chose to do as the tech-priest had suggested; beyond the bio-pool chamber the throat-corridors branched and he ordered Dane to break off, taking Corae and Serun with him. Brother Dane's element would move anti-spinwards through the hive ship's interior spaces, while Nord and his commander ventured along the other path.

The psyker threw the veteran a questioning look when he voiced the orders; in turn Kale's expression remained unchanged. 'Xeren and I agree on one point,' he noted. 'We both wish this mission to be concluded as quickly as possible.'

Nord had to admit he too shared that desire. He thought of Gorolev's words aboard the *Emathia*. The ship-master was right; this monstrous hulk was an insult every second it was allowed to exist.

Dane's team vanished into the clammy darkness and Nord followed Kale onwards. They passed through more rendering chambers, then rooms seemingly constructed from waxy matter, laced with spherical pods, each one wet and dripping ichor. They encountered other strange spaces that defied any interpretation of form or function; hollows where tooth-like spires criss-crossed from floor and ceiling; a copse of bulbous, acid-rimed fronds that resembled coral polyps; and great bladders that throbbed, thick liquid emerging from them in desultory jerks.

And there were the creatures. The first time they came across the alien forms, Nord's axe had come to his hand before he was even aware of it; but the tyranids they encountered were in some state that mirrored death, a strange hibernative trance that rendered them inert.

They crossed a high catwalk formed from spinal bone, and Kale used the pin-lamp beneath the barrel of his boltgun to throw a disc of light into the pits below. The glow picked out the hulking shape of a massive carnifex, its bullet-shaped head tucked into its spiny chest in some mad parody of a sleeping child.

The rasping breaths of the huge assault organism fogged the air, bone armour and spines scraping across one another as its chest rose and fell. Awake, it could have killed the Blood Angels with a single blast of bio-poison from its slavering venom cannons.

Around the gnarled hooves of the slumbering carnifex, a clutch of deadly hormagaunts rested, shiny oil-black carapaces piled atop one another, clawed limbs folded back, talons sheathed. Nord gripped the force axe firmly, and it took a near physical effort for him to turn from the gallery of targets before him. Instead they moved on, ever on, picking their way in stealth through the very heart of the hive's dozing populace.

'Why do they ignore us?' Kale wondered, his question transmitted to the vox-bead in Nord's ear.

'They are conserving their strength, brother-sergeant,' he replied. 'Whatever incident caused this ship to fall away from the rest of its hive fleet, it must have drained them to survive it. I would not question our luck.'

'Aye,' Kale replied. 'Terra protects.'

'I–'

The force axe fell from Nord's fingers and the impact upon the bone deck seemed louder than cannon fire. Suddenly, without warning, *it* was there.

A black and cloying touch enveloping his thoughts – the same sense of something alien he had felt aboard the *Emathia*.

A presence. A mind. Clouds, billowing wreaths of black and red, surrounding him, engulfing him.

'There… is something else here,' he husked. 'A psychic phantom, just beyond my reach. Measuring itself against me.' Nord's heart hammered in his chest; he tasted metal in his mouth. 'Not just the xenos… More than that.'

He grimaced, and strengthened his mental bulwarks, shoring them up with raw determination. The dark dream uncoiled in his thoughts, the rumbling pulse of the Red Thirst in his gullet, the churn of the Black Rage stiffening his muscles. All about him, the shadows seemed to lengthen and loom, leaking from the walls, ranging across the sleeping monsters to reach for the warrior with ebon fingers.

Nord gasped. 'Something is awakening.'

ACROSS THE PLANE of the hive ship's hull, Brother Dane brought up his fist in a gesture of command, halting Corae and Serun. 'Do you hear that?' he asked.

Corae turned, the flamer in his grip. 'It's coming

from the walls.' They were the last words he would utter.

Flesh-matter all around the squad ripped and tore into bleeding rags as claws shredded their way towards the Astartes. With brutal, murderous power, a tide of chattering freaks boiled in upon them, spines and bone and armoured heads moving in blurs. They were so fast that in the dimness they seemed like the talons of single giant animal, reaching out to take them.

Gunfire lit the corridor, the flat bang of bolter shells sounding shot after shot, the chugging belch of fire from the flamer issuing out to seek targets. In return came screaming – the blood-hungry shrieks of a warrior brood turned loose to find prey.

The horde of tyranid soldier organisms rolled over the Space Marines with no regard for their own safety; mindless things driven on by killer instinct and a desire to feed, they had no self to preserve. They were simply the blades of the hive, and the very presence of the intruders was enough to drive them mad.

Perhaps beings with intellect might have sensed the hand of something larger, something at the back of their thoughts, compelling them, driving them to destroy. But the termagants knew nothing but the lust to rip and rend.

Symbiotic phero-chemical links between the tyranids and the engineered bio-tools in their claws sent kill commands running before them. Like everything in their arsenal, the weapons used by the warriors were living things. Their fleshborers, great bell-mouthed flutes of chitin, spat clumps of fang-toothed beetles that chewed through armour and flesh in a destructive frenzy.

Numberless and unstoppable, the brood swallowed up Corae and Serun, opening them to the air in jets of red. Dane was the last to fall, his legs cut out from under him, his bolter running dry, becoming a club in his mailed fists. At the end of him, a storm of tusk blades pierced his torso, penetrating his lungs, his primary and secondary hearts.

Blood flooded his mouth and he perished in silence, his last act to deny the creatures the victory of his screams.

BROTHER NORD STUMBLED and fell to one knee, clutching at his chest in sympathetic agony. He felt Dane perish in his thoughts, heard the echo of the warrior's death, and that of Corae and Serun. Each man's ending struck him like a slow bullet, filling his gut with ice.

Nord's heart and its decentralised twin beat fast, faster, faster, his blood singing in his ears in a captured tempest. The same trembling he had felt back in the chapel returned, and it was all he could do to fight it off.

He became aware of Brother-Sergeant Kale helping him to his feet, dimly registering his squad commander guiding him away from the hibernaculum chamber and into the flesh-warm humidity of the corridor beyond.

'Nord! Speak to me!'

He tried to answer but the psychic undertow dragged on him, taking all his effort just to stay afloat and sensate. The shocking resonance was far worse than he had ever felt before. There had been many times upon the field of combat where Nord had tasted the mind-death of others, sometimes his foes, too often his battle-brothers... But this... This was of a very different stripe.

At once alien and human, unknowable and yet known to him, the psychic force that had compelled the termagant swarm reached in and raked frigid claws over the surface of his mind. A part of him screamed that he should withdraw, disengage and erect the strongest of his mental barriers. Every second he did not, he gave this force leave to plunge still deeper. And yet, another facet of Nord's iron will dared to face this power head-on, driven by the need to know it. To know it and *destroy* it.

Against the sickness he felt within, Nord tried to see the face of his enemy. The mental riposte was powerful; it hit him like a wall and he recoiled, his vision hazed crimson.

With a monumental psychic effort, Nord disengaged and slumped against a bony stanchion, his dark skin sallow and filmed with sweat.

He blinked away the fog in his vision and found his commander. Kale's pale face was grave in the dimness. 'The others?' he whispered.

'Dead,' Nord managed. 'All dead.'

The sergeant gave a grim nod. 'The Emperor knows their names.' He hesitated a moment. 'You felt it? With your witchsight, you saw... the enemy?'

'Aye.' The psyker got to his feet. 'It tried to kill me. Didn't take.'

Kale stood, drumming his fingers on the hilt of his chainsword. 'This… force that assaulted you?'

He shook his head, 'I've never sensed the like before, sir.'

'Do you know where it is?' The veteran gestured around at the walls with the chainsword.

Nord nodded. 'That, I do know.'

He heard the hunter's smile in the sergeant's voice. 'Show me.'

AT THE HEART of every tyranid nest, one breed of creature was supreme. If the carnifexes and termagants, ripper swarms and biovores were the teeth and talons of the tyranid mass, then the commanding intellect was the hive tyrant. None had ever been captured alive, and few had been recovered by the Imperium intact enough for a full dissection. If the lictors and the hormagaunts and all the other creatures were common soldiery, the hive tyrants were the generals. The conduit for whatever passed as the diffuse mind of this repugnant xenos species.

Some even said that the tyrants were only a sub-genus of something even larger and more intelligent; a cadre of tyranid capable of reasoning and independent thought. But no such being had ever been seen by human eyes – or if it had, those who had gazed upon it did not live to tell.

It was the hive ship's tyrant that the Blood Angels sought as they entered the orb-like hibernacula, the tech-priest's objective now ranked of lesser importance. If a tyrant was awake aboard this vessel, then none of them were safe.

'It's not a tyranid,' husked Nord. 'The thought-pattern I sensed... It wasn't the same as the lictor's.' He paused. 'At least, not in whole.'

Kale eyed him. 'Explain, brother. Your gift is a mystery to me. I do not understand.'

'The mind that touched my thoughts, that rallied the creatures who attacked us. It is neither human nor xenos.'

The sergeant halted. 'A daemon?' He said the word like a curse.

Nord shook his head. 'I do not sense the taint of Chaos here, sir. This is different...' Even as the words fell from his lips, the psyker felt the change in the air around them. The wet, damp atmosphere grew sullen and greasy, setting a sickly churn deep in his belly.

Kale felt it too, even without the Codicier's preternatural senses. The sergeant drew his chainsword and brandished it before him, his thumb resting on the weapon's activation stud.

A robed figure, there in the dimness. Perhaps a man, it advanced slowly towards them, feet dragging as if wounded. And then a voice, brittle and cracked.

'Me,' rasped the newcomer. 'You sense me, Adeptus Astartes.' The figure moved at the very edge of the dull light from the lamp-beetles. Nord's eyes narrowed; threads of clothing, cables perhaps, seemed to trail behind the man, away into the dark.

Kale aimed his gun. 'In the Emperor's name, identify yourself or I will kill you where you stand.'

Hands opened in a gesture of concession. 'I do not doubt you already know who I am.' He bowed slightly, and Nord saw cords snaking along his back. 'My name is Heraklite Indus, adept and savant, former Magis Biologis Minoris of the Adeptus Mechanicus.'

'*Former?*' echoed Kale.

Indus's shadowed head bobbed. 'Oh, yes. I attend a new master now. Let me introduce you to him.'

The strange threads pulled taut and lifted Indus off his feet, to dangle as a marionette would hang from the hands of a puppeteer. A shape that dwarfed him lumbered out of the black, drawing into the pool of light.

White as bleached bone, crested with purple-black patches of armour shell, it bent to fit its bulk inside the close quarters of the hibernacula; a hive tyrant, in all its obscene glory.

TWO OF ITS four arms were withered and folded to its torso, the pearlescent surface of their claws cracked and fractured. The other arms ended in ropey whips of sinew that threaded across the floor and into the adept's flayed spine, glittering wetly where bone was revealed beneath his torn robes.

And yet... The towering tyranid's breathing was laboured and rough, and from its eye-spots, its great fanged jaws, its fleshy throat-sacs, thin yellow pus oozed over crusted scabs. For all the horror and scale, the tyrant seemed slack and drained, without the twitchy, insectile frenzy of its lessers. A stinking haze of necrotic decay issued from it; Nord had tasted the scent of death enough times to know that this alien beast was mortally wounded.

'What have you done, Indus?' demanded Kale, his face twisted in disgust. In all his years, the veteran sergeant had never seen the like.

'Neither human nor xenos.' Nord repeated his earlier statement, the words suddenly snapping into hard focus. With a whip-crack thought, he sent a savage mental probe towards the adept; Indus spun to face him with a glare and the telepathic feint was deflected easily.

The adept nodded slowly. 'Yes, Blood Angel. We are the same. Both blessed with witchsight. Both psykers.' Indus cocked his head. 'Xeren never told you. How like him.'

'No matter,' growled Kale. Without hesitation, the sergeant opened fire and Nord followed suit, both Space Marines turning their weapons on the ugly, abhorrent pairing.

The hive tyrant shifted, drawing Indus close in a gesture of protection, shielding the adept from the bolt-rounds that whined off its chitinous armour. Its head lolled back and a high screech issued from between its teeth; in reply there were hoots and howls from all around the Adeptus Astartes.

In moments, sphinctered rents in the hibernacula walls drew open, spilling dozens of mucus-slicked hormagaunts into the chamber. The chattering beasts rose up in a wave and the Blood Angels went to their blades. Kale's chainsword brayed as it chewed through bone; Nord's force axe cut lightning-flash arcs into meat, as barbed grasping claws dragged them down.

Nord caught a telepathic spark as blood from a cut gummed his right eye shut; he drew up his mental shields just as the hive tyrant released a scream of psychic energy upon them.

The wave of pain blasted across the chamber and the Codicier saw his battle-brother stumble, clutching his hands to his head in agony. Nord fared little better, the tyranid's telepathic onslaught sending him spinning. For long moments he waited for death to fall upon him, for the mass of hormagaunts to take the opportunity to rip him apart – but they did not.

Instead, the hissing monsters retreated, forming into a wall before the Space Marines, shielding Indus and the tyrant.

Nord went to Kale and helped him to his feet. The sergeant had lost his bolter in the melee, and he still shook from the after-effect of the psychic scream.

'We could have killed you,' said Indus. 'We chose not to.'

'You speak for the xenos now?' spat Nord.

Indus gave a crooked smile. 'A soldier's limited mindset. I had hoped for better from one with the sight.' He came forwards, the shuffling tyrant at his back. 'I found this creature near death, you understand? Too weak to fight me. I pushed in, touched its thoughts…' The adept gave a gasp of pleasure. 'And what I saw there. Such riches. The knowledge of flesh and bone, nerve and blood, an understanding! More than the scribes of the Magis Biologis could ever hope to learn. Race memory, Adeptus Astartes. Millions of years of it, to drink in…'

* * *

'FOOL,' REPLIED THE Blood Angel. 'Can you not see what you have done? The creature is near death! It used what strength it had to lure you in, place you in its thrall! It uses you like it uses these mindless predators!' He gestured at the hormagaunts. 'When it is healed, it will reawaken every horror that walks or crawls within this hive, and turn again to the killing of men!'

'You are wrong,' Indus retorted. 'I have control here! I spared your lives!'

'I?' snapped Kale. 'A moment ago you said "we". Which is it?'

'The hive answers to me!' he shouted, the warrior creatures howling in empathy. 'I gave myself to the merging, and now see what I have at my hands...' Indus drew in a rattling breath. 'That is why Xeren sent you here. He is like you. Afraid. Jealous of what we are.'

'The priest knew of this?' hissed Kale.

Indus chuckled. 'Xeren saw it happen. He fled! He sent you to find us, praying you would destroy us so his cadre could take this hive for itself.'

Nord nodded to himself. 'Aboard a ship filled with killing machines, a deed only an Astartes could do.'

'You've seen the power of these creatures,' said the adept. 'This is only a tiny measure of what the swarm is capable of.' He extended a skeletal cybernetic arm towards the psyker. 'There is such majesty here, red in tooth and claw, Blood Angel. Come see it. Join me.' New, fang-mouthed tentacles issued forth from the tyrant's stunted arms, questing towards the Codicier. 'Our union is vast and giving, for those with the gift...'

His eyes narrowed, and with one sweeping blow, Brother Nord sliced down with his axe, severing the probing limbs in a welter of acidic blood. The tyrant screamed and rocked backwards.

'A grave mistake,' snarled Indus. 'You have no idea what you have denied yourself.'

'I know full well,' came the reply. 'My blood stays pure, by the Emperor's grace and the might of Sanguinius! You have willingly defiled yourself, debased your humanity... For that there can be no forgiveness.'

'We are not monsters!' shouted Indus, amid his howling chorus. 'You are the destroyers, the disunited, the infection! You are the hate! The rage and the thirst!'

Too late, Nord's mind sensed the build of warp energy once more, resonating between the tyrant and the Mechanicum psyker. Too late, the cold understanding reached him. 'No...' he breathed, staggering backwards. '*No!*'

'Nord?' The question on Brother Kale's lips was suddenly ripped away by a new, thunderous shockwave of dark power.

Perhaps it was the hive tyrant, with its hate for all things alien to it, perhaps it was Indus in his crazed fury. Whatever the origin, the burning blade of madness swept across the Blood Angels and ripped open their minds.

Nord held on to the ragged edge of the abyss, as once more the red and black clouds enveloped him. The dream! The vision in his roaring heart was upon him! His moment of foresight damning and terrifyingly real.

The strength of the psychic blast tore away any self-control, burning down to the basest, most *monstrous* instincts a man could conceal; and for an Adeptus Astartes of the Blood Angels Chapter, the fall to such madness was damning.

The gene-curse. The flaw. The Red Thirst's wild and insatiable desire for blood, the Black Rage's uncontrollable berserker insanity. These were the twin banes Nord fought to endure. Fought and held against. Fought... And finally... resisted.

But Brother-Sergeant Brenin Kale had none of the Codicier's psychic bulwarks. His naked mind absorbed the power of the tyrant's fury... and *fell*.

THE MAN THAT Nord's comrade had been was gone; in his place was a beast clothed in his flesh.

Kale threw himself at the Codicier, his chainsword discarded and forgotten, hands in claws, his mouth wide to release a bellow of pure anger. The Blood Angel's fangs glittered in the light, and darkness filled his vision.

Nord collided with Kale with a concussion that sounded across the chamber, scattering dithering hormagaunts, crushing others with the impact. Kale's mailed fists rained blow after blow upon Nord's battle armour, the crimson tint of fury in the sergeant's aura stifling him.

He cried out the other man's name, desperately trying to reach through the fog of madness, but to no avail. Nord fought to block the impacts as they struggled against one another, locked in close combat; he could not bring himself to hit back.

His skull rang with each strike, his vision blurring. There was no doubt that Kale could kill him. He was no match for the old veteran's strength and prowess, even in such a state. Kale's frightening speed and instinctive combat skills would overwhelm him. He had little choice. If he could not end this madness quickly, Kale would tear open his throat and drink deep.

He glimpsed a rent in Kale's armour, a deep gouge that had penetrated the ceramite sheath. 'Brother,' he whispered, 'Forgive me.'

Nord's hand closed around the hilt of his combat blade, turning the fractal-edged knife about. Without pause, he buried it deep in his old friend's chest, down to the hilt. The blade penetrated plasteel, flesh and muscle; it punctured Kale's primary heart and the veteran's back arched in a spasm of agony.

Nord let him fall, and the other man dropped to the bony deck, pain wracking him, robbing him of his rage.

A DIFFERENT KIND of fury burned in the psyker. One pure and controlled, as bright as the core of a star. Blue sparks gathering around the crystal matrix of his psychic hood, Nord turned and found his force axe, sweeping it up to aim at Indus.

'You will pay in kind for this, adept,' he snarled. 'Know that. In the name of Holy Terra, you will pay.'

Nord closed his eyes and let the power flow into him. Blazing actinic flares of warp energy sputtered and flew around the Blood Angel's head as the hormagaunts shook off their pause and came at him.

Channelling the might of heroes though his bones, through his very soul itself, he unleashed his telepathic might through the force axe.

The blast turned the air into smoke and battered away the xenos beasts, sending them shrieking into the dark. Indus bellowed in pain as his flesh was wracked with agony, and the tyrant hooted in synchrony with him.

It took unbearable minutes for the psychic blast to dissipate, for the adept's crooked mind to shake off the aftershock.

Finally, through the myriad senses of the howling, confused tyranids, he saw only the scorched bone deck of the hibernacula.

The Adeptus Astartes were gone.

WITH KALE'S BODY across his shoulder, Brother Nord ran as swiftly as the bulk of his battle armour would allow, always onwards, never looking back. His storm bolter ran hot in his hand as the Codicier placed shots into any tyranid that crossed his path. He did not stop to engage them, did not pause in his headlong flight.

Nord could feel Indus reaching out, probing the hive ship for him, drawing more and more of the sleeping xenos from their hibernation with each passing moment. He crossed the high bone bridge above the pits and saw the carnifex stirring, moaning as it rose towards wakefulness.

The psyker understood a measure of what had transpired here; Indus or the hive tyrant – or whatever unholy fusion of the two now existed – must have sensed him for the very first time as the *Emathia* made its approach. Hungry for another thrall, the hive mind allowed Nord and Kale to approach the core of the ship, while dispatching Dane and the other battle-brothers. He suppressed a shudder; it wanted *him*. It wanted to engulf him, subsume him into that same horrific unity.

Nord spat in loathing. Perhaps a weakling mind, a man like the bio-adept, perhaps he might have fallen to such a thing… But Nord was a Blood Angel, an Adeptus Astartes – the finest warrior humanity had ever created. Whatever dark fate awaited him, his duty came before them all.

His duty…

'Brother…' He heard the voice as they came to the chamber where the boarding torpedo had made its breach.

Nord lowered his comrade to the ground and he saw the light of recognition in the sergeant's eyes. The mental force Indus had turned on Kale was, at least for the moment, dispelled. 'What… did I do?' Kale's voice was a gasp, thick with blood and recrimination. 'The xenos…'

'They are close,' he replied. 'We have little time.'

KALE SAW NORD'S dagger deep in his chest and gave a ragged chuckle. 'Should… I thank you for this?'

The psyker dragged the injured warrior into the boarding capsule, ignoring the question. 'You will heal, sir. Your body's implants are already destroying infection, repairing your wounds.' He stood up and punched a series of commands into a control panel.

Kale's pale face darkened. 'Wait. What… are you doing?'

Nord didn't meet his gaze. 'Indus will find us again soon enough. He must be dealt with.' The psyker scowled at the vox-link and gave a low curse; the channel was laced with static, likely jammed by some freakish tyranid organism bred just for that task.

Kale tried to lift himself off the deck, ignoring the pain of his fresh, bloody scars, but the acid burn of tyranid venom in his flesh left him gasping, shaking with pain. 'You can't… go back. Not alone…'

The other warrior reached into a weapons locker, searching for something. 'I beg to differ, sir. I am the *only* one who can go back. This enemy has already claimed the lives of three Blood Angels. There must be payment for that cost.' He glanced at the veteran. 'And Xeren's perfidy cannot stand unchallenged.'

Through his blurred vision, the sergeant saw the Codicier gather a gear pack to him, saw him slam a fresh clip of bolt shells into his weapon. 'Nord,' he growled. 'You will stand down!'

The psyker hesitated at the airlock, looking back into the gloom of the hive ship beyond. 'I regret I cannot obey you, brother. Forgive me.'

Without another word, Nord stepped through, letting the brass leaves of the hatch close behind him. Then the razor-cogs began to turn, the boarding torpedo drawing back into the void amid gushes of outgassing air.

FUMING, KALE DRAGGED himself to the viewport, a trail of dark blood across the steel deck behind him, in time to see the hive ship's hull falling away.

The capsule turned away to find the *Emathia* hanging in the blackness, and with a pulse of thrusters, it set upon a return course towards the frigate.

NORD THREW HIMSELF into the melee, storm bolter crashing, his force axe a spinning cascade of psychic fury. 'Indus!' He cried, 'I am here! Face me if you dare!'

In the confines of the corridors, he fought with termagants and warriors, stamped ripper swarms into paste beneath his boots, killed and tore and blazed a path of destruction back through the hive. Nord became a whirlwind of blade and shell, deep in the mad glory of combat.

His body sang with pain from lacerations, toxins and impacts, but still he fought on, bolstering himself with the power of his own psionic quickening. The shadows of the Rage and the Thirst were there at his back, reaching for him, ready to take him, and he raced to stay one step ahead. He could not be consumed: *not yet*. His heavy burden rattled against his chest plate.

*Soon*, he told himself, sensing the red and the black. *Very soon*.

Crossing the bone bridge once more, he shouted his defiance – and the tyranids replied in kind.

Winged fiends and fluttering, gas-filled spores fell around him, the gargoyle broods tearing through the air, daring him to attack. He unloaded the storm bolter, tracer shells cutting magnesium-bright flashes in the dark; but for each he killed there were five more, ten more, twenty. The spores detonated in foetid coughs of combustion and without warning the bridge was severed.

Nord fell, his weapons lost, down into the pit where the carnifex lurked. Impact came hard and suffocating, as the Blood Angel sank into a drift of soft, doughy matter collecting around the hive's egg sacs. Tearing the sticky strings of albumen from his armour, he tore free–

And faced his foe.

'You should have fled while you had the chance.' Indus's voice had taken on a fly-swarm buzz. 'We will take you now.'

Flanked by mammoth thorn-backed beasts, the hive tyrant bowed, as if mocking him, allowing Indus to dangle before Nord upon his tendrils. More tentacles snaked forwards, questing and probing.

The aliens waited to taste the stink of his fear, savouring the moment; Nord gave them nothing, instead bending to recover his axe where it had fallen.

'This will be your end, adept,' he said. 'If only you could see what you have become.'

'We are the superior!' came the roar in return. 'We will devour all! You are the prey! You are the beasts!'

Nord took a breath and let the dark clouds come. 'Yes,' he admitted, 'perhaps we are.'

The Black Rage and the Red Thirst, the curses that he had fought against for so long, the twin madness at the core of his being... The psyker let his defences fall before them. He gave himself fully to the heart of the rage, let it fill him.

Power, burning nova-bright, swept away every doubt, every question in his mind. Suddenly it was so very clear to him; there was only the weapon and the target. The killer and the killed.

The aliens charged, and Nord ripped open the gear pack at his belt, drawing the weapon within, running to meet them, racing towards the hive tyrant.

Indus saw the lethal burden in the Blood Angel's hand and felt a cold blade of fear lance through him; the tyrant shook in sympathetic panic. 'No–' he whispered.

'In the name of Sanguinius and the God-Emperor,' the Codicier snarled, baring his fangs. 'I will end you all!'

Captain Gorolev jerked up from the console, his expression set in fear. 'The cogitators register an energy increase aboard the hive ship!'

Xeren's head turned to face him atop his snake-like neck. 'I am aware.'

Gorolev took a step towards the Mechanicus magi. 'That ship is a threat!' he snapped. 'We have completed recovery of the boarding torpedo, and your scouts are lost! We should destroy the xenos! There is no reason to let them live a moment longer!'

'There is every reason!' Xeren's manner of cold, silky dismissal suddenly broke. He rounded on the frigate's commander, his mechadendrites and cyber-limbs rising up behind him in a fan, angry serpents hissing and snapping at the air. All trace of his false politeness faded. 'You test me and test me, ship-master, and I will hear no more! You *will* do as I say, or your life will be forfeit!'

'You have no right–' Gorolev was cut off as Xeren reached out a hand, showing brass micro-lasers where fingers should have been.

'I have the authority to do anything,' he grated. 'That hive is worth more than your life, captain. More than the lives of your worthless crew, more than the lives of Kale and his Space Marines! I will sacrifice every single one of you, if that is what it will cost!'

A silence fell across the bridge; Gorolev's eyes widened, but not in fear of Xeren. He and his officers stared beyond the tech-priest, to the open hatchway behind him.

There, filling the doorway, was a figure clad in blood-red. Xeren spun, his limbs, flesh and steel, coming up before him in a gesture of self-protection.

Brother-Sergeant Kale entered, carrying himself with a limp, his pale face stained with spilled vitae and smoke. His eyes were black with an anger as cold and vast as space.

ARMOUR SCARRED FROM tyranid venom and claw, blemished with bitter fluids, he took heavy, purposeful steps towards the tech-priest. 'My brothers lie dead,' he intoned. 'The blame is yours.'

'I… I was not…' Xeren's cool reserve crumbled.

'Do not cheapen their sacrifice with lies, priest,' growled Kale, his ire building ever higher as he came closer. 'You sent us to our deaths, and you smiled as you did it.'

Xeren stiffened, drawing himself up. 'I only did what was needed! I did what was expected of me!'

'Yes,' Kale gave a slow nod, and reached up to his chest, where the hilt of a combat knife protruded from a scabbed wound. 'Now I do the same.'

With a shout of rage and pain, Kale tore the knife free and swept it around in a fluid arc. The blade's mirror-bright edge found the tech-priest's throat and cut deep, severing veins and wires, bone and metal. The Blood Angel leaned into the attack and took Xeren's head from his neck. The cyborg's body danced and fell, crashing to the deck in a puddle of oil.

'Energy surge at criticality...' Gorolev reported, as alert chimes sounded from the cogitator console.

Kale said nothing, only nodded. He stepped up to the viewport, over Xeren's headless corpse, and watched the hive ship. His hands drew up to his chest in salute, taking on the shape of the Imperial aquila.

'In His name, brother,' he whispered.

HE WAS FALLING.

Somewhere, far beyond his thoughts in the world of meat and bone, he was dying. Claws tearing at him, serpentine tendrils cutting into him, cilia probing to find grey matter and absorb it.

Nord fell into the cascade of sensation. The blood roaring through him. The flawless, diamond-hard perfection of his anger driving him on, into the arms of the enemy.

He had never feared death; he had only feared that when the moment came, he would be found wanting.

That time was here, and he was more certain of his rightness than ever before.

The clouds of billowing crimson, the swelling mist of deep, deep night; they came and took him, and he embraced it.

Somewhere, far beyond his thoughts, a bloody, near-crippled hand curled about the grip of a weapon, tight upon a trigger. And with a breath, a slow and steady breath, that hand released. Let go. Gave freedom to the tiny star building and churning inside.

The fusion detonator Nord had recovered from the weapons locker, the secret burden he had carried back into the heart of the hive ship. Now revealed, now empowered and unleashed.

The new sun grew, flesh and bone crisping, becoming pale sketches and then vapour; and in that moment, as the light became all, in its heart Brother Nord saw an angel, golden and magnificent. Reaching for him. Offering his hand.

Beckoning him towards honour, and a death most worthy.

# BUT DUST IN THE WIND

## by Jonathan Green

THE THUNDERHAWK GUNSHIP dropped through the planet's exosphere like a star falling from heaven, its scorched and scarred hull-plating glowing hot as molten gold. Beneath it lay a vast shroud of cloud cover and beneath that the frozen world of Ixya.

Clouds boiled and evaporated at the caress of the burning craft, and as the vessel continued its descent, those on board were afforded their first view of the snowball world at last.

Ixya might look no more than a vast planet-sized chunk of ice drifting silently through space at the far reaches of the freezing depths of the Chthonian Subsector, but according to the data the Chapter's archivists on board the *Phalanx* had been able to coax from the ancient Archivium's cogitators, it was the foremost provider of essential ores and precious metals to the forge worlds of the Chthonian Chain.

Platinum, iridium, plutonium and uranium were all found buried within the crust of the planet, even though it was compressed beneath ten kilometres of crushing ice in some places. Iron ore was found in vast quantities in great seams running practically the entire circumference of the planet's equator and it was the only attainable source of a number of rarer elements for twelve parsecs.

But all that was currently visible to the Thunderhawk's pilot was kilometre after kilometre of fractured ice sheet, crawling glaciers and frost-formed blades of frozen mountain ridges.

'Any lock on the source of the signal yet?' Sergeant Hesperus enquired of the battle-brother piloting the craft.

'Triangulating now, sir,' Brother-Pilot Teaz replied via the vessel's internal comm.

There was a pause, accompanied by an insistent pinging sound as the *Fortis*'s machine spirit gazed upon the blue-white world through its auspex arrays, seeking to pinpoint the source of the distress signal. Mere moments later, the servitor hard-wired into the gunship's systems in the co-pilot's position began to burble machine code, its eyes glassy and unblinking as it continued to stare perpetually out of the front glasteel shield of the Thunderhawk's cockpit.

'Scanners indicate that it is coming from a location three hundred kilometres from our current position. Signs are that it is uninhabited. But...' Teaz trailed off.

'What is it, brother? What else is the *Fortis* telling you?"

'Very little at that location. But there is a large settlement – a Mechanicus facility of some kind two hundred kilometres from here.'

'The miners,' Hesperus mused. 'And the distress signal isn't coming from there?'

'No, brother-sergeant.'

'And yet the facility is inhabited?'

'Reading multiple life-signs, sergeant. Cogitator estimates somewhere within the region of three thousand souls.'

'And are you reading any other settlements of comparable size anywhere else upon the planet's surface?'

'No, sir. This would appear to be the primary centre of human occupation.'

'Then I think we should pay our respects to the planetary authorities, don't you, Brother Teaz?'

'Shall I hail them, sergeant?' the pilot asked.

'No, brother, that won't be necessary. Besides, I am sure they already have us on their scopes and if they don't already know of our imminent arrival, then they soon will. I think it only right that we meet with those charged with the care of this world face to face. After all, first impressions matter.'

'You think they will brave this blizzard to meet us, brother?'

'If they have any sense, they would brave the warp itself rather than leave a detachment of Imperial Fists unattended.'

'Very good, sir. Landing site acquired. Planetfall in five minutes.'

Keying his micro-bead, Sergeant Hesperus addressed the other battle-brothers on board, strapped within the ruddy darkness of the Thunder-hawk's belly hold.

'Brothers of Squad Eurus, the time has come,' Hesperus said, taking up the venerable thunder hammer that it was his honour to wield in battle along with the storm shield that bore his own personal battle honours. 'Lock helmets, bolters at the ready. We make planetfall in five.'

LIKE A SPEAR of burning gold, cast down from heaven by the immortal Emperor Himself, Thunderhawk *Fortis* made planetfall on the snow-bound world.

With a scream of turbofan afterburners and attitude thrusters – the jet-wash from the craft momentarily disrupting the blizzard sweeping across the barely-visible mass of chimneys, pylons and refinery barns – the *Fortis* touched down on the landing pad located within the facility's outer defensive bulwark.

Power to the engines was cut and the Doppler-crashing white noise of the fans descended to a deafening whine, the craft's landing struts flexing as they took the weight, as the great golden bird settled on the plasteel and adamantium-reinforced platform.

By the time the disembarkation ramp descended and Sergeant Hesperus led the battle-brothers of Squad Eurus out onto the hard standing of the firebase, the Space Marines' ceramite boots crunching on the ice-patched rockcrete, the welcoming committee was already trooping out onto deck to greet them. The blunt shapes of shuttle craft and grounded orbital tugs squatted on the platform, their hard profiles softened by drifts of snow.

Three men, diminutive by the standards of the Emperor's finest, made the long walk from the shelter of an irising bunker door to where Squad Eurus had formed themselves up in a perfectly straight line, ready to receive them.

Although he was at least half a head shorter than either of his two companions, from his bearing, along with the red sash and ceremonial badge of office, to his straining dress jacket, ursine fur cloak, and polished grox-hide jackboots, Hesperus knew at once that the Space Marines' arrival on Ixya had brought none other than the planetary governor – the Emperor's representative himself – to receive them. It was a good sign; Sergeant Hesperus liked to be appreciated.

The three men faced the nine mighty Adeptus Astartes of the Imperial Fists Chapter, resplendent in their black-iron trimmed golden yellow power armour, the jet packs they wore making them appear even more intimidating. Every member of the welcoming committee had to look up to meet Hesperus's visored gaze.

With a hiss of changing air pressures, Sergeant Hesperus removed his helmet and peered down at the shortest of the three. He had to admire the man; his steely expression of resolute determinedness did not falter once.

The governor had a face that looked like it had been carved from cold marble. His pate was balding but the white wings of hair that swept back from his temples and covered his chin gave him an appropriately aristocratic air.

The man held the Space Marine's gaze for several seconds and then bowed, his ursine-skin cloak sweeping the powdered snow from the landing deck. 'We are honoured, my lords.' He rose again and carefully considered the smart line of Space Marines. 'I am Governor Selig, Imperial administrator of this facility and by extension this world. I bid you welcome to Aes Metallum.' Hesperus considered that the man's chiselled expression did not offer the same welcome his words offered. Governor Selig was suspicious of them.

A wry smile formed at the corner of the sergeant's mouth. And so would I be, Hesperus thought, if I were governor and a fully-armed assault squad of Imperial Fists Space Marines arrived unannounced on my watch.

Governor Selig turned to the man at his right hand, a military man wearing a cold-weather camo-cloak over the uniform of a PDF officer. 'May I introduce Captain Derrin of the Ixyan First Planetary Defence Force,' – the man saluted smartly and the governor turned to the towering, semi-mechanoid thing shrouded by a frayed crimson robe to his left – 'and Magos Winze of the Brotherhood of Mars who oversees our mining operation.'

Hesperus noted the huge ceramite and steel representation of the Cult Mechanicus's cybernetic skull heraldry on the towering facade of the structure before the landing pad, the details of the huge icon blurred by the snow that had settled upon it.

'Welcome to Aes Metallum,' the tech-priest hissed in a voice that was rusty with age and underlain by the wheezing of some augmetic respiratory function. A buzzing cyber-skull – looking like a miniature version of the Cult's crest – hovered at the adept's shoulder.

Hesperus acknowledged the tech-priest's greeting with a curt nod of his head.

'What can we do for you, sergeant?' Selig asked.

'Ask not what you can do for us,' Hesperus countered, 'but what we can do for you.'

'My lord?'

'The strike cruiser *Fury's Blade* picked up a faint automated distress call being broadcast from this world three standard days ago. Our glorious Fourth Company was en route on the *Phalanx*, our fortress-monastery, to the Roura Cluster, to bolster the defence of the Vendrin Line against the incursions of the alien eldar. However, it was deemed appropriate to send a single Thunderhawk and accompanying assault squad to assess the level of threat that had triggered this distress beacon accordingly. I presume you are aware of this distress signal yourselves, are you not?'

To his credit, Governor Selig's steely expression didn't change one iota. 'Yes we are, thank you, brother,' he stated unapologetically.

'An explorator team is currently carrying out a survey of that region,' Magos Winze explained, 'searching for new mineral reserves we suspect may be located in the area.'

'And have you sent rescue squads to investigate?' Hesperus challenged.

Governor Selig turned his gaze from the looming Astartes to the PDF officer at his side. 'Captain Derrin?'

'No, sir.'

Hesperus looked at him askance.

'And might I ask why not?'

Captain Derrin indicated the blizzard howling about them with a gesture. The clinging flakes were steadily turning the Imperial Fists' armour from dazzling yellow to white gold.

'It's the ice storm, sir,' he said, pulling his cold-weather camo-cloak tighter about him as he shivered in the face of the freezing wind. 'We're only at the edge of it here but further north it's at its most intense – so cold it'll freeze the promethium inside the tanks of a Trojan. The planes and armour we have at our disposal are not able to withstand its full force.'

Hesperus turned from the captain to the tech-priest, the altered adept's mechadendrites seeming to twitch with an epileptic life all of their own.

'You can confirm this, magos?'

'Captain Derrin is quite correct,' Winze wheezed. 'Aes Metallum's been locked down for three days. However, our meteorological auspex would seem to suggest that the storm is moving east across the Glacies Plateau. In two days it should be safe to send out a team to investigate.'

'Have you had any pict-feed or vox-communication with the explorator team since the storm began?' Hesperus pressed.

'No. Nothing but the signal put out by the automated beacon.'

The Imperial Fist on Hesperus's right, Battle-Brother Maestus, keyed his micro-bead. 'Do you think it could be the eldar, brother-sergeant?'

At mention of the enigmatic alien raiders, Governor Selig's expression faltered for the first time since he had welcomed the Astartes to Ixya.

'The distress beacon could be explained by any one of a dozen or more scenarios,' Magos Winze interjected. 'A snowplough could have fallen into an ice fissure, or the team saw the storm coming and triggered the distress beacon hoping for a quick extraction. We would not wish to keep you from your holy work, brother.'

'We may yet be needed here,' Hesperus countered. He turned to Maestus. 'Remaining here will not tell us whether the eldar are poised to attack this world as well. It is time we followed the signal to its source.'

He addressed each of the Ixyan welcoming committee in turn. 'Captain Derrin, ice storm or no, mobilise your men. Magos Winze, see that your servants run diagnostics of all this facility's defences; I want them primed and ready for action. Governor, good day to you.'

'But–' Selig began before Hesperus cut him off with a curt wave of an armoured hand.

'It is better that you prepare for the worst and ultimately face nothing than it is to do nothing and reap the bitter harvest that follows as a result of your inaction. Look to your defences. Secure the base. We shall return presently. Squad Eurus, move out.'

And with that the nine golden giants boarded the *Fortis* again. Only a minute later, as Governor Selig and the rest of the welcoming committee returned to the shelter of the bunker, the *Fortis* lifted off from the landing platform, the snow flurries returning as the Thunderhawk was swallowed up by the blizzard.

THE FORTIS SHOOK as the freezing winds assailed it, the constant staccato of hailstones pounding its hull-plating like a remorseless barrage of autocannon fire. But the Thunderhawk, as capable of short range interplanetary travel as it was of atmospheric flight, resisted and held firm, Brother-Pilot Teaz steering a course through the hurricane winds and hail towards the spot indicated by the chiming distress signal.

'This is the place,' Teaz said as the Thunderhawk's forward motion suddenly slowed, holding it in a hover above the ice and the snow for a moment before bringing it down in the middle of a whiteout so intense that for all the visibility there was, they might as well have landed on the dark side of the planet; if that had been the case, at least then the Thunderhawk's lamps would have been able to make a difference.

Squad Eurus disembarked from the craft again, Teaz remaining on board as before, in case there was the need for a hasty extraction or the Space Marines found themselves involved in an encounter that required heavier firepower to resolve it than was carried by the members of Hesperus's team.

And yet continued sensor sweeps carried out by the *Fortis's* instruments during the short hop from the Aes Metallum facility, now one hundred kilometres to the south-west, had revealed nothing. No signs of life, no indication of an alien presence, nothing at all. It seemed that there was nothing out there beyond the howling ice storm, other than whatever anomalous geological feature it was that had led the explorators here in search of mineral deposits in the first place.

'Search pattern delta. Battle-Brother Ngaio, I want you up front,' Hesperus instructed his squad members via the helmet comm. He would have struggled to make himself heard by his battle-brothers otherwise, even with their Lyman's ear implants.

In response the nine Imperial Fists began to fan out from the landing site, sweeping the snow-shriven wilderness with their weapons, each alike – bolter in one hand, chainsword in the other, except in Battle-Brother Verwhere's case, who targeted the illusory shapes created by the flurries of gale-blown snow with his plasma pistol. Battle-Brother Ngaio advanced at the forefront, at the apex of the expanding semi-circle of warriors, his chainsword mag-locked to his hip, replaced in his gauntleted hand by the auspex he was carrying.

Hesperus moved forwards, between Ngaio and Battle-Brother Ahx. Then came Ors and Jarda. To Ngaio's left were arrayed, in the same formation, Battle-Brothers Maestus, Verwhere, Haldrich and Khafra.

Not one of them had been born on the same world – Jarda had not even set foot on one of the vassal worlds of the galaxy-spanning Imperium until after he had been inducted into the Imperial Fists Chapter, having been void-born, while Khafra was from the desert necropolis world of Tanis – but they were all brothers nonetheless. They might not have the same predominant eye colour, skin tones, hair or bone structure, but thanks to the gene-seed they all bore inside them now, they were all Imperial Fists and shared the common physiological traits of a Space Marine.

The Imperial Fists gathered their aspirants from a whole network of worlds, many of which they had visited before in the ten millennia since the *Phalanx* had set out upon its never-ending quest to bring the Emperor's mercy and justice to the galaxy. But although the brothers of Squad Eurus might not have come from a common culture or been born of a common ancestry before joining the ranks of the Imperial Fists, since their induction into the Chapter – second only, other agencies claimed, to Great Guilliman's Adeptus Astartes paragons, the Ultramarines – they were all Sons of Dorn now, the superhuman essence of the primarch having been passed down to them through his blessed gene-seed.

Hesperus peered through the whiteout, everything coloured now by the heat spectrum of his helmet's infrared arrays. But even the HUD struggled to reveal any more than he could already see with his own occulobe-enhanced sight.

Shapes came into relief out of the impenetrable whiteness, ice-obscured objects delineated by the subtle variations in light and shade that existed even within this white darkness. Huge things with tyred wheels and caterpillar track-sections, twice as tall as a Space Marine, and bucket scoops large enough to contain a land speeder emerged from the storm-wracked ice-desert.

Servos in his suit whirred as Hesperus scanned left and right, surveying the frozen wrecks of earth-moving machines and the explorators' abandoned equipment.

'Where are the bodies?' he heard Brother Jarda wonder aloud over the helmet comm.

Hesperus had been thinking the same thing. Here were the explorator team's machines, left to be claimed by the ice and snow, but there was no sign of the crews that had driven the hundred kilometres across the ice sheet to bring them to this place.

'Sergeant Hesperus,' Brother Ngaio voxed. 'I have something.'

'It's all right, brother, I see it too,' Hesperus replied.

'No, I mean there's a structure, sir.'

'A structure?'

'It should be right in front of us.'

A gust of biting wind suddenly swept the ice sheet all about them clear of snow and – beyond the frozen, broken shapes of the earthmovers and drilling rigs – Hesperus saw it. It was a great rift in the glacier, as if a great cube had been cut out of the ice where the explorators had dug down into the ice, exposing...

Hesperus tensed.

It was a pyramid. It was caked in ice, half-buried by the drifts of snow. What little of it that was visible appeared to be made from a seamless piece of some unrecognisable compound that looked like dark silver, but it was pyramidal in form and there was no mistaking its origin.

'The soulless ones,' Hesperus growled. Not the renegade eldar they had been expecting perhaps, but xenos
nonetheless – something even more alien than the
piratical raiders. Something utterly inimical to life.

'BROTHERS, WITH ME,' Sergeant Hesperus instructed,
leading the march down the rutted slope of ice that
had been carved from the ice sheet by the
explorators' machines. 'Brother Teaz, remain with the
*Fortis*,' he commanded the Thunderhawk's pilot. 'We
may be in need of the *Fortis*'s legendary firepower
before too long.'

The rest of the Imperial Fists formed up behind
him, trooping after him into the hole, which was ten
metres deep and more than six times that across, that
had been carved into the ice of Ixya.

Over the keening of the wind Sergeant Hesperus
imagined he could hear another sound, like the
echoes of the desperate cries and terrified screams of
those who had met their end here. For there was no
one left to find. They would not find anyone alive
this day; of that fact Hesperus was certain.

THE NINE SPACE Marines gathered before the looming
pyramidal spike of alien metal, their weapons
trained on the xenos structure.

'You think they're in there?' Brother Maestus asked.
He and Hesperus had a unique relationship within
the squad, since they had been aspirants together
almost sixty years before.

'I think that something unspeakable woke, walked
from this tomb and took them.'

'Do we attempt a rescue?' Brother Verwhere asked, his plasma pistol ready in his hand, trained at the curious spherical and hemispherical hieroglyphs etched into the otherwise perfectly smooth surface of the pyramid.

'And rescue what, exactly?' Hesperus challenged his brother. 'We would find nothing alive in there, I can assure you.'

He took a step back from the towering structure.

'This is only the tip of the iceberg,' he said, smiling darkly. 'No, we pull back, return to the Aes Metallum facility. We send an astropathic message to our brethren aboard the *Phalanx* and the *Fury's Blade* and we prepare for a battle the like of which I'll wager this world has never seen.'

'Sir, I have something on the auspex,' Ngaio announced, the adrenaline-rush detectable in his tone.

'Range?' Hesperus demanded, scanning the ice-locked structure in front of him, searching for any sign that the sepulchre was about to open and disgorge its unholy host.

'Sixty metres. Moving this way.'

'Vladimir's bones! Where did that come from?'

'Nowhere, sir. It came out of nowhere!'

'Direction!' Hesperus demanded.

'Heading two-seven-nine degrees!' Ngaio stated, turning to face the approaching menace, bolter in one hand, auspex still gripped tightly in the other.

'Squad Eurus!' Hesperus called to his companions over the sheet ice and howling gale. 'Ready yourselves. The enemy chooses to show itself.'

And then he saw it through the blizzard, a black beetle shape gliding towards the Imperial Fists through the whirling snow.

More than twice as large as a Space Marine, the construct hovered over the frozen ground towards them, its flight unaffected by the powerful wind shear.

Eight articulated metal limbs hung from the iron carapace of its body. The thing reached out with its forelimbs and with a ringing of blades the tips each ratcheted open to form three savage cutting claws. Multiple asymmetrical artificial eyes scanned the Space Marines, pulsing with the eerie green light of an unfathomable xenos intelligence.

'Fire at will!' Hesperus commanded and a cacophony of bolter fire immediately filled the ice hole like the barking of angry hate-dogs.

Mass-reactive shells exploded from the resilient carapace of the construct. The arachnoid-thing jerked and faltered, rotating wildly about its centre of gravity as the battle-brothers found their target.

The spyder-like construct surged forwards again, closing the distance between the Space Marines and it. And was it merely the strange acoustics set up by the flesh-scouring wind keening through the teeth of the weird ice formations that clung to the pyramid, or at that moment did the xenos-construct give voice to a disharmonic shriek of its own?

With a high-pitched scream, a pulse of rippling blue-white energy burned through the whipping winds of the ice storm and struck the soaring spyder. There was an explosion of sparks and one of the construct's fore-claws went whirling away into the storm. The limb landed in a wind-blown drift, still twitching with a macabre life of its own. As the spyder recovered and closed, Brother Verwhere stood his ground, his plasma pistol still trained on the construct as he waited for the weapon to recharge.

Sergeant Hesperus strode forwards, ready to bolster Verwhere's defence. If the spyder evaded the next shot from his plasma pistol, he would ensure that the thing did not escape the wrath of his thunder hammer.

As the spyder construct closed on them, Brother Verwhere fired again, the shot making a molten mess of the thing's head and sending it ploughing into the ice in a sparking, crackling mess, bolts of green lightning arcing from its metal carcass.

'We have multiple contacts,' Ngaio declared clearly over the comm, one eye on the blizzard of returns now painting the scope of his auspex.

And then the snowstorm birthed a host of figures even more macabrely grotesque and yet, at the same time, hauntingly familiar. They possessed the form of hunched humanoid creatures and advanced at a gambolling gait, darting through the ice and snow, reaching for the Space Marines with hands shaped into glinting razor-sharp talons, as long as a man's arm, dripping blood and sticky with gore.

And as if the presence of such soulless, inhuman things was not bad enough, then the grisly trophies with which they had adorned themselves made their very existence all the more mind-wrenching. Their ghoulish garb – the shredded skins they had flayed from the bodies of their victims – eradicated any lingering doubt within the minds of the Space Marines as to the fate of the lost survey team.

As the sinister silver and crimson figures stalked towards them out of the blizzard, Squad Eurus opened fire with their bolt pistols, the rattle of gunfire warped by the wind into something that sounded not unlike the drumming of iron bones on a taut skin of human hide.

Metal bodies jerked and spun, clipped by the mass-reactive shells, or were thrown backwards into the snow when a direct hit was scored.

Hearing a thrumming, insistent buzzing noise, Sergeant Hesperus's attention was drawn away from the approaching alien automatons and onto the approach of another three of the hovering spyder-things.

'Defence pattern gamma,' Hesperus commanded and the eight battle-brothers present reacted immediately, forming a tight circle of ceramite and adamantium armour between the pyramid and the Thunderhawk. With every angle covered, they lay down suppressing fire, dropping spyders and the flayed ones before they could even get close.

'Sergeant,' Teaz's voice came over the comm, 'look to the pyramid.'

Hesperus stepped forwards and dropped another of the skin-wrapped metal skeletons with his crackling thunder hammer and stared at the frozen structure even though he already knew what he would see there.

Under its cladding of ice and snow, part of the

pyramid's solid surface appeared to have liquefied and now rippled like quicksilver. Defying all the laws of physics, the liquid surface remained at a slant, ripples gliding out from its centre as if a pebble had been dropped into a pool of mercury.

All this happened in only a matter of seconds. His attention still half on the approaching xenos constructs, Hesperus turned and spun, bringing his hammer down on another of the spyder-things even as it reached for him with snapping pincer-claws.

Something was emerging from the pool of liquid metal that had formed in the side of the pyramid. At the periphery of his vision, Hesperus saw a skeletal metal thing step out from the fluid shimmering surface and begin to stalk towards the Space Marines' line. Its gleaming metal skull was hung low between its armoured shoulders, its crystal eyes glowing with a malign intelligence. In its gauntlet-like hands the inhuman warrior carried a bizarre-looking weapon of alien design, but nonetheless lethal for all that. Hesperus had read a treatise disseminated by the Cult Mechanicus that postulated how such weapons operated and recognised the glowing green rods that formed what could best be described as the barrel of the gun as a linear accelerator chamber. Beneath this, the firearm sported a cruel, scything blade – a lethal close quarters combat attachment.

'We're not prepared for this,' Hesperus muttered. It was not the way of an Imperial Fists commander to readily give the order to retreat. The Chapter was notorious amongst the Adeptus Astartes for the stubborn determination of its warriors, who would stand

and fight long after the brethren of other Chapters would have quit the field of battle. But nor was it the Imperial Fists way to waste such a precious commodity as experienced battle-brothers, by fighting a suicidal action which would not win them the day and which, in the case of Ixya and the Aes Metallum facility, would leave the Emperor's loyal subjects open to attack, with no hope of victory in the face of the xenos threat.

There was a steady stream of the skeletal warriors emerging from the quicksilver pool now, without there being any indication as to when the reinforcements might come to an end.

Beside him Brother Ors's chainsword bit through the spine of a warrior, sending chewed-up chunks of metal vertebrae flying and leaving shorn gold wiring exposed.

In the face of ever-increasing numbers, having no idea how many there might still be to come, Hesperus called the retreat.

'Squad Eurus! Ignite jump packs and fall back to the *Fortis*. We are leaving – now!'

He did not fall back lightly; it was not the Imperial Fists' way. But Hesperus knew from bitter experience, that where there was one necron, a multitude might follow.

'Brother-Pilot Teaz,' he called into the comm, once again. 'Covering fire, now!'

One after another, in quick succession, the Space Marines' jump packs ignited with a roar and Squad Eurus rocketed skywards.

A split second later searing laser light streaked over

their heads and down into the excavation site, exploding spyders and warriors where it struck as the grounded Thunderhawk's strafing fire found targets even through the obscuring blizzard.

Pulses of sick green lightning burst from the weapons of the advancing warriors, chasing them from the depths of the whiteout, evaporating the falling snow and lending the snowstorm an eerie, otherworldly cast.

Almost as quickly as the Thunderhawk's laser barrage had begun it cut out again.

'Brother Teaz!' Hesperus called into the comm as he began to descend again towards the waiting Thunderhawk. 'We need covering fire, now!'

He could make out the silhouette of the great adamantium craft on the ice beneath them now. What he could not hear, however, was the roar of turbofan engines running up to take-off speed and he could not see pulses of laser-light spitting from the *Fortis's* guns.

As he and his brother Space Marines dropped lower he understood the reason for the Thunderhawk's unprepared condition. The hull of the craft appeared to ripple as if its adamantium plates had fractured and acquired some unnatural form of life.

As they came closer still, Hesperus could see that the undulating surface was in fact formed from myriad beetle-like constructs that were swarming all over the *Fortis*, jamming its flight controls, clogging its propulsion systems and interfering with its weapon arrays.

There were more of the beetling machines

burrowing up through the ice to join the host already smothering the Thunderhawk. If the craft was to be of any use to the Imperial Fists in their flight from this xenos-cursed place, the silver scarabs had to be eliminated.

'Squad Eurus, deploy grenades.'

As well as being armed with bolt pistols and chainswords, each of the Space Marines also carried a number of grenades. Mag-locking their chainswords to their armoured suits, the battle-brothers of Squad Eurus slowed their rapid descent, dropped the primed frag charges where the swarm was thickest, training their pistols on the scarabs interfering with the weapons systems and the Thunderhawk's engines, removing them with precision shots to free the more delicate parts of the craft from the xenos swarm infestation.

The grenades detonated as they hit, sending fragments of alien artifice flying, turning the beetle-things into just so much more shrapnel, clearing a score of the creatures from the fuselage with every blast.

As the Space Marines dropped the last twenty metres to the landing site, they opened up with their bolters, their own strafing fire clearing yet more of the insidious scuttling things from the stricken *Fortis*.

Hesperus landed hard, the ice shuddering beneath his feet. He was up and at the swarm in the time it took him to rise from the crouch in which he braced himself as he landed, batting the scrabbling scarabs clear of the wings of the Thunderhawk, sending a dozen flying with every powerfully concussive blow of his hammer.

But the Space Marines' action against the Thunderhawk was making a difference now. Slowly, the flyer's turbofan engines began to whine as the cockpit controls came online again and Brother-Pilot Teaz coaxed the great craft into life.

Striding into the thick of the skittering beetle-things, Hesperus made his way to the *Fortis's* hold access and, with well-placed sweeps of his crackling hammer head, he beat the scarabs clear of the hatch.

'Brother Teaz, can you hear me now?'

'Re– *czzz*– ving you now, s– *czz*– geant.'

'Then open up and let us in.'

With a grinding whine the embarkation hatch opened and Squad Eurus boarded the Thunderhawk. Brother Khafra, the last on board punched the switch to activate the closing mechanism as the *Fortis* lifted off, shaking the snow from its landing struts and sending the last of the scarabs tumbling from its surface where they had persistently clung onto the outer hull.

As the Thunderhawk continued to gain altitude, Brother-Pilot Teaz swung its nose round, pointing it back in the direction of the mining facility. Sergeant Hesperus, his hearts still racing within the hardened shell of his ribs, peered through the closing crack of the outer hatch and uttered a heartfelt prayer to Dorn and the Emperor. A multitude filled the excavation site before the frozen pyramid, the legions woken by the explorers' innocent interference darkening the snow and ice with their innumerable host.

'Brothers,' he said, 'we return to the facility to prepare for a siege.'

'What news, sergeant?' Governor Selig asked as the great and the good of Aes Metallum met the Imperial Fists again upon the adamantium skirt of the shuttle pad.

Hesperus removed his helmet again before answering the governor.

'Nothing good I fear,' he said, his face hard.

'But did you find the missing explorators?'

'What was left of them.'

The governor stared at him aghast. Hesperus took a long, slow breath, carefully composing what he was about to say in his mind first.

Selig blanched as Sergeant Hesperus told him what had befallen the explorator team and what would soon befall the mining facility. For those who had once claimed this frozen hell as their own had woken from the slumber of aeons to take it back.

'Governor, were it not for our presence upon this world, I would say that the fate of this world was sealed, that Ixya was doomed. But you see here before you ten of the Emperor's finest warriors, each one worth a hundred of those who fight within the Emperor's inestimable armies, and as a result this world is not yet doomed. For as long as you have us to bolster your defence of this bastion, there is still hope.'

'Throne be praised,' Selig gasped, making the sign of the aquila across his chest.

'The Emperor protects.'

Magos Winze's circling mechadendrites formed the holy cog symbol in supplication to the Omnissiah of Mars, accompanied by a chirrup of machine code-prayer.

'Captain Derrin,' Hesperus said, turning to the commander of Ixya's planetary defence force. 'What armour have you? Aircraft? Gun emplacements? How many men do you have at your command? What other defensive measures? I need an inventory of everything you have got at your disposal. You too, Magos Winze. Tell me everything.'

When Captain Derrin had finished running through the PDF's resources on Ixya – from the flight of Valkyries, through to Hades breaching drills, Sentinel power-lifters and Trojan support vehicles – aided by the tech-priest's indefatigable augmented memory, Sergeant Hesperus looked at each of the three men and said, 'Then we prepare for war!'

'PERMISSION TO SPEAK honestly, brother-sergeant,' Brother Maestus said over a closed comm channel so that only Hesperus could hear him.

'For you, Maestus, always.'

'Sir, it is not enough,' the battle-brother said, gravely.

'I know that, brother,' Hesperus replied, 'but what would you have me tell Selig and the others? Take away their hope and we take away the best weapon these people have at their disposal. As it stands, this facility may well be doomed, but if we can hold the enemy at bay long enough, then it is still possible that reinforcements may arrive in time.'

He hesitated and then turned back, calling after the departing tech-priest. 'Magos Winze, a word if you would be so kind.'

Winze appeared to rotate at the waist and then glided back across the hard deck towards them. 'How may I assist you, sergeant?'

'How are the refined minerals you produce here transported to the forge worlds of this subsector?'

'Why,' the adapted adept croaked rustily, 'Mechanicus transport vessels arrive on a regular basis to transport the ores and isotopes we refine here to Croze, Incus and Ferramentum III.'

'And when is the next shipment due to leave?'

'Why, the *Glory of Gehenna* is coming in-system as we speak,' Magos Winze announced, augmetic nictitating eyelids clicking in quick succession. 'Would I be correct in the assumption that you are now cogitating what I predict you to be cogitating, sergeant?'

'Hail the *Glory of Gehenna*. We shall have need of the might of Mars as well as the might of the strength of Dorn's legacy this day.'

LIKE SOME LEVIATHAN void-spawn birthed in the cold, dark depths of space, the Mechanicus vessel *Glory of Gehenna* coasted in the exosphere of the frozen planet a thousand kilometres below, like some vast and ancient cetacean trawling the shallows of an arctic sea.

The servitor bound from the waist down into the ordnance post of the nave-like bridge rotated to face the command pulpit and a string of machine code emanated from the speaker grille that stood in place of a mouth.

The tech-priest at the pulpit-comm smiled in satisfaction, a hundred artificial muscle-bundles articulating the near-dead flesh of his mouth into something approximating the correct facial expression.

'Target confirmed,' Magos Kappel said.

While on the surface of the snowball world everyone and everything – from caterpillar-tracked servitors, as large as a full-grown grox and twenty times as strong, to huge earthmoving machines – was pressed into service in preparing the mining facility for the siege that was to come, the *Glory of Gehenna* prepared to deliver a dolorous blow against the enemy and pre-empt the xenos attack on Aes Metallum Hive.

Dropping into low orbit, the Mechanicus vessel locked onto the coordinates relayed from the surface by Thunderhawk *Fortis*'s machine spirit, the signal boosted by Magos Winze's Mechanicus-maintained communication arrays.

A seismic shudder passed along the length of the *Glory of Gehenna* as with a silent scream the vessel's port and starboard laser batteries fired on the surface of Ixya. They hit the ground with a deviation of only point zero six degrees, due to atmospheric distortion, and pounded the excavation site and the xenos ruins with everything the servants of the Machine-God on board could coax from the ancient weapons batteries, channelling as much energy as they could from the leviathan's ancient plasma core.

Atmospheric gases were split into their component elements as the beams of focussed retina-searing light, as hot as the heart of a sun, speared down through the cloud-festooned atmosphere of the planet, setting the sky on fire, mere nanoseconds later reaching their target on the ground.

Ice melted and water boiled as the furious heat of the *Glory of Gehenna*'s attack burned away the layers of frozen glacier within which the doomed explorator team had found the alien pyramid waiting for them.

Hundreds of the inhuman constructs were wiped out in the initial phase of the bombardment. The skeletal warriors were reduced to their component parts, as units of tomb spyders and swarms of scarabs, too numerous to count, were eradicated alongside them.

In only a matter of seconds half the emerging necron force had been eradicated by one decisive, pre-emptive strike.

But as the clouds of steam drifted clear of the burn site and the whirling snow returned, it soon became apparent to those monitoring the results of the orbital barrage, from both the heavens and one hundred kilometres away within the rockcrete bunkers of the Aes Metallum base, that despite wiping out a significant portion of the burgeoning necron host, the blasphemous structure on the ground – the pyramid itself – still stood. The only thing that had altered about its status was that much more of it had been uncovered by the scouring laser lances as their furious barrage cut through ice many metres deep, exposing not just the primary pyramid, but the peaks of two smaller structures that lay in its deathly shadow.

'Magos Winze,' the adept-master of the *Glory of Gehenna* said, speaking into the pulpit comm-link, addressing the senior adept on the surface. 'I regret to report that the target still stands.'

'Understood, Magos Kappel,' a static-distorted voice replied, echoing back across the gulf of space from the planet below, echoing like the voice of some disembodied machine spirit between the orna-mented metal ribs of the bridge nave. 'Our initial sensor scans suggest that too.'

'We are charging batteries for a second attempt,' Magos Kappel continued, and then broke off abruptly. 'Wait, auspex arrays are detecting fresh activity in the vicinity of the structures.' He stared at the data-splurge scrolling across the pulpit monitor screen. 'Just a nanosecond...'

A series of live-feed data-inputs from the various servitor scanner stations ranged throughout the bridge spiked as a dramatic change in energy output was detected, centred upon the three xenos struc-tures.

No more than four kilometres from the pyramidal hibernation sepulchres, the compacted snow cover-ing the ice sheet fractured like the sun-baked clay bed of a receding summer watering hole. Three crescent-shaped pylon structures shuddered up out of the snow, seismic tremors rippling through the glacier, quantities of the white powder falling from them in fresh cascades as more and more of the pylons were revealed. Each supported a huge green crystal emitter, and all three were already pulsing with pent-up esoteric energies. Finally the alien devices shuddered to a halt, the last of the clinging snow dropping from them in blocks of melting slush.

With the whining thrum of ancient machinery grinding into operation again after countless millennia of inaction, the three pylons rotated slowly, like morning flowers turning to follow the sun. As one they turned and as one their energising crystals glowed into deadly life, as an aetheric light began to trickle like a shower of pulverised emerald dust from the tips of each crescent. With a crack, like the ignition of a thousand rocket launchers, the gauss annihilators fired.

Whips of coruscating energy lashed out from the crystals, focussed by the vanes that projected from the pylons to either side of each emitter that harnessed their unimaginable power, streaming it into a lethal crackling discharge kilometres in length.

The annihilator beams merged a thousand metres up, cutting through the tortured atmosphere, their combined lethal lightning fingertips reaching into the exosphere, not stopping until they made contact with the *Glory of Gehenna* itself.

The annihilating beams stripped the shields from the Mechanicus vessel within seconds setting the port weapons batteries on fire and tearing through the hull plating. The carefully regulated artificial atmosphere on board the ship ignited as it bled out into the void in rippling waves of flame a hundred metres long.

As the beams continued to rip through the Mechanicus vessel, the *Glory of Gehenna* was clearly doomed. Listing badly to port, the ship commenced its descent, its blunt prow glowing magma-red as it plunged head-long through Ixya's upper atmosphere.

THE BLAZING WRECKAGE of the *Glory of Gehenna* fell on Ixya like the divine wrath of the God-Emperor of Mankind Himself. It struck the ice sheet two hundred kilometres east of Aes Metallum, the shockwave of its crash-landing rippling through the crust of ice and rock, hitting Aes Metallum only a minute later, followed by a dense white cloud, a tsunami of snow that was thrown up into the freezing air as the concussive energies raced outwards from the epicentre of the crash site.

The distant crump and boom of its reactor core was also the sound that signalled the beginning of the assault on Aes Metallum.

'Brother-sergeant, they are here,' Ngaio announced from his place on the northern bulwark of the defended facility.

Before its catastrophic death, perpetrated by the gauss annihilators, the *Glory of Gehenna* had eradicated much of the necron force as Magos Kappel tried to destroy the pyramidal structure. But out of the thousands that had already emerged from the tomb, hundreds had still survived the orbital bombardment. And that surviving vanguard force had now reached the walls of the mining facility.

Aes Metallum already had two semi-circular rings of defences, based on the Phaeton pattern – the rear of the facility being shielded by the towering cliff face against which it had been built – but the Imperial Fists had worked hard to bolster these by barricading the gates with earthmoving vehicles. Magos Winze's tech-priests had done what they could to hard-wire a number of the servitors available to them into the gun emplacements in redoubts and atop the bulwarks of the base. Atop the cliffs behind the refinery works and the ore-processing sheds stood yet more servitor-tasked Tarantula gun turrets, covering the reverse approach.

But the Imperial Fists had also used the mining equipment and facilities available to them to prepare a few other surprises with which to challenge the enemy's assault.

Skimming towards them now, over the wind-whipped ice, advanced the destroyers. To the untrained eye they looked like anti-gravitic speeders, only where a land speeder needed a separate pilot, in this example of heretical xenos machinery, the vehicle and its pilot were one and the same. Rising from the prow of each of the skimmer bodies was the torso, arms and head of a humanoid automaton. These mechanoids were more heavily armoured than the warriors Squad Eurus had encountered at the excavation site and were noticeably more heavily armed as well.

As Hesperus peered through a pair of magnoculars at the approaching skimmers he could see that each of the constructs had had its right arm melded into an energy cannon that pulsed with malevolent emerald energy.

'On my mark,' Hesperus announced into his helm comm, 'activate forward countermeasures.'

The Imperial Fists, the serried ranks of the PDF and even the miners of Aes Metallum, who had exchanged hammer-drills for autoguns, waited. The sense of tense anticipation shared by the Space Marines, the half-human things of the Adeptus Mechanicus, and the mortal defenders of Aes Metallum, was a living breathing thing, and its breathing was shallow and its pulse panic-fast.

'Wait for it,' Hesperus muttered under his breath. 'Wait for it.'

They waited. The destroyers drew nearer.

And now scuttling swarms of scarabs, the trooping warriors of the necron host and other skulking or swiftly darting things appeared as the snowstorm abated at last.

Gauss weapons glowed with a foetid green light as the advancing host prepared to fire on the mining facility's defenders.

The destroyers were in range of the defenders' guns now and, more worryingly, the aliens' own weapons were in range too, ready to give the defenders a taste of their lethal lightning discharges.

'Mark!' Hesperus shouted into the comm.

A split second later, the bulwarks of the base were rocked by a series of detonations that threw up great clouds of white snow and black rock that enveloped the speeding necron destroyers. As the Imperial Fists and PDF conscripts had worked to strengthen the base's forward defences, teams of miners, under the supervision of tech-priests, had cut trenches in the ice in which they had laid the explosives they normally used as part of the mining process to open new seams of precious ore. But they had been put to a more war-like use this day.

A moment later, the destroyers emerged from the smoke and fresh-falling snow, trailing smoke, their carapaces scorched and dented. Some were listing badly. One had almost lost its cannon-arm to the charge it had passed over. Another skewed sideways, collided with one of its fellows and the two of them then ploughed into the frozen ground, triggering another detonation that had failed to fire first time round.

Broadcasting on all channels, Sergeant Hesperus cried, 'For Ixya, for Aes Metallum, and for the *Glory of Gehenna*!' His cry was echoed by the miners and PDF troopers while their tech-priest overseers made the sign of the cog and offered up prayers of supplication to the Omnissiah for the thousand souls that had perished aboard the mighty Mechanicus vessel.

Then Hesperus spoke again, standing atop the battlements overlooking the main gate of the facility, behind which had been parked a host of heavy, earth-moving and drilling machinery to form an additional barricade behind the vulnerable entrance. Thrusting his thunder hammer into the sky, he shouted – so that all could hear – 'Primarch. Progenitor, to your glory!'

'And to the glory of Him on Earth!' his brothers bellowed in response.

* * *

THE NECRON ADVANCE hit the outer bulwark like a hammer blow. Destroyers and tomb spyders sprouting particle projectors blasted battlements, gun emplacements and defenders alike with coruscating beams of molecule-shredding energy and searing bolts of hard-white light.

A turret-mounted autocannon magazine cooked off, not thirty metres from the main gate, the gun emplacement disappearing in an expanding ball of black smoke and oily orange flame.

Men caught in the coruscating emerald beams screamed briefly and then died as layer after layer of their bodies was stripped away by the gauss guns.

Necron warriors advanced by the score, rank after rank of the relentless warriors, each locating their targets on the battlements and then picking them off with mechanical precision. Other things, only partially humanoid in form – the elongated spines of their armoured skeleton bodies tapering to lethal shocking blades – moved with bewildering speed, blinking in and out of existence, vanishing in one position only to reappear at the foot of the base's defences. Then they would blink out of existence again and re-materialise atop the battlements, striking with whip-like arms and deadly scalpel-fingers.

More of the facility's guardians screamed and died, in horror as much as in agony as they were cut down by a grotesque vision of their own mortality made manifest.

The ground itself appeared to be moving. And then, through the drifting smoke and whirling snow, the panicked defenders of the curtain defences saw the seething mass of scarabs closing on them, crawling over everything in sight.

With a roar of turbofans, the Thunderhawk *Fortis* swept low over the icy no-man's-land before the walls of Aes Metallum, twin-linked heavy bolters raking the troops massed on the ground in front of the siege works. Where the massive-reactive shells hit, necrons were blown into their component parts, mechanoid body parts raining back down onto the sullied snow in a shower of twisted black metal and fused components.

A second later, Captain Derrin's Valkyries screamed overhead, great blooms of orange fire blossoming in their wake and more of the undying legion fell – destroyers, spyders and warriors alike.

A dreadful scream – like the rending of reality itself – ripped the heavens asunder. Green fire blazed across the firmament and tore the snow-white skies apart as the trailing Valkyrie disintegrated in shredding flames.

The red harvest had begun.

SERGEANT HESPERUS BATTED aside another darting robotic wraith-form, the crackling head of his thunder hammer pulverising its living metal cranium. The thing slid back down the second curtain wall, throwing up a stream of sparks behind it as it scraped against the adamantium-reinforced bulwarks.

The defenders of Aes Metallum had had to abandon the outer defensive ring after a concerted pounding attack by a trio of heavy destroyers had breached the main gate. But losses had been heavy on both sides. As the Imperial Fists performed a rear-guard action, the surviving PDF troopers and others involved in the defence of the facility retreated behind the second curtain wall and the refinery barns and processing manufactorums beyond. Battle-Brother Verwhere triggered another trap, igniting the promethium store that had been positioned between the two gates with a well-placed shot from his plasma pistol.

Flames rose twenty metres into the freezing air, licking at the mechanoid forms pouring through the breach in the base's defences, but doing little in the way of any real harm.

A coruscating cord of dread lightning tore across the sundered ice-field, shredding the tyres from a massive spoil plough and sending the machine sliding sideways.

The particle whip reached out again, sending half a dozen of the curtain wall's defenders to their deaths.

Sergeant Hesperus's gaze immediately went to the source of this devastating attack.

Standing serenely at the centre of the necron strike force, clad in crumbling vestments, was a thing apart from the others of its kind now marching into the compromised mining facility. Its body was the colour of antique silver inlaid with hieroglyphs of gold, its skull tarnished with the fractal patterns of the patina of epochs past. It scanned the progress of the battle raging all around it with tactical interest as it directed its forces into the fray.

It was the calm at the centre of the storm, the eye of the hurricane, and in its hands it clasped its staff of power. With a silent gesture it guided its warriors forwards, towards the breach, glittering arcs of energy crackling between its skeletal digits, its entire being suffused with ancient power.

This was the focus of the necron force's esoteric energies. For this was their lord. As their mechanoid master passed by, those among their number that had already fallen to the Imperials rose to fight again, living metal re-knitting itself, repairing damaged limbs and forging their armoured shells anew.

'Brothers,' Hesperus spoke into the comm, directing his own troops into the fray, 'we have our target. The xenos lord cannot be allowed to stand any longer. It is a blasphemy in the sight of the Emperor. In the name of Dorn, ignite jump packs.'

To which the battle-brothers of Squad Eurus replied in unison, 'And Him on Earth!'

HESPERUS'S BODY SMASHED through the ranks of the milling necrons, sending a number of the xenos flying as his armour-hard body collided with them. His hurtling flight was brought to a sudden stop by the dozer blade of a heavy earth-mover. The bodywork of the huge digger buckled at the impact and Hesperus dropped to the ground, momentarily stunned by the blast from the necron's arcane weapon.

Recovering quickly, he got to his feet again, grey tendrils of smoke rising from the scorched ceramite plates of his power armour. If it hadn't been for the now dented storm shield that he still held fast in his left hand, he would have been lucky to survive the staff of light's unkind ministrations at all.

Raising his thunder hammer above his head once more, he began to pound towards the silver and gold ancient a second time, hammer held high, an unintelligible bellow of battle-rage on his lips. The pace of his pounding footfalls began to pick up as he covered the expanse of ice before his target.

As he ran, servos in his armoured greaves squealing, the necron prepared itself for another onslaught from the Imperial Fists. With his eyes locked on the necron lord, Hesperus could still see the broken and mangled metal carcasses of fallen xenos warriors knit themselves back together – as if he was watching a pict-feed of the destruction of the alien host running backwards – the undying automatons rising from the sullied snow to fight again at their master's side.

Hesperus readied himself both physically and mentally for the necron's retaliatory attack that was sure to come, but kept running.

Hearing the hot roar of a jump pack above him, he looked up and saw Battle-Brother Maestus, shorn of one arm already, descend upon the necron from the sky like the wrath of Dorn himself.

As Maestus dropped on the necron, Hesperus could tell that something was wrong with his battle-brother's jump pack immediately. The Space Marine was doing his damnedest to direct his wild plunge directly onto the target, rather than making a controlled leap across the ice-field. The trail of smoke trailing from the port gravitic thruster attested to the problem as well.

But Hesperus had no idea just how badly damaged Brother Maestus's jump pack was until, preceded by a cry of 'For Dorn!' from the plunging Space Marine, the pack's power core overloaded, resulting in a detonation as powerful as that of a cluster of thermal charges.

Time suddenly slowed for Hesperus as he watched the scene unfold before him as if he were watching a pict-feed playing at half-speed.

He saw the jump pack rip apart like burnt paper as the blast consumed it. He saw Brother Maestus reduced to his component atoms as the resulting fireball from the sub-atomic explosion consumed him. He saw the necron's tattered robes burn away to nothing on the nuclear wind. He watched as the skeletal lord warped, melted and disintegrated nanoseconds later. Then the hungry flames were washing over him and the shockwave hit, sending him somersaulting backwards once more across the vaporised ice-field.

SERGEANT HESPERUS PICKED himself up for a second time and gazed in stunned shock across the ice-field, knowing what he would see there. Nothing at all.

Brother Maestus was gone. Of the necron master, there was no sign either. What there was, was the solidifying bowl of a melted crater focussed on the epicentre of the catastrophic blast. For thirty metres in every direction lay the fallen of the necron host: warriors and wraiths, scarabs and spyders, all obliterated by the blast, their cybernetic components fused into lumps of useless metal, the flicker of artificial automaton intelligence in their eyes fading to the black of oblivion.

The loss of Battle-Brother Maestus was a dolorous wound in the very heart of Squad Eurus, but his passing had dealt an even more dolorous blow against the enemy. Maestus's sacrifice had taken down the entity that had led the necrons into battle. With the ancient's passing the attacking force was as good as defeated.

'Squad Eurus,' Hesperus commanded. 'Sound off!'

As the seven surviving battle-brothers under his immediate command signalled their condition to their sergeant and the rest of the squad, Hesperus stared in wonder at the debris littering the battlefield all around them.

Even as the remaining necron warriors continued to stride towards the mining facility over the ice with lethal purpose blazing in their incandescent eye-sockets, they began to shimmer, their armoured bodies becoming blurred and hazy. And then suddenly Hesperus was staring right through them until they weren't actually there at all.

Even the battle debris of necron constructs besmirching the snow and the crater-gouged ice – up-ended spyders and sparking scarabs included – shimmered and phased out of existence. Soon even the spectral forms of the steel skeletons were no more.

If it had not been for the great smouldering wounds scarring the bulwarks of the base, the wrecked earth-movers, the devastated Trojans, the downed Valkyrie and the bodies of those who had died defending the facility, Hesperus could have believed that there hadn't been an attack launched on the base at all. Of the enemy there was now no sign.

The Imperial allies had won. Aes Metallum had been saved but at a price, a price that had been paid in the blood and the lives of PDF troopers, tech-adepts and one battle-brother of the lauded Imperial Fists Chapter.

A leaden silence descended over the blizzard-blown wastes, falling across the battlefield like a funerary shroud, as autoguns, las weapons and the huge autocannon emplacements ceased firing.

Then, intermittently at first, Hesperus's acute hearing registered the utterances of disbelief of the Ixyans. Many men had died, but Aes Metallum still stood and the enemy had been vanquished.

Gathering pace and momentum, like a snowball rolling downhill, the gasps turned to emotional whoops of joy and of relief, mixed with wailing cries of intense emotion and heartfelt howls of grief.

But, as the sounds of jubilant celebration increased, overwhelming all other expressions of emotion, ringing from the cliffs behind the base, the Imperial Fists remained silent. Their sergeant's dour mood reflected how they all felt.

Hesperus's helm comm crackled into life.

'Sergeant? Are you receiving me?' It was Brother-Pilot Teaz.

'Receiving,' Hesperus confirmed. 'Where are you, brother?'

'Sir, I'm eighty kilometres north of the facility.'

'What news?'

For a moment Hesperus could hear nothing but

the hiss of static over the helm comm. He knew immediately that the news was going to be bad.

'Reinforcements are moving in on your position from the north-east.'

Hesperus took a deep breath, trying hard to dispel the chill that had now permeated even his ossmodula-hardened bones. 'Reinforcements, brother?'

'Well, no, sir, not really, I suppose. It would appear that the force that attacked Aes Metallum was only the vanguard of a much larger reaper force that has risen from inside the pyramid.'

'How much larger, Brother Teaz?'

'A thousand times, sir.'

'Their number is legion,' Hesperus breathed.

THE REMAINING MEMBERS of Squad Eurus met with Governor Selig, Captain Derrin and Magos Winze in the shell of a manufactorum temple. None of them had escaped the battle for the base unscathed. The governor had acquired a haunted, hollow-eyed expression. Captain Derrin's right arm was bound up in a sling that was now soaked with blood. Even the magos showed signs of having played his part in the battle for Aes Metallum: a half-shorn mechadendrite convulsed spastically and there was no sign of his attendant cyber-skull.

'But the battle is won, brother-sergeant,' Selig protested, a haunted look in his eyes. 'The necrontyr are defeated. I witnessed their destruction with my own eyes. You and your men bested them and in their rout the blasphemies quit not only the battle-field but reality itself!'

'The force we defeated was merely the vanguard,' Hesperus stated bluntly, 'but a fraction of the legion of undying xenos constructs that is even now marching on this base.'

'But our hard-won victory cost us dear,' Derrin said hollowly. 'We shall not survive another battle like it, I fear.'

'Whatever else happens, we must not despair,' Sergeant Hesperus told the Ixyans.

'You have been in touch with your brethren?' the magos queried, his croaking words washed through with a static buzz.

'We have reported our status but they are too far away to be able to relieve Ixya and are already on course for the Chthonian Chain. Even if they broke off from that Chapter-sanctioned campaign, they would not reach us in time. The only ones who stand between the necrontyr and their re-conquest of this world is us.'

'But Captain Derrin has made an accurate assessment of the situation. Those who remain cannot hope to win this day.'

'Perhaps not,' Hesperus admitted, 'but that does not mean that the necrontyr shall either.'

'Please explain yourself, Astartes,' the tech-priest crackled.

'Magos, from where does Aes Metallum get its power?'

'We take our energy from the boiling heart of this world, deep, deep below the ice.'

'As I suspected, geothermally.'

'Your point being, sergeant?'

'Captain Derrin, you are right; I fear none of us shall see another dawn, but our deaths shall not be in vain.'

The governor's shoulders sagged, his head hung low.

'We must prepare to sell ourselves dear. We shall die this day, yes, but we shall die as heroes all. For it is in our power to ensure that no more Imperial lives are lost. Through our actions here, this day, we can keep the rest of the Imperium safe from the menace being birthed here.

'Magos Winze – broadcast a repeating signal via your satellite network that Ixya is *Terra Perdita*. Then do all that is necessary to ensure that you overload the geothermal grid. We shall use Aes Metallum's very power source, the beating heart of this Emperor-given world, to split it asunder. This base, and everything in it, shall be destroyed in a volcanic eruption the like of which Ixya has not seen in ten thousand years. We may die this day, but so shall the undying legions of the necrontyr!'

Hesperus's tone was all vehement righteousness.

'In time our battle-brothers will visit this world and our deaths shall be avenged. But for the time being we shall tear this planet apart and blow this place sky high, in His name!'

SERGEANT HESPERUS STOOD atop the inner curtain wall of Aes Metallum, with the battle-brothers of Squad Eurus at his side.

Behind them were gathered the remnants of the PDF, indentured miners and Mechanicus-mustered servitors, battle-weary but resolute the lot of them. The Imperial Fist's rhetoric had lent them the strength they needed to face the end with courage and resolve. Every man, tech-adept and servitor was ready to sell himself dear if it meant they might deny the necrontyr this world and, through their own deaths, bring about the destruction of their hated enemy.

Bowing his head, Hesperus led his battle-brothers in prayer. 'Oh Dorn, the dawn of our being. Lead us, your sons, to victory.'

Hesperus stared, his immovable gaze focussed beyond the limits of the ice-field. As far as his occulobe-enhanced eyes could see, to both left and right, the far horizon glinted silver. The ice storm had blown itself out at last, revealing the necrontyr in all their morbid might as they advanced in a solid line of living metal.

Hesperus hefted his hammer in his hand, the blackened storm shield already in place on his left arm, and heard the hum of Brother Verwhere's energising plasma pistol, accompanied by the clatter of bolt pistols being primed and the growl of chainswords running up to speed.

'In the name of Dorn!' Hesperus bellowed, his eyes still locked on the seething tide of dark metal.

'And Him on Earth!' his fellow battle-brothers shouted, giving the antiphonal response, their battle-cry almost drowned out by the roar of turbofan engines as the *Fortis* roared overhead, to meet the enemy head-on and make the first strike against the xenos hordes.

Through the cockpit of the craft Brother-Pilot Teaz could see the advancing horde in all its terrible glory. Truly could the term innumerable be applied to the host. Where the Imperial Fists had faced hundreds of the mechanical warriors during the initial attack on Aes Metallum, here thousands advanced on the right flank, thousands on the left, thousands more forming the central block, an unstoppable mass of moving metal. From this height individual necrons looked not unlike the scarab swarms that now turned the sky black above them as millions of the beetle-form constructs took to the air.

Hesperus cast his eyes from the soaring Thunderhawk to the seething mass of silent metal warriors that stretched from the ancient sepulchre complex to the very gates of the devastated refinery, covering every centimetre of the ice wastes in between.

The planet's ancient masters had returned: the necrontyr. Their number was legion.

And they would show no mercy to the servants of the Emperor – not that the Imperial Fists would have sought it – for their name was death.

And today, Sergeant Hesperus decided, was a good day to die.

*That we, in our arrogance, believed that humankind was first among the races of this galaxy will be exposed as folly of the worst kind upon the awakening of these ancient beings. Any hopes, dreams or promises of salvation are naught but dust in the wind.*

Excerpted from the *Dogma Omniastra*

# EXHUMED

## by Steve Parker

THE THUNDERHAWK GUNSHIP loomed out of the clouds like a monstrous bird of prey, wings spread, turbines growling, airbrakes flared to slow it for landing. It was black, its fuselage marked with three symbols: the Imperial aquila, noble and golden; the 'I' of the Emperor's Holy Inquisition, a symbol even the righteous knew better than to greet gladly; and another symbol, a skull cast in silver with a gleaming red, cybernetic eye. Derlon Saezar didn't know that one, had never seen it before, but it sent a chill up his spine all the same. Whichever august Imperial body the symbol represented was obviously linked to the Holy Inquisition. That couldn't be good news.

Eyes locked to his vid-monitor, Saezar watched tensely as the gunship banked hard towards the small landing facility he managed, its prow slicing through the veils of windblown dust like a knife through silk. There was a burst of static-riddled speech on his headset. In response, he tapped several codes into the console in front of him, keyed his microphone and said, 'Acknowledged, One-Seven-One. Clearance codes accepted. Proceed to Bay Four. This is an enclosed atmosphere facility. I'm uploading our safety and debarkation protocols to you now. Over.'

His fingers rippled over the console's runeboard, and the massive metal jaws of Bay Four began to grate open, ready to swallow the unwelcome black craft. Thick toxic air rushed in. Breathable air rushed out. The entire facility shuddered and groaned in complaint, as it always did when a spacecraft came or went. The Adeptus Mechanicus had built this station, Orga Station, quickly and with the minimum systems and resources it would need to do its job. No more, no less.

It was a rusting, dust-scoured place, squat and ugly on the outside, dank and gloomy within. Craft arrived, craft departed. Those coming in brought slaves, servitors, heavy machinery and fuel. Saezar didn't know what those leaving carried. The magos who had hired him had left him in no doubt that curiosity would lead to the termination of more than his contract. Saezar was smart enough to believe it. He and his staff kept their heads down and did their jobs. In another few years, the tech-priests would be done here. They had told him as much. He would go back to Jacero then, maybe buy a farm with the money he'd have saved, enjoy air that didn't kill you on the first lungful.

That thought called up a memory Saezar would have given a lot to erase. Three weeks ago, a malfunction in one of the Bay Two extractors left an entire work crew breathing this planet's lethal air. The bay's vid-pictors had caught it all in fine detail, the way the technicians and slaves staggered in agony towards the emergency airlocks, clawing at their throats while blood streamed from their mouths, noses and eyes. Twenty-three men dead. It had taken only seconds, but Saezar knew the sight would be with him for life. He shook himself, trying to cast the memory off.

The Thunderhawk had passed beyond the outer pictors' field of view. Saezar switched to Bay Four's internal pictors and saw the big black craft settle heavily on its landing stanchions. Thrusters cooled. Turbines whined down towards silence. The outer doors of the landing bay clanged shut. Saezar hit the winking red rune on the top right of his board and flooded the bay with the proper nitrogen and oxygen mix. When his screen showed everything was in the green, he addressed the pilot of the Thunderhawk again.

'Atmosphere restored, One-Seven-One. Bay Four secure. Free to debark.'

There was a brief grunt in answer. The Thunderhawk's front ramp lowered. Yellow light spilled out from inside, illuminating the black metal grille of the bay floor. Shadows appeared in that light – big shadows – and, after a moment, the figures that cast them began to descend the ramp. Saezar leaned forwards, face close to his screen.

'By the Throne,' he whispered to himself.

With his right hand, he manipulated one of the bay vid-pictors by remote, zooming in on the figure striding in front. It was massive, armoured in black ceramite, its face hidden beneath a cold, expressionless helm. On one great pauldron, the left, Saezar saw the same skull icon that graced the ship's prow. On the right, he saw another skull on a field of white, two black scythes crossed behind it. Here was yet another icon Saezar had never seen before, but he knew well enough the nature of the being that bore it. He had seen such beings rendered in paintings and stained glass, cut from marble or cast in precious metal. It was a figure of legend, and it was not alone.

Behind it, four others, similarly armour-clad but each bearing different iconography on their right pauldrons, marched in formation. Saezar's heart was in his throat. He tried to swallow, but his mouth was dry. He had never expected to see such beings with his own eyes. No one did. They were heroes from the stories his father had read to him, stories told to all children of the Imperium to give them hope, to help them sleep at night. Here they were in flesh and bone and metal.

Space Marines! Here! At Orga Station!

And there was a further incredible sight yet to come. Just as the five figures stepped onto the grille-work floor, something huge blotted out all the light from inside the craft. The Thunderhawk's ramp shook with thunderous steps. Something incredible emerged on two stocky, piston-like legs. It was vast and angular and impossibly powerful-looking, like a walking tank with fists instead of cannon.

It was a Dreadnought, and, even among such legends as these, it was in a class of its own.

Saezar felt a flood of conflicting emotion, equal parts joy and dread.

The Space Marines had come to Menatar, and where they went, death followed.

'MENATAR,' SAID THE tiny hunched figure, more to himself than to any of the black-armoured giants he shared the pressurised mag-rail carriage with. 'Second planet of the Ozyma-138 system, Hatha Subsector, Ultima Segmentum. Solar orbital period, one-point-one-three Terran standard. Gravity, zero-point-eight-three Terran standard.' He looked up, his tiny black eyes meeting those of Siefer Zeed, the Raven Guard. 'The atmosphere is a thick nitrogen-sulphide and carbon dioxide mix. Did you know that? Utterly deadly to the non-augmented. I doubt even you Adeptus Astartes could breathe it for long. Even our servitors wear air tanks here.'

Zeed stared back indifferently at the little tech-priest. When he spoke, it was not in answer. His words were directed to his right, to his squad leader, Lyandro Karras, Codicier Librarian of the Death Spectres Chapter, known officially in Deathwatch circles as Talon Alpha. That wasn't what Zeed called him, though. 'Tell me again, Scholar, why we get all the worthless jobs.'

Karras didn't look up from the boltgun he was muttering litanies over. Times like these, the quiet times, were for meditation and proper observances, something the Raven Guard seemed wholly unable to grasp. Karras had spent six years as leader of this kill-team. Siefer Zeed, nicknamed Ghost for his alabaster skin, was as irreverent today as he had been when they'd first met. Perhaps he was even worse.

Karras finished murmuring his Litany of Flawless Operation and sighed. 'You know why, Ghost. If you didn't go out of your way to anger Sigma all the time, maybe those Scimitar bastards would be here instead of us.'

Talon Squad's handler, an inquisitor lord known only as Sigma, had come all too close to dismissing Zeed from active duty on several occasions, a terrible dishonour not just for the Deathwatch member in question, but for his entire Chapter. Zeed frequently tested the limits of Sigma's need-to-know policy, not to mention the inquisitor's patience. But the Raven Guard was a peerless killing machine at close range, and his skill with a pair of lightning claws, his signature weapon, had won the day so often that Karras and the others had stopped counting.

Another voice spoke up, a deep rumbling bass, its tones warm and rich. 'They're not all bad,' said Maximmion Voss of the Imperial Fists. 'Scimitar Squad, I mean.'

'Right,' said Zeed with good-natured sarcasm. 'It's not like you're biased, Omni. I mean, every Black Templar or Crimson Fist in the galaxy is a veritable saint.'

Voss grinned at that.

There was a hiss from the rear of the carriage where Ignatio Solarion and Darrion Rauth, Ultramarine and Exorcist respectively, sat in relative silence. The hiss had come from Solarion.

'Something you want to say, Prophet?' said Zeed with a challenging thrust of his chin.

Solarion scowled at him, displaying the full extent of his contempt for the Raven Guard. 'We are with company,' he said, indicating the little tech-priest who had fallen silent while the Deathwatch Space Marines talked. 'You would do well to remember that.'

Zeed threw Solarion a sneer, then turned his eyes back to the tech-priest. The man had met them on the mag-rail platform at Orga Station, introducing himself as Magos Iapetus Borgovda, the most senior adept on the planet and a xeno-heirographologist specialising in the writings and history of the Exodites, offshoot cultures of the eldar race. They had lived here once, these Exodites, and had left many secrets buried deep in the drifting red sands.

That went no way to explaining why a Deathwatch kill-team was needed, however, especially now. Menatar was a dead world. Its sun had become a red giant, a K3-type star well on its way to final collapse. Before it died, however, it would burn off the last of Menatar's atmosphere, leaving little more than a ball of molten rock. Shortly after that, Menatar would cool and there would be no trace of anyone ever having set foot here at all. Such an end was many tens of thousands of years away, of course. Had the Exodites abandoned this world early, knowing its eventual fate? Or had something else driven them off? Maybe the xeno-heirographologist would find the answers eventually, but that still didn't tell Zeed anything about why Sigma had sent some of his key assets here.

Magos Borgovda turned to his left and looked out the viewspex bubble at the front of the mag-rail carriage. A vast dead volcano dominated the skyline. The mag-rail car sped towards it so fast the red dunes and rocky spires on either side of the tracks went by in a blur. 'We are coming up on Typhonis Mons,' the magos wheezed. 'The noble Priesthood of Mars cut a tunnel straight through the side of the crater, you know. The journey will take another hour. No more than that. Without the tunnel–'

'Good,' interrupted Zeed, running the fingers of one gauntleted hand through his long black hair. His eyes flicked to the blades of the lightning claws fixed to the magnetic couplings on his thigh-plates. Soon it would be time to don the weapons properly, fix his helmet to its seals, and step out onto solid ground. Omni was tuning the suspensors on his heavy bolter. Solarion was checking the bolt mechanism of his sniper rifle. Karras and Rauth had both finished their final checks already.

If there is nothing here to fight, why were we sent so heavily armed? Zeed asked himself.

He thought of the ill-tempered Dreadnought riding alone in the other carriage.

And why did we bring Chyron?

THE MAG-RAIL CARRIAGE slowed to a smooth halt beside a platform cluttered with crates bearing the cog-and-skull mark of the Adeptus Mechanicus. On either side of the platform, spreading out in well-ordered concentric rows, were scores of stocky pre-fabricated huts and storage units, their low roofs piled with ash and dust. Thick insulated cables snaked everywhere, linking heavy machinery to generators; supplying light, heat and atmospheric stability to the sleeping quarters and mess blocks. Here and there, cranes stood tall against the wind. Looming over everything were the sides of the crater, penning it all in, lending the place a strange quality, almost like being out-doors and yet indoors at the same time.

Borgovda was clearly expected. Dozens of acolytes, robed in the red of the Martian Priesthood and fitted with breathing apparatus, bowed low when he emerged from the carriage. Around them, straight-backed skitarii troopers stood to attention with lasguns and hellguns clutched diagonally across their chests.

Quietly, Voss mumbled to Zeed, 'It seems our new acquaintance didn't lie about his status here. Perhaps you should have been more polite to him, paper-face.'

'I don't recall you offering any pleasantries, tree-trunk,' Zeed replied. He and Voss had been friends since the moment they met. It was a rapport that none of the other kill-team members shared, a fact that only served to further deepen the bond. Had anyone else called Zeed *paper-face*, he might well have eviscerated them on the spot. Likewise, few would have dared to call the squat, powerful Voss *tree-trunk*. Even fewer would have survived to tell of it. But, between the two of them, such names were taken as a mark of trust and friendship that was truly rare among the Deathwatch.

Magos Borgovda broke from greeting the rows of fawning acolytes and turned to his black-armoured escorts. When he spoke, it was directly to Karras, who had identified himself as team leader during introductions.

'Shall we proceed to the dig-site, lord? Or do you wish to rest first?'

'Astartes need no rest,' answered Karras flatly.

It was a slight exaggeration, of course, and the twinkle in the xeno-heirographologist's eye suggested he knew as much, but he also knew that, by comparison to most humans, it was as good as true. Borgovda and his fellow servants of the Machine-God also required little rest.

'Very well,' said the magos. 'Let us go straight to the pit. My acolytes tell me we are ready to initiate the final stage of our operation. They await only my command.'

He dismissed all but a few of the acolytes, issuing commands to them in sharp bursts of machine code language, and turned east. Leaving the platform behind them, the Deathwatch followed. Karras walked beside the bent and robed figure, consciously slowing his steps to match the speed of the tech-priest. The others, including the massive, multi-tonne form of the Dreadnought, Chyron, fell into step behind them. Chyron's footfalls made the ground tremble as he brought up the rear.

Zeed cursed at having to walk so slowly. Why should one such as he, one who could move with inhuman speed, be forced to crawl at the little tech-priest's pace? He might reach the dig-site in a fraction of the time and never break sweat. How long would it take at the speed of this grinding, clicking, wheezing half-mechanical magos?

Eager for distraction, he turned his gaze to the inner slopes of the great crater in which the entire excavation site was located. This was Typhonis Mons, the largest volcano in the Ozyma-138 system. No wonder the Adeptus Mechanicus had tunnelled all those kilometres through the crater wall. To go up and over the towering ridgeline would have taken significantly more time and effort. Any road built to do so would have required more switchbacks than was reasonable. The caldera was close to two and a half kilometres across, its jagged rim rising well over a kilometre on every side.

Looking more closely at the steep slopes all around him, Zeed saw that many bore signs of artifice. The signs were subtle, yes, perhaps eroded by time and wind, or by the changes in atmosphere that the expanding red giant had wrought, but they were there all the same. The Raven Guard's enhanced visor-optics, working in accord with his superior gene-boosted vision, showed him crumbled door-ways and pillared galleries.

Had he not known this world for an Exodite world, he might have passed these off as natural structures, for there was little angular about them. Angularity was something one saw everywhere in human construction, but far less so in the works of the hated, inexplicable eldar. Their structures, their craft, their weapons – each seemed almost grown rather than built, their forms fluid, gracefully organic. Like all righteous warriors of the Imperium, Zeed hated them. They denied man's destiny as ruler of the stars. They stood in the way of expansion, of progress.

He had fought them many times. He had been there when forces had contested human territory in the Adiccan Reach, launching blisteringly fast raids on worlds they had no right to claim. They were good foes to fight. He enjoyed the challenge of their speed, and they were not afraid to engage with him at close quarters, though they often retreated in the face of his might rather than die honourably.

Cowards.

Such a shame they had left this world so long ago. He would have enjoyed fighting them here.

In fact, he thought, flexing his claws in irritation, just about any fight would do.

SIX MASSIVE CRANES struggled in unison to raise their load from the circular black pit in the centre of the crater. They had buried this thing deep – deep enough that no one should ever have disturbed it here. But Iapetus Borgovda had transcribed the records of that burial, records found on a damaged craft that had been lost in the warp only to emerge centuries later on the fringe of the Imperium. He had been on his way to present his findings to the Genetor Biologis himself when a senior magos by the name of Serjus Altando had intercepted him and asked him to present his findings to the Ordo Xenos of the Holy Inquisition first.

After that, Borgovda had never gotten around to presenting his work to his superiors on Mars. The mysterious inquisitor lord that Magos Altando served had guaranteed Borgovda all the resources he would need to make the discovery entirely his own. The credit, Altando promised, need not be shared with anyone else. Borgovda would be revered for his work. Perhaps, one day, he would even be granted genetor rank himself.

And so it was that mankind had come to Menatar and had begun to dig where no one was supposed to.

The fruits of that labour were finally close at hand. Borgovda's black eyes glittered like coals beneath the clear bubble of his breathing apparatus as he watched each of the six cranes reel in their thick poly-steel cables. With tantalising slowness, something huge and ancient began to peek above the lip of the pit. A hundred skitarii troopers and gun-servitors inched forwards, weapons raised. They had no idea what was emerging. Few did.

Borgovda knew. Magos Altando knew. Sigma knew. Of these three, however, only Borgovda was present in person. The others, he believed, were light years away. This was *his* prize alone, just as the inquisitor had promised. This was *his* operation. As more of the object cleared the lip of the pit, he stepped forwards himself. Behind him, the Space Marines of Talon Squad gripped their weapons and watched.

The object was almost entirely revealed now, a vast sarcophagus, oval in shape, twenty-three metres long on its vertical axis, sixteen metres on the horizontal. Every centimetre of its surface, a surface like nothing so much as polished bone, was intricately carved with script. By force of habit, the xeno-heirographologist began translating the symbols with part of his mind while the rest of it continued to marvel at the beauty of what he saw. Just what secrets would this object reveal?

He, and other Radicals like him, believed mankind's salvation, its very future, lay not with the technological stagnation in which the race of men was currently mired, but with the act of understanding and embracing the technology of its alien enemies. And yet, so many fools scorned this patently obvious truth. Borgovda had known good colleagues, fine inquisitive magi like himself, who had been executed for their beliefs. Why did the Fabricator General not see it? Why did the mighty Lords of Terra not understand? Well, he would make them see. Sigma had promised him all the resources he would need to make the most of this discovery. The Holy Inquisition was on his side. This time would be different.

The object, fully raised above the pit, hung there in all its ancient, inscrutable glory. Borgovda gave a muttered command into a vox-piece, and the cranes began a slow, synchronised turn.

Borgovda held his breath.

They moved the vast sarcophagus over solid ground and stopped.

'Yes,' said Borgovda over the link. 'That's it. Now lower it gently.'

The crane crews did as ordered. Millimetre by millimetre, the oval tomb descended.

Then it lurched.

One of the cranes gave a screech of metal. Its frame twisted sharply to the right, titanium struts crumpling like tin.

'What's going on?' demanded Borgovda.

From the corner of his vision, he noted the Deathwatch stepping forwards, cocking their weapons, and the Dreadnought eagerly flexing its great metal fists.

A panicked voice came back to him from the crane operator in the damaged machine. 'There's something moving inside that thing,' gasped the man. 'Something really heavy. Its centre of gravity is shifting all over the place!'

Borgovda's eyes narrowed as he scrutinised the hanging oval object. It was swinging on five taut cables now, while the sixth, that of the ruined crane, had gone slack. The object lurched again. The movement was clearly visible this time, obviously generated by massive internal force.

'Get it onto the ground,' Borgovda barked over the link, 'but carefully. Do not damage it.'

The cranes began spooling out more cable at his command, but the sarcophagus gave one final big lurch and crumpled two more of the sturdy machines. The other three cables tore free, and it fell to the ground with an impact that shook the closest slaves and acolytes from their feet.

Borgovda started towards the fallen sarcophagus, and knew that the Deathwatch were right behind him. Had the inquisitor known this might happen? Was that why he had sent his angels of death and destruction along?

Even at this distance, some one hundred and twenty metres away, even through all the dust and grit the impact had kicked up, Borgovda could see sigils begin to glow red on the surface of the massive object. They blinked on and off like warning lights, and he realised that was exactly what they were. Despite all the irreconcilable differences between the humans and the aliens, this message, at least, meant the same.

Danger!

There was a sound like cracking wood, but so loud it was deafening.

Suddenly, one of the Deathwatch Space Marines roared in agony and collapsed to his knees, gauntlets pressed tight to the side of his helmet. Another Adeptus Astartes, the Imperial Fist, raced forwards to his fallen leader's side.

'What's the matter, Scholar? What's going on?'

The one called Karras spoke through his pain, but there was no mistaking the sound of it, the raw, nerve-searing agony in his words. 'A psychic beacon!' he growled through clenched teeth. 'A psychic beacon just went off. The magnitude–'

He howled as another wave of pain hit him, and the sound spoke of a suffering that Borgovda could hardly imagine.

Another of the kill-team members, this one with a pauldron boasting a daemon's skull design, stepped forwards with boltgun raised and, incredibly, took aim at his leader's head.

The Raven Guard moved like lightning. Almost too fast to see, he was at this other's side, knocking the muzzle of the boltgun up and away with the back of his forearm. 'What the hell are you doing, Watcher?' Zeed snapped. 'Stand down!'

The Exorcist, Rauth, glared at Zeed through his helmet visor, but he turned his weapon away all the same. His finger, however, did not leave the trigger.

'Scholar,' said Voss. 'Can you fight it? Can you fight through it?'

The Death Spectre struggled to his feet, but his posture said he was hardly in any shape to fight if he had to. 'I've never felt anything like this!' he hissed. 'We have to knock it out. It's smothering my... gift.' He turned to Borgovda. 'What in the Emperor's name is going on here, magos?'

'Gift?' spat Rauth in an undertone.

Borgovda answered, turning his black eyes back to the object as he did. It was on its side about twenty metres from the edge of the pit, rocking violently as if something were alive inside it.

'The Exodites...' he said. 'They must have set up some kind of signal to alert them when someone... interfered. We've just set it off.'

'Interfered with what?' demanded Ignatio Solarion. The Ultramarine rounded on the tiny tech-priest. 'Answer me!'

There was another loud cracking sound. Borgovda looked beyond Solarion and saw the bone-like surface of the sarcophagus split violently. Pieces shattered and flew off. In the gaps they left, something huge and dark writhed and twisted, desperate to be free.

The magos was transfixed.

'I asked you a question!' Solarion barked, visibly fighting to restrain himself from striking the magos.

'What does the beacon alert them to?'

'To that,' said Borgovda, terrified and exhilarated all at once. 'To the release of… of whatever they buried here.'

'They left it alive?' said Voss, drawing abreast of Solarion and Borgovda, his heavy bolter raised and ready.

Suddenly, everything slotted into place. Borgovda had the full context of the writing he had deciphered on the sarcophagus's surface, and, with that context, came a new understanding.

'They buried it,' he told Talon Squad, 'because they couldn't kill it!'

There was a shower of bony pieces as the creature finally broke free of the last of its tomb and stretched its massive serpentine body for all to see. It was as tall as a Warhound Titan, and, from the look of it, almost as well armoured. Complex mouthparts split open like the bony, razor-lined petals of some strange, lethal flower. Its bizarre jaws dripped with corrosive fluids. This beast, this nightmare leviathan pulled from the belly of the earth, shivered and threw back its gargantuan head.

A piercing shriek filled the poisonous air, so loud that some of the skitarii troopers closest to it fell down, choking on the deadly atmosphere. The creature's screech had shattered their visors.

'Well maybe *they* couldn't kill it,' growled Lyandro Karras, marching stoically forwards through waves of psychic pain, 'But *we* will! To battle, brothers, in the Emperor's name!'

\* \* \*

SEARING LANCES OF las-fire erupted from all directions at once, centring on the massive worm-like creature that was, after so many long millennia, finally free. Normal men would have quailed in the face of such an overwhelming foe. What could such tiny things as humans do against something like this? But the skitarii troopers of the Adeptus Mechanicus had been rendered all but fearless, their survival instincts overridden by neural programming, augmentation and brain surgery. They did not flee as other men would have. They surrounded the beast, working as one to put as much firepower on it as possible.

A brave effort, but ultimately a wasted one. The creature's thick plates of alien chitin shrugged off their assault. All that concentrated firepower really achieved was to turn the beast's attention on its attackers. Though sightless in the conventional sense, it sensed everything. Rows of tiny cyst-like nodules running the length of its body detected changes in heat, air pressure and vibration to the most minute degree. It knew exactly where each of its attackers stood. Not only could it hear their beating hearts, it could feel them vibrating through the ground and the air. Nothing escaped its notice.

With incredible speed for a creature so vast, it whipped its heavy black tail forwards in an arc. The air around it whistled. Skitarii troopers were cut down like stalks of wheat, crushed by the dozen, their rib cages pulverised. Some were launched into the air, their bodies falling like mortar shells a second later, slamming down with fatal force onto the corrugated metal roofs of the nearby storage and accommodation huts.

Talon Squad was already racing forwards to join the fight. Chyron's awkward run caused crates to fall from their stacks. Adrenaline flooded the wretched remains of his organic body, a tiny remnant of the Astartes he had once been, little more now than brain, organs and scraps of flesh held together, kept alive, by the systems of his massive armoured chassis.

'Death to all xenos!' he roared, following close behind the others.

At the head of the team, Karras ran with his bolter in hand. The creature was three hundred metres away, but he and his squadmates would close that gap all too quickly. What would they do then? How did one fight a monster like this?

There was a voice on the link. It was Voss.

'A trygon, Scholar? A mawloc?'

'No, Omni,' replied Karras. 'Same genus, I think, but something we haven't seen before.'

'Sigma knew,' said Zeed, breaking in on the link.

'Aye,' said Karras. 'Knew or suspected.'

'Karras,' said Solarion. 'I'm moving to high ground.'

'Go.'

SOLARION'S BOLT-RIFLE, A superbly-crafted weapon, its like unseen in the armouries of any Adeptus Astartes Chapter but the Deathwatch, was best employed from a distance. The Ultramarine broke away from the charge of the others. He sought out the tallest structure in the crater that he could reach quickly. His eyes found it almost immediately. It was behind him – the loading crane that served the mag-rail line. It was slightly shorter than the cranes that had been used to lift the entombed creature out of the pit, but each of those were far too close to the beast to be useful. This one would do well. He ran to the foot of the crane, to the stanchions that were steam-bolted to the ground, slung his rifle over his right pauldron, and began to climb.

The massive tyranid worm was scything its tail through more of the skitarii, and their numbers dropped to half. Bloody smears marked the open concrete. For all their fearlessness and tenacity, the Mechanicus troops hadn't even scratched the blasted thing. All they had managed was to put the beast in a killing frenzy at the cost of their own lives. Still they fought, still they poured blinding spears of fire on it, but to no avail. The beast flexed again, tail slashing forwards, and another dozen died, their bodies smashed to a red pulp.

'I hope you've got a plan, Scholar,' said Zeed as he ran beside his leader. 'Other than *kill the bastard*, I mean.'

'I can't channel psychic energy into *Arquemann*,' said Karras, thinking for a moment that his ancient force sword might be the only thing able to crack the brute's armoured hide. 'Not with that infernal beacon drowning me out. But if we can stop the beacon… If I can get close enough–'

He was cut off by a calm, cold and all-too-familiar voice on the link.

'Specimen Six is not to be killed under any circumstances, Talon Alpha. I want the creature alive!'

'Sigma!' spat Karras. 'You can't seriously think... No! We're taking it down. We have to!'

Sigma broadcast his voice to the entire team.

'Listen to me, Talon Squad. That creature is to be taken alive at all costs. Restrain it and prepare it for transport. Brother Solarion has been equipped for the task already. Your job is to facilitate the success of his shot, then escort the tranquilised creature back to the *Saint Nevarre*. Remember your oaths. Do as you are bid.'

It was Chyron, breaking his characteristic brooding silence, who spoke up first.

'This is an outrage, Sigma. It is a tyranid abomination and Chyron will kill it. We are Deathwatch. Killing things is what we do.'

'You will do as ordered, Lamenter. All of you will. Remember your oaths. Honour the treaties, or return to your brothers in disgrace.'

'I have no brothers left,' Chyron snarled, as if this freed him from the need to obey.

'Then you will return to nothing. The Inquisition has no need of those who cannot follow mission parameters. The Deathwatch even less so.'

Karras, getting close to the skitarii and the foe, felt his lip curl in anger. This was madness.

'Solarion,' he barked, 'how much did you know?'

'Some,' said the Ultramarine, a trace of something unpleasant in his voice. 'Not much.'

'And you didn't warn us, brother?' Karras demanded.

'Orders, Karras. Unlike some, I follow mine to the letter.'

Solarion had never been happy operating under the Death Spectre Librarian's command. Karras was from a Chapter of the Thirteenth Founding. To Solarion, that made him inferior. Only the Chapters of the First Founding were worthy of unconditional respect, and even some of those...

'Magos Altando issued me with special rounds,' Solarion went on. 'Neuro-toxins. I need a clear shot on a soft, fleshy area. Get me that opening, Karras, and Sigma will have what he wants.'

Karras swore under his helm. He had known all along that something was up. His psychic gift did not extend to prescience, but he had sensed something dark and ominous hanging over them from the start.

The tyranid worm was barely fifty metres away now, and it turned its plated head straight towards the charging Deathwatch Space Marines. It could hardly have missed the thundering footfalls of Chyron, who was another thirty metres behind Karras, unable to match the swift pace of his smaller, lighter squadmates.

'The plan, Karras!' said Zeed, voice high and anxious.

Karras had to think fast. The beast lowered its foresections and began slithering towards them, sensing these newcomers were a far greater threat than the remaining skitarii.

Karras skidded to an abrupt halt next to a skitarii sergeant and shouted at him, 'You! Get your forces out. Fall back towards the mag-rail station.'

'We fight,' insisted the skitarii. 'Magos Borgovda has not issued the command to retreat.'

Karras grabbed the man by the upper right arm and almost lifted him off his feet. 'This isn't fighting. This is dying. You will do as I say. The Deathwatch will take care of this. Do not get in our way.'

The sergeant's eyes were blank lifeless things, like those of a doll. Had the Adeptus Mechanicus surgically removed so much of the man's humanity? There was no fear there, certainly, but Karras sensed little else, either. Whether that was because of the surgeries or because the beacon was still drowning him in wave after invisible wave of pounding psychic pressure, he could not say.

After a second, the skitarii sergeant gave a reluctant nod and sent a message over his vox-link. The skitarii began falling back, but they kept their futile fire up as they moved.

The rasping of the worm's armour plates against the rockcrete grew louder as it neared, and Karras turned again to face it. 'Get ready!' he told the others.

'What is your decision, Death Spectre?' Chyron rumbled. 'It is a xenos abomination. It must be killed, regardless of the inquisitor's command.'

Damn it, thought Karras. I know he's right, but I must honour the treaties, for the sake of the Chapter. We must give Solarion his window.

'Keep the beast occupied. Do as Sigma commands. If Solarion's shot fails…'

'It won't,' said Solarion over the link.

It had better not, thought Karras. Because, if it does, I'm not sure we *can* kill this thing.

* * *

SOLARION HAD REACHED the end of the crane's arma-
ture. The entire crater floor was spread out below
him. He saw his fellow Talon members fan out to
face the alien abomination. It reared up on its hind-
sections again and screeched at them, thrashing the
air with rows of tiny vestigial limbs. Voss opened up
on it first, showering it with a hail of fire from his
heavy bolter. Rauth and Karras followed suit while
Zeed and Chyron tried to flank it and approach from
the sides.

Solarion snorted.

It was obvious, to him at least, that the fiend didn't
have any blind spots. It didn't have eyes!

So far as Solarion could tell from up here, the furious fusillade of bolter rounds rattling off the beast's
hide was doing nothing at all, unable to penetrate
the thick chitin plates.

I need exposed flesh, he told himself. I won't fire
until I get it. One shot, one kill. Or, in this case, one
paralysed xenos worm.

He locked himself into a stable position by pushing his boots into the corners created by the crane's
metal frame. All around him, the winds of Menatar
howled and tugged, trying to pull him into a deadly
eighty metre drop. The dust on those winds cut visibility by twenty per cent, but Solarion had hit targets
the size of an Imperial ducat at three kilometres. He
knew he could pull off a perfect shot in far worse
conditions than these.

Sniping from the top of the crane meant that he
was forced to lie belly-down at a forty-five degree
angle, his bolt-rifle's stock braced against his

shoulder, right visor-slit pressed close to the lens of his scope. After some adjustments, the writhing monstrosity came into sharp focus. Bursts of Astartes gunfire continued to ripple over its carapace. Its tail came down hard in a hammering vertical stroke that Rauth only managed to sidestep at the last possible second. The concrete where the Exorcist had been standing shattered and flew off in all directions.

Solarion pulled back the cocking lever of his weapon and slid one of Altando's neuro-toxin rounds into the chamber. Then he spoke over the comm-link.

'I'm in position, Karras. Ready to take the shot. Hurry up and get me that opening.'

'We're trying, Prophet!' Karras snapped back, using the nickname Zeed had coined for the Ultramarine.

Try harder, thought Solarion, but he didn't say it. There was a limit, he knew, to how far he could push Talon Alpha.

THREE GRENADES DETONATED, one after another, with ground-splintering cracks. The wind pulled the dust and debris aside. The creature reared up again, towering over the Space Marines, and they saw that it remained utterly undamaged, not even a scratch on it.

'Nothing!' cursed Rauth.

Karras swore. This was getting desperate. The monster was tireless, its speed undiminished, and nothing they did seemed to have the least effect. By contrast, its own blows were all too potent. It had already struck Voss aside. Luck had been with the

Imperial Fist, however. The blow had been lateral, sending him twenty metres along the ground before slamming him into the side of a fuel silo. The strength of his ceramite armour had saved his life. Had the blow been vertical, it would have killed him on the spot.

Talon Squad hadn't survived the last six years of special operations to die here on Menatar. Karras wouldn't allow it. But the only weapon they had which might do anything to the monster was his force blade, *Arquemann*, and, with that accursed beacon drowning out his gift, Karras couldn't charge it with the devastating psychic power it needed to do the job.

'Warp blast it!' he cursed over the link. 'Someone find the source of that psychic signal and knock it out!'

He couldn't pinpoint it himself. The psychic bursts were overwhelming, drowning out all but his own thoughts. He could no longer sense Zeed's spiritual essence, nor that of Voss, Chryon, or Solarion. As for Rauth, he had never been able to sense the Exorcist's soul. Even after serving together this long, he was no closer to discovering the reason for that. For all Karras knew, maybe the quiet, brooding Astartes had no soul.

Zeed was doing his best to keep the tyranid's attention on himself. He was the fastest of all of them. If Karras hadn't known better, he might even have said Zeed was enjoying the deadly game. Again and again, that barbed black tail flashed at the Raven Guard, and, every time, found only empty air. Zeed kept himself a split second ahead. Whenever he was close enough, he lashed out with his lightning claws and raked the creature's sides. But, despite the blue sparks that flashed with every contact, he couldn't penetrate that incredible armour.

Karras locked his bolter to his thigh plate and drew *Arquemann* from its scabbard.

This is it, he thought. We have to close with it. Maybe Chyron can do something if he can get inside its guard. He's the only one who might just be strong enough.

'Engage at close quarters,' he told the others. 'We can't do anything from back here.'

It was all the direction Chyron needed. The Dreadnought loosed a battle-cry and stormed forwards to attack with his two great power fists, the ground juddering under him as he charged.

By the Emperor's grace, thought Karras, following in the Dreadnought's thunderous wake, don't let this be the day we lose someone.

Talon Squad was *his* squad. Despite the infighting, the secrets, the mistrust and everything else, that still meant something.

SOLARION SAW THE rest of the kill-team race forwards to engage the beast at close quarters and did not envy them, but he had to admit a grudging pride in their bravery and honour. Such a charge looked like sure suicide. For any other squad, it might well have been. But for Talon Squad...

Concentrate, he told himself. The moment is at hand. Breathe slowly.

He did.

His helmet filtered the air, removing the elements that might have killed him, elements that even the Adeptus Astartes implant known as the Imbiber, or the multi-lung, would not have been able to handle. Still, the air tasted foul and burned in his nostrils and throat. A gust of wind buffeted him, throwing his aim off a few millimetres, forcing him to adjust again.

A voice shouted triumphantly on the link.

'I've found it, Scholar. I have the beacon!'

'Voss?' said Karras.

There was a muffled crump, the sound of a krak grenade. Solarion's eyes flicked from his scope to a cloud of smoke about fifty metres to the creature's right. He saw Voss emerge from the smoke. Around him lay the rubble of the monster's smashed sarcophagus.

Karras gave a roar of triumph.

'It's… it's gone,' he said. 'It's lifted. I can feel it!'

So Karras would be able to wield his psychic abilities again. Would it make any difference, Solarion wondered.

It did, and that difference was immediate. Something began to glow down on the battlefield. Solarion turned his eyes towards it and saw Karras raise *Arquemann* in a two-handed grip. The monster must have sensed the sudden build-up of psychic charge, too. It thrashed its way towards the Librarian, eager to crush him under its powerful coils. Karras dashed in to meet the creature's huge body and plunged his blade into a crease where two sections of chitin plate met.

An ear-splitting alien scream tore through the air, echoing off the crater walls.

Karras twisted the blade hard and pulled it free, and its glowing length was followed by a thick gush of black ichor.

The creature writhed in pain, reared straight up and screeched again, its complex jaws open wide.

Just the opening Solarion was waiting for.

He squeezed the trigger of his rifle and felt it kick powerfully against his armoured shoulder.

A single white-hot round lanced out towards the tyranid worm.

There was a wet impact as the round struck home, embedding itself deep in the fleshy tissue of the beast's mouth.

'Direct hit!' Solarion reported.

'Good work,' said Karras on the link. 'Now what?'

It was Sigma's voice that answered. 'Fall back and wait. The toxin is fast acting. Ten to fifteen seconds. Specimen Six will be completely paralysed.'

'You heard him, Talon Squad,' said Karras. 'Fall back. Let's go!'

Solarion placed one hand on the top of his rifle, muttered a prayer of thanks to the weapon's machine spirit, and prepared to descend. As he looked out over the crater floor, however, he saw that one member of the kill-team wasn't retreating.

Karras had seen it, too.

'Chyron,' barked the team leader. 'What in Terra's name are you doing?

The Dreadnought was standing right in front of the beast, fending off blows from its tail and its jaws with his oversized fists.

'Stand down, Lamenter,' Sigma commanded.

If Chyron heard, he deigned not to answer. While there was still a fight to be had here, he wasn't going anywhere. It was the tyranids that had obliterated his Chapter. Hive Fleet Kraken had decimated them, leaving him with no brothers, no home to return to. But if Sigma and the others thought the Deathwatch was all Chyron had left, they were wrong. He had his rage, his fury, his unquenchable lust for dire and bloody vengeance.

The others should have known that. Sigma should have known.

Karras started back towards the Dreadnought, intent on finding some way to reach him. He would use his psyker gifts if he had to. Chyron could not hope to beat the thing alone.

But, as the seconds ticked off and the Dreadnought continued to fight, it became clear that something was wrong.

From his high vantage point, it was Solarion who voiced it first.

'It's not stopping,' he said over the link. 'Sigma, the damned thing isn't even slowing down. The neuro-toxin didn't work.'

'Impossible,' replied the voice of the inquisitor. 'Magos Altando had the serum tested on–'

'Twenty-five... no, thirty seconds. I tell you, it's not working.'

Sigma was silent for a brief moment. Then he said, 'We need it alive.'

'Why?' demanded Zeed. The Raven Guard was crossing the concrete again, back towards the fight, following close behind Karras.

'You do not need to know,' said Sigma.

'The neuro-toxin doesn't work, Sigma,' Solarion repeated. 'If you have some other suggestion…'

Sigma clicked off.

I guess he doesn't, thought Solarion sourly.

'Solarion,' said Karras. 'Can you put another round in it?'

'Get it to open wide and you know I can. But it might not be a dosage issue.'

'I know,' said Karras, his anger and frustration telling in his voice. 'But it's all we've got. Be ready.'

CHYRON'S CHASSIS WAS scraped and dented. His foe's strength seemed boundless. Every time the barbed tail whipped forwards, Chyron swung his fists at it, but the beast was truly powerful and, when one blow connected squarely with the Dreadnought's thick glacis plate, he found himself staggering backwards despite his best efforts.

Karras was suddenly at his side.

'When I tell you to fall back, Dreadnought, you will do it,' growled the Librarian. 'I'm still Talon Alpha. Or does that mean nothing to you?'

Chyron steadied himself and started forwards again, saying, 'I honour your station, Death Spectre, and your command. But vengeance for my Chapter supersedes all. Sigma be damned, I *will* kill this thing!'

Karras hefted *Arquemann* and prepared to join Chyron's charge. 'Would you dishonour all of us with you?'

The beast swivelled its head towards them and readied to strike again.

'For the vengeance of my Chapter, no price is too high. I am sorry, Alpha, but that is how it must be.'

'Then the rest of Talon Squad stands with you,' said Karras. 'Let us hope we all live to regret it.'

SOLARION MANAGED TO put two further toxic rounds into the creature's mouth in rapid succession, but it was futile. This hopeless battle was telling badly on the others now. Each slash of that deadly tail was avoided by a rapidly narrowing margin. Against a smaller and more numerous foe, the strength of the Adeptus Astartes would have seemed almost infinite, but this towering tyranid leviathan was far too powerful to engage with the weapons they had. They were losing this fight, and yet Chyron would not abandon it, and the others would not abandon him, despite the good sense that might be served in doing so.

Voss tried his best to keep the creature occupied at range, firing great torrents from his heavy bolter, even knowing that he could do little, if any, real damage. His fire, however, gave the others just enough openings to keep fighting. Still, even the heavy ammunition store on the Imperial Fist's back had its limits. Soon, the weapon's thick belt feed began whining as it tried to cycle non-existent rounds into the chamber.

'I'm out,' Voss told them. He started disconnecting the heavy weapon so that he might draw his combat blade and join the close-quarters melee.

It was at that precise moment, however, that Zeed, who had again been taunting the creature with his lightning claws, had his feet struck out from under him. He went down hard on his back, and the tyranid monstrosity launched itself straight towards him, massive mandibles spread wide.

For an instant, Zeed saw that huge red maw descending towards him. It looked like a tunnel of dark, wet flesh. Then a black shape blocked his view and he heard a mechanical grunt of strain.

'I'm more of a meal, beast,' growled Chyron.

The Dreadnought had put himself directly in front of Zeed at the last minute, gripping the tyranid's sharp mandibles in his unbreakable titanium grip. But the creature was impossibly heavy, and it pressed down on the Lamenter with all its weight.

The force pressing down on Chyron was impossible to fight, but he put everything he had into the effort. His squat, powerful legs began to buckle. A piston in his right leg snapped. His engine began to sputter and cough with the strain.

'Get out from under me, Raven Guard,' he barked. 'I can't hold it much longer!'

Zeed scrabbled backwards about two metres, then stopped.

No, he told himself. Not today. Not to a mindless beast like this.

'Corax protect me,' he muttered, then sprang to his feet and raced forwards, shouting, '*Victoris aut mortis*!'

Victory or death!

He slipped beneath the Dreadnought's right arm, bunched his legs beneath him and, with lightning claws extended out in front, dived directly into the beast's gaping throat.

'Ghost!' shouted Voss and Karras at the same time, but he was already gone from sight and there was no reply over the link.

Chyron wrestled on for another second. Then two. Then, suddenly, the monster began thrashing in great paroxysms of agony. It wrenched its mandibles from Chyron's grip and flew backwards, pounding its ringed segments against the concrete so hard that great fractures appeared in the ground.

The others moved quickly back to a safe distance and watched in stunned silence.

It took a long time to die.

WHEN THE BEAST was finally still, Voss sank to his knees.

'No,' he said, but he was so quiet that the others almost missed it.

Footsteps sounded on the stone behind them. It was Solarion. He stopped alongside Karras and Rauth.

'So much for taking it alive,' he said.

No one answered.

Karras couldn't believe it had finally happened. He had lost one. After all they had been through together, he had started to believe they might all return to their Chapters alive one day, to be welcomed as honoured heroes, with the sad exception of Chyron, of course.

Suddenly, however, that belief seemed embarrassingly naïve. If Zeed could die, all of them could. Even the very best of the best would meet his match in the end. Statistically, most Deathwatch members never made it back to the fortress-monasteries of their originating Chapters. Today, Zeed had joined those fallen ranks.

It was Sigma, breaking in on the command channel, who shattered the grim silence.

'You have failed me, Talon Squad. It seems I greatly overestimated you.'

Karras hissed in quiet anger. 'Siefer Zeed is dead, inquisitor.'

'Then you, Alpha, have failed on two counts. The Chapter Master of the Raven Guard will be notified of Zeed's failure. Those of you who live will at least have a future chance to redeem yourselves. The Imperium has lost a great opportunity here. I have no more to say to you. Stand by for Magos Altando.'

'Altando?' said Karras. 'Why would–'

Sigma signed off before Karras could finish, his voice soon replaced by the buzzing mechanical tones of the old magos who served on his retinue.

'I am told that Specimen Six is dead,' he grated over the link. 'Most regrettable, but your chances of success were extremely slim from the beginning. I predicted failure at close to ninety-six point eight five per cent probability.'

'But Sigma deployed us anyway,' Karras seethed. 'Why am I not surprised?'

'All is not lost,' Altando continued, ignoring the Death Spectre's ire. 'There is much still to be learned from the carcass. Escort it back to Orga Station. I will arrive there to collect it shortly.'

'Wait,' snapped Karras. 'You wish this piece of tyranid filth loaded up and shipped back for extraction? Are you aware of its size?'

'Of course, I am,' answered Altando. 'It is what the mag-rail line was built for. In fact, everything we did on Menatar from the very beginning – the construction, the excavation, the influx of Mechanicus personnel – all of it was to secure the specimen alive, still trapped inside its sarcophagus. Under the circumstances, we will make do with a dead one. You have given us no choice.'

The sound of approaching footsteps caught Karras's attention. He turned from the beast's slumped form and saw the xeno-heirographologist, Magos Borgovda, walking towards him with a phalanx of surviving skitarii troopers and robed Mechanicus acolytes.

Beneath the plex bubble of his helm, the little tech-priest's eyes were wide.

'You… you bested it. I would not have believed it possible. You have achieved what the Exodites could not.'

'Ghost bested it,' said Voss. 'This is his kill. His and Chyron's.'

If Chyron registered these words, he didn't show it. The ancient warrior stared fixedly at his fallen foe.

'Magos Borgovda,' said Karras heavily, 'are there men among your survivors who can work the cranes? This carcass is to be loaded onto a mag-rail car and taken to Orga Station.'

'Yes, indeed,' said Borgovda, his eyes taking in the sheer size of the creature. 'That part of our plans has not changed, at least.'

Karras turned in the direction of the mag-rail

station and started walking. He knew he sounded tired and miserable when he said, 'Talon Squad, fall in.'

'Wait,' said Chyron. He limped forwards with a clashing and grinding of the gears in his right leg. 'I swear it, Alpha. The creature just moved. Perhaps it is not dead, after all.'

He clenched his fists as if in anticipation of crushing the last vestiges of life from it. But, as he stepped closer to the creature's slack mouth, there was a sudden outpouring of thick black gore, a great torrent of it. It splashed over his feet and washed across the dry rocky ground.

In that flood of gore was a bulky form, a form with great rounded pauldrons, sharp claws, and a distinctive, back-mounted generator. It lay unmoving in the tide of ichor.

'Ghost,' said Karras quietly. He had hoped never to see this, one under his command lying dead.

Then the figure stirred and groaned.

'If we ever fight a giant alien worm again,' said the croaking figure over the comm-link, 'some other bastard can jump down its throat. I've had my turn.'

Solarion gave a sharp laugh. Voss's reaction was immediate. He strode forwards and hauled his friend up, clapping him hard on the shoulders. 'Why would any of us bother when you're so good at it, paperface?'

Karras could hear the relief in Voss's voice. He grinned under his helm. Maybe Talon Squad was blessed after all. Maybe they would live to return to their Chapters.

'I said fall in, Deathwatch,' he barked at them; then he turned and led them away.

ALTANDO'S LIFTER HAD already docked at Orga Station by the time the mag-rail cars brought Talon Squad, the dead beast and the Mechanicus survivors to the facility. Sigma himself was, as always, nowhere to be seen. That was standard practice for the inquisitor. Six years, and Karras had still never met his enigmatic handler. He doubted he ever would.

Derlon Saezar and the station staff had been warned to stay well away from the mag-rail platforms and loading bays and to turn off all internal vid-pictors. Saezar was smarter than most people gave him credit for. He did exactly as he was told. No knowledge was worth the price of his life.

Magos Altando surveyed the tyranid's long body with an appraising lens before ordering it loaded onto the lifter, a task with which even his veritable army of servitor slaves had some trouble. Magos Borgovda was most eager to speak with him, but, for some reason, Altando acted as if the xeno-heirographologist barely existed. In the end, Borgovda became irate and insisted that the other magos answer his questions at once. Why was he being told nothing? This was *his* discovery. Great promises had been made. He demanded the respect he was due.

It was at this point, with everyone gathered in Bay One, the only bay in the station large enough to offer a berth to Altando's lifter, that Sigma addressed Talon Squad over the comm-link command channel once again.

'No witnesses,' he said simply.

Karras was hardly surprised. Again, this was standard operating procedure, but that didn't mean the Death Spectre had to like it. It went against every bone in his body. Wasn't the whole point of the Deathwatch to protect mankind? They were alien-hunters. His weapons hadn't been crafted to take the lives of loyal Imperial citizens, no matter who gave the command.

'Clarify,' said Karras, feigning momentary confusion.

There was a crack of thunder, a single bolter-shot. Magos Borgovda's head exploded in a red haze.

Darrion Rauth stood over the body, dark grey smoke rising from the muzzle of his bolter

'Clear enough for you, Karras?' said the Exorcist.

Karras felt anger surging up inside him. He might even have lashed out at Rauth, might have grabbed him by the gorget, but the reaction of the surviving skitarii troopers put a stop to that. Responding to the cold-blooded slaughter of their leader, they raised their weapons and aimed straight at the Exorcist.

What followed was a one-sided massacre that made Karras sick to his stomach.

When it was over, Sigma had his wish.

There were no witnesses left to testify that anything at all had been dug up from the crater on Menatar. All that remained was the little spaceport station and its staff, waiting to be told that the excavation was over and that their time on this inhospitable world was finally at an end.

\* \* \*

SAEZAR WATCHED THE big lifter take off first, and marvelled at it. Even on his slightly fuzzy vid-monitor screen, the craft was an awe-inspiring sight. It emerged from the doors of Bay One with so much thrust that he thought it might rip the whole station apart, but the facility's integrity held. There were no pressure leaks, no accidents.

The way that great ship hauled its heavy form up into the sky and off beyond the clouds thrilled him. Such power! It was a joy and an honour to see it. He wondered what it must be like to pilot such a ship.

Soon, the black Thunderhawk was also ready to leave. He granted the smaller, sleeker craft clearance and opened the doors of Bay Four once again. Good air out, bad air in. The Thunderhawk's thrusters powered up. It soon emerged into the light of the Menatarian day, angled its nose upwards, and began to pull away.

Watching it go, Saezar felt a sense of relief that surprised him. The Adeptus Astartes were leaving. He had expected to feel some kind of sadness, perhaps even regret at not getting to meet them in person. But he felt neither of those things. There was something terrible about them. He knew that now. It was something none of the bedtime stories had ever conveyed.

As he watched the Thunderhawk climb, Saezar reflected on it, and discovered that he knew what it was. The Astartes, the Space Marines… they didn't radiate goodness or kindness like the stories pretended. They were not so much righteous and shining champions as they were dark avatars of destruction. Aye, he was glad to see the back of them.

They were the living embodiment of death. He hoped he would never set eyes on such beings again. Was there any greater reminder that the galaxy was a terrible and deadly place?

'That's right,' he said quietly to the vid-image of the departing Thunderhawk. 'Fly away. We don't need angels of death here. Better you remain a legend only if the truth is so grim.'

And then he saw something that made him start forwards, eyes wide.

It was as if the great black bird of prey had heard his words. It veered sharply left, turning back towards the station.

Saezar stared at it, wordless, confused.

There was a burst of bright light from the battle-cannon on the craft's back. A cluster of dark, slim shapes burst forwards from the under-wing pylons, each trailing a bright ribbon of smoke.

*Missiles!*

'No!'

Saezar would have said more, would have cried out to the Emperor for salvation, but the roof of the operations centre was ripped apart in the blast. Even if the razor sharp debris hadn't cut his body into a dozen wet red pieces, the rush of choking Menatarian air would have eaten him from the inside out.

'No witnesses,' Sigma had said.

Within minutes, Orga Station was obliterated, and there were none.

* * *

DAYS PASSED.

The only thing stirring within the crater was the skirts of dust kicked up by gusting winds. Ozyma-138 loomed vast and red in the sky above, continuing its work of slowly blasting away the planet's atmosphere. With the last of the humans gone, this truly was a dead place once again, and that was how the visitors, or rather returnees, found it.

There were three of them, and they had been called here by a powerful beacon that only psychically gifted individuals might detect. It was a beacon that had gone strangely silent just shortly after it had been activated. The visitors had come to find out why.

They were far taller than the men of the Imperium, and their limbs were long and straight. The human race might have thought them elegant once, but all the killings these slender beings had perpetrated against mankind had put a permanent end to that. To the modern Imperium, they were simply xenos, to be hated and feared and destroyed like any other.

They descended the rocky sides of the crater in graceful silence, their booted feet causing only the slightest of rockslides. When they reached the bottom, they stepped onto the crater floor and marched together towards the centre where the mouth of the great pit gaped.

There was nothing hurried about their movements, and yet they covered the distance at an impressive speed.

The one who walked at the front of the trio was taller than the others, and not just by virtue of the high, jewel-encrusted crest on his helmet. He wore a rich cloak of strange shimmering material and carried a golden staff that shone with its own light.

The others were dressed in dark armour sculpted to emphasise the sweep of their long, lean muscles. They were armed with projectile weapons as white as bone. When the tall, cloaked figure stopped by the edge of the great pit, they stopped, too, and turned to either side, watchful, alert to any danger that might remain here.

The cloaked leader looked down into the pit for a moment, then moved off through the ruins of the excavation site, glancing at the crumpled metal huts and the rusting cranes as he passed them.

He stopped by a body on the ground, one of many. It was a pathetic, filthy mess of a thing, little more than rotting meat and broken bone wrapped in dust-caked cloth. It looked like it had been crushed by something. Pulverised. On the cloth was an icon – a skull set within a cog, equal parts black and white. For a moment, the tall figure looked down at it in silence, then he turned to the others and spoke, his voice filled with a boundless contempt that made even the swollen red sun seem to draw away.

'Mon-keigh,' he said, and the word was like a bitter poison on his tongue.

*Mon-keigh.*

# PRIMARY INSTINCT

## by Sarah Cawkwell

*Victory does not always rest with the big guns.*
*But if we rest in front of them, we shall be lost.*
— Lord Commander Argentius,
Chapter Master, Silver Skulls

THE SOARING FORESTS of Ancerios III steamed gently in the relentless heat of the tropical sun. Condensation beaded and rose, shimmering in a constant haze from the emerald-green and deep mauve of the leaves. This was a cruel, merciless place where the sultry twin suns raised the surface temperature to inhospitable levels. The atmosphere was stifling and barely tolerable for human physiology.

However, the party making their way through the jungle were not fully human.

The dark Anceriosan jungle had more than just shape, it had oppressive, heavy form. There was an eerie silence, which might once have been broken by the chattering of primate-like creatures or the call of exotic birds. In this remote part of the jungle, there was no sign of the supposed native fauna. What plant life that did exist had long since evolved at a tangent, adapting necessarily to the living conditions. Everything that grew reached desperately upwards, yearning towards the suns. Perhaps there was a dearth of animal life, but these immense plants thrived and provided a home for a countless variety of insects.

There was a faint stirring of wind, a shift in the muggy air, and a cloud of insects lifted on the breeze. They twisted lazily, their varicoloured forms catching and reflecting what little smattering of dappled sunlight managed to penetrate this far down. They twirled with joyful abandon on the zephyr that held them in its gentle grasp, riding the updraught through to a clearing.

The cloud abruptly dissipated as a hand clad in a steel-grey gauntlet scythed neatly through it. Startled, the insects scattered as though someone had thrown a frag grenade amongst them. The moment of confusion passed swiftly, and they gradually drifted back together in an almost palpably indignant clump. They lingered briefly, caught another thermal and were gone.

Sergeant Gileas Ur'ten, squad commander of the Silver Skulls Eighth Company Assault squad 'The Reckoners', swatted with a vague sense of irritation at the insects. They flew constantly into the breathing grille of his helmet and whilst the armour was advanced enough and sensibly designed in order not to allow them to get inside, the near-constant *pit-pit-pit* of the bugs flying against him was starting to become a nuisance.

He swore colourfully and hefted the weight of the combat knife in his hand. It had taken a great deal more work than anticipated to carve a path through to the clearing, and the blade was noticeably dulled by the experience.

Behind him, the other members of his squad were similarly surveying the damage to their weapons caused by the apparently innocent plant life. Gileas stretched out his shoulders, stiff from being hunched in the same position for so long, and spun on his heel to face his battle-brothers.

'As far as I can make out, the worst threats are these accursed insects,' he said in a sonorous rumble. His voice was deep and thickly accented. 'Not to mention these prevailing plant stalks and the weather.'

The Assault squad had discovered very quickly that the moisture in the air, coupled with spores from the vegetation that they had hacked down, was causing a variety of malfunctions within their jump packs. Like so much of the rediscovered technology that the Adeptus Astartes employed, the jump packs had once been things of beauty, things that offered great majesty and advantage to the Emperor's warriors. Now, however, they were starting to show signs of their age. Fortunately, the expert and occasionally lengthy ministrations of the Chapter's Techmarines kept the machine-spirits satisfied and ensured that even if the devices were not always perfect, they were always functional.

Gileas sheathed his combat knife and reached up to snap open the catch that released his helmet. There was an audible *hiss* of escaping air as the seals unlocked. Removing the helmet, an untidy tumble of dark hair fell to his shoulders, framing a weather-tanned, handsome face that was devoid of the tattoos that covered the rest of his body beneath the armour. Like all of the Silver Skulls, Gileas took great pride in his honour markings. He had not yet earned the right to mark his face. It would not be long, it was strongly hinted, for the ambitious Gileas was reputedly ear-marked for promotion to captain. It was a rumour which had stemmed from his own squad and had been met with mixed reactions from others within the Chapter. Gileas repeatedly dismissed such talk as hearsay.

He cast dark, intelligent eyes cautiously around the clearing, clipping his helmet to his belt and loosening his chainsword in the scabbard worn down the line of his armoured thigh. The twisted, broken wreckage of what had once been a space-going vessel lay swaddled amidst fractured trees and branches. Whatever it was, it was mostly destroyed and it most certainly didn't look native to the surroundings. This was the first thing they had encountered in the jungle which was clearly not indigenous.

Reuben, his second-in-command, came up to Gileas's side and disengaged his own helmet. Unlike his wild-haired commanding officer, he wore his hair neat and closely cropped to his head. He considered the destroyed vessel, sifting through the catalogue of data in his mind. It was unlike anything he had ever seen before. Any markings on its surface were long gone with the ravages of time, and it was nearly impossible to filter out any sort of shape. Any form it may have once taken had been eradicated by the force of impact.

'It doesn't look like a wraithship, brother,' he said.

'No,' grunted Gileas in agreement. 'It certainly bears no resemblance to that thing we were pursuing.' He growled softly and ran a hand through his thick mane of hair. 'I suspect, brother, that our quarry got away from us in the webway. Unfortunate that they escaped the Emperor's justice. For now, at least.' His hand clenched briefly into a fist and he swore again. He considered the vessel for a few silent moments. Finally, he shook his head.

'This has been guesswork from the start,' he acknowledged with reluctance. 'We all knew that there was a risk we would end up chasing phantoms. Still...' He indicated the wreck. 'At least we have something to investigate. Perhaps this is what the eldar were seeking. There's no sign of them in the atmosphere. We may as well press our advantage.'

'You think we're ahead of them?'

'I would suggest that there's a good chance.' Gileas shrugged lightly. 'Or maybe we're behind them. They could already have been and gone. Who knows, with the vagaries of the warp? The *Silver Arrow's* Navigator hadn't unscrambled her head enough to get a fix on chronological data when we left. Either way, it's worth checking for any sign of passage. Any lead is a good lead. Even when it leads nowhere.'

'Is that you or Captain Kulle speaking?' Reuben

smiled as he mentioned Gileas's long-dead mentor.

The sergeant did not reply. Instead, he grinned, exposing ritualistically sharpened canines that were a remnant of his childhood amongst the tribes of the southern steppes. 'It matters little. Whatever this thing is, it's been here for a long time. This surely can't be the ship we followed into the warp. It isn't one of ours and that's all we need to know. You are all fully aware of your orders, brothers. Assess, evaluate, exterminate. In that order.'

He squinted at the ship carefully. Like Reuben, he was unable to match it to anything in his memory. 'I feel that the last instruction might well be something of a formality though. I doubt that anything could have survived an impact like that.'

The ship was practically embedded in the planet's surface, much of its prow no longer visible, buried beneath a churned pile of dirt and tree roots. Hardy vegetation, some kind of lichen or moss, clung to the side of the vessel with grim determination.

The sergeant glanced sideways at the only member of the squad not clad head-to-foot in steel-grey armour and made a gesture with his hand, inviting him forwards.

Resplendent in the blue armour of a psychic battle-brother, Prognosticator Bhehan inclined his head in affirmation before reaching his hand into a pouch worn on his belt. He stepped forwards until he was beside the sergeant, hunkered down into a crouch and cast a handful of silver-carved rune stones to the ground. As Prognosticator, it was important for him to read the auguries, to commune with the will of the

Emperor before the squad committed themselves. To a man, the Silver Skulls were deeply superstitious. It had been known for entire companies to refuse to go into battle if the auguries were poor. Even the Chapter Master, Lord Commander Argentius, had once refused to enter the fray on the advice of the *Vashiro*, the Chief Prognosticator.

This was more, so much more than ancient superstition. The Silver Skulls believed without question that the Emperor projected His will and His desire through His psychic children. These readings were no simple divinations of chance and happenstance. They were messages from the God-Emperor of Mankind, sent through the fathomless depths of space to His distant loyal servants.

The Silver Skulls, loyal to the core, never denied His will.

Prognosticators served a dual purpose in the Chapter. Where other ranks of Adeptus Astartes had Librarians and Chaplains, the Silver Skulls saw the universe in a different way. Those battle-brothers who underwent training at the hands of the Chief Prognosticator offered both psychic and spiritual guidance to their brethren. Their numbers were not great: Varsavia did not seem to produce many psykers. As a consequence, those who did ascend to the ranks of the Adeptus Astartes were both highly prized and revered amongst the Chapter.

Gileas knew that the squad were deeply honoured to have Bhehan assigned to them. He was young, certainly; but his powers, particularly those of foresight, were widely acknowledged as being amongst the most veracious and trustworthy in the entire Chapter.

'I'm feeling nothing from the wreck,' said Bhehan in his soft, whispering voice. The young Prognosticator hesitated and frowned at the runes, passing his hand across them once again. He considered for a moment or two, his posture stiff and unyielding. Finally, he relaxed. 'If it were a wraithship, if it were the one we were pursuing, its psychic field would still be active. This one is assuredly dead. Stone-cold dead.' He frowned, pausing just long enough for Gileas to quirk an eyebrow.

'Is that doubt I'm detecting there?' The Prognosticator looked up at Gileas, his unseen face, hidden as it was behind his helmet, giving nothing away. He glanced back down at the runes thoughtfully. The scratched designs on their surfaces were a great mystery to Gileas. However, the Prognosticators understood them, and that was all that mattered. An eminently pragmatic warrior, Gileas never let things he didn't understand worry him. He would never have vocalised the thought, but it was an approach he privately felt many others in the Chapter should adopt.

Bhehan shifted some of the runes with a practiced hand, turning some around, lining others up, making apparently random patterns on the ground with them. A pulsing red glow briefly animated the Space Marine's psychic hood as he brought his concentration to bear on the matter at hand.

Finally, after some consideration, he shook his head.

'An echo, perhaps,' he mused, 'nothing more,

nothing less.' He nodded firmly, assertiveness colouring his tone. 'No, Brother-Sergeant Ur'ten,' he said, 'no doubt. The Fates suggest to me that there was perhaps something alive on board this ship when it crashed. Any sentience within its shell has long since passed on. Subsumed, perhaps, into the jungle. Eaten by predators, or simply died in the crash.'

He gathered up the runes, dropping them with quiet confidence back into his pouch, and stood up. 'The Fates,' he said, 'and the evidence lying around us.' He nodded once more and removed his helmet. The face beneath was surprisingly youthful, almost cherubic in appearance, and reflected Bhehan's relative inexperience. For all that, he was a field-proven warrior of considerable ferocity. Combined with the powers of a Prognosticator, he was a formidable opponent, something the sergeant had already tested in the training cages.

Gileas nodded, satisfied with the outcome. 'Very well. Reuben, take Wulfric and Jalonis with you and search the perimeter for any sign of passage. All of this…' He swept his hand around the clearing to indicate the crash site. 'All of this may simply be an eldar ruse. I have no idea of the extent of their capabilities, but they are xenos and are not to be trusted. Not even in death. Tikaye, you and Bhehan are with me. Seeing as we're here anyway, let's get this ship and the surrounding area checked out. The sooner it's done, the sooner we can move on to the next location.' He grinned his wicked grin again and rattled his chainsword slightly.

The entire group moved onwards, aware of a shift in the weather. A storm front was rolling in. It told in the increased ozone in the air, the faint tingle of electricity that heralded thunder. Following his unit commander, Bhehan absently dipped a hand into the pouch at his side and randomly selected a rune. The tides of Fate were lapping against his psyche strongly, and the closer they got to the craft, the more intense that sensation became.

He briefly surfaced from his light trance to stare with greater intensity at the rune he had withdrawn and he stiffened, his eyes wide. He considered the stone in his hand again and tried to wind the rapidly unravelling thoughts in his mind back together. As though a physical action could somehow help him achieve this, he raised a hand and grabbed at his fair hair.

Noticing the sudden movement, Gileas moved to the Prognosticator's side immediately. 'Talk to me, brother. What do you see?'

A faint hint of wildness came into the psyker's eyes as he turned to look up at the sergeant. 'I see death,' he said, his voice notably more high-pitched than normal. 'I see death, I smell corruption, I taste blood, I feel the touch of damnation. Above all, above all, above all, I *hear* it. Don't you hear it? I hear it. The screams, brothers. The screaming. They will be devoured!'

He pulled wretchedly at his hair, releasing the rune which fell to the floor. A thin trail of drool appeared at the side of the psyker's mouth and he repeatedly drummed his fist against his temple. Gileas, despite the respect he had for the Prognosticator, reached out and caught his battle-brother's arm in his hand.

'Keep your focus, Brother-Prognosticator Bhehan,' he rebuked, his tone mild but his manner stern. 'We need you.' He'd seen this before; seen psykers lose themselves to the Sight in this way. Disconcertingly, where Bhehan was concerned, the Sight had never been wrong.

It did not bode well.

'We are not welcome here,' the psyker said, his voice still edged with that same slightly unearthly, eerie, high-pitched tone. 'We are not welcome here and if we set one foot outside of the ship, it will spell our doom.'

'We *are* outside the ship…' Tikaye began. Gileas cast a brief, silencing glance in his direction. The young psyker was making little sense, but such were the ways of the Emperor and it was not for those not chosen to receive His grace to question. The sergeant patted Bhehan's shoulder gruffly and gave a grim nod. 'The faster this task is completed, the better. Double-time, brothers.'

He leaned down and picked up the rune that Bhehan had dropped, offering it back to the psyker without comment.

THE OTHER PARTY, led by Reuben, had skirted the perimeter of the clearing. At first there had been nothing to suggest anything untoward had occurred. Closer investigations by Wulfric, a fine tracker even by the Chapter's high standards, had eventually revealed recently trampled undergrowth.

Reuben took stock of what little intelligence they had gathered on this planet, far out on the Eastern Fringe of the galaxy. There had been suggestions of some native creatures, but as of yet, they had encountered none. Worthless and of little value, the planet had been passed over as unimportant and uninhabited with no obviously valuable resources or human life.

Just because there were no previous sightings of any of the indigenous life forms, of course, did not mean that there were none to actually *be* seen.

Reuben waved his bolter to indicate that Wulfric should lead on and the three Space Marines plunged back into the jungle, following what was a fairly obvious trail. They did not have to travel far before they located their quarry, a few feet ahead of them, in a natural glade formed by a break in the trees.

The creature seemed totally ignorant of their presence, affording them a brief opportunity to assess it. An overall shade of dark, almost midnight-blue, the alien was completely unfamiliar. Without any frame of visual reference, the thing could easily be one of the presumably indigenous life forms. Muted conversations amongst the group drew agreement.

A slight adjustment to his optical sensors allowed Reuben a closer inspection. The thing had neither fur, nor scales or even insectoid chitin covering its body. It was smooth and unblemished with the same pearlescent sheen to its form that the insects seemed to have. Its limbs were long and sinewy; the musculature of the legs suggesting to Reuben's understanding of xenobiology that it could very probably run and jump exceptionally well. The arms ended in oddly human-like five-fingered hands. Frankly, Reuben didn't care about its lineage or whether it had ever displayed any intelligence. In accordance with every belief he held, with every hypno-doctrination he had undergone, he found it utterly repulsive.

He reacted in accordance with those beliefs and teachings at the exact moment the alien turned its head in their direction, emitting a bone-chilling screech that tore through the jungle. It was so piercing as to be almost unbearable. Reuben's enhanced auditory senses protected him from the worst of it, but it was the sort of noise that he genuinely suspected could shatter crystal. Unearthly. Inhuman.

*Alien.*

Acting with the intrinsic response of a thousand or more engagements, Reuben flicked his bolter to semi-automatic and squeezed the trigger. Staccato fire roared as every projectile found its target. It was joined, seconds later, by the mimicking echo of the weapons in his fellow Space Marines' hands.

At full stretch, the xenos was easily the size of any of the Space Marines shooting at it. It showed no reaction to the wounds that were being ripped open in its body by the hail of bolter fire. It was locked in a berserk rage, uncaring and indifferent to the relentless attack. As the explosive bolts lacerated its body, dark fluid sprayed onto the leaves, onto the ground, onto the Silver Skulls.

Still it kept coming.

Reuben switched to full-automatic and unloaded

the remainder of the weapon's magazine. Wulfric and Jalonis followed his example. Eventually, mortally wounded and repelled by the continuous gunfire, the abomination emitted a strangled scream of outrage. It crumpled to the ground just short of their position, spasms wracking its hideous form, and then all movement ceased.

Smoke curled from the ends of three bolters and the moment was broken only by the crackle of the vox-bead in Reuben's ear.

'Report, Reuben.'

'Sergeant, we found something. Xenos life form. Dead now.'

Reuben could hear the scowl in his sergeant's voice. 'Remove its head to be sure it *is* dead, brother.' Reuben smiled. 'We're coming to your position. Hold there.'

'Yes, brother-sergeant.'

Not wishing to take any chances, Reuben swiftly reloaded his weapon and stepped forwards to examine the xenos. It had just taken delivery of a payload of several rounds of bolter fire and had resisted death for a preternaturally long time. As such, he was not prepared to trust to it being completely deceased. His misgivings proved unfounded.

Moving towards the alien, any doubt of its state was dismissed: thick, purple-hued blood oozed stickily from multiple wounds in its body, pooling in the dust of the forest floor, settling on the surface and refusing to soak into the ground. It was as though the planet itself, despite being parched, rejected the fluid. The pungent, acrid scent of its essential vitae was almost sweet, sickly and cloying in the thick, humid air around them. Wrinkling his nose slightly against its stench, Reuben moved closer.

Lying on the ground, the thing had attempted to curl into an animalistic, defensive position, but was now rapidly stiffening as rigor mortis took hold. Reuben could see its eyes, amethyst-purple, staring glassily up at him. Even in death, sheer hatred shone through. The Adeptus Astartes felt sickened to the stomach at its effrontery to all that was right.

Just to be on the safe side, he placed the still-hot muzzle of his bolter against its head and fired a solitary shot at point-blank range into it. Grey matter and still more of the purplish blood burst forth like the contents of an over-ripe fruit.

Reuben crouched down and considered the xenos more carefully. The head was curiously elongated, with no visible ears. The purple eyes were over-large in a comparatively small face. A closer look, despite the odour that roiled up from it, suggested that they may well have been multi-faceted. The head was triangular, coming to a small point at the end of which were two slits that Reuben could only presume were nostrils.

Anatomically, even by xenos standards it seemed *wrong*. In a harsh environment like the jungle, any animal would need to adapt just in order to survive. This thing, however, seemed as though it was a vague idea of what was right rather than a practical evolution of the species. It was a complex chain of thought, and the more Reuben considered it, the more the explanation eluded him. It was as though the answer was there, but kept just out of his mental grasp.

For countless centuries, the Silver Skulls had claimed the heads of their victims as trophies of battle, carefully extracting the skulls and coating them in silver. Thus preserved, the heads of their enemies decorated the ships and vaults of the Chapter proudly. However, the longer Reuben stared at the dead alien, any urge he may have had to make a prize of it ebbed away. Forcing himself not to think on the matter any further, he turned back to the others.

Wulfric had resumed his search of the surrounding area and even now was gesturing. 'It wasn't alone. Look.' He indicated a series of tracks leading off in scattered directions, mostly deeper into the jungle.

Reuben gave a sudden, involuntary growl. It had taken three of them with bolters on full-automatic to bring just one of these things to a halt, and even then he had half-suspected that if he hadn't blasted its brains out, it would have got back up again.

'Can you make out how many?'

'Difficult, brother.' Wulfric crouched down and examined the ground. 'There's a lot of scuffing, plus with our passage through, it's obscured the more obvious prints. Immediate thoughts are perhaps half a dozen, maybe more.' He looked up at Reuben expectantly, awaiting orders from the squad's second-in-command. 'Of course, that's just in the local area. Who knows how many more of those things are out there?'

'They probably hunt in packs.' Reuben fingered the hilt of his combat knife.

Unspoken, the thoughts passed between them. If one was that hard to put down, imagine what half a dozen of them or more would be like to keep at bay. Reuben made a decision and nodded firmly.

'Good work, Wulfric. See if you can determine any sort of theoretical routes that these things may have taken. Do a short-range perimeter check. Try to remain in visual range if you can. Report anything unusual.'

'Consider it done,' replied Wulfric, getting to his feet and reloading his bolter. Without a backwards glance, the Space Marine began to trace the footprints.

The snapping of undergrowth announced the impending arrival of the other three Adeptus Astartes. Straightening, Reuben turned to face his commanding officer. He punched his left fist to his right shoulder in the Chapter's salute and Gileas returned the gesture.

All eyes were immediately drawn to the dead creature on the floor.

'Now that,' said Gileas after a few moments of assessing the look and, particularly, the stench of the alien, 'is unlike anything I have ever seen before. And to be blunt, I would be perfectly happy if I never see one again.'

Reuben dutifully reported the incident to his sergeant. 'Sorry to disappoint you, but Wulfric believes there could be anything up to a half-dozen other creatures similar to this one in the vicinity. I sent him to track them.'

Gileas frowned as he listened, his expression

darkening thunderously. 'Any obvious weaknesses or vulnerable spots?'

'None that were obvious, no.'

Gileas glanced at Reuben. They had been brothers-in-arms for over one hundred years and were as close as brothers born. He had never once heard uncertainty in Reuben's tone and he didn't like what he heard now. He raised a hand to scratch at his jaw thoughtfully.

'These things are technically incidental to our mission,' he said coolly, 'but we should complete what we have started. It may retain some memory, some thought or knowledge about those we seek.' He turned to the Prognosticator, who was standing slightly apart from the others. 'Brother-Prognosticator, much as it pains me to ask you, would you divine what you can from this thing?'

'As you command.' Bhehan lowered his head in acquiescence and moved to kneel beside the dead alien. The sight of its bloodied and mangled body turned his stomach – not because of the gore, but because of its very inhuman nature. He took a few deep, steadying breaths and laid a hand on what remained of the creature's head.

'I sense nothing easily recognisable,' he said, after a time. He glanced up at Reuben. 'The damage to its cerebral cortex is too great. Virtually all of its residual psychic energies are gone.' His voice held the slightest hint of reproach.

Gileas glanced sideways at Reuben, who smiled a little ruefully. 'It was you who suggested I remove its head to be sure it was dead, Gil,' he said, the use of the diminutive form of his sergeant's name reflecting the close friendship the two shared. 'I merely used my initiative and modified your suggestion.'

The sergeant's lips twitched slightly, but he said nothing. Bhehan moved his hand to the other side of the being's head without much optimism.

*A flash of something. Distant memories of hunting…*

As swiftly as it had been there, the sensation dwindled and died. Instinctively, and with the training that had granted him the ability to understand such things, Bhehan knew all that was needed to be known.

'An animal,' said Bhehan. 'Nothing more. Separated from the pack. Old, perhaps.' He shook his head and looked up at Gileas. 'I'm sorry, brothersergeant. I cannot give you any more than that.'

'No matter, Prognosticator,' said Gileas, grimly. 'It was worth a try.' He surveyed the surrounding area a little more, looking vaguely disappointed. 'This is a waste of time and resources,' he said eventually. 'I propose that we regroup, head back the way we came, destroy the ship in case it is, or contains, what the eldar were seeking, and get back to the landing site. We'll have time to kill, but I'm sure I can think of something to keep us occupied.'

'Not another one of your impromptu training sessions, Gileas,' objected Reuben with good-natured humour. 'Don't you ever get tired of coming up with new and interesting ways to get us to fight each other?'

'No,' came the deadpan reply. 'Never.'

Bhehan allowed the Reckoners to discuss their next

course of action amongst themselves, waiting for the inevitable request to see what the runes said. He kept his attention half on their conversation, but the other half was caught by something in the dirt beside the dead alien's head. From his kneeling position, he reached over and scooped it up in one blue-gauntleted hand.

Barely five centimetres across, the deep wine-red stone was attached to a sturdy length of vine: a crudely made necklace. Bhehan's brow furrowed slightly as he glanced again at the corpse. It had felt feral and not even remotely intelligent, but then most of its synapses had been shredded by Reuben's bolter. Putting a hand back against its head yielded nothing. He was feeling more psychic emanations from the trees themselves than from this once-living being. Of course, the charm may not have belonged to the animal; perhaps it had stolen it. It was impossible to know for sure without employing full regression techniques. For that option, however, the thing needed to be alive.

The young Prognosticator brought the stone closer to his face to study it more intently, and another flash of memory seared through his mind. This one, though, was not the primal force of nature that he had felt from the dead xenos. This was something else entirely. Sudden flashes emblazoned themselves across his mind. Shadowy images wavered in his mind's eye, images that were intangible and hard to make out.

A shape. Male? Maybe. Human? Definitely not. Eldar. It was eldar. Wearing the garments of those known as warlocks. It was screaming, cowering.

It was dying. It was being attacked. A huge shape loomed over it, blocking out the sunlight...

'Prognosticator!'

Gileas's sudden bark brought the psyker out of the trance that he had not even realised he'd fallen into. He stared at the sergeant, the brief look of displacement on his face swiftly replaced by customary attentiveness.

'My apologies, brother-sergeant,' he said, shaking his mind clear of the visions. He got to his feet and stood straight-backed and alert, the images in his mind already faded. 'Here, I found this. It might give us some clue to what happened here.' He proffered the stone and Gileas stared at it with obvious distrust before taking it. He held it up at arm's length and studied it as it spun, winking in the sunlight.

'I've seen something like this before,' he said thoughtfully. 'The eldar wear them. Something to do with their religion, isn't it?'

'In honesty, I'm not completely sure,' replied Bhehan. 'I haven't had an opportunity to study one this closely. We, I mean the company Prognosticators, have many theories...' Seeing that the sergeant wasn't even remotely interested in theories, the psyker tailed off and accepted the object back from Gileas, who seemed more than pleased to be rid of it.

'If this is an eldar item,' said Gileas, grimly, 'then it's not too much of a leap of faith to believe that they've been present, or *are* present, on this planet. Increases the odds of that wreck being eldar and also that this planet may well have been their ultimate destination.'

The others concurred. The sergeant nodded abruptly. 'Then we definitely return to the ship and we destroy the whole thing. We make damn sure that they find nothing when they get here. Are we in accord?'

He glanced around and all nodded agreement. They clasped their hands together, one atop the other. Gileas looked sideways at Bhehan who, surprised by this unspoken invitation into the brotherhood of the squad, laid his hand on the others.

'Brothers all,' said Gileas, and the squad responded in kind.

'Fetch Wulfric back,' commanded Gileas. Tikaye nodded and voxed through to his battle-brother.

There was no reply.

'Wulfric, report,' Tikaye said into the vox, even as they began heading in the direction he had taken, weapons at the ready.

THEY MOVED DEEPER still into the jungle.

It was rapidly becoming far more densely packed, the vibrant green of the trees and plants creating an arboreal tunnel through which the five giants marched. Despite the overriding concern at their companion's whereabouts, the Adeptus Astartes welcomed the moment's relief from the constant squinting brought about by standing in the direct sunlight. As they made their way with expediency through the trees, light filtered through to mottle the dirt and scrub of the forest floor. Parched dust marked their passage, rising up in clouds around their feet.

'Brother Wulfric, report.' Tikaye continually tried

the vox, but there was still nothing. Bhehan extended the range of his psychic powers, reaching for Wulfric's awareness, and instead received something far worse. His nostrils flared as a familiar coppery scent assailed him, and he turned slightly to the west.

'It's this way,' he said, with confidence.

'You are sure, brother?'

'Aye, brother-sergeant.'

'Jalonis, lead the way. I will bring up the rear.' Gileas, with the practical and seemingly effortless ease that he did everything, organised the squad. They had travelled a little further into the trees when a crack as loud as a whip caused them all to whirl on the spot, weapons readied and primed. The first fall of raindrops announced that it was nothing more than the arrival of the tropical storm. The thunder that had barely been audible in the distance was now directly above them.

The vox in Gileas's ear crackled with static and he tapped at it irritably. These atmospherics caused such frustrating communication problems. It had never failed to amaze Gileas, a man raised as a savage in a tribe for whom the pinnacle of technological advancement was the longbow, that a race who could genetically engineer super-warriors still couldn't successfully produce robust communications.

More static flared, then Jalonis's voice broke through. It was a scattered message, breaking up as the Space Marine spoke, but Gileas had no trouble extrapolating its meaning.

'…Jal… found Wulfric… t's left… him anyway. Dead ah… maybe… dred metres or so.'

Gileas acknowledged tersely and accelerated his pace.

Another crack of thunder reverberated so loudly that Gileas swore he could feel his teeth rattle in his jaw. The light drizzle gave way rapidly to huge, fat drops of rain. The canopy of the trees did its best to repel them, but ultimately the persisting rain triumphed. The bare heads of the Silver Skulls were soaked swiftly. Gileas's hair, wild and untamed at the best of times, soon turned to unruly curls that clung tightly around his face and eyes. He put his helmet back on, not so much to keep his head dry, but more to reduce the risk of his vision being impaired by his own damp hair getting in the way.

The moment he put his helmet back on, he knew what he would find when he reached Jalonis. The information feed scrolling in front of his eyes told him everything that he needed to know. A sense of foreboding stole over him, and he murmured a prayer to the Emperor under his breath.

The precipitation did nothing to dispel the steaming heat of the forest, but merely landed on the dusty floor where it was immediately swallowed into the ground as though it had never been.

'Sergeant Ur'ten.'

Jalonis stood several metres ahead, a look of grim resignation on his face. 'You should come and see this. I'm afraid it's not pretty.'

Jalonis, a practical man by nature, had ever been the master of understatement. What Gileas witnessed as he looked down caused his choler to rise immediately. With the practice of decades, he carefully balanced his humours.

Wulfric's armour had been torn away and discarded, scattered around the warrior's corpse. The Space Marine's throat had been ripped apart with speed and ferocity, which had prevented him from alerting his battle-brothers or calling for aid.

The thorax had been slit from neck to groin, exposing his innards. In this heat, even with the steady downpour of rain, the stink of death was strong. The fused ribcage had been shattered, leaving Wulfric's vital organs clearly visible, slick with blood and mucus. Or at least, what remained of them.

Where Wulfric's primary and secondary hearts should have been was instead a huge cavity. Gileas stared for long moments, his conditioning and training assisting his deductive capability. Whatever had attacked Wulfric had gone for the throat first, rendering his dead brother mute. It had torn through his armour like it was shoddy fabric rather than ceramite and plasteel. The assailant, or more likely the assailants, had then proceeded to shred the skin like parchment and defile Wulfric's body.

The details were incidental. One of Gileas's brothers was dead. More than that, one of his closest brothers was dead. For that, there would be hell to pay.

'Take stock,' he said to Tikaye, who whilst not an Apothecary was the squad's primary field medic. 'I want to know what has been taken.' His voice was steady and controlled, but the rumble and pitch of the words hinted strongly at the anger bubbling just under the surface.

The stoic Tikaye moved to Wulfric and began to

examine the body. He murmured litanies of death fervently under his breath as he did so.

'You understand, of course,' said Gileas, his voice low and menacing, 'this means someone… or *something* is going to regret crossing my path this day.'

The falling rain, evaporating in the intense heat, caused steam to rise in ethereal tendrils from the ground. It loaned even more of a macabre aspect to the scene, and the coils partially swathed Wulfric's body as they rose. It was a cheap mockery of the tradition of lighting memorial pyres on the Silver Skulls' burial world and it did little to ease their collective grief and rage.

Staring down at their fallen brother, each murmuring his own personal litany, the remaining Silver Skulls were fierce of countenance, ready for a fight in response to this atrocity.

'Several of his implants are gone,' came Tikaye's voice from the ground. There was barely masked outrage in his tone.

'Gone? What does *gone* mean?'

'Taken, brother-sergeant. The biscopea, Larraman's organ, the secondary and primary hearts, and from what I can make out, his progenoid is gone, too. I'd suggest that whoever or whatever did this knew what they wanted and took it. It's too clean to be an arbitrary or random coincidence.'

'You said they were animals, Prognosticator.' Gileas couldn't keep the accusation out of his tone. 'That conflicts directly with what Brother Tikaye suggests. One of you is wrong.' Bhehan shook his head.

'The creature we found *was* an animal,' he

countered. 'That was before I found the stone, however. It's possible that it had been wearing it as some sort of decoration. I acknowledge that may potentially suggest intelligence. I–'

'I did not ask for excuses, neither did I ask for a lecture. The runes, Prognosticator.' Gileas's voice was barbed. The sergeant had a reputation amongst the Silver Skulls as a great warrior, a man who would charge headlong into the fray without hesitation and also as a man who did not suffer fools gladly, particularly when his wrath was tested. Da'chamoren, the name he had brought with him from his tribe, translated literally as 'Son of the Waxing Moon'. Gileas's power and resilience had always seemed to grow proportionately to his rising fury.

It was a fitting name.

'Yes, sir,' Bhehan replied, suitably chastened by the change in the sergeant's attitude. Without further comment, he commenced another Sighting. He felt a moment's uncertainty, but didn't dwell on it. At first, nothing came to him and he could not help but wonder if he was going to experience what his psychic brethren termed the 'Deep Dark', a moment of complete psychic blindness. Prognosticators considered this to be a sign that they had somehow fallen from the Emperor's grace. Bhehan had tasted the sensation once before and it had left a bitter flavour of ash in his mouth. He firmly set aside all thoughts of failure and closed his eyes. The Emperor was with them, he asserted firmly. Had He not already communicated His will through His loyal servant?

Reassured, his mental equilibrium ceased its

churning and settled again. Bhehan allowed the reading of the runes to draw him. The stones served well as a focus for his powers, helping him to draw in all the psychic echoes that flitted around this charnel house like ghosts. Each Prognosticator found their own focus; some, like Bhehan, chose runes whilst others divined the Emperor's will through a tarot.

'The perpetrators of this butchery... I sense that they want something from us. To learn, perhaps? To understand how we are put together.' The Prognosticator's eyes were still closed, his voice barely more than a whisper. 'Why? If they were animals, they would have just torn the flesh from his bones. They have not. They have intelligence, yes, great intelligence... or at least... no. Not all of them. Just one, perhaps? A leader of sorts?' The questioning was entirely rhetorical and nobody answered or interrupted him during the stream of consciousness. The rain drummed on their armour, creating a background rhythm of its own.

Bhehan's hand closed around the eldar stone still in his hand. To his relief, a flood of warmth suffused him, a sensation he had long equated as the prelude to a vision. No Deep Dark for him, then. His powers were intact. The feeling of relief was quickly replaced by one of intense dislike as he sensed a new presence in his mind.

*They know what you are because of us. Because of what we know. The gift unintentionally given.*

The words were perfectly sharp and audible, but the image of the being who spoke them was not. Tall and willowy, the apparition shimmered before his closed eyelids like an imprint of the sun burned onto his retina.

*They absorbed what we were, what we are. They seek to do the same to you through nothing more than a primitive urge to survive, to evolve. To change. Is this not the instinct that drives us all? Aspiration to greatness? A need to be better than we were?*

Bhehan, made rational and steady through years of training, concentrated on the image.

You are eldar. He did not speak the words aloud. There was no need to.

*I was eldar. Now I am nothing more than a ghost, a faint remnant of what once was.*

I will not speak to you, xenos.

*Such arrogance as this brought my own brothers and our glorious sister to their end. It will be your undoing, mon-keigh.*

Bhehan sensed a great sigh, like the last exhalation of a dying man, and as rapidly as the spectre had materialised inside his mind, it was gone. With a sharp intake of breath, Bhehan's eyes snapped open.

'We should not linger,' he said, slightly unfocussed. 'We should take our brother and we should go.'

'Is this what the Fates suggest?'

'No,' said Bhehan, hesitating only momentarily. 'It is what *I* feel we should do.'

Gileas practically revered the majesty of the Prognosticators. Divine will or not, he would never question a Prognosticator's intuition. He nodded.

'The will of a Prognosticator and the will of the Fates are entwined as one. We will do as you say.'

Reuben stepped forwards. 'Perhaps...' he began. 'Perhaps we should not. Not yet.'

'Explain.' Gileas shot a glance at Reuben.

'We interrupted them. The aliens. We could lure them back out in the open.'

'Reuben, are you suggesting that we use our dead brother as *bait*?' Gileas didn't even bother keeping the disgust out of his tone. 'I can't believe you would even entertain such a thought.'

'Bait,' echoed Bhehan, his eyes widening. 'Bait. Yes, that's it. Bait!' He drew the force axe he wore across his back. 'That's exactly what he is.'

'Prognosticator? You surely aren't agreeing to this ridiculous scheme?'

'No! For *us*, sergeant. He's been left here to lure *us* out.'

Another echo of thunder rolled around the skies overhead in accompaniment to this grim pronouncement. The rain had slowed once again to a steady *drip-drip-drip*. It pooled briefly in the vast, scoop-like leaves of the trees and splashed to the ground, throwing up billows of dust before evaporating permanently.

None of the Reckoners other than Bhehan had psychic capability, but all of them could sense the sudden shift in the air, sense the threat hiding somewhere.

Just waiting.

'Keep your weapons primed,' snapped Gileas, his thumb hovering over the activation stud of his chainsword. 'Be ready for anything.'

'I sense three psychic patterns,' offered the

Prognosticator, his hands tight around the hilt of the force axe. 'Different directions, all approaching.'

'Only three?' Gileas said. 'You are sure of this?'

'Yes.'

'Three of them, five of us. It will be a hard fight, my brothers, but we will prevail. We are the Silver Skulls.' Gileas's voice swelled with fierce pride. 'We *will* prevail.' Jalonis and Bhehan pulled their helmets back on at the sergeant's words.

With the squad at full battle readiness, Gileas turned his attentions to the reams of data which began scrolling in front of his eyes. He blink-clicked rapidly, filtering out anything not pertinent to the moment of battle, including the winking iconograph that had previously represented Wulfric's lifesigns. The brief glimpse of that particular image served as a visible reminder of the desire for requital, however, and fire-stoked battle-lust raced through the sergeant's veins.

'They are coming,' Bhehan breathed through the vox.

Gileas made a point to double-check the functionality of his jump pack at the Prognosticator's warning. He diverted his attention to the relevant streams of data that fed the device's information into his power armour, and was satisfied to note that it was at approximately seventy per cent. Certainly not representative of its full, deadly performance, but good enough for a battle of this size. He ordered the rest of the squad to do the same. If these animals were seeking a fight, then the Reckoners would willingly deliver. They would deliver a fight and they would deliver what they gave best and what had earned them their name.

A reckoning.

For most Space Marines, engaging an enemy was all about honour to the Chapter, pride in the company or loyalty to the Imperium. Sometimes, like now, it was about righteous vengeance. Occasionally, it was simple self-defence. For Sergeant Gileas Ur'ten it was about all of these things. Above and beyond all else, however, it was the thrill that came with the anticipation of a fight. The burst of adrenaline and increased blood flow as his genetically enhanced body geared up to beget the hand of retribution that was the rightful role of all the Adeptus Astartes.

Another moment of silence followed and then a tumult of screaming voices rose as one. It preceded the charge of a slew of enemies from the undergrowth, each as massive as the one they had already encountered. Gileas thumbed the activation stud of his chainsword and it roared into deadly life, the weapon's fangs eager to feast.

The sudden appearance of so many of the xenos caused a moment's pandemonium, but that was all it was: a single moment during which the Assault squad formed a tight-knit, ceramite-clad wall of stoic defence. There was vengeance to be taken and they were ready to take it.

Each of the xenos radiated a palpable desire to kill. They walked upright, although with a certain stumbling gait that implied they may not always have done so. It seemed probable that their hind legs hadn't been used in this way for long. As though confirming these suspicions, three of them dropped to all fours.

As they prowled closer to the Adeptus Astartes, their movements became snake-like, a sinuous flow that allowed them to undulate across the uneven ground with hypnotic ease and disconcerting speed.

The skin of one creature's mouth drew back to reveal a double set of razor-sharp teeth. It didn't take much of a stretch of the imagination to work out how it was that the xenos had removed internal organs so swiftly and efficiently. Every single one of those teeth looked capable of tearing through flesh and muscle with ease. The attackers moved as a unit, almost as though they were as tightly trained and drilled as the Adeptus Astartes themselves.

A rapid headcount told the Silver Skulls that there were nine of them, and with determination every last one of the Assault squad entered the fray. Bhehan, his force axe at the ready in his right hand, raised the other, palm outstretched in front of him, ready to cast a psychic shield around his battle-brothers. The crystals in the psychic hood attached to the gorget of his armour began to pulsate as he channelled the deadly power of the warp, ready to unleash it at a moment's notice.

Gileas and Tikaye both charged the alien on the far right with their chainswords shrieking bloody murder. Jalonis and Reuben levelled their bolters and began firing.

Fury descended on the previously silent jungle. Orders were shouted, and the cries of alien life and the indignant, defensive answering retorts of the squad's weapons flooded the surrounding area in a cacophony of sound.

Gileas drove his chainsword deeper into the flesh of the alien he was fighting, putting all his strength into the blow. The thing lashed out at him, howling and chittering. Talons flashed like deadly knives before his helmet, but he ducked and weaved with easy agility, avoiding its blows. As far as he was concerned, as long as it remained affixed to the end of his chainsword, it was a suitable distance away from him and was dying at the same time. An additional bonus.

Reuben coaxed his weapon into life, discharging a hail of bolter shells at the onslaught. Beside him, Bhehan swept his hand forwards and round in a semi-circular arc, almost as though he were simply thrusting the xenos away from him. The one directly facing him stumbled backwards and howled its displeasure.

With a grunt of effort, Gileas yanked the chainsword out of the alien's flesh and swung it round, almost severing one of the wicked, scythe-like talons from its hand. He moved in harmony with the weapon as though it was merely an extension of his own body. Watching Gileas Ur'ten fight was aesthetically pleasing; even in the heavy power armour of the Adeptus Astartes he was agile, lithe and, more than that, he was a master at what he did. He enacted his deadly dance of death with practiced aplomb.

Tikaye, engaged as he was with his own opponent, did not immediately notice that another was prowling towards him. It reached out with a clawed hand

and swept it towards the Space Marine. It caught him between his helmet and breastplate, and with a sudden display of strength sent him flying backwards. He landed heavily with an audible crunch of ceramite at Bhehan's feet. The Prognosticator, briefly distracted from gathering force for his next attack, glanced down at his battle-brother.

Within seconds, Tikaye was back on his feet, his weapon back in his hand, and he tore into the nearest enemy with a vengeance, letting his chainsword do the talking.

One of the three beasts that had been slithering towards the psyker leapt suddenly with a yowl of triumph. Instinctively, Bhehan trusted to the power of his force axe rather than his psychic ability and channelled his rage and righteousness into its exquisitely forged blade. The hidden runes carved deep into its metal heart kindled and throbbed with an otherworldly glow.

Years of training and dedication to the arts of war at the hands of the masters on Varsavia automatically took over and Bhehan planted his feet firmly on the ground, prepared for the moment of impact. The axe sang through the air towards its target, a low whine audibly marking its trajectory as it swept towards the enemy.

To his consternation, the force axe passed right through the alien's body. The unexpected follow-through of his own swing unbalanced him and he fell to one knee. He scrambled immediately back to his feet, ready to resume combat, only to realise that the thing was gone, utterly vanished before his very eyes. All that remained was a strange psychic residue, streamers of barely visible non-corporeal form that were consigned fleetingly to the air, and then to nothing more than memory.

'Something isn't right here,' he voxed, puzzlement implicit in every syllable.

'Really, Prognosticator? You think so?' The pithy reply from Gileas was harsher than perhaps it might otherwise have been, but given that the sergeant was locked in a bloody battle to the death with a creature seemingly quite capable of slicing through him like he was made of mud, it was understandable. 'Any chance that you'd care to elaborate on this outstanding leap of logic?'

Clenching his force axe with an iron grip, Bhehan whirled to intercept another xenos which was catapulting itself at him. He swung the weapon again and once more his blow met with no resistance.

He had sensed three minds. No more, no less. With the two illusory attackers dispelled, they were now facing seven.

'They are not all real, my brothers,' he stated urgently. 'Only three of them present a real threat.'

'They feel real to me,' responded Jalonis, who had just been viciously swept into the trunk of one of the vast trees. The armour plating across his back was cracked. His helmet flashed loss-of-integrity warnings at him and, ignoring them, he resumed his fighting. One of Reuben's arms hung limp at his side as his body worked swiftly to fix the damage that had been caused to it.

Gileas and Tikaye had fallen into battle harmony

with each other and were battering determinedly at one of the enemy. As one, they both fired their jump packs, performing a vertical aerial leap that caused the xenos to snap its head up sharply, its eyes fixed on the now-airborne targets. The range of the jump packs was severely limited due to the tree cover, but they remained aloft, well out of its reach.

It dropped its long body low, coiling like a spring and readying itself to launch. Bhehan, thinking swiftly, took the opportunity to blast a psychic attack into the creature's mind.

It did not vanish.

'That one!' he shouted into the vox, gesticulating ferociously at the xenos and alerting his airborne brothers. 'That one, brother-sergeant! It's solid.'

The sergeant nodded brusquely. He had no desire to understand the whys or hows of the situation. Bhehan's words were little more than meaningless background noise to him at this moment. Only the solution was of importance at this stage. Only the battle mattered.

In full synchronicity, Gileas and Tikaye both bore their full weights downwards to land on the xenos beneath them. Close-quarters combat was one thing. During such a pitched battle, a being could fight back and stand a chance of being a danger. Being crushed beneath the full might of two power armour-wearing Space Marines was something else entirely, and not something so easily eluded.

The alien, anticipating its own demise, wailed in murderous rage for a few seconds before both Space Marines plummeted solidly onto it. Bones crunched and arterial blood spurted from puncture wounds caused by the creature's exoskeleton shredding through its flesh. Crude brutality, perhaps, but effective nonetheless.

Devoid of their source, two more of the psychic projections immediately melted into the ether. Gileas and Tikaye fired their jump packs again and blasted grimly towards the rest of the fray. Bhehan, witnessing the scene, paused momentarily as realisation bloomed.

It was suddenly so clear to the Prognosticator. So very, very simple.

'They are manipulating your minds! Brother-Sergeant Ur'ten, you must listen to me! They have extremely strong psychic capability. My mind should be awash with all these things, but it is not!' The Prognosticator bit down on the excitement and forced his mind to focus. He knew he was making little sense and that was no use to anybody.

He had removed two of the illusory aliens by passing his force axe through their psychically generated forms. With the death of one of the true alien forms, two more had dispersed.

From the nine who had attacked, the Silver Skulls now faced four. If Bhehan's theory proved correct, only two of them were real. Kill those, his theory suggested, and their intangible counterparts would vanish; eliminate the phantasms and only the real xenos would remain. It seemed that whatever trick they were playing with the squad's minds meant that they were unable to tell them apart. For them, the two decoy enemies were each as solid and real as the two who were weaving the illusion. They seemed immune to all but extrasensory attack. Only he could do anything about it.

His thought processes were lightning-fast and Bhehan began to gather his psychic might once more. The most decisive way he could think of to end this situation was to crush the opposing will of the xenos with a psychic flood of the Emperor's righteous fury. Whilst the melee had been tight and kept largely confined due to the jungle's enforced restrictions, it was still a reasonably large area. The desired result would be effective, but it would tax his constitution considerably.

It did not matter. His gift might temporarily be exhausted, but he was a fully trained battle-brother. He would never be totally defenceless. With an exultant cry, he flung both hands out in front of him. His voice carrying into the jungle with strident fervour, Bhehan called forth the powers of the warp.

With a fizzing crackle, a massive burst of energy lit his hood up in a flicker of blue sparks. The resultant shock wave not only targeted the xenos, but also caused the four battling Space Marines to pause briefly as their own minds were assailed from no longer one, but two directions. For them, a mental battle for supremacy took place as the will of the Prognosticator worked to force out the intruders.

Bhehan was trained, disciplined and strong. The aliens were clever, certainly, but they fought on instinct and did not truly know how to counter such a devastating blow to their defences. For a heartbeat, Bhehan could feel his advantage slipping as the barb of the aliens' mental hooks worked in deeper. The silent struggle continued and then abruptly, he felt the fingers of deception release their hold and fall away.

Two of the attackers instantly disappeared. One screamed with fury and began to lope away into the undergrowth. Bhehan, staggering slightly from the sheer potency of his attack, automatically reached out for its mind. Instantly, he was filled with a sense of pain and, even better as far as he was concerned, of fear. It was injured, probably dying. It was unimportant. The final alien was also mortally wounded. It would be the work of but moments to end its foul existence.

Good work, Bhehan,' said Gileas, his breathing heavy through the vox-channel.

The remaining creature slunk around the Assault squad, fluidity implicit in its every movement. Before any of them could open fire or attack, the xenos reared back, a crest-like protrusion standing up on top of its head, and emitted a screech that was staggeringly high-pitched. Had the auto-senses in the warriors' helmets not instantly reacted, it would surely have ruptured eardrums. In the event, it achieved nothing.

The xenos clamped its jaws tightly shut and stared with renewed malevolence at its enemy as it realised the futility of its last defences. Without hesitation Gileas roared the final order, his voice like the crack of doom.

'Open fire! Suffer not the alien to live!'

With resounding cries that echoed those

sentiments most emphatically, bolter fire razored through the air and tore into the alien's armour-hard exterior. Every last bolt was unloaded into it, spent shells rapidly littering the ground. Blood fountained out of the wounds in the xenos's body, the sheer force of it suggesting they had successfully hit something vital, and Gileas found renewed vigour in the scent of its imminent demise. A sudden, desperate desire to eliminate this foul abomination once and for all took hold.

With a roar of determination, he took out his bolt pistol and aimed it with deadly, pinpoint accuracy between the thing's eyes. Reuben discarded his spent weapon, taking his own pistol from its holster. Falling in beside his sergeant, he stepped forwards with him as they fired together.

Every bolt that burst against the alien's skull caused its head to snap back and drew further eardrum-splitting screeches.

Bhehan responded with a psychic blow, although due to his exhaustion, the effect was greatly diminished. Heedless of this fact, he focussed all of his fury, sense of retribution and hatred, and flung it towards the xenos with a practised heft of his mental acuity. He was drained, but it provided a useful diversion. The enemy hesitated, crouching low, ready to spring at Reuben. It moved with uncanny alacrity, propelling itself with deadly grace for something that should surely have been dead by now towards the Space Marine, bearing him to the ground. It reared up, blood and saliva flying from its jaws as it prepared to strike.

'No!'

Bhehan brandished his force axe. He urged a ripple of power across its surface and bounded the short distance to his fallen brother. With an easy, accurate swing, he buried the axe deep in the alien's chest.

It stumbled back, licks of warp-lightning crackling across its carapace. It writhed on the ground in agony for a few moments and then was still.

A silence fell, disturbed only by the heavy breathing of everyone present.

Gileas lowered his pistol and nodded in grim satisfaction. 'It is done,' he said. 'Status report.'

Apart from several light wounds and Jalonis's fractured backplate, the squad had escaped almost completely unscathed from the encounter. Bhehan's weariness showed in the Prognosticator's posture and in his voice as he communicated via the vox, but he had expended a remarkable amount of energy in a very short space of time. The strength of will it must have taken for each of the xenos to maintain replicas had been quite the barrier for him to overcome. It gave him great satisfaction to acknowledge that not only had he overcome it but had also emerged triumphant.

'Are you well, Bhehan?' Gileas addressed the psyker directly, his tone brusque and formal. 'Do you require time to gather yourself?'

'No, brother! I do not "require time". I am tired, but I am not some weakling straight out of his chamber. I am fine.' The indignation in the young Prognosticator's voice put a smile on Gileas's face beneath the helmet. He might be young, but Bhehan already had the true fire of a Silver Skull with many more years of service behind him. The Emperor willing, the youth would undoubtedly go far.

'Puts you in mind of yourself, does he, brother?'

At his side, Reuben murmured the words softly enough for only the sergeant to hear. The squad commander's smile deepened.

'Just a little, aye.' Gileas leaned down slightly and wiped his bloodied chainsword on the ground. He stared up at the sky visible through the canopy. Daylight was beginning to give way to the navy-blue of what he had always known as the gloaming. The Thunderhawk would return just after dusk. For now, there was one thing only left to do.

'Brother-Prognosticator,' he said, turning to Bhehan. 'Would you do us the great honour of claiming the squad's trophy from this battle?'

Bhehan understood the largesse implicit in the gesture and was deeply flattered by the offer. He made the sign of the aquila and bowed his head in respect to the sergeant. He stepped up and raised his force axe above his head.

'The honour would be mine, brother-sergeant. In the name of the Silver Skulls, for the glory of Chapter Master Argentius and for the memory of our fallen brother, Wulfric, I claim your head as my prize. Let those who walk the halls of our forefathers gaze upon your countenance and give thanks for your end.' The axe flashed through the air and struck the neck of the dead xenos.

The moment the head and the body parted, there was a hazy shimmering and the unknown alien's body was replaced by something entirely more recognisable. Bhehan realised it first, but the others were not very far behind him.

'An illusion,' the Prognosticator breathed. 'It's woven a psychic disguise around itself!'

'No. No, that's impossible,' countered Jalonis, perturbation in his voice. 'That can't be correct. Kroot don't have psychic abilities.'

Indeed, the headless body on the ground was most definitely that of a kroot. It had the same wiry, sinewy build and avian-like features that matched every image that had ever been pict-flashed at them through doctrination tapes and training sessions. Yet despite its instantly familiar form, there were subtle differences. It varied from what was presumably the norm in a number of ways, not least of which was the most obvious which Jalonis had just voiced.

It was imbued with psychic powers. Unheard of, at least in the Silver Skulls' experience. Reports and research had never once suggested that the kroot, the fierce, mercenary warrior troops regularly employed by tau armies, were psychic. Moreover, this kroot wore no harness, carried no weapon. It was far more primitive than what they expected of such beings. An evolutionary throwback maybe, but one in possession of something perhaps far more deadly than a rifle or any other kind of physical weapon.

'A feral colony home world?' Jalonis made the suggestion first. 'A breed of kroot who have taken a different genetic path to their brethren?'

Gileas frowned. 'It is said that these things eat the flesh of their enemies, that they have the ability to assimilate their DNA. There have certainly been reports that this planet once sported animal life. It is surely not unreasonable to guess that the kroot have systematically destroyed whatever may have existed on this planet.'

He considered the dead beasts. 'These things, at least... the things that look like they did before we exposed the truth... are all we have encountered.' A thought occurred to the sergeant. 'When Reuben shot that other one in the head, it did not change its shape or form, did it?'

'The cerebral connection remained intact,' Bhehan commented absently. 'Brother Reuben obliterated its brain, yes. However, he didn't disconnect the spinal cord. Nerve impulses continued to flow after death. The mental disguise it wove remained stable until full brain death. We didn't stay there long enough to witness it change back.'

'Aye,' said Reuben, remembering the unnatural need to ignore the alien. Bhehan would have been better equipped to avoid that psychic shielding.

Something was niggling at the back of Bhehan's mind, but he couldn't quite put his finger on it. It danced tantalisingly outside his grasp and he reached out for it.

'Psychic kroot... This is a vital discovery for us. They cannot be suffered to live. This planet must be cleansed.' Tikaye offered up his opinion.

Gileas glanced up at Bhehan and remembered the deep red stone that he had found. 'Bhehan, you have a theory, I suspect. Tell me.'

Bhehan nodded slowly. 'There are, to the best of

our knowledge, no psychic kroot. Not any that we've met before,' he hypothesised. 'However, what if it were to assimilate a psychic species? Say… the eldar?' He held up the red stone so that all the battle-brothers could see it. 'What would stop it from killing and eating one of the eldar? What would prevent it from the freedom to filter out the required genetic strands that would give it the most useful result?'

'Surely it must take several generations for a kroot to assimilate such powers?' The query came from Tikaye, and the others considered his words.

'We don't know what constitutes a kroot genera-tion. We have no idea how old that ship is. We don't even know if it *is* an eldar ship. Perhaps it is a kroot vessel. Maybe they arrived before the eldar, maybe after.' Gileas's voice was grim. His patience was already strained to breaking point. 'It is without question, brothers, that both those xenos races have tainted this planet one way or the other. There are far too many unknown variables, and I have little inter-est in philosophical postulation about which came first.'

He put his chainsword back into its scabbard and reloaded the chamber of his pistol.

'Brother Bhehan,' he said, without another glance, 'collect the trophy. We will take Wulfric's body to the predetermined extraction coordinates and we will leave. This must be reported to Captain Meyoran. I do not presume to second-guess his actions on hear-ing the news, but I would not want to be on this planet when he found out.'

The Prognosticator tucked the eldar stone into the pouch with his runes and moved to the dead kroot. The very thought of such a being filled him with passionate hatred: a foul crossbreed of two xenos races with the most lethal features of both. It was an atrocity of the highest order, an abomination that had no right to exist. Yet here it was, albeit not for much longer once the Silver Skulls returned to the *Silver Arrow*.

The sudden truth of what the murderer had wanted with Wulfric's body hit the Prognosticator head-on. A kroot, with the psychic abilities and memories of an eldar, would have had some knowledge of Astartes physiology, even if only as a basic, barely recalled memory. Imagine, then, a kroot, with the psychic abilities and memories of an eldar... and the strength and resilience of a Space Marine...

Bhehan straightened his shoulders and bent down to pick up the head of the kroot. Thanks to the Reckoners, such a thing would never come to pass.

WHAT HEAT REMAINED in the day began to sap steadily as the suns continued their slow descent towards the horizon. The air was thick with heat stored by the trees and the rocks. This, coupled with residual moisture from the rainstorm, left the air feeling thick and greasy.

The squad trampled through the trees for several more minutes, all senses on full alert. They had barely arrived at the extraction point when the general vox-channel fizzed into life. The Thunderhawk would be in position in fifteen minutes.

Nocturnal life began to flood the jungle with a dis-cordant symphony over which the approaching whine of the Thunderhawk could swiftly be heard. Once in situ, there was a hiss of servos and hydraulics and the front boarding ramp of the vessel opened, the light from within spilling out and bathing the jungle.

Gileas waited for the others to board before he joined them. He had always maintained that, as sergeant, it was his place to arrive first and leave last. He fired his jump pack, rose to the Thunderhawk and dropped to the floor with a clatter.

'All on board, Correlan. Give us a few moments to ensure that our fallen battle-brother is secure.'

'Understood. Good to have you back, sergeant.'

Gileas removed his helmet and ran his fingers through his hair. Already the words for his report to Captain Meyoran were forming clearly in his mind. They had been sent down to this planet for one thing and yet had found something entirely different and unexpected.

Bhehan remained standing at the edge of the land-ing ramp, staring down at the jungle. He reached into his pouch to draw a random rune and instead pulled out the eldar stone. Considering it thoughtfully, he indulged in a moment's wild curiosity as to what sort of portent the Emperor was sending him.

As his hand closed around it, he became aware of a strong push against the wards he had set in place, wards that had no doubt gone a long way towards allowing him to see through the kroot's duplicitous scheming. This mental touch was no wild and instinctual thing, though. This press against his defences was nearly as disciplined and practiced as his own. A sudden flicker of movement caught his eye.

At the jungle's edge, barely visible in the dusk and what remained of the light cast by the Thunderhawk, Bhehan saw it. A solitary figure. Tall, seemingly all whipcord muscle and sinew, the huge kroot stood boldly in direct sight of the Thunderhawk. To all intents and purposes it was little different to its kin, but it was not difficult to surmise that it was a more powerful or at least a more evolved strain of these twisted xenos. A cloak of stitched animal hide was slung around its shoulders and in one hand it held a crudely fashioned staff, from which hung feathers and trinkets of decoration. A number of stones also dangled from the staff, stones that looked remarkably like the very one in the psyker's hand.

He felt its vicious touch against his mind again and clamped the wards down tighter. The lesser kroot had been disorganised and fierce. This, though, was a calculated, scheming mind. This was a mind that would gladly extract the very soul of you and leave you to crumble to dust in its wake. It was barbed and brutal and uncannily self-aware.

The crystals on his psychic hood flickered, attracting the sergeant's attention.

'Brother-Prognosticator?' He moved to stand beside the younger Adeptus Astartes and his sharp eyes quickly made out what the psyker had seen.

'Throne of Terra!' he exclaimed and drew his pistol, ready to fire it at the alien. But by the time the weapon was out of its holster and in his hand, the kroot had gone, vanished into the jungle. Gileas lowered his weapon, his disappointment obvious.

Bhehan turned to the sergeant. His young face showed nothing of the vile revulsion he had felt at the kroot's mental challenge.

He felt one last, sickening touch on his mind and then the alpha, if indeed that had been what it was, let him go.

'This place needs to be purified,' said the psyker, fervently. 'To be cleansed of this filth.'

'It will be, brother,' acknowledged Gileas with absolute sincerity. As the gaping maw of the landing ramp finally sealed off the last sight of the Anceriosan jungle, he turned to Bhehan. 'It will be.'

# SACRIFICE

## by Ben Counter

THE WARP TORE at him.

The unearthly cold shot right through him.

He could see for a billion kilometres in every direction, through the angry ghosts of dead stars and the glowing cauls of nebulae, dark for aeons. Alaric fought it, tore his eyes away from the infinities unravelling around him. The psychic wards built into his armour were white hot against his skin, tattooing him with burns in the shape of their sacred spirals.

Alaric's lungs tried to draw breath, but there was no air there. He tried to move, but space and movement had no meaning here. And beyond his senses, far in the black heart of the universe, he could sense vast and god-like intelligences watching him as he flitted through their domain.

Man, he managed to think, was not meant to be teleported.

The air boomed out as Alaric emerged in real space again, several hundred kilometres from the teleporter array on the *Obsidian Sky* where he had started the journey. Even a Space Marine, even a Grey Knight, was not immune to the disorientation of being hurled through the warp to another part of space, and for a second his senses fought to make definition of reality around him.

The squad had been teleported onto the grand cruiser *Merciless*. The familiar architectures of an Imperial warship were everywhere, from the aquilae worked into the vault where the pillars met overhead to the prayer-algorithms stamped into the ironwork of the floor by Mechanicus shipwrights.

The air was a strange mix peculiar to spaceships. Oil and sweat, incense from the constant tech-rituals, propellant from the ship's guns. It was mixed with the tongue-furring ozone of the squad's sudden arrival.

Alaric took a couple of breaths, forcing out the supercooled air in his lungs. 'Brothers!' he gasped. 'Speak unto me.'

'I live, brother,' came Dvorn's reply from where he lay, a few metres away, ice flaking from his armour.

'I too,' said Haulvarn. Alaric's second in the squad leaned against a wall of the corridor. His journey had been one of intense heat instead of cold and his armour hissed and spat where it met the wall.

Brother Visical coughed violently and forced himself to his feet. In reply to Alaric, he could only meet the Justicar's eyes. Visical was inexperienced for a Grey Knight, and he had never been teleported before. It was rare enough even for a veteran like Alaric. The technology that made it possible could not be replicated, and was restricted to a handful of the oldest Imperial warships.

The whole squad had made it onto the *Merciless*. That was something to give thanks for in itself. Teleportation was not an exact science, for even the oldest machines could simply fling the occasional man into the warp to be lost forever. He could be turned inside out, merged with a wall upon re-entry or fused with one of his fellow travellers. Luckily this had not happened to any of Alaric's squad. Fate had smiled on them so far.

'We're in the lower engineering decks,' said Haulvarn, checking the data-slate built into the armour of his forearm.

'Damnation,' spat Dvorn. 'We're off course.'

'I...' spluttered Visical, still suffering from disorientation. 'I am the hammer... I am the point of His spear...'

Alaric hauled Visical to his feet. 'Our first priority is to find Hyrk,' said Alaric. 'If we can find a cogitator or take a prisoner, we can locate him.'

As if in reply, a monstrous howl echoed from further down the corridor. This part of the ship was ill-maintained and the patchy light did not reach that far down. The sound was composed of a hundred voices, all twisted beyond any human range.

'First priority is survival,' said Dvorn.

'Where is your faith, brother?' said Haulvarn with a reproachful smile. 'Faith is the shield that never falters! Bear it up, brothers! Bear it up!'

Dvorn hefted his Nemesis hammer in both hands. 'Keep the shield,' he said. 'I'll stick to this.'

Alaric kicked open one of the doors leading off from the corridor. He glimpsed dusty, endless darkness beyond, an abandoned crew deck or cargo bay. He took shelter in the doorway as the howling grew closer, accompanied by the clatter of metal-shod feet on the floor. Sounds came from the other direction, too, this time the rhythmic hammering of guns or clubs on the walls.

'Hyrk has wasted little time,' said Alaric. 'Barely a month ago, he took this ship. Already it is crewed by the less-than-human.'

'Not for long,' said Dvorn. He looked down at Visical, who was crouching in another doorway, incinerator held ready to spray fire into the darkness. 'You were saying?'

'I am the hammer!' said Visical, voice returned and competing with the growing din. 'I am the shield! I am the mail about His fist! I am the point of His spear!'

'I see them!' yelled Haulvarn.

Alaric saw them, too. They had once been the crew of the *Merciless*, servants of the Emperor aboard a loyal warship. Now nothing remained of their humanity. The first glimpse Alaric had was of asymmetrical bodies, limbs moving in impossible configurations, stretched and torn naval uniforms wrapped around random tangles of bone and sinew.

He saw the stitches and the sutures. The humans they had once been had been cut up and rearranged. A torso was no more than an anchor for a random splay of limbs. Three heads were mounted on one set of shoulders, the jaws replaced with shoulder blades and ribs to form sets of bony mandibles. A nest of razor-sharp bone scrabbled along the ceiling on dozens of hands.

'This side, too!' shouted Dvorn, who was facing the other way down the corridor.

'Greet them well!' ordered Alaric.

The Grey Knights opened fire. The air was shredded by the reports of the storm bolters mounted onto the backs of their wrists. A wave of heat from Visical's incinerator blistered the rust off the walls. Alaric's arm jarred with that familiar recoil, his shoulder hammered back into its socket.

The mutant crewmen came apart in the first volleys. The corridor was awash with blood and torn limbs. Carried forwards on the bodies, as if riding a living tide, came a thing like a serpent of sundered flesh. Torsos were stacked on top of one another, sewn crudely together at shoulder and abdomen. Its head was composed of severed hands, fastened together with wire and metal sutures into the approximation of a massive bestial skull. Its teeth were sharpened ribs and its eyes were beating hearts. The monstrous face split open in a serpentine grin.

It moved faster than even Alaric could react. Suddenly it was over him, mouth yawning wide, revealing thousands of teeth implanted in its fleshy gullet to crush and grind.

Alaric powered to his feet, slamming a shoulder up into the underside of the thing's jaw. He rammed his fist up into the meat of its neck and trusted that his storm bolter was aiming at some vital place, some brain or heart the thing could not live without.

Words of prayer flashed through his mind.

Alaric fired.

*The light was worse than the dark.*

*He was bathed in it. He felt it illuminating not just his body, but his mind. All his sins, his very fears in that moment, were laid open to be read like the illuminations of a prayer book.*

*Up above him was the dome of the cathedral. Thousands of censers hung from it, smouldering in their clouds of pungent smoke. The dome was painted with a hundred methods of torture, each one inflicted on a famous sinner from the Imperial creed. A body, broken on a wheel, had its wounds picked out in clusters of rubies. The victim of an impaling, as he slid slowly down a spear through his stomach, wept tears of gold leaf.*

*The light came not from the dome, but from below. Faith was like fire – it could warm and comfort, and it could destroy, Fire, therefore, filled the cathedral floor. Hundreds of burners emitted a constant flame, so the cathedral seemed to contain an ocean of flame. The brazen walkways over the fire, where the clergy alone were permitted to tread, were so hot they glowed red and the clergy went about armoured in shielded and cooled vestments.*

*The man who knelt at the altar was not one of the clergy. He was not shielded, and he could barely draw breath in the scalding heat. His wrists were burned where his manacles had conducted the heat. He knelt on a prayer cushion, but even so his shins and knees were red*

raw. He wore only a tabard of cloth-of-gold, and his head
had been shaven with much ceremony that very morning.

A silver bowl on the metal floor in front of him was
there, he knew, to catch his blood.

One of the cathedral's many clergy walked up to where
the man knelt. His Ecclesiarchy robes almost completely
concealed him, forming a shell of ermine and silk that
revealed only the clergyman's eyes. His robes opened and
an arm reached out. The hand, gloved in crimson satin,
held a single bullet.

The bullet was dropped into the silver bowl. The kneeling man winced at the sound.

Other clergy were watching, assembled on the metal
walkways, lit from beneath by the lake of fire. The reds,
purples and whites of their robes flickered with the flames.
Only their eyes were visible.

One of them, in the purple and silver of a cardinal,
raised his hand.

'Begin,' he said, and his words were amplified through
the sweltering dome of the cathedral.

The priest in front of the sacrificial altar drew a knife
from beneath his robes. It had a blade of gold, inscribed
with High Gothic prayers. The prisoner – the sacrifice –
flinched as the tip of the knife touched the back of his
neck.

The city outside was dark and cold. It was a city of
secrets and dismal hope. It was a place where for a normal man – the kind of man the sacrifice had once been –
to get by, rules had to be broken. In every side street and
basement, there was someone who would break those
rules. Fake identity papers, illicit deals and substances,
even murder for the right price. Some of those criminals

would open up a slit in a customer's abdomen and implant an internal pouch where a small item could be concealed so well that even if the carrier was stripped to the waist and forced to kneel at a sacrificial altar, it would remain hidden.

The sacrifice had also paid what little he had to have one of his fingernails replaced with a miniature blade. As the priest in front of him raised the knife into the air and looked up towards the dome, the sacrifice used this tiny blade to open up the old scar in the side of his abdomen. Pinpricks of pain flared where the nerve endings had not been properly killed in that dingy basement surgery. The sacrifice's stomach lurched as his finger slipped inside the wound and along the slippery sides of the implanted pouch.

His fingers closed on the grip of the gun.

'By this blood,' intoned the priest, 'shed by this blade, shall the weapon be consecrated! Oh Emperor on high, oh Lord of Mankind, oh Father of our futures, look upon this offering!'

The sacrifice jumped to his feet, the metal scorching his soles. With his free hand he grabbed the priest's wrist and wrenched it behind his back, spinning the man around. With the other, he put the muzzle of the miniature pistol to the back of the priest's head.

A ripple of alarm ran around the cathedral. Clergy looked from the altar to one another, as if one of them would explain that this was just another variation on the ritual they had all seen hundreds of times before.

'I am walking out of here!' shouted the sacrifice. 'Do you understand? When I am free and deep in the city, I will let him go. If you try to stop me, or follow me, I will kill him. His life is worth a lot more than one sacred bullet. Don't make me a murderer.'

The assembled clergy took a collective step backwards. Only the cardinal did not move.

Even with his face hidden, the presence and authority that had made him a cardinal filled the cathedral. Voxcasters concealed in the dome sent his voice booming over the sound of the flames.

'Do not presume to know,' said the cardinal, 'what a life is worth to me. Not when I serve an Imperium where a billion brave men die every day. Not when the Emperor alone can number those who have died in His name. Do not presume to know. Be grateful, merely, that we have given you the chance to serve Him in death.'

The sacrifice forced the priest forwards a few steps, the pistol pressed against the layers of silk between it and the priest's skull. The sacrifice held the priest in front of him as if shielding himself from something the cardinal might do. 'No one needs to know you let me go,' he said. 'The priests will do whatever you say. They will hold their tongues. And I will simply disappear. No one will ever know.'

'The Emperor watches,' replied the cardinal. 'The Emperor knows.'

'Then cut a hundred men's throats on this altar to keep him happy!' retorted the sacrifice. 'A hundred killers. There are plenty of them out there. A hundred sinners. But not me. I am a good man. I do not deserve to die here!'

The cardinal held out his hands as if he was on the pulpit, encompassing a great congregation. 'That is why it has to be you,' he said. 'What worth is the blood of a sinner?'

'Then find someone else,' said the sacrifice, walking his

prisoner forwards a few more paces. The main doors were beyond the cardinal, a set of massive bronze reliefs depicting the Emperor enthroned.

'Brother,' said the cardinal, his voice still calm. 'A thousand times this world blesses a bullet with the blood of a good man. A thousand other worlds pay the same tithe to our brethren in the Inquisition. Do you think you are the first sacrifice to try to escape us? The first to smuggle a weapon through the ritual cleansings? Remember your place. You are but one man. There is nothing you can do which another has not tried and failed before. You will not leave this place. You will kneel and die, and your blood will consecrate our offering.'

'This man will die,' hissed the sacrifice, 'or I will be free.'

The cardinal drew something from inside his robes. It was a simple silver chain, with a single red gemstone in its setting. It had none of the ostentatiousness of the cardinal's own diamonds and emeralds which encrusted the heavy golden chain around his neck. It looked out of place dangling from his silk-gloved fingers.

The sacrifice froze. Recognition flooded his face as his eyes focussed on the necklace in the cardinal's hand.

'Talaya,' he said.

'If you do not kneel and bare your throat to the Emperor's blade,' said the cardinal, 'then she will take your place. She is a good person, is she not?'

The sacrifice stepped back from his prisoner. He did not look away from the necklace as the backs of his legs touched the scalding metal of the altar.

He threw the gun off the walkway, into the flames.

He knelt down, and bowed his head over the silver bowl with its bullet.

'Continue,' said the cardinal.

*The sacrifice did not have time to cry out in pain. The sacrificial knife severed his spinal cord with a practised thrust, and opened up the veins and arteries of his throat. He just had time to see the bullet immersed in his dark red blood before the darkness fell.*

THE CONSECRATED BULLET ripped up into the serpent's skull and detonated, blowing clots of a dozen brains across the ceiling.

The weight of the mutant thing fell onto Alaric's shoulders. He shrugged it off, glancing behind him to the rest of the squad. Dvorn was breaking the neck of a thing with too many limbs and Haulvarn was shredding the last of the crewmen seething down the corridor with bolter fire. Fire licked along the walls and ceiling beyond, clinging to the charred remnants of the mutants Visical had burned.

'Keep moving!' yelled Alaric. 'They know we are here!'

Alaric ran down the corridor, his armoured feet skidding on the spilt blood and crunching through corpses. Up ahead were what had once been the crew decks. Upwards of thirty thousand men had lived on the *Merciless*, their lives pledged to crewing and defending the grand cruiser. Between the mutiny and disappearance of the ship and the confirmation that Bulgor Hyrk was on board, only a few weeks had passed. That was more than enough time for Hyrk to turn every single crewman on board into something else.

Some of those transformations had taken place in

the crew quarters. The walls and ceiling were blistered up into cysts of translucent veiny metal, through which could be seen the fleshy forms of incubating mutants. The crewmen had been devolved into foetal forms and then reborn as something else.

Every one would be different, obscene in its own way. Hyrk considered himself, among other things, an artist.

'Would that we could burn it all,' said Visical.

'We will,' said Dvorn. 'The fleet will. This place will all burn, once we know Hyrk is dead.'

One of the cysts near Visical split open. The thing that fell out looked like two human torsos fused together at the waist end-to-end, forming something like a serpent with a lumpily deformed head at each end. For limbs it had hands attached to the sides of its length at the wrists, fingers like the legs of a centipede.

Visical immolated the mutant in a blast of flame. It shrivelled up, mewling. 'How can honest human flesh become such a thing?' he said.

'Think not of how far a human is from these abominations,' said Alaric. 'Think how close he is. Even a Grey Knight is not so far removed from Hyrk's creations. The line is thin. Do not forget that, brother.' Alaric checked his storm bolter and reloaded. Each shell was consecrated, blessed by the Ecclesiarchy. Many, many more would be fired before Alaric saw the last of the *Merciless*.

Haulvarn had ripped a panel off the wall and was examining the wiring inside. 'The cogitator data-lines

run through here,' he said. He hooked one of the
lines into his data-slate. 'There is a lot of power running to the astronav dome. Far beyond normal
tolerances. Whatever Hyrk's doing here, it has something to do with the dome.'

'The dome on the *Merciless* is archeotech,' said
Alaric. 'It's older than anything in the fleet. It must be
why Hyrk chose this ship.'

'The only thing I care about,' said Dvorn with a
snarl, 'is where it is.'

The floor shook, as if the fabric of the *Merciless* was
coming apart and sending quakes running through
the decks. A sound ran through the ship – a howl –
the sound of reality tearing. The air turned greasy and
thick, and rivulets of brackish blood ran down the
walls of the warped crew quarters.

'Daemons,' spat Alaric.

'Hyrk has torn the veil,' said Haulvarn.

'That is why it had to be us,' said Alaric. 'That is why
no one else could kill him.'

The sound of a thousand gibbering voices filtered
down from the decks above. Howling and inhuman,
they were echoes of the storms that ripped through
the warp. Every voice was a fragment of a god's own
voice, each of the daemons now pouring into the
*Merciless*.

'Upwards,' said Alaric. 'Onwards. Take the fight to
them and kill every one that gets in your way! We are
the tip of His spear, brothers!'

Dvorn squared up to the door at the far end of the
crew quarters, hammer held ready. Though Dvorn
was as skilled with the storm bolter as any Grey

Knight, it was face-to-face, hammer to daemon hide, that he loved to fight. Dvorn was the strongest Adeptus Astartes Alaric had ever met. He had been born to charge through a bulkhead door and rip through whatever foe waited for him beyond.

Visical and Haulvarn stacked up against the bulkhead wall beside Dvorn.

'Now, brother!' ordered Alaric.

Dvorn kicked the bulkhead door off its hinges. The roar that replied to him was a gale, a storm of foulness that roared through the decks beyond.

Dvorn had opened the door into the wet, beating heart of the ship, a stinking mass of pulpy flesh lit by ruddy bioluminescence. Daemons, their unnatural flesh glowing, flowed along the walls and ceiling in a seething tide welling up from hell itself.

'Come closer, vomit of the warp!' yelled Dvorn. 'Let us embrace, in the fire of the Emperor's wrath!'

Knots of iridescent flesh formed a dozen new limbs and eyes every second. One-eyed, one-horned monstrosities bulged with masses of corrosive decay. Skull-faced cackling creatures with skin the colour of blood. Lithe, leaping things, with an awful seductiveness in their impossible grace.

Alaric planted his feet and braced his halberd, like a spearman ready to receive a cavalryman's charge.

The tide hit, in a storm of flesh and corruption boiling straight up from the warp.

*Xanthe knelt, as if in prayer, but she was not praying.*

*In the pitch-black hangar, she could pretend she was alone. A hundred more souls were locked in there with* her, manacled to the floor or the walls, but they were silent. They had been silent for weeks now. At the start of the voyage, when they had been herded from the holding cells into the ship's hangar, they had screamed and sobbed and begged for mercy. They had learned by now that the crew did not listen. The crew, who went about the ship masked and robed, had never once spoken to any of the prisoners, no matter how the prisoners pleaded to know where they were going, or what would happen to them. Even the children had given up asking.

Xanthe knew why they were all there. They were witches. Some of them were wise women or medicine men, healers and sages on primitive worlds who had been rounded up and handed over to the men from the sky in return for guns, or just to make the spacecraft leave. Others were killers and spies for hire whose skills had made them valuable to noble houses and underhive gangs, but had also made them targets for the planetary authorities. Xanthe was one of them, a spy, and though she had scrupulously avoided making any deadly enemies among the cutthroat nobles of her home world, her pains had not helped her when the Arbites with their riot shields and shotguns had purged the hive of its psykers.

Psykers. Witches. Heretics. Just by existing, they were committing the foulest of sins. Where they were going, none of them knew, except that punishment would be waiting for them when they got there.

Xanthe let her mind sink down deeper. Her senses rippled out from her. She could perceive the bright minds of the other psykers in the hold. Some of them winked feebly, for they were the most dangerous ones who had been sedated for the whole trip. Others were still twinkling with hope. Most were dull with the acceptance of fate.

She could taste the wards built into the ship, too. They were complex geometric designs, pentagrams and interlocking spirals etched with psychoactive compounds and inked with sacred blood. They covered every surface of the hold, forming a shield blocking all psychic power. Xanthe's own powers, far greater than the ship's crew suspected, were barely a glimmer in the back of her mind.

On one wall was a rivulet of water, trickling down the wall. Xanthe had noticed it four months before, when the prisoners had first been shackled. Some imperfection in the wall was allowing condensation from the breathing of the prisoners to collect and pool, and then run down the wall. Over the months it had eroded the metal in a tiny channel of rust, to the naked eye little more than a reddish stain. Xanthe had not seen it – not with her normal senses – for many weeks, since the last time there had been light in the hangar.

The sacred oils, with which the wards had been inked, were washed away. The pattern was broken. The single rivulet had erased a channel far too small for all but the most powerful minds to exploit.

Xanthe's mind was very powerful indeed.

Xanthe let her mind slither out of her body. It was an insane risk, and in any other situation she would never have dared do it. If she was trapped outside her body she would die, with her spirit withering away and her body shutting down. If the wards were strengthened during her time outside her body, she would be cut off from her body entirely and would be at the mercy of the predators that lurked at the edges of reality waiting for unharnessed minds.

*But these circumstances were different. It was worth the risk.*

*Xanthe's mind slipped out of her and through the tiny gap in the wards. The patterns scraped at her, lines of psychic pain across her soul. The fire passed and she was through.*

*The Black Ship stretched out around her. Impenetrable barriers were everywhere and Xanthe realised that there were many hangars, each presumably full of psykers. Thousands of them, perhaps, all alone and afraid.*

*The corridors and decks were tinged with suffering and arrogance. The crew were blank spots, their minds shielded from psychic interference so thoroughly that they were black holes in Xanthe's perceptions.*

*The Black Ship was far larger than Xanthe had expected. It stretched off into the distance in both directions, as big as a city. Xanthe stumbled blindly through the structure, slipping through walls and between decks, trying to keep moving while steering clear of the banks of wards blocking her path.*

*Cells stretched off in a long row. The minds inside them were broken and smouldering, little more than embers. The cells were drenched in pain and Xanthe had the sensation of being bathed in blood, the coppery taste and smell filling her.*

*Xanthe hurried away from the cells, but a worse sensation greeted her. A circular anatomy theatre, walls hung with diagrams of dissected brains and spinal columns, was layered in such intense pain and hate that Xanthe recoiled from it and flitted away like an insect.*

*Xanthe knew she was losing her mind. Losing it literally – the connection between her mind and the brain that still controlled it might snap and her mind would be trapped outside her, circling around the Black Ship until some anti-psychic ward snuffed it out. Perhaps there were other ghosts here, other orphaned minds wandering the decks.*

*She forced herself to concentrate. She would not end that way. In desperation she located one of the black holes, one of the mind-shielded crew, and followed it. Candles were everywhere, miniature wax-caked shrines built into every alcove and iron chandeliers hanging from every ceiling. Relics – painted icons, mouldering bones, scraps of armour, inscribed bullet casings – lay in glass-fronted cabinets to flood the ship's decks with holiness and keep the taint of the thousands of psykers out of the crew's minds.*

*They were gathering in a chapel. The holiness of it was tainted with a cynicism and cruelty that clashed with the taste of the altar, which was consecrated to the Emperor as Protector. The blank minds gathered there were kneeling in prayer, with one of them sermonising them atop a pulpit hung with manacles. More candles abounded, many of them cramped in masses of wax and wicks behind stained glass windows. Each crewman held a candle, too, and their shoulders were hunched with the symbolic weight of the light they carried.*

*Xanthe sent her mind in close to one of the crewmen. She could make out none of his features, for the cowl of his uniform contained an inhibitor unit that kept his thoughts and his face from her. But the echoes of his perception just got through, enough for Xanthe to make out the words he could hear.*

*The crewman on the pulpit was an officer. Xanthe could make out a medallion around his neck in the shape of the* letter 'I'. His uniform of red and black had a collar so high he could not turn his head, and he wore ruby-studded laurels on his brow. His voice was deep and dark, enhanced by an amplifier unit in his throat.

'And so let us pray,' he was saying, 'that our sacred duty might go unimpeded. Though we near our destination, let us not allow our attention to waver. A scant few days remain, and no doubt we give thanks that our proximity to our cargo will soon be over. Yet until the last second, we must remain vigilant! Our duty is greater than any of us. In its fulfilment, our purpose as servants of the Emperor is fulfilled. Be not content, be not lax. Be suspicious of all, at all times!'

The words continued but Xanthe let them go. She could taste the meaning of them, and they went on in the same vein. She slipped away through the chapel, following the concentrations of crewmen up through the bewildering structures of the ship's upper decks. She made out the soaring arches and sweeping stage of an opera house, a cluster of tiny buildings forming a mock village under a ceiling painted to resemble a summer sky – things that had no place on a spaceship. In her bewilderment she almost lost her way but she glimpsed a collection of black voids where more crew were gathered.

Xanthe soared along a corridor lined with statues and portraits, each one of a subject with his face covered. She emerged in a map room where several crew were gathered around an enormous map table. A servitor clung to the ceiling, scribbling annotations on a stellar map with autoquills – Xanthe could taste the tiny flicker of life inside it, for like all servitors it was controlled by a crudely reprogrammed human brain.

*In the back of the room was another servitor. A holo-device, it projected a huge image that took up most of the map room, shimmering above the heads of the blank-minded crew. Xanthe perceived it through the echo of their eyes.*

*It was a vast furnace, its every dimension picked out in shimmering lines of light. The sight of it filled Xanthe with revulsion, turning the stomach in her body several decks below. The image was so detailed that Xanthe could shrink her perception and enter it, flitting through its vast vaulted rooms and side chapels. She was drawn to it as if by some appalling gravity of fascination. The pediments of Imperial saints and enormous pipe organ chambers enthralled her, and the yawning maw of the furnace entrance reeled her in as if hooks were latched into her soul.*

*The cavern of the furnace billowed around her, pure darkness harnessed in the holo-unit's bands of light. Above the furnace, suspended over the place where the flames would rage, was a circular platform on which a single suit of armour was mounted on a rack. The armour was beautiful, ornate and massive, too large for a normally-proportioned human. Cables and coils hung everywhere, and servo-skulls hovered ready to manipulate the armour as it was forged.*

*Xanthe withdrew her mind from the sight. She did not understand why it was at once fascinating and repellent to her. It held meaning, this place, so powerful and con-centrated that it affected her even though she did not know anything about it.*

*The crewmen were talking. Their faces were still cowled by their psychic protection, but their words echoed. Xanthe could not help but listen, even though some cruel precognition told her that she would not like what she heard. Xanthe could not match the voices to the shadowy figures grouped around the map table, but their meaning was clear to her, as if some force wanted her to understand.*

'Do they know?'

'Of course they do not.'

'What if they did? It is of no concern anyway. Without them to fuel the forge, the armour's wards will not be imbued with their power. The only concern we have is that the armour is forged and the Grey Knights receive their tithe.'

'The witches are vermin. The galaxy is better off without them.'

'It is a duty we do to mankind. That one Grey Knight fights on is worth a million of these sinners.'

*Xanthe felt her stomach turn again, and her heart flutter in her chest. The link between body and mind shuddered and she was flying, hurtling backwards through the decks of the Black Ship towards where her body lay. White pain shrieked through her soul as she was torn back through the tiny gap in the hangar's wards, and she slammed into her body with such force that her first physical sensation was the metal floor cracking into her head as she fell onto her side.*

*Hands were on her. Gnarled and cracked, the hands of her fellow prisoners.*

'Xanthe?' *said one. It was the old woman, one of the few prisoners who had been willing to speak with Xanthe, for some of them suspected what she really was.* 'Did you do it? Did you venture out of this place?'

'I... I did,' *gasped Xanthe. She tasted blood in her mouth.*

*'Where are we? Where are we going?'*

*Xanthe opened her eyes. The other prisoners were gathered around, their eyes glinting in the only light – a flame cast from the old woman's palm. It was the only power she could manifest in the psychically dampened hangar. The old woman was powerful, too.*

We are going to a furnace, *thought Xanthe.* We are going to be incinerated so that our power will be transferred into a suit of armour, that its wearer might be protected from people like us.

*The faces looked at her, waiting for her answer. The children wanted to know even more than the adults.*

*'They are taking us to camps,' said Xanthe. 'We will be studied by their scientists. It will be a hard life, I think, and we will never go back. But we will live there, at least. We will live.'*

*'You have seen this?' said the old woman.*

*'I have,' said Xanthe. 'I saw it all.'*

*'Then let us place ourselves in the hand of fate,' said the old woman. She bowed her head, and the other prisoners did the same. 'Let us give thanks. Even in this place, the Emperor is with us.'*

*Xanthe almost choked back her lie and told the truth. But it would do no good.*

*She stayed silent as the old woman let the flame die out.*

THE WARDS BUILT into Alaric's armour flared up, white-hot as they absorbed the force of the sorcery cast at the Grey Knights. Without that armour and its coils of psychically impregnated wards he and his fellow Grey Knights would have been stripped to the bone by the purple flame that washed over them.

They would have been shredded by the razor-sharp wind shrieking around the astronav dome of the *Merciless*.

Alaric crouched behind a shard of the dome, fallen from above and speared into the wind-scoured floor. The storm shrieked around him and he fought to keep from being thrown off his feet. The others of his squad were taking cover too, hammering fire up at the daemons that rode the storm overhead and left contrails of spinning knives.

Alaric could not worry about the eel-like daemons flying above him. He had to trust his squad to deal with them. His only concern was Bulgor Hyrk.

Hyrk flew on wings of steel in the centre of the astronav dome, suspended, unaffected by the storm of power around him. Hyrk had once been a man but now he looked more like a primitive vision of a god, some daemon worshipped by savages on a far-flung world. His six arms were held open in gestures of benediction and prayer. Instead of legs he had long plumes of iridescent feathers, crawling with imp-like familiars that cackled and leered. Hyrk's face was still that of a man, albeit with blank skin where his eyes should be. Those eyes had migrated to his bare chest, from which two large yellow orbs stared unblinking.

Rows of vestigial limbs ran down the sides of his abdomen, carrying scrolls with glowing letters. A crown of horns ringed his head, tipped with gold and inlaid with diamonds. The sacred implements of the rites through which he communed with his gods – chains, brass-plated skulls, sacred daggers, a lash of purple sinew – orbited around him, dripping silvery filaments of power.

'Brother,' said Hyrk, the lipless mouths in his palms speaking in unison with him. 'Grey Knight. Son of the Emperor. Child of the universe. Thank you. Thank you for being my witness. My glory is nothing without the greatest of men to behold it.'

'I spit on your glory!' shouted back Alaric, his own voice almost lost in the screaming wind.

A daemon fell from above, snaking torso torn open by bolter fire. In his peripheral vision Alaric saw Brother Visical dragging another daemon down to the floor and scorching it to corrupted bones with his incinerator.

'You do now,' replied Hyrk, his voice impossibly loud and yet possessing an awful calm and reason, for the mind had long since given up the sanity required to harbour doubt. 'But you will kneel.'

Alaric looked beyond Bulgor Hyrk. The astronav dome had shattered. Shards of its transparent dome littered what remained of the dome's holomap projectors and command pulpit. Normally, the broken dome would expose the place to hard vacuum, for the dome blistered up from the hull of the *Merciless* and looked out on the void. But nothing on the *Merciless* was obeying the rules of normality.

Through the shattered dome was a vortex of power, a vision of madness mixed with the raw stuff of reality. At its heart was a glimpse through the veil to the warp. A man without the mental training of a Grey Knight might have been transfixed by that shard of insanity, condemned to stare at it until his body gave out on him or he was drawn by it through to the warp itself. As Alaric looked on the shard of the warp split and opened; a silvery eye looked down at him.

It was from that vortex that Hyrk drew his power. That power coalesced into sights from Hyrk's depraved life, churning randomly as the vortex echoed the seething pit of Hyrk's mind. A million bodies writhed in joy, smiles on their faces, as they were burned in the golden flame that Hyrk taught them to summon down upon themselves. The blasphemies in the Library of Absalaam tore themselves free of their pages, flocking like ravens around the figure of Hyrk. A hive city's population wept with such sorrow at the heretic's crimes that their tears rose up in a flood and drowned them.

Alaric tore his eyes away. Hyrk's many arms were making the gestures with which he channelled his own form of witchcraft. Pulses of golden fire, like miniatures comets, rained down. Alaric broke cover and ran forwards, powering through the storm. Hyrk's face broke into a faint smile, as if amused by some trifle, and another gesture hurled a spear of ice into Alaric's chest. The spear splintered against his breastplate, the armour's wards discharging purple spirals of power away from the impact.

Alaric was knocked onto one knee. He forced himself another step forwards, planting the haft of his Nemesis halberd in the dome's floor to give him purchase against the storm.

'I have seen a thousand like you, Hyrk!' shouted Alaric. 'A thousand gods. A thousand vessels of the warp's glory. And I know what you cannot.'

'And what,' said Hyrk, 'is that?'

'You all die,' replied Alaric, forcing himself another step closer.

Hyrk conjured a shield of energy the colour of moonlight, covered in runes of invulnerability taught to him by his patrons in the warp. 'I am immortal,' he said simply.

'Then your masters will have forever to punish you for your failure,' said Alaric.

'You cannot hurt me,' replied Hyrk, one of his hands waving dismissively, as if he was bored of Alaric's presence at his court and was commanding him to leave.

Alaric did not reply to that.

He drew back his arm, the head of the halberd hovering beside his head. Hyrk's eyes glimmered with amusement at the motion, for he knew that even a Nemesis weapon hurled by a Grey Knight could not get through the magics he commanded.

Alaric's gaze went upwards. He focussed on the eye in the heart of the vortex overhead, the eye that stared directly from the warp.

He was strong. He would have to be. It was not an easy shot.

Alaric hurled the Nemesis halberd straight up. The force of his throw kept it flying true even through the storm. It seemed to take an hour for it to spin upwards through the vortex, past the endless atrocities pulled from Hyrk's mind.

Hyrk realised, a split second before it hit, what Alaric was trying to do.

The blade of the halberd speared the eye through

the centre of its pupil. The eye recoiled, folds of time-space rippling around it, and a bolt of iridescent blood squirted from the ruined pupil.

The vortex went dark. The power drained away. The daemons and the victims in Hyrk's visions dissolved away to skeletons, then darkness.

The storm died down. Alaric could hear the gunfire from his battle-brothers now, he could stand at full height without being swept aside by the storm. The gods who watched Hyrk and granted him his power were blinded for a moment, and turned away from their champion. Hyrk could not call on them now.

Hyrk was stunned. Alaric was too quick for him. Alaric dived forwards and grabbed a handful of Hyrk's feathered tail. He dragged Hyrk down to the floor, fighting against the psychic force keeping him aloft.

'I can hurt you now,' said Alaric. He wrapped an elbow around Hyrk's jaw and twisted. Bulgor Hyrk's neck snapped in his grasp.

*The first time, Thorne was ready.*

*The room into which they wheeled him was of polished steel, so harshly lit that the reflection of the glowstrips in the mirror-like walls turned it into a cube of light. Thorne was strapped into a wheelchair, for the nerve stimulation had rendered him malcoordinated and unable to walk without fear of falling. His hands shook and he sweated constantly, his body still geared up for the next tide of bafflement and pain.*

*Instructor Gravenholm sat in the room, a thick file on the table in front of him. He was haloed in the light, as if he was a bureaucrat sorting through sins and virtues in the Emperor's own court. Gravenholm was an old man, too old to live were it not for the juvenat machine sighing on the floor by his feet. Gravenholm was important enough for the Ordo Malleus to keep alive through arcane technology. Once, long ago, he had been a lowly trainee like Thorne. That was one of the thoughts that kept Thorne going.*

*'Trainee,' said Gravenholm, his words accompanied by the stuttering of the juvenat machine hooked up to his ancient lungs. 'Speak your name.'*

*'Explicator-Cadet Ascelan Thorne,' replied Thorne, forcing the strength into his voice.*

*'Good,' said Gravenholm. 'What process have you just undergone?'*

*Thorne swallowed. 'Direct-pattern nerve stimulation.'*

*'Why?'*

*'Part of my training as an interrogator. We must resist interrogation techniques ourselves.'*

*'I see.' Gravenholm leafed through the file. 'Prior to this process you were given data to memorise. Describe to me the content of that data.'*

*'No.'*

*Gravenholm looked Thorne in the eye. 'Tell me, Cadet Thorne.'*

*'I will not do so.'*

*'I see. That will be all.'*

*The orderlies returned to the room to wheel Thorne away. 'Did I pass, sir?' he said. The words came unbidden, blurted out. In reply Gravenholm merely gave him a last look, before turning a page in the file and starting to make notes with a quill.*

\* \* \*

*The second time, Thorne was not ready.*

He knew there had been nerve stimulation again. But there had been more, too. He had watched pict-grabs of destruction and death, cities burning, murders and mutilations spliced with images taken of himself doing things he couldn't remember. In a dark room, men had screamed at him to confess his treachery with witches and aliens. He had woken up on an examining table with doctors describing the mutations they said he possessed. He did not know where the nerve stimulation ended and his own thoughts began.

He had seen Gravenholm many times. Perhaps it had been one of the pict-grabs, perhaps a nightmare. Perhaps he had actually been there. But now he was in the cube of light again, this time lying on a medical gurney with intravenous lines in the backs of his hands.

'What is your name?' asked Gravenholm.

Thorne coughed, and arched his back in pain. The nerve stimulation had been applied this time along his spine, and the points of pain remained where the probes had punctured between his vertebrae. 'Thorne,' he said. 'Thorne. Explicator-cadet.'

'I see. What processes have you undergone?'

'I don't... I'm not sure.'

Gravenholm made a few notes. He had not changed since the first bout of resistance training. The juvenat machine still did his breathing for him and his bald, lined face still tilted oddly so he could look over his spectacles at Thorne.

'You were given data to remember. Tell it to me.'

'No.'

Gravenholm made another note. 'If you do not, further

*processes will be performed on you. They will include further nerve stimulation.'*

'No. I won't tell you.'

'I see.'

Thorne smiled. It was the first time he had done so in a long time. 'I did well, right?' he said. 'I didn't break. Have I done it? Will you make me an interrogator?'

Gravenholm didn't bother to look up this time. He waved a hand, and the orderlies took Thorne away again.

The third time, Thorne barely recognised the room at all. The cube of light had been there before, but he did not know if it was in his mind or whether he had really been there. The inside of his mind was full of half-truths and random fragments. Faces loomed at him, and gloved hands holding medical implements. He saw hideous creatures, many-eyed beasts squatting in pits of rotting bodies and swarms of tiny things devouring his arms and body. He saw his hands become charred skeletal limbs and his face bloated and decaying in a mirror.

Maybe there had been nerve stimulation. Maybe not. Maybe a key word brought back the pain without any need for attaching the probes to his spine. It all ran together. There had been no passing of the days – just an infinite ribbon of time, a few loops illuminated in memory, most of it in darkness.

Thorne was again on the gurney. He had been lying on it for some time. His limbs were too weak to support him. Orderlies had to turn him onto his side so Gravenholm could speak to his face.

'What is your name?' said Gravenholm, the juvenat machine sighing in unison.

*Thorne took a long time to answer.*

*'I don't know,' he said. 'Throne alive. Oh... merciful Emperor! I don't know any more...'*

*Gravenholm smiled, made a final annotation, and closed the file.*

*'Then you are ready,' he said. 'I have no use for an interrogator with his own personality. With his own name. Only when the vessel is empty can it be refilled with something the Ordo Malleus can use. Your training can begin, explicator-cadet. You shall be an interrogator.'*

ALARIC WATCHED THE interrogator at work through the one-way window that looked onto the explicator suite. Like the rest of the *Obsidian Sky* it was dressed with stone, more like the inside of a sepulchre than a spacecraft. The interrogator, wearing the plain uniform of an Ordo Malleus functionary, was speaking to Bulgor Hyrk. Hyrk was bracketed to the wall of the explicator suite, with his neck braced so his head did not loll on his useless neck. His spine was severed and his body paralysed, and it had been quick work by the ship's medicae to save the heretic's life when Alaric brought the dying body back to the *Obsidian Sky*.

'Thorne is good,' said Inquisitor Nyxos. The *Obsidian Sky* was Nyxos's ship for the duration of the mission to capture Hyrk. He was an old, bleak-humoured man who seemed ancient enough to have seen everything the life of a daemon hunter could throw at him. He looked frail, but Alaric knew this was an illusion Nyxos cultivated with his bent body and ragged black robes. 'He is already getting answers from Hyrk. Hyrk thinks his gods have abandoned him so he is telling all out of spite more than anything. Much of what he has told us is rather interesting.'

'How so?' said Alaric. He had spent many hours cleaning the filth off his armour and reconsecrating it, and now it gleamed in the dim light coming through the window.

'It seems he took over the *Merciless* because he had somewhere to go in a hurry,' replied Nyxos. 'Nothing to do with the crew or the Imperial Navy. He just needed a spaceship. Everything he did to the crew was for his own amusement, as far as we can tell.'

'Where was he going?'

'To the Eye.'

Alaric shook his head. The Eye of Terror had opened and the forces of Chaos had poured through. Billions of Imperial Guardsmen and whole Chapters of Space Marines were fighting there to stem the tide, which threatened to break through into the Imperial heartlands of the Segmentum Solar. Heretics like Hyrk were flocking there, too, to pledge themselves to the cause of the Chaos lords.

'Specifically,' Nyxos was saying, 'a planet named Sarthis Majoris. A call has gone out to filth like Hyrk and Throne knows how many have answered already. It seems that Hyrk was summoned by a creature there called Duke Venalitor. I have sent to the Eye for confirmation, but either way, I intend to see your squad reinforced and sent to Sarthis Majoris as soon as we have gotten everything we can out of Hyrk.'

'I see. Could Hyrk be lying?'

'Perhaps. But as I said, Thorne is really very good.'

Nyxos said this with a telling smile that told Alaric all he needed to know about what would happen to the paralysed Hyrk.

'Look at this ship,' said Alaric. 'At the crew and the resources we have spent. How much did it take to put my squad on the *Merciless*? What sacrifices are made so we can do what we must do?'

'Indeed, even I cannot count them all,' said Nyxos. 'We must take more from our Imperium than any of us can understand. This thought troubles you?'

'I can allow nothing to trouble me,' said Alaric. 'If we turn our thoughts to these things, we lose our focus. Our sense of duty is eroded. If our task is not worth sacrifice, then no task is.'

'Good.' Nyxos's face darkened. 'But speak not these thoughts too freely, Justicar. To some, they might sound like moral weakness. Like the thoughts of one who harbours doubt. Would that you were an inquisitor, Alaric, that you could speak freely and unveil the inquisitor's seal to anyone who dared question you! But you are not.'

'I know,' said Alaric. 'But someone must think of them. Otherwise, what are we? It is the Imperium we are supposed to be protecting, and yet it must suffer for our efforts to protect it. How far can we go before all become madness? Someone must watch over what we do.'

'Leave that to us. And in the meantime, prepare your men. Sarthis Majoris will not be easy, and we are thin on the ground in the Eye. You and your squad will be on your own, whatever you might encounter there.'

'I shall lead their prayers,' said Alaric.

For a while after Nyxos left, Alaric watched Thorne work. Even without eyes, the expression on Hyrk's face was that of a broken man.

It had taken untold sacrifices to break him. But Nyxos was right – that was a dangerous thing to think of. Alaric closed his eyes and meditated, and soon the thoughts were gone.

# ABOUT THE AUTHORS

## SARAH CAWKWELL

Sarah is a north-east England-based freelance writer. Old enough to know better, she's still young enough not to care. Married, with a son (who is the grown up in the house) and two intellectually challenged cats, she's been a determined and prolific writer for many years. She hasn't yet found anything to equal the visceral delights of the Warhammer universe and is thrilled that her first piece of published work is within its grim, dark borders.

When not slaving away over a hot keyboard, Sarah's hobbies include reading, running around in fields with swords screaming incomprehensibly and having her soul slowly sucked dry by online games.

## BEN COUNTER

Author of the Souldrinkers and Grey Knights series, freelance writer Ben Counter is one of Black Library's most popular SF authors. An Ancient History graduate and avid miniature painter, he lives near Portsmouth, England.

## JONATHAN GREEN

Jonathan Green is a freelance writer well known for his contributions to the Fighting Fantasy range of adventure gamebooks, as well as his novels set within Games Workshop's worlds of *Warhammer* and *Warhammer 40,000*, which include the Black Templars duology *Crusade for Armageddon* and *Conquest of Armageddon*. He has written for such diverse properties as Sonic the Hedgehog, Doctor Who, Star Wars The Clone Wars and Teenage Mutant Ninja Turtles. He is also the creator of the popular steampunk Pax Britannia line, published by Abaddon Books, and has an ever-increasing number of non-fiction books to his name. To keep up with what he is doing, go to www.jonathangreenauthor.com

## STEVE PARKER

Steve Parker was born and raised in Edinburgh. Scotland, and now lives and works in Tokyo, Japan. As a video-game writer/designer, he has worked on titles for various platforms. In 2005, his short fiction started appearing in American SF/Fantasy/Horror Magazines. In 2006, his story 'The Falls of Marakross' was published in the Black Library's *Tales from the Dark Millennium* anthology. His first novel, *Rebel Winter*, was published in 2007 and his latest book, *Rynn's World*, was the first book in the Space Marine Battles series.

## ROB SANDERS

Rob Sanders is a freelance writer, who spends his nights creating dark visions for regular visitors to the 41st Millennium to relive in the privacy of their own nightmares. By contrast, as Head of English at a local secondary school, he spends his days beating (not literally) the same creativity out of the next generation in order to cripple any chance of future competition. He lives off the beaten track in the small city of Lincoln, UK.

## JAMES SWALLOW

James Swallow is an award-winning New York Times bestselling author whose stories from the dark worlds of Warhammer 40,000 include the Horus Heresy novels *Nemesis* and *The Flight of the Eisenstein*, along with *Faith & Fire*, the Blood Angels books *Deus Encarmine*, *Deus Sanguinius*, *Red Fury* and *Black Tide*. His short fiction has appeared in *Inferno!*, *What Price Victory*, *Legends of the Space Marines*, *Tales of Heresy* and *The Book of Blood*, along with the audiobook tales *Heart of Rage*, *Oath of Moment* and the forthcoming *Legion of One*. Swallow's other credits include the non-fiction book *Dark Eye: The Films of David Fincher*, writing for Star Trek Voyager, and scripts for videogames and audio dramas.

He lives in London.

## GAV THORPE

Prior to becoming a freelance writer, Gav Thorpe worked for Games Workshop as lead background designer, overseeing and contributing to the Warhammer and Warhammer 40,000 worlds. He has written numerous novels and short stories set in the fictional worlds of Games Workshop, including the Time of Legends 'The Sundering' series, the seminal Dark Angels novel *Angels of Darkness*, and the *Last Chancers* omnibus. He lives in Nottingham, UK, with his mechanical hamster, Dennis.

## C. L. WERNER

C. L. Werner was a diseased servant of the Horned Rat long before his first story in *Inferno!* magazine.

His Black Library credits include the Chaos Wastes books *Palace of the Plague Lord* and *Blood for the Blood God, Mathias Thulmann: Witch Hunter, Runefang* and the Brunner the Bounty Hunter trilogy. Currently living in the American south-west, he continues to write stories of mayhem and madness set in the Warhammer World.

Visit the author's website at www.vermintime.com

## CHRIS WRAIGHT

Chris Wraight is a writer of fantasy and science fiction, whose first novel was published in 2008. Since then, he's published books set in the Warhammer Fantasy, Warhammer 40K and Stargate: Atlantis universes. He doesn't own a cat, dog, or augmented hamster (which technically disqualifies him from writing for Black Library), but would quite like to own a tortoise one day. He's based in a leafy bit of south-west England, and when not struggling to meet deadlines enjoys running through scenic parts of it.

# BATTLE OF THE FANG

CHRIS WRAIGHT

UK ISBN 978-1-84970-046-7 US ISBN 978-1-84970-047-4